THE GLORY OF THE KINGS

DAN CLOSE

THE TAMARAC PRESS
WARREN, VERMONT

ILLUSTRATIONS
Front Cover: photograph by George Steinmetz/National Geographic Stock. The interior of Abuna Yemata Church, Axum, Tigre Province, Ethiopia. 1970. Used by permission

Map of Ethiopia, 1895: Marc Hughes Illustrations, Richmond, Vermont, frontis

Battle Map of Adua: Dan Close, Underhill, Vermont; p. 272

"MENELIK": from an illustration in Le Petit Jornal, August 28, 1898, done by staff illustrators. In Public Domain. PD-1923; p. 282

"Avanti, i mei alpini!" : from Sul Campo di Adua, Diario. Marzo Guigno, 1896. In Public Domain. PD-1923, cc-by-sa 2.5-It; p. 299

"The Battle of Adowa": from staff artists of The Guardian, a British weekly, based on details supplied by survivors. 1896. In Public Domain. PD-1923; p.302

"Reap! Reap!" : from Sul Campo di Adua, Diario. Marzo Guigno, 1896. In Public Domain. PD-1923; cc-by-sa 2.5-It; p. 307

SPECIAL LIMITED EDITION, NUMBERED AND SIGNED.

ISBN: 978-0-9706620-9-5

Published by The Tamarac Press, Warren, Vermont
November, 2013

ETHIOPIA in 1895
Arabia
Red Sea
ERITREA
Massawa
Asmara
Mareb River
Axum
Adua
Adigrat
Makele
Gondar
TIGRE
Begemder
Amba Alagie
Danakil Depression
Lk. Tana
Gojjam
Lk. Hayk
French Somaliland
Gulf of Aden
The Blue Nile
Lalibela
AMHARA
Wollega
Wara Illu
Ankober
British Somaliland
Debre Berhan
SHOA
Addis Ababa
Awash River
Mt. Zuquala
Harar
Adama
Ilubabor
Lk. Zwai
Assella
ARUSI
Kaffa
Lk. Langana
Bekoji
Omo River
Marero
Bonga
OROMO LANDS
BALE
Wabi Shibeli River
Ogaden Desert
SIDAMO
Lake Rudolph
Kenya
Somalia

This book is dedicated to the people of Bekoji,
Arusi District, Oromia, Ethiopia – the runners, the scholars,
the teachers, the farmers, the merchants,
the administrators, the families.
This book would never have been written without the
grand and glorious memories I have of this
great little mountain town.

CONTENTS

The Glory of the Kings is the story of two young men, Chala and Bedane Negassa, of the Shoa Oromo people of southern Ethiopia, who join the Ethiopian army and go off to battle against the Italian invaders in 1895. It is also the story of an Amhara bishop, Haile Mikael Tesfaye, whom they encounter in their travels. Their story is set within the context of the military campaign waged by Emperor Menelik II that culminated in Ethiopian victory at the Battle of Adua in March of 1896.

A WORD ON THE OROMO PEOPLES

In the past, the Oromo were frequently called the Galla. The term "Galla" means "Outsiders". It can also be used as a pejorative or demeaning word of abuse. In 1895, although certain of the Oromo cultures such as the Shoa Oromo were allied with the Emperor, and had been a major influence in Ethiopian history for centuries, they were still called "The Galla" by the Amharas, the Tigreans, the Eritreans, the Italians, European historians, ethnologists, and observers. Evidently nobody ever asked the Oromo what they would like to be called until about 1975.

Nowadays, the term "Galla" is no longer in use, except as a derogatory term. But for purposes of this story, I wanted to reflect the reality of more than a century ago. Thus, certain of the characters in this novel – good enough people in themselves – call the Oromo "Galla", very likely not thinking twice about it. This is the name they went by. As an Italian soldier cries out during the battle of Adua, "Galla cavalry! Galla cavalry! Horror! Horror!" Oh, yes, the Oromo were, and still are, great riders. They had quite a reputation as warriors.

NAMES AND SPELLINGS

A note on names and spellings: in Ethiopia, the Amharic language was predominant at the time of this story, and still is. It is a Semitic language based on the ancient Ge'ez script, and therefore its alphabet and appearance bear no discernible relationship to western European alphabets. (There are many sites on the internet where you can see the script.) When translated into English, words come out spelled in all kinds of ways, depending on the ear of the translator. Thus, Adua, Adwa, Adowa. I have used the most common spellings found in English-language sources. As for meanings of certain words, there is a glossary in the back of the book which contains place names, individual names, and military and court titles and their translations.

PART I

THE HIGHLANDS OF ETHIOPIA, 1895

CHAPTER 1

THE GREEN AND THE GOLD

Chala ran like the wind. The summons from his father, brought by a young servant boy, had been direct and to the point. "Come home immediately."

Suddenly, the boy had appeared in the doorway of the classroom, startling Debtera Markos and Chala's classmates, requesting that Chala be allowed to leave. Markos shifted his bulk under his clerical robes and nodded to Chala, and Chala headed for the door.

"What has happened?" he asked the boy.

The boy shrugged his shoulders. He didn't know. "He just said to get home fast."

So Chala ran like the wind. Out of the town of Bekoji he ran, heading south. Soon he was out in the fields, following the faint track that led to the little town of Meraro, eight miles distant. Two miles beyond Meraro, up in the hills in the rolling grasslands, beyond the hill that people called *The Bag of Gold* because of its beautiful golden grasses, stood the *tukul* of his parents, Negassa and Tsehai.

Chala ran across the grassland of the high Arusi plateau of southern Ethiopia, the midday sun above, the green and gold of the highland valleys giving way to the knife edge of Mount Encuolo's ridge in the east. Running was no strange thing to Chala. Everybody ran. Small boys ran and squealed. Girls ran together and chased each other and laughed. Boys ran to the fields and herded the cattle, goats, and sheep. Women ran to catch up to their friends on their way to fetch great bundles of firewood and fill huge jars of water. Men ran to catch their horses in the golden morning sun. Everyone ran, except the *shemagales*, the elders who stood in the doorways of their tukuls and kept the chickens out of the houses with their sticks.

Everyone either ran or rode horses, for this was great horse country. Horses had come to this tableland with each nation that had settled there, but there were no horses like Shoa Oromo horses. The ones that survived the lowland crossing from Shoa grew into beautiful strong specimens on the highland grass and in the highland air. They snorted and pranced and ran like thunder, startling herds and runners alike.

Today Chala ran smiling as he went, sometimes brandishing his spear at an imaginary enemy or hyena. He was fourteen years old and full of life, with never a thought that his lungs might tire or his legs might weaken. That just didn't happen.

The grassland plateau through which he ran rolled and swelled into ridges and hills like a golden ocean caught in a second of time. The land was wide, some twenty-five miles across, east to west. It stretched from the north some hundred miles, two days' travel by fast horse, and another hundred miles to the south, where it finally went down to meet the Wabe Shebelle River. On each side of this plateau, both on the east and west, great mountains rose to 14,000 feet. In between, the plateau, all of it between 8,000 and 10,000 feet high, rolled and glowed in the sun.

The mountains were full of game. Beyond the mountains to the east the land turned dry and canyonlike and was inhabited by *shifta* bandits, and to the west the land suddenly stopped. Cliffs dropped away 5,000 feet straight down to a wide valley full of lakes and big game and mosquitoes and too much sickness. In those huge valley lakes there were islands, and on some of the islands there were devils.

That was what Chala knew. He had been to the west, to the top of the cliffs. That was a full day's ride. He had been to the top of the mountain ridge to the east just that past Easter Week, when he had gone with his father and brother and all the other men to spear game. He had never been more than one day's ride to the north or one day's ride to the south.

Looking straight down the wide grassland to the south, Chala could see that the land was not flat, but cut by many streams and rivers that helped to give the land its rolling appearance. The rivers came down from the mountains and either flowed north to the Awash River or south to the Wabi Shebelle. One stream flowed west to the cliffs, where it tumbled into space and fell to the valley floor far below.

Chala's high grassland was dotted with tukuls, round houses of bound sticks over which was cemented a brown plaster made of cattle dung and mud and straw. The roof of a tukul was conical, made of thick thatched grasses. Inside, the space was divided into a living room, kitchen, and sleeping rooms. A tukul was usually around thirty feet in diameter, so it was a pretty good size. Each one was surrounded by out-buildings: perhaps a stable for the horses, a granary for feed and food and next year's seed, and a fence either of sharp sticks or a living hedge.

Sometimes two or three tukuls would be together, built close for protection and neighborliness. Many times, though, a tukul stood alone, surrounded by a sea of grass and trees. Around the tukuls were vast fields, some for grazing and some for growing *teff* and barley.

From where Chala ran along a high ridge, he could see two dozen tukuls. But that was just a small portion of the thousands of homes on the Arusi Plateau. The Shoa Oromo were a strong people.

CHAPTER 2

THE SONS OF NEGASSA MERGA

Chala arrived home at four o'clock, the tenth hour of the day, when the sun was just beginning its decline over the western mountain. He entered the tukul, where he found his father and uncle and elder brother Bedane seated on mats in the living room, drinking coffee. He bowed low to his father and uncle, and less low to his brother, all the while exchanging the traditional greetings with them.

"Akam oltan!"

"Akam olte!"

"How are you? Have you been well?"

"By the grace of God, we are all well. "

"And the horses?"

"They are well."

"And the animals? "

"They too are well."

"And the crops? "

"We have enough for once, thanks be to God."

"What is that you are drinking? It smells strong."

"Coffee from Kaffa," said Negassa Merga. "They are growing it there again, since the fighting is over. It is much stronger than the Harari kind. Have some," he said, and clapped his hands.

This was a great honor for Chala. He usually would be told to sit over by the wall and keep silent. But in deference to his growing up, or his schooling, or whatever the reason, Negassa Merga had determined to honor the boy.

Chala's mother, Tsehai, appeared in the opening to the kitchen.

"Coffee for the younger son," said Negassa. Tsehai disappeared, and reappeared almost immediately, carrying a pitcher, a bowl, and a cloth draped over her forearm.

Chala stood and bowed to his mother, who approached, smiling softly. She held out the bowl and Chala placed his hands over it. Tsehai tipped the pitcher and cool water poured over Chala's hands. He washed his hands carefully, then bowing again to his mother, he took the cloth and dried his hands.

"I am honored, Mother," he said.

"Ah!" said Tsehai, as quietly as the wind in the grass.

"You deserve a little honor," said his uncle, Bedasa Merga. "You've grown a little, and you've learned a little. Not much, probably, but a little, and that's good." The two older men and Bedane laughed quietly.

With the laughter, the happy glow occasioned by the knowledge of this new honor drained from Chala's face, and he sat on the mat, puzzled. He had not been rebuked. The men had not been fooling with him. He couldn't understand what they were driving at.

"I will get the coffee," said Tsehai, and she stood and went to the kitchen.

As soon as Tsehai left the room, Negassa Merga said, "Chala, my younger son, you may have to grow up sooner than you or we had planned. The fighting in Kaffa and Sidamo has ended, it is true, but there is still more fighting ahead. The Ferengi are on the move again in the north. They are not satisfied with the treaties. They seem to want to take Axum and all Tigre for themselves. Ras Mengesha has already been in battle with them. It seems they won't stop. So we will have to go and stop them. Your uncle Bedasa has ridden all day from the north to bring us this news."

"*Indet!*" exclaimed Chala, using the Amharic expression of surprise.

"Menelik *yimut!*" said Bedasa, raising his hand. Again, an Amharic expression. "May Emperor Menelik die if I do not tell the truth!"

"From this family, Bedane will go to war," said Negassa. "But this leaves us short-handed for the farming. You are still a little too small for the plowing, but there are other things you will be able to do. I don't know what yet. What I do know, though, Chala, is that life will change for all of us. This is as it must be."

Emotions were strong in Chala's heart, and came fast. First, disappointment.

"I will have to leave school?"

Negassa Merga nodded.

"I will not tend the goats," Chala said emphatically.

"Your young cousin Ariti will do that."

"What am I to do?"

"You will train to run the farm," said Negassa Merga. "Beyond that, we will have to see. It will be whatever the times give to us or force us to do."

Tsehai returned to the room with coffee for Chala. With both her hands she placed the warm cup in his. The aroma of the coffee was strong.

"Thank you, my mother," he said. He put the cup to his lips. The coffee was hot, strong, dark, and bitter. But it was sweet at the same time. There was honey in it.

"I am ready, my father," said Chala. "I will do whatever needs to be done." He looked up at his father with steady, serious eyes. "But as soon as I am old enough, I will go off to war," he said sternly.

"That is the way of a man," said Negassa Merga, looking at him with pride.

A smile spread slowly across Bedasa Merga's face as he listened to Chala proclaim his readiness to go to battle when it was his time, but the smile faded and his face became serious as he turned toward Bedane.

Bedane was in his sixteenth year; therefore, a man; therefore, a soldier. He had grown up tall, with a strong body and intelligent, reserved eyes. He held his own counsel, and was not swayed by stories and opinions. He would wait until he had heard everything about a subject. Then he would ask questions—good questions—questions that would bring more talk and more information. Then when he had all the information he could gather, he would not hesitate. He would make his decision. He would act. Bedane would be more than just a farmer.

Now Bedasa said to Bedane, "Nephew, it is my duty to inform you that it is your turn to fight for the Emperor; and it is my duty to tell you why you must do this." Bedasa paused. Bedane listened intently.

"We Shoa Oromo are a favored race," said Bedasa. "The Emperor granted us these lands for our service to him in the wars in Wollega and Jimma. We are newcomers here, and we came here just in time, I think. You remember the cattle plague five years ago, and the famine that followed, and the diseases that took so many of your friends. You remember how hungry we were, how we had to hunt in the hills for anything that moved, how we ate roots and insects. How we were saved from death by the locusts that ate our crops. How we roasted them and ate everything but their wings. You remember all this and you must say to yourself, 'Has my uncle gone mad? How can he say we are favored?'"

Bedasa snorted and said, "Believe me, Bedane, and Chala, too, when I say that it was good here through those times. It was worse everywhere else. Everything died. There are stories. People ate horses and donkeys. Men ate other men. A woman of Wollo ate her own child. Lions, leopards, and hyenas ate men everywhere. Here, at least, we had green hills, and grass enough for our horses, and plenty of water. For all of this, we owe thanks to the Emperor.

"But we owe the Emperor more than this," continued Bedasa. "We owe him allegiance for the many gifts he has given us over the years. And he owes much to us, also. We kept his kingdom strong when he was young and held prisoner by Theodore. We are of Shoa, and the Oromo and Amhara of Shoa are like this." Bedasa folded his hands together. "We are of them and they are of us. Thus it has been for hundreds of years, and it works well."

Bedasa paused and then said, "Bedane, we are the Spear of the Emperor, and it is your turn to be the point of that spear. The Emperor has called us, and we must go. I speak now not as your uncle, but as Meto Aleka of the Wareda of Meraro. I will be your war leader, your military leader. I will need good soldiers. You are the first among them. I am finished."

Bedane was silent. Then he looked at his uncle and said, "I am honored, Aleka Bedasa. I will follow you, and protect you, and protect the Emperor."

"Good," replied Bedasa. He drained the last of his coffee and stood to go.

"Where do you go now?" asked Negassa.

"Ah!" said Bedasa. "It has been a long ride from the north. Now I go home and rest. Tomorrow I ride south, close to the Western Hill, down to the Wabe Shebelle. Then I ride north again, further to the east this time, under the shadow of Mount Encuolo, through Siltana, and back here, raising the troops the whole way. We meet at Bekoji on the day after the Feast of Meskel. It too will be a special feast day, and the governor will read Menelik's proclamation to us. Is this enough news for you?" Bedasa laughed.

"Yes," said Negassa, "except that you ride long and hard. Before that, you should stay and eat with us."

"I thank you for your hospitality," said Bedasa, "and nobody makes *injera* like Tsehai, but I must go home. I will have little enough time to be there. This honor of being the Wareda Aleka is not all it seems. I have had enough of it. This will be my last campaign." Bedasa grinned. "I will take the title and go home and sit in my door like the other *shimagales*, accepting the praise of everyone who comes to visit and living out my remaining years mostly sleeping."

"It will be many a year before you are an old man," said Negassa, laughing.

"That's what you think," said Bedasa. "For now, goodbye, my brother. Chala, goodbye. Bedane, I will be expecting you next week at Bekoji."

"I will be there," said Bedane, smiling.

It was a brilliant, beautiful, cloudless week, that week before Meskel. Two weeks earlier the Big Rains had stopped, and for the first time in three months people could move about without skipping around in the mud.

Bedasa had come from the north as soon as it was possible to travel and had arrived a week after the sun had begun drying out everything. Now the yellow Meskel daisies were in bloom, covering the green fields as far as you could see, peppering the green grass with a shimmer of gold under the cool blue sky. And not just here in Arusi did they bloom like this. All over the highlands of the Empire golden Meskel daisies were blowing in the breeze, gladdening the hearts of the people, making the horses snort and prance, and the oxen bellow, and the donkeys bray, and the dogs bark, and the baboons screech, and the leopards scream in the night.

What in the West would be September was the month of Meskarem in Ethiopia, and for the West what would have been Summer – June, July, and August—was called in Ethiopia *Krempt*—Winter—and in Winter it rained all the time and it was cold and miserable, and only a constant fire in the hearth kept you warm.

But suddenly the Big Rains ended, and suddenly there was Spring and the month of Meskarem, and Meskel daisies, and Meskel itself: Meskel, the Feast of the Finding of the True Cross, and suddenly the world became new again, and there was hope once more, and the people were happy.

For what did these happy people hope?

"I hope there is meat at the church feast," thought Chala. "I hope someone has donated a cow, or even two cows, to the priests. That would be good."

"I hope I am in time," thought Bedasa, riding to the south in search of his troops. "I hope we are all in time. If the Ferengi come down fast, if they get over Amba Alagie, they will be in Shoa before you can whistle."

"I hope it's a good year," thought Negassa Merga. "It will be hard enough with Bedane gone, and Chala too little and too big at the same time. But if the Little Rains are soft, and if the Ferengis and the shiftas leave us alone, it will be good. God, protect Bedane."

"I hope I am brave," thought Bedane, peering out over his father's fields. "I know I can ride, and spear, and use the sword well if I get one, and I think I am brave. I do well in the games, and the other boys seem to listen to me. I just hope I am brave."

"I hope this new child in me is a girl," thought Tsehai, hurrying about her homemaking. "There are enough men in this family. Who will help me with my work when I am old?" She almost cried, standing there in the dark house, when she remembered the two girls, ten and eight they were, and the boy who was six—all of them taken two years ago by the sicknesses.

Taking a deep breath, she thought, "I must go about my work. Oh, and I should look to see about my white chemise and *shamma*—they must be pretty for Meskel."

Debtera Markos, Chala's teacher, standing in the courtyard of St. George's Church in Bekoji, thought, "Those little scoundrels had better march well in the procession or I'll slap them silly. Now, where will I collect them? And speaking of collecting, I wonder if Abba Gelawdewos has managed to get a cow out of any of the societies? We must have a cow. What is Meskel without a feast? Famine, that's what. A famine the year before; a famine the year after. Where can we get a cow?"

Far to the north, a thousand miles away, General Oreste Baratieri sat in his headquarters in Asmara, looking at his maps of Africa. "If I can just get these devils to attack," he thought. "If I can just get them down out of their hills and pick the ground, I can easily grind them up. Then a movement south from here and another in from the Somali coast, and we crush them in a vise. That puts an end to their pretensions, and Italy has an immense, beautiful colony. And I, Baratieri, have provided it."

In his new Gibbi Palace at Entoto, Menelik II pondered his problem: how to send an army of overwhelming strength north to defeat the Ferengi while keeping sufficient men in the south to maintain his newly-expanded empire. He could feel forces tugging his mind back and forth. "I will have to weigh these strengths carefully," he said to himself. "My *rases* will have to be clear about who comes and who stays, and how many, and where, or all hell will break loose. Where did I put that devil of a Kaffa princeling anyway? In Wollo or Lasta? Wollo. Dessie, yes. He's in the dungeon in the castle at Dessie. That should keep him." Menelik strode off to find his Minister of the Pen. The rases had been summoned. In two days they would all be together. All the leaders of Shoa, all the dignitaries, the leaders of the Church— the Itchegie and the Abuna, the entire power structure of the Ethiopian leadership would assemble.

Then the fur would fly and the armies would move. By the glory of God, and by the strength of Saint Michael and Saint George, Menelik the Second, King of Kings, Elect of God, Emperor of All the Ethiopias, Conquering Lion of the Tribe of Judah—Menelik and his armies would march north, and woe to any enemy in his path.

It was at the sixth hour of the day of Meskel Eve, when the sun stood highest in the sky, that Chala Negassa, Bedane Negassa, and Negassa Merga rode their horses away from the tukul on the slopes of the Western Mountain and trotted them down the path to Bekoji. Tsehai Jara would stay home this day and tend the fire. This would not be the usual fire, but instead the special one outside the door of the house. Only the men would ride to Bekoji for this Meskel Eve. The women would come the next day. Meskel Eve was reserved for the men.

Just before the track from Meraro met the main track going toward Bekoji from the south, Negassa Merga raised his hand and signaled them to stop. They halted by a stand of a half-dozen great trees. It was a pleasant place to stop and rest, but rest was not on Negassa's mind this day. "Quiet!" he ordered, and the three of them sat on the horses and waited until they could all hear the hooves of the cantering horses coming up the main track from the south.

It was a beautiful sight. Less than a thousand meters away, two riders appeared out of the trees, heading north. Their horses were magnificent— huge animals that loped along like the wind, almost effortlessly; one black, one gray—two stallions.

"Look at that!" said Negassa Merga.

The two riders sat their horses like English gentlemen—straight up in their saddles—their spears and shields grasped in their left hands, their Gras rifles slung across their backs, their right hands guiding the reins with the lightest of touches.

"Ah!" said Negassa to his sons. "I wish I could have trained you to ride like that. I wish you had horses like that." The father looked at the disappearing horsemen with wistful eyes.

"Our horses are fine, Father," said Bedane, feeling sullen over his father's sadness. "I would put up Star here against any horse, especially against one of those high-strung purebreds."

"I want a shirt like that," said Chala, watching the riders disappear into the trees to the north.

"I could sooner buy Bedane a horse to equal those two than I could buy you a shirt like that, Chala," said Negassa. "Those shirts are blue silk. Would you give me five years of crops in return?"

"Are they our leaders?" asked Bedane, his eyes narrowing in thought.

"I know exactly who they are," said Negassa. "They are the sons of Ras Gobena of Ba'le. They may not be your immediate leaders, but if I were you, I would expect to see them again soon. At your side. And if I were you, I would be happy to have them there."

"They looked good," admitted Bedane.

"They are good, son," said Negassa, "and so are you!" he exclaimed, slapping Bedane on the arm. "Come! Let us go! Our friends are waiting. Already it is time for the feast to begin!"

Negassa and his sons spurred their mounts with their bare heels and cantered away up the trail to Bekoji, less than five kilometers away.

The town of Bekoji rose on the slopes of a small hill that climbed up out of the grasslands. It was right in the middle of the Arusi Plateau, and there were streams nearby in ravines that gave growth to trees. The whole place was fertile with trees, and so from a distance it could not be distinguished from any other treed ridge around. But suddenly, Negassa and his sons were there, splashing their horses through one of the streams outside the town and moving up the rising road toward the wide open marketplace surrounded by its houses and shops made of chicka.

Turning up the hill from the marketplace, they rode up the gravel street, the houses on each side getting a bit larger and better as they went, until at the top they arrived at the center of the town. Here on the left on its own little hill was the compound of the Church of St. George where Chala studied with Debtera Markos. To the right were the town offices and the jail, and across the street was the best inn in the town, with a bar and a restaurant and six rooms in back. It was called "*Yegabareoch Buna-Bet*"—"The Farmers Hotel" and it was owned by Makonnen Legassie, who had come from the north two years before with a lot of money and built the place.

Turning to the right there, Negassa and his sons had two choices: they could either go further up the hill to its top, where a small hilltop gave a tremendous view of the surrounding land and served as part of the village's defenses; or they could angle down the hill on the road to the north, where there were more houses and small farms. That is what they did, riding for the house of Negassa's friend Tamrat, down at the bottom of the hill.

Negassa, Bedane, and Chala reined in their horses at the gate to Tamrat's compound and Negassa shouted out, "Tamrat, by the grace of God we hope that you are well, that your animals are fine, that your fields are filled with crops, and that you are happy this Meskel Eve! How are you, my good friend?"

At this, Tamrat appeared at the doorway of his house and, stepping out onto the porch, said "Negassa, my brother! How are you? How is your wife? How are your sons? How are your animals and fields? Come in. Come in and water and feed your horses and yourselves."

They rode through the gate of the large compound, slipped off their horses, and Negassa and Tamrat bowed and shook hands, all the time asking each other how they were. Then, formalities aside, Tamrat hugged Negassa around the shoulders and shouted, "But you must come in! Have some *tej*, old friend. You must be thirsty."

Inside, Tamrat shouted, "Emebet! Emebet! Wife! Quick, bring some tej for my friend Negassa and his sons. Where are the girls?" Almost at once, Tamrat's and Emebet's two little girls, Birtukan and Tirunesh, who were perhaps eight or nine years old, appeared at the doorway to the main room. They carried the pitcher and bowl and cloth for the men to wash and dry their hands in exactly the same manner as Tsehai had done for Chala when he had arrived home. Behind them, and seeming to shepherd them and shoo them into the room, came a young serving girl with glasses and bottles of tej.

The main room had been turned into a meeting room. Rude benches had been brought in and placed around its walls. In front of the benches were tables made simply with wide board slabs, similar to the benches but higher. There would be twenty-five men and older boys eating here this afternoon.

This was to be the feast of the St. Michael Society, a group of twenty-five who met once each month to sit and talk and eat and drink and exchange the news and help each other. The St. Michael Society was one of six societies in and around Bekoji and, along with the extended families and clans and the lesser nobility and appointed officials, they formed the backbone of the community. This kind of society was what made the Oromo strong. Here it was that men gathered together, after their schooling and initiations and marriages, to keep listening to each other and working for each other. The society moved around from house to house, month by month, for its meeting and feast. This month of Meskerem, and by coincidence the Feast of Meskel, would be celebrated at Tamrat Bekele's house. This was a meeting of great importance.

Tamrat's wife, Emebet, had arranged the feast, and she had everything under control. The sheep were slaughtered, the *tej* and *tella* were ready, the potatoes had been cleaned, the *teff* was ground, the huge iron cooking pots borrowed, enough wives and girls and servants gathered, and the floor strewn with new, sweet-smelling straw. Within the hour the guests would begin to arrive. Emebet was a good wife. Tamrat had captured her twelve years ago on a raid down in Ba'le, in Muslim territory, near the Muslims' sacred Caves of Ginir. He had come swooping down into the village and saw the figure running, trying to escape. He bent low from his galloping horse and scooped her up.

Emebet was thirteen at the time, just at marriageable age, bright-eyed and full of fight. She pounded away at Tamrat's head and screamed at him while Tamrat held her and laughed.

That was how Tamrat and Negassa had become such good friends. While Tamrat was laughing, his horse whirling around, the girl flailing away, Negassa rode up and put a spear between the shoulder blades of the defending Muslim villager who was about to shoot Tamrat off his horse.

And the unwritten law declared at that time, and still does, that if a man saves the life of another man, that man is responsible for the saved man's life forever. So then, Negassa felt responsible for Tamrat, and Tamrat felt grateful to Negassa. Fortunately, they had been friends before the incident and bore each other no grudges, had joked with each other during the long rides of the southern campaigns, and so this binding together caused them no pain. This too was the way of the land, and in this instance it worked, and worked well.

Now twelve years had passed, and here in the home of Tamrat and Emebet, Tamrat was speaking to Negassa:

"This tej is good. Last year the flowers must have been good for the bees. Whatever, this new tej is great."

"You sound like you have already sampled a good bit of it," said Negassa. "Will there be enough of it for the others?"

"Two rounds for each, then we can switch to tella. Drink up. Drink up."

The tej *was* good. Served in large clear glasses, the golden color of the honey mead was cheering. The taste was an excellent mixture of sweet honey combined with the sharp tang of the ferment. Tej could make you forget the nip in the air and the cold ground under your feet. It could give you a golden glow on a crisp afternoon and make you feel very good about the world, at least until you went out later into the dark night.

The night was sobering. In a night without the moon, with just starlight, you could not see a thing. But the hyenas could. They were out there, and they could see in the dark. They could see you as you stumbled along through the dark streets, feeling with your toes so that you would not fall into a hole. They could see you bumbling along, and you could hear them laugh. Ah, what a chilling cry that was—the laugh of a hyena. It was worse than anything in the world, unless it was the scream of a baboon, or the cry of the leopard, or the rumbling bellow of the roaring lion. Tej would not take care of those things, nor of the cattle disease which stole your wealth, nor of the disease which took your children, your wife, your friends, or you yourself. Nor would tej stop armies from marching through your land, looting, raping, burning the crops and acting like giant locusts, consuming all before them, leaving a swath of pillaged grey land in their wakes. No, tej could not do anything against any of those things, but on a sunny, cool afternoon in Meskerem, it could make things seem a whole lot better for a little while.

"This will be a good Meskel Eve," Negassa was saying. "This past year has been fortunate. How are your crops? The rains were so good this winter, my teff is shooting up like crazy."

"So is mine," said Tamrat, "and my barley. Emebet's potatoes are coming along, and the onions are, well, the onions are onions. Nothing seems to stop them."

"Has any new *berbere* arrived at the market?"

"Tuesday some came in. And, if you believe it, some fish."

"Fish?"

"Some fool caught a donkey-load of fish down in Lake Langano, wrapped it in *ensete* leaves, beat his donkey all the way up the cliffs, and brought the damn smelly fish to market. Thought he'd make a killing, I suppose, but he guessed wrong. Got here too late."

"Did you buy any?"

"Do I look like an idiot? Of course not. Nobody did. That damned fish smelled worse than hides left for tanning. He left the whole mess on the ground in the marketplace Tuesday night."

"That really must have pleased the people who live around the marketplace," Chala chimed in, laughing.

"Waugh!" snorted Tamrat. "The hyenas took care of it all early on.

You could hear them yelping and snarfling and fighting each other over the disgusting stuff. They ate it all. Got what they deserved, too. We haven't heard any hyenas around here since Wednesday night. We could hear them all right then, though, out in the woods beyond the creek. Howling and puking and farting and sounding like the tree gods were pounding them with their limbs. Ahwooo!" howled Tamrat.

The feast had begun. It was more dignified than you might suppose from listening to Tamrat alone. Each man came in, greeted his neighbors, and washed his hands. Then he was treated to a glass of tej, and soon the gathering became less formal as the men relaxed. In time there came a rapping on the table from Tilahun Berdida, this year's leader of the society. The room quieted and Tilahun rose to speak.

"Friends, brothers," intoned Tilahun, a wide smile creasing his square face. "Welcome to this month's feast of our Saint Michael's Society. We thank Tamrat Bekele and Emebet Fasil for hosting today's meeting, and we look forward to tonight's and tomorrow's festivities. We did donate a cow to the Church for their Meskel feast tomorrow, but we kept a sheep for ourselves. We'll have some fine mutton today, and we'll get some of that good beef back tomorrow....."

At this there was general applause.

"That's all the business today," said Tilahun. "We salute and commemorate the finding of the True Cross. We are thankful for what looks like a good year coming, and that's all I have to say."

"Good," said Tamrat. "Emebet, send in the food. Let's eat!"

First the girls brought in one *injera* pancake for each of the men, placing it unfolded in front of each man. Injera was made from ground teff, the small grain of the highlands. Each pancake was about eighteen inches in diameter. On top of the pancake was placed the meal itself. In this instance it was *beg wat*—mutton cooked in its own juices, spiced lightly. Then came *alicha wat*—vegetables cooked in a light, delicate sauce; then *beg tibs*—small roasted pieces of mutton simmered in a chewy red-brown stew. Then it was *kai wat*—red-hot wat, simmered in *berbere*, the vicious red pepper of the Horn of Africa. Waugh! Berbere could make your eyes sweat. It could make steam come out of your hair and fire come out of your nose. It could burn your tongue and sear your stomach and keep your gut warm for a week. Like tej, it could make you forget the cold, and the fact that frost could form in your hair overnight in these high hills. When applied directly to meat, berbere could make the toughest sheep or cow taste like candy. When allowed to simmer in a pot with the meat for a few hours—waugh! —it became the center of life itself. You could make a stew out of berbere and a stone and a little butter, and dip a piece of injera in it and when you tasted it, you would believe that you were at a feast in the palace at Addis Ababa. Berbere gave you strength and courage. It was important. Ah, yes. It was very important.

So the men sat and ate and drank and laughed at each others' jokes and wolfed down the food; and when the tej ran out they switched to *tella*, home-brewed beer that looked evil, with twigs and leaves still floating around in it. The beauty of tella was that it took less than a week to brew, and the bush that grew the leaves that started the ferment grew in everyone's back yard.

It was when the men were about halfway through their second round of tella that the *azmari* with the *masinko* chose to appear in the doorway of the house.

Now an azmari was a wandering minstrel, and a masinko was an old-fashioned one-stringed violin, of sorts, that the minstrel played with a bow fashioned out of a curved tree branch and horsehair. These minstrels would go from town to town and play for special occasions: feasts, weddings, funerals, and the like, and they were very smart. They would find out all about the people who were going to be at a feast and devise songs especially for them.

Silhouetted in the setting sun, the minstrel ran his bow across the one-stringed violin to announce his presence and walked into the room, where he stood silently. Conversation and laughter stopped as the men at the tables looked at him. When the room was silent he began to sing. In a high-pitched, quavering voice, he sang:

> "Now here in the house of good Tamrat Bekele,
> A man who has cows and a good-sized beer belly,
> I sing for my supper from Waizero Emebet;
> If it were up to Tamrat, I'd sit and I'd wait.
> Ah, ha ha ha, ha ha ha, ha ha ha!"

"What!" shouted Tamrat. "Who is this arrogant singer? Who invited this beggar?" He could hardly be heard through the laughter, and the minstrel paid no attention to him at all. Instead, he entered the house further, and turning toward Tilahun Berdida, he sang,

> "Good health to his honor, the right-thinking Tilahun,
> Who knows a great singer whenever he hears one.
> I'll sing for the pleasure of this great company
> And even include this jerk Tamrat Bekele.
> Ah, ha ha ha, ha ha ha, ha ha ha!"

"Aha!" cried Tamrat. "So, Tilahun, it was you who invited this scurvy dog! Aha! I'll fix you! I'll fix you!"

Tilahun, sitting with his back against the wall, was convulsed with laughter. His eyes began to well with tears, and his breaths came in great gasps of laughter. The singer began to work his way around the room. Each man there knew there would be a song about him, and there was a general searching of pockets for coins to give to the singer as a reward. When he got to Negassa, he sang:

> "Old Negassa here seems fit for the job
> Of planting and sowing enough for a mob.
> Though elderly now and with two full-grown sons,
> He's just planted his wife with another one.
> Ah, ha ha ha, ha ha ha, ha ha ha!"

And when he came to Bedane, he picked up the tempo and sang:

> "Bedane here now is the point of our spear;
> With him in the first line we've nothing to fear.
> We'll send him up north with his Enfield and horse;
> Let him kill the Ferengis and come home a great ras!
> Ah, ha ha ha, ha ha ha, ha ha ha!"

To Asrate Asfaw, who had mistaken a bull for a cow while crossing a field in the mist and rain a few months ago, he sang:

> "Now here we have Asrate, a traveler of fame
> Who set out for home in the mist and the rain;
> Mistaking a bull for a cow with great ease,
> He spent the whole night way up in the trees -
> On the high branches -
> *He* says, anyway,
> So his *wife* thinks!
> Ah, ha ha ha, ha ha ha, ha ha ha!"

When he came to Chala, he chanted in a low, understanding voice:

> "Here's a young boy bound for manhood;
> Doesn't know which way to turn.
> Thinks his head will break asunder,
> Doesn't know which way his dream.

Oh, to be once more that youthful
With a wide and rolling track
Leading onward, ever onward -
I'm so glad I can't go back!
Ah, ha ha ha, ha ha ha, ha ha ha!"

And he sawed away at his one-stringed violin until it burst forth with mock melancholy and despair. Chala sat and watched him with a solemn face, his lips curled upward in just the start of a smile. He shrugged, and Bedane, sitting next to him, slapped him on the back and laughed, and to be truthful, Chala didn't feel too bad at all. For one thing, minstrels didn't sing to children. They sang to men. This was a splendid honor.

While all that was going through Chala's head, the minstrel had already moved on to the next man. It was Babilla Wami, the one everybody called The Wild Warrior Of Kofele. To him the minstrel sang:

"No one ever knows what Babilla is thinking,
Sitting there staring, scowling, and drinking;
Put him on the field of battle
With the lightning in his hand
Place the charger's thunder under him
Then the world will understand him -
Then the world will understand.
Oh, ho ho ho, ho ho ho, ho ho ho!"

"Good minstrel," said Babilla, coming out for a second from under a sullen cloud of thought. No one ever knew whether Babilla was going to say "Good whatever," or "Spear him." Babilla, like all great warriors, was unpredictable, and thus greatly to be feared.

Around the room the azmari went, bringing laughter and warmth and cheer, until he came back to Tamrat. His fiddling ceased, and he stood with a twinkle in his eye until all were looking at him with great anticipation. Then he began to sing again to Tamrat:

"Here in the house of Tamrat Bekele,
I have found such good cheer and a spirit so merry
That I have decided to stay for a while.
I know, my friend Tamrat, that will make you smile!
You say you already have enough mouths to feed?

Ah, well. Then I'm off, with all good speed.
Farewell to you all, all good men and bold,
And may you never, no never, grow old.
And as for our host, may his days be spent
In laughter and good cheer. Now I fold my tent."

"Aha!" cried Tamrat, waggling his finger at the minstrel, "You have redeemed yourself at the last moment! Well done, minstrel, and thanks to you, friend Tilahun, for this grand surprise."

While all these festivities were taking place, the sun never ceased its journey across the sky. The colors of the earth changed from the bright blues, whites, and greens of the early afternoon through the mellow purple shades and shadows of early evening; and now the reds and golds of sunset gave way to the newly-lit torches in the courtyard of Tamrat's house. It was now just past sunset, at the twelfth hour of the day, and night with its darkness and mystery crept upon the land.

In Tamrat's compound, dusky figures moved about. The men of the society, like the day, were transforming themselves. Off came the festive white Sunday clothes. Out of shaggy bundles came the war clothes, the monkeyskin headdresses, the leopard capes, the cloth cummerbund body armor. Out of shadowy corners came the spears and lances and blunt throwing sticks. Out of scabbards slung off saddle horns came the Enfields and the Mausers and the Remingtons and the Gras long rifles.

As the day had become converted into night, so the pleasant and satisfied men of a society dedicated to self-improvement had become converted into their dark shadow-warrior selves of old. And in truth, these dark shadows were just as real as the daytime farmers. It is something that we have never lost in our country. We Ethiopians can kill and die as quickly and beautifully as anyone in any land. We are, at heart, warriors.

Now it was the time to honor Christ, to honor the True Cross and the Feast of Meskel. The men of the society gathered together and lit long rag-tipped staves dipped in oil. With torches held high, they made their way out of the gate of the compound and turned up the hill. Jostling and joking, they began their march to the church.

Out of other houses and compounds streamed other bands of men. Across the plains you could see other lights coming too, converging on the hill of Bekoji. The men began to sing and chant, keeping time with their footfalls, which now began a sort of half-step cadence. "Yah-hey! Yah-hey! Yah-hey!" they chanted softly, moving up the road. "Yah-hey! Yah-hey! Yah-hey!"

At the very top of the hill, in a flat place outside the church compound, the priests of the Church of Saint George had built a pyre out of long, long staves. The length of these saplings exceeded twenty feet, and they were propped up against each other like a tepee frame stretching to the stars. At the base of this pyre the priests had piled brush and scrap wood, and now the youngest priest bent low, and with a glowing brand he lit the brush. The Meskel bonfire had begun.

Then came the men of Bekoji and Meraro and Siltana and Mojji and all the surrounding farms and districts. From all directions they approached, chanting and dancing and yelling and brandishing their lighted lances. And now as they approached the light on the hilltop, one by one they broke loose from their bands. Running, screaming, howling their war cries, they ran toward the bonfire and hurled their lances into it. The flaming arcs of fire hurtled through the sky, meeting the flames rising from the insides of the bonfire itself. The sparks leapt into the sky, and the sparks and the stars became as one. It was like heaven meeting earth, like a fire of shooting stars. "Ah," thought Debtera Markos, "it is the fire of each soul coming to join in the light of Christ."

Still more men and more lights came, and men formed groups and bands, and danced in circles together, and suddenly, Tilahun yelled out, "Look out! Here they come!" And in the dark you could hear the horses pounding up the road, and hear above that thunder the wild cries of the riders. In the dark, the light of the burning lances came, describing wild gyrations, and the riders shot their rifles into the sky. Rifles in one hand, torches in the other, on the riders came and let the horses have their lead. On they galloped, firing their rifles, hurling their lances into the fire, and they disappeared into the dark on the other side of the hill.

Even more men came. More brands were hurled. More dancers formed circles. The priests beat the sacred drums. The circles of jumping, dancing men were framed in the light of the huge bonfire. Shadows of monkeyhair headdresses, circles of shields, glimmering spear-tips—a mass of warriors danced through the night, shaking the earth and time itself.

And at the height of that, at the absolute height of the howling and the yelling and the thunder of hooves and feet and drums, Negassa went into the circle of the Saint Michael dancers and laid his hands on the shoulders of his sons and drew them outside the circle.

"Come," he said. "There will be many more circles for you, but this you must see."

And he took them and led them away from the fire, away from the flame. He took them away past the compound of the Church of Saint George, to the edge of the hill of Bekoji, and bade them stare into the darkness toward the east. "Look," said Negassa.

Bedane and Chala looked into the night, and the night was filled with stars. There was no difference between the sky and the earth. The stars filled both the earth and the sky.

For in the sky the stars held forth in beauty, showing the way of the path to Eternity.

And on this special night, on earth, before each tukul in the land, the women of the Shoa Oromo had built their own fires. There were thousands of fires. The hills were on fire.

You could not tell the difference between earth and sky. It was all one.

"Truly," said Negassa, "this is the beauty of the earth."

"Yes," said Bedane, resting on his spear.

Chala said nothing. He looked, and stared, and drank it all in. He took all those fires and all those stars into him, and held them there in his heart and his soul and his mind.

And the earth stars and the sky stars burned silently through the crystal-clear night, even unto the dawn.

All through the night, long after the men had dispersed and the fires had burned low and turned to small curlicues of white smoke and grey ash, there was a faint sound, like whispering, coming from the deepest recesses of the Church of Saint George. It was the sound of the priests chanting. All through the night they chanted, locked away in the innermost third circle of the church, in the Holy of Holies, where only they could enter, where the Writings were kept. They chanted their praise of God, of the Christ, of the True Cross. They kept time to their chanting with low beats of the sacred drums, with the whispering of the silver systrums. All through the night they chanted, until the sky turned light with that special hue it holds just before sunup. Then the dawn came up; then the day had once again taken hold against the night. And still the priests chanted, on and on, the chanting growing in intensity and fervor until it suddenly ended with a roar of drums.

Then the priests began to sing the morning mass. All the while, people had been gathering outside the church, called by the chanting and the drums. The men and boys gathered inside the compound; the women and girls, dressed in their holiday finest, outside the waist-high compound wall.

At the end of the mass came the procession. The priests emerged from the round church in their ecclesiastical garments. Embroidered in gold and green, red and purple, the garb handed down through generations of priests bespoke a tradition itself handed down through fifteen hundred years. Great sacred umbrellas fashioned with all the colors of the rainbow sheltered the priests as they walked in procession around the compound. Incense wafted through the mountain air as the priests sanctified the way for the Ark.

For it was for the Ark of the Covenant, the Tabot, that all this finery was displayed. The ancient writings of the Commandments were taken from the church only on high holy days. In grand procession, they were shown to the people as proof of the sacredness of religion and of life itself.

Now the Ark emerged from the church, borne atop the head of a distinguished elderly priest. The Ark was a flat book, large and heavy, some two feet long and a foot wide. It was bound in leather and covered in glorious colors of richly embroidered cloth. The priest balanced it on his head, and other priests marched at his side in attendance. Some walked with their eyes glued to the Ark, lest it fall; others walked with eyes downcast, watching the ground before the honored bearer, lest he stumble. As the Ark was carried out into the sunlit day, the head priest raised his cross on high and said in a loud voice, "Behold the Ark!"

At once the men cheered and clapped, and the women, beyond the wall, sent up a wail of joy, an ancient sound, one that first echoed off the walls of desert caves so long ago that no one knew when women began to make this sound. They made it at times of great happiness, such as when their children were baptized or when their men rode off to battle. It was a trilling sound, made by singing a high note from the back of the throat, and flicking the tongue back and forth so rapidly that the note quavered in the mouth. When hundreds of women made this sound together it was startling and almost frightening. This sound is a part of the women that is very ancient. These cries reach the sky faster than a falcon can dive back from heaven to earth.

Now the women sent up their cry of joy, and all the men honored the sacred Ark with their applause, and the priests wafted incense at the Ark from their incense holders made of gold and brass. Then suddenly everything was silent as the people begin to pray.

After that time of prayer, when time itself seemed to stop, the high priest lowered his cross and the procession, completing its way around the compound, turned, and all the priests and deacons and debteras slowly and with great stateliness entered the church once again. The procession was over. The congregation moved away from the church to an adjoining hill where there was a large, flat space. There they waited for the priests.

The priests, meanwhile, released from their spiritual duties, doffed their ecclesiastical garments and emerged from the church once again, this time dressed in their everyday white clothing, and wearing over that the long black robes of the priesthood. On their heads they wore white turbans. They carried long staffs upon which were mounted glorious silver and gold Coptic crosses. Some priests carried systrums, and some carried the great sacred drums.

When the priests arrived at the hillside, the crowd retreated, leaving them room. Then the priests formed two long lines facing each other, and they began to sing and dance.

It was a sacred dance. It was the Dance of David, the very dance King David himself devised to teach to the priests of Israel so long ago. The great King David was not just a great warrior and administrator, but also a great poet and musician. He gave the world the psalms and the harp. And he gave us this dance as well.

Now the priests danced to the rhythm of the drums. Their eyes lit with spiritual fervor, loudly they sang the psalms. The drum rhythms grew stronger. Their steps grew lighter. Soon both lines swayed back and forth, dancing to the Lord. The priests smiled. They almost laughed. They did laugh! They laughed in their delight of the Lord. With a final triumphant chant and a thunderous bellow from the drums, the dancing ended.

The day was almost half-finished, but there was still more to do. The dance ended, the crowd swept back toward the church. It was time for the feast. There would be a final blessing, and then anyone who wished to do so could stay at the church and help the priests eat.

The students were enthusiastic about this. They swarmed into the compound and sat against the eastern wall where it was warm. The debteras brought platters of raw beef and flung huge chunks of meat to the boys. It was like watching some kind of a game. The students had to remain seated or they were whipped. But there was great competition for the meat. Arms flailed around, searching the air for the sailing meat. There was a lot of laughter. The littlest boy snared the largest piece of meat. His classmates applauded. Everyone was happy.

The few beggars that were in this small mountain town joined the students. The rest of the crowd milled around, talking, meeting friends, discussing families, history, the weather, the crops. They waited for the final blessing...

Gebre Medhin Teshome, the high priest of the Church of Saint George, raised his hands for silence.

"Men," he intoned. "Women. Today, before I give you my blessing, I must tell you something. You must all come back here tomorrow, at the sixth hour of the day. A proclamation is to be read. It is a very important proclamation; possibly one of the most important in the history of our Empire. You must all be here. It is a market day anyway, and you will all be in town. But the market will be closed between the sixth and seventh hours. So come here when you hear the drums. Now I give you the special blessing of The Finding of the True Cross." He raised his staff in the blessing, and said, "Go now, and enjoy yourselves on this fine Meskel day."

The people went off to their own private feasts. After that, in the afternoon, there would be the games.

At the eighth hour of the day, with the sun still high in a sky almost free of clouds, Negassa and his sons walked their horses out of the trees and onto the great flat field to the west of Bekoji. No one farmed this field. It was the Field of Games, and was left open for the few times each year that the games were held. The games were that important.

Already there were a few horsemen on the field, trotting and cantering their horses, warming them up. Anyone could join the games, but only the youngest, strongest, and most wiry men could do well at them. Anyone else looked like a fool.

You didn't need much to enter the games, but the little you needed was very important. First, you had to have courage. Second, you needed the blood lust of the warrior. Third, a good sense of humor. Fourth, a good horse that you knew well and that knew you well. That horse was the most important part, and if you didn't have the courage and skill to match his, you would meet certain disaster.

The horse needed a good saddle and blanket, a good bridle, and strong stirrup straps stretching down to small round stirrups, which were really no more than iron rings.

Then what little more you needed in the way of equipment was a good strong hippopotamus leather shield, good body armor around your middle, a good wrapping cloth for your head, three well-balanced blunt spears, a ready willingness to play the game, and a thick skull. That's all you needed, and you were ready.

Negassa, Bedane, and Chala joined the long line of horsemen gathered along the sideline of the field. Groups of men stood together, quieting their horses, bantering, telling tales of other games on other days, reliving the stories of the games, giving history to this day. They laughed at the mishaps of their friends and of they themselves. Those stories helped the older riders recall their oldest memories. And those tall tales, accurate and otherwise, gave a welcome to the younger riders who would be entering the games for the first time. At the same time, those groups of men never took their eyes off the other riders on the field, commenting on their horses, their riding ability, their strength, their grace. There they stood, judging their chances.

Suddenly, Bedane leapt onto Star's back and the big horse, sensing the excitement of the rider, reared and pawed the air. The two were off across the field, Bedane guiding the horse more with his knees than with the bridle, warming him up for the chase. Then they came back across the wide field, up to a group of the standing men. Wielding one of his blunt spears, Bedane whacked one of the men who was not facing him over the shoulder and shouted out, "Hey, Mamo! Let's see what you're made of, if anything!"

Mamo Galata spun around fast and glared up at Bedane. "When I catch you, you'll find out what I am made of!" he shouted, and he, too, leapt onto his horse.

Bedane, laughing, wheeled Star around and walked him a little way out into the field. For the first time, he used his stirrups. He placed his big toes into the metal rings. The rest of his toes hung down into space. Bedane would support himself only with the tendons between his big toe and the rest of his foot. This was the way it was done.

Mamo followed on his mount. Bedane, half turning, and laughing, hurled a challenge to him. "Let's see, Mamo, if your hyena of a horse can run at all!" Suddenly, Bedane dug his heels into Star's ribs and the horse surged forward, with Mamo yowling threats behind him.

The two horses galloped at full speed down the field, Bedane on Star laughing, and Mamo on his mount yelling "I'll get you, you dog! I'm catching up. I'm catching you!"

Bedane sensed that Mamo was closing in and so, jamming his big toes all the way into those iron rings, Bedane stood up in the saddle and turned all the way around, just in time, too, as Mamo's first spear came hurtling through the air. It was an easy parry. Bedane simply flicked his arm and the spear flipped off his shield, coming to rest harmlessly in the field.

Yes, that is how it was done. People sometimes ask me if I am telling the truth. Yes, I am. That is how this game is played in my country. But how, they say, can this be? How can a man stand on a galloping horse with only his big toes in two small metal rings and have his feet take all that pressure? It would rip his feet in two, they say. Well, that is not true. But you know, you have to see it to believe it.

Down the field they charged. Mamo let go his second and then his third spears. The second went wide and missed entirely. The third came close, and Bedane again parried it away with his shield.

Slowly the horses came to a halt. The two riders sat side by side, joking and letting the horses rest. All of a sudden, Mamo kicked his horse in the ribs and away they went, Bedane galloping Star close behind.

Now it was Bedane's turn to throw. Twice Bedane threw, and twice he missed. He galloped Star closer and closer to Mamo, who had to twist around more and more in the saddle to defend himself. Then in just one instant it was too much for Mamo, who lost his balance, almost fell, and had to hunch forward to stay in the saddle. It was Bedane's opportunity, and he used it well. Up came the spear arm and off went the spear, right to its mark halfway between Mamo's backbone and his right shoulder blade. Mamo let out a yelp, Bedane gave a whoop of victory, and the game was over.

Bending out of their saddles to pick up spears on the way, the two friends cantered their mounts to the edge of the field. There they sat and watched the others play. Some men would challenge as many as half a dozen others to the chase, and whole squadrons would go thundering off over the field. Others would challenge one or two chasers, but would ride without shields and parry the spears with only their own spears, held out so that they acted like swords, flicking the thrown spears away. Sometimes, two or three chasers would throw at once, from different sides. That was exciting to watch, and if a man escaped a volley like that, either from skill or luck or the work of his horse, great applause would swell from the large crowd of onlookers on the side of the field.

Once there was a tremendous crash. Imagine now a man chased by three or four others, turned back in the saddle to defend against them. Imagine another horseman charging across the field from another direction, followed by another group of attackers with exactly the same thing going on. Imagine the shouts of the chasers, trying to warn the lead riders. Imagine the lead riders believing their attackers were just playing the game, yelling at them to turn around simply so that they could spear them easier. And then, imagine the awful sound as two horses smashed together at full speed, the horses going down in a tangled heap, the riders flying through the air, ponies neighing in terror and galloping every which way, trying to avoid each other, and men running to help the horses and riders, pounding on horse and on foot from all over the field, and the gasp of disbelief from the crowd.

Now imagine all that, and believe me when I say that crashes like that happened all the time. On this fine Meskel day of 1895, just this one crash occurred, but it was a spectacular one. Believe me when I say that, miracle of miracles, both horses staggered to their feet, and both men, too. Well, one man did. The other was carried from the field, but he came round a short while later. And wonder of wonders, neither of the horses and neither of the men were very much injured. How could this be possible? But it was.

That was not always the case. This was a most dangerous game. Horses were injured and had to be destroyed. Men broke arms, legs, ribs, and noses. They lost eyes. I saw a man once who took a blunt spear with such force that it entered the inside of his mouth and came out his cheek. A blunt spear! How could this be possible? Yet it was. In two months he was almost as good as new, with a very wonderful scar to help him tell his tales of courage to the ladies.

This day, the games went on until almost dusk, and the red sun went down amid large threatening clouds that came up in the late afternoon, hung in the sky for sunset, and then disappeared in the first hours of the night.

Truly it was a beautiful day of blue sky and white clouds, of green grass and yellow Meskel daisies, of air as crisp and clean as wine, and not too much of red-running blood.

Truly it is said that nine-tenths of all the courage given to mankind was given to the Ethiopians.

Truly, the Shoa Oromo are great warriors.

CHAPTER 6

THE PROCLAMATION

The day after Meskel began as a typical market day in Bekoji, but quickly changed. Starting with the fifth hour of the day, people singly and in groups began to wander up the hill to the open area between the church and the inn.

At fifteen minutes to noon the drums began to beat. These were not the sacred drums of the church. These were the great war drums—the *negarit*— of Ras Gobena of Ba'le. There were two of them, so large that each drum had to be slung between two mules to be carried along. Now they were set up on the hill of Bekoji. The people gathered in front of them, and the drummers pounded out the call to assemble.

At midday the leaders rode down from the hilltop fort to take their places behind the drums. These leaders were as follows: the two sons of Ras Gobena; five *Meto Alekas*—leaders of a hundred—including Bedasa Merga; the *Chika Shum,* or Mayor, of Bekoji; three *Wareda* governors of nearby districts; the chief priest of the Church of Saint George; and *Kanyazmach* Didda, the leader of the Alekas.

All of these dignitaries were dressed in their best. Leopard capes; monkeyskin, lion mane, or feathered headdresses; curved scimitars held in bejeweled scabbards; traditional war dress—they looked splendid in their seriousness and importance.

At a signal from the Chicka Shum, the crowd became entirely still.

At a signal from the Kanyazmach, a tall warrior unrolled a parchment and began to read in a stentorian voice. And this is what he read, direct from the hand of the Emperor himself, direct from Menelik:

ASSEMBLE THE ARMY!
BEAT THE DRUMS!

God by his goodness in striking down my enemies and in extending my Empire has preserved me until this time. Up to now I have reigned by the grace of God. If my death is at hand I am not afraid, for death is the fate of us all. But so far God has never humiliated me and I am confident that He will not humiliate me in the future.

An enemy has arrived who ruins the country, changes the religion, and has crossed the sea which God has given us as a frontier. Considering that the livestock had perished and that the people were worn out by the famine I did not want to take action until now.

But these enemies have begun to advance and to dig into the country like moles. With the aid of God I will not deliver my country to them. Men of my country, up to this day I do not believe I have been guilty toward you, and you have never given me cause for pain.

Today you who are strong help me according to your strength, and you who are weak help me with your prayers and in thinking of your children, your wife, and your faith! But if because of your negligence you fail to follow me, take care! You will hate me because I will not fail to punish you! I swear to you by Mary that I will not accept any prayer for your pardon! I leave in the month of Tekemt. Men of Shoa, wait for me at Wara Ilu and be ready, all of you, in the middle of the month!

Men of Gojjam and Dambea, of Qwara and Begemder and all that part of the country, rally near Lake Ashange.

Men of Semien, Walqayt and Tegedi, make your way to Makelle.

Fitawrari Takle of Wallaga, move north to Gondar. Proceed from there.

I have finished! Beat the drums!

As the last syllable of the proclamation dropped from the lips of the tall warrior, Kanyazmach Didda bellowed:

"I will add to this the following: three armies of the south will march north. The army of Harar, led by Ras Makonnen, will march from that city to the Awash, then strike directly north to the old capital of Ankober, thence to the north. The army of Ba'le and Sidamo will march up the low valley to our west and again move toward Ankober. We shall go before them, and instead of Ankober, we will head toward the northwest and camp halfway between Ankober and Debra Berhan. There we will await the Emperor and the Empress." The Kanyazmach paused.

"Here is the reason for that," he continued. "We are to protect the Emperor and the Empress. We will escort them to the north, clearing their way, being their eyes and their ears. The Emperor must know everything, and we will be the ones to tell him everything he must know. Also, we must protect the persons of the Emperor and the Empress and their followers. We are chosen for this for two reasons. One, our bravery and skill and loyalty is well known to the Emperor. Two, our cavalry is in the best shape of any in the country. Many horses have been lost to the diseases and famine. The Emperor needs good strong troops, including cavalry. That's why he needs us. So don't go getting swelled heads about this honor.

"Here is how we will do this. Two weeks from today—listen to me carefully—two weeks from today, the troops of the Meto Alekas of Robi, Meraro, and Bekoji will meet here at Bekoji, and sort out and encamp for the night on the Field of Games. One night only. Then you will depart for the north, picking up the squadrons of the Alekas of Lemu, Sagure, and Mojji on the way.

"Within three days, you must be at Assella. The troops from Assella will assign you your camping space to the east of the town, near Mount Chillalo. There we will gather. We will have the troops of twenty alekas with us. We will train there. We will have new Remingtons for you there. And meat.

"There, beside me, you will meet your *dejazmach* and *grazmach*, your leaders of the center and left wing.

"After you train enough so that you can do more than spear yourself in the foot, we will proceed to Debre Berhan, where we will join with the troops of our Oromo brothers who remained in Shoa. Together, we shall have the troops of fifty alekas. We shall be as a shield of iron for His Majesty."

The Kanyazmach again paused for effect, then continued:

"We march against a strong and vicious enemy. These are not the troops of the Mahdi, whom our Emperor Yohannes destroyed at Galabat. These are not the Egyptians that our rases destroyed at Ginbot and Gundula. This is not the Mad Mullah, sweeping out of the desert to destroy our people and our religion. These are the Ferengi, and they want our land and us as slaves. Tell me, my warriors, can you see us as slaves? Can you imagine other men plowing your land, sleeping with your wives, taking your horses and making you walk behind them as their servants?

"If you can live with such disgrace, stay home. I don't want you. We will deal with your cowardly kind after the fight. But if you are ready to defend your homes and your land and above all, your Emperor, come with me. Come with me to the north! Beat the drums! I am finished!"

PART II

WAR

"From this moment you are at war," said Negassa Merga. Bedane had just entered his father's tukul and was standing in the doorway, startled. His father had dispensed with any greeting. That had never happened before.

"You are relieved of your home duties as of now," continued Negassa. "From this time, you will think only of war. Come, sit down. I will instruct you."

It was late in the afternoon of the proclamation day. After the drums had stopped beating, Bedasa Merga had gathered together the ten warriors who would be his squad leaders. Bedane was among them. They had been instructed to recruit their squad members. Each squad would have ten warriors. They would need two tents, ten mules, and at least six servants strong enough to protect their belongings. Any soldier who had a wife or knew a trustworthy woman could bring her along. It was better that way, instead of having men running all over the place looking for women who might bring trouble in the form of disease or jealousy among the cohort members. Drinking was to be held to a minimum, especially as the troops moved closer to the enemy. No drinking was allowed during training. Each soldier was to bring as much grain as possible for himself, his horse, his animals, and his followers. Meat would be provided as necessary and possible.

All who came had to be young and strong. An Ethiopian army might look unwieldy, but it moved fast. It was descended from the moving capital of the ancient Ethiopian feudal kings. It was self-contained, even more so now since Menelik had, three years ago, proclaimed an end to armies living off the land as they had done for centuries.

"Bedane, your first duty is to protect your men," said Negassa. "This does not mean that you should run from the fighting. This means that you should be sure that all of them are trained to the utmost, so that they are all so skilled at fighting and marching and doing without and surviving anything that they have the best chance at growing old. You must give them all of your knowledge. You must find out what each one knows and get him to share it with the others. That will make you all stronger. Have you chosen your men yet?"

"I have chosen four," said Bedane. "Mamo Galata, Wondimu Gemechu, Tula Urga, and Dabale Ariti. All big and smart, and with great hearts for battle." He hesitated. "The others, I am not so sure of. Egersa Regasa asked to join with me, but I don't know. He is so thin. Last year, he was sick. His lungs. He seems to have recovered, but..."

"Ah!" said his father. "Egersa. I know him. Here is what you must ask. Find out if he is well enough. Perhaps you can give him a test of some kind. A footrace. Some long run or ride. Something that tests his endurance. If he is in good shape, he should be the first on your list."

Bedane was puzzled.

Negassa went on. "I once walked to the mountains with Regasa. Egersa came with us. Even at so young an age, he was amazing. He knew every root, every plant, every herb, and what it could do. Egersa could keep every one of your soldiers healthy if anyone could. He would be your *hakim*, your doctor. Take him if you can."

"Good advice, Father," said Bedane. "I will test him and if he is well, he will come. I will test him tomorrow."

"Good," said Negassa. "Now, how about Shasho Megenasa?" Negassa sat and waited.

"Shasho!" huffed Bedane, not believing his ears. "Shasho is a shrimp. He's almost as small as Chala, and two years older."

"Not quite two years older," said Negassa thoughtfully, "but tell me, Bedane, have you ever seen him shoot?"

"Yes," said Bedane. "He can shoot the eye out of a running jackal at a hundred paces. That is true."

"And have you ever seen the look in his eye in a sport or fight?"

"Fierce," said Bedane. He was silent for a full minute, then he said, "This is excellent advice, Father."

"I am happy that you have listened," said Negassa. "Sometimes people cannot listen. They must learn for themselves. But this is too important to learn by yourself. Take all the information and advice that you can get, especially from those who have been to war before. Bedasa will be especially helpful to you. Listen well to him. Now, do you have ideas for the other three?"

"I am considering half a dozen of them," said Bedane.

"Get by yourself for a time. Listen to yourself, then choose. Choose quickly. You do not have too much time. Those choices must be made, and they must be made right. Above all, you don't want any complainers. Those who do not complain about anything now will complain about everything as you go along. That is natural. But you don't want to start with complainers. You will want to spear them before you are ten days out. Have you chosen your servants?"

"No, Father, I have not. I have wondered about Chala..."

"You cannot have him. I cannot spare him," said Negassa. "Besides, Chala would not be a servant. He would fight. If you did not allow him to fight, he would fight you. It would be bad. You do not need that. Why don't you take two of those day laborers who work our western lands? They are great workers. Loyal, truthful people. They would be good. Ask your men about others."

"This begins to be more work than adventure," said Bedane.

"War *is* work," said Negassa. "And the more work you do, the less you and your men will suffer. But about work: do not burden yourself with all of it. Give as much as possible away to your men. They will be stronger for it, and so will you. But be warned, whatever work you give to them to do, you must also give them credit and praise for what they have done. Then you will have a strong unit. Are you going to take a woman?"

"Father," said Bedane, "what would I do with a woman? The way it looks, I am going to be father to twenty-five sons, daughters, horses, mules, chickens, and donkeys. Where is there time for a woman?"

"I thought you might want to take Askale," said Negassa, a twinkle in his eye.

"Askale!" exclaimed Bedane, his color deepening. "She is only twelve!"

"One year to marriage age," said Negassa, grinning. "Tsehai!" Negassa called. "Our son has chosen a bride!"

"What? Who?" called Tsehai, running from the kitchen.

"Askale," said Negassa.

"No no no no no," laughed Bedane, hiding his face in his hands.

"Look at his face," said Negassa to Tsehai. "There is no doubt."

"She is so pretty," said Tsehai, smiling like she believed the whole conversation. "And such good hips. Easy childbirths for her. Congratulations, son."

"By the time you return, she will be ready," said Negassa.

"Do not say anything to anybody," said Bedane, sternly.

"Don't worry, son," said Tsehai, patting his cheek, "we'll keep your secret."

"I don't *have* a sec...," said Bedane, but Negassa was saying, more to the air than to anyone, "Unless we hear of anyone else seeking her hand. Then we'll have to say something, won't we, Tsehai?"

"Oh, of course, Ato Negassa," said Tsehai. "We will run right over there and put a stop to whatever we think is going on!"

"Mother!" said Bedane. "What are you saying!"

"Son," said Negassa, "Your mother is saying that we love you very much and we are not going to see you again for almost a year. That is a long time, so we are playing with you as much as we can before you leave. War is a terrible thing. You may not come back for years." Negassa turned serious. "You may never come back," he said. "That would be a terrible thing for us. We have had too many of our children taken from us already."

"Be sure you come back, son," said Tsehai. "Of what use is the future if we do not see our children making use of it?"

CHAPTER 8

HORSEMEN

"Bedane," said Negassa, "there are four horsemen who ride with every army. They are called Death, Disease, Famine, and Pestilence. You have heard stories about them from the priests. I tell you they are real. I tell you that they are *very* real. They either ride with you or against you, but they are always there. You must protect yourself and your men against them, or Death will surely turn against you and take you.

"The best defense against Disease is this: always be sure your food and water are clean. If any of your men get sick, be sure Egersa sees them at once. There are so many diseases I can't count them all. If a man gets dysentery, leave him behind with a servant. Be careful of the women you meet: some of them will have what we call the Muslim disease. It is the same disease that Muslims call the Christian disease. You know the one I mean. Stay away from crowds as much as possible. Always camp where the air is fresh if you can.

"There are two kinds of pests you must guard against. The first: the rats. They will find an army as soon as it is formed. They will eat anything they can, and get into everything. They carry lice and fleas with them. Keep clean. Keep your clothes clean. One good thing—you will be sleeping outside where it is cold. You can move around. If you get fleas, find a river, take off your clothes, and jump in. Pound your clothes with rocks before you put them back on. Examine them closely. Even one flea can make life miserable. A dozen can make life hell. Keep your hair cut short, no matter how good you think it looks long. Less hair, fewer lice, and easier to find.

"The second group of pests are the camp-followers. They travel in hordes. They are excruciating, and you will want to take your spear to them after a while. They will always know a friend of a relative, or a relative of a friend, and they will drive you crazy begging to work for you. If you order them away, they will give you a look like you have just sentenced them to death. They are very good at this. Do not even talk to them. Let your servants take care of them. They will, if only from their own self-interest. Do not bother yourself with these people. You will have other things to think about. And do not be envious of great chiefs. You will see them on the march, surrounded by hundreds of these leeches. Just know that each of these great chiefs has just one thing on his mind: how to get rid of most of his devoted servants before they eat him out of house and home."

Bedane started to laugh, and kept laughing.

"Go ahead and laugh," said his father. "Believe me. I have seen it! It is not funny!"

"I am sorry, Father," said Bedane, "but it sounds like you have experienced some of these people first-hand."

It was Negassa's turn to chuckle, and he said, "You are very observant, my son. That is good. And that is one good piece of advice I just gave you. Now, let me talk about something that is not so funny. Let me tell you about Death."

Bedane stopped laughing, and looked solemnly at his father, standing there in the dim light of the tukul.

"Against Death, there are two defenses: truth and quickness. You must report everything you see as quickly as possible to those who must know. Do not hesitate for a moment. Hesitation is the death of fools who do not wish to appear foolish. I have seen entire armies destroyed because some fool did not wish to appear foolish, or because he hesitated too long to report something. Report it right away, whatever it is.

"The second defense is speed. You must be quicker than the cat. Get your men to where they are supposed to be quickly. Retreat quickly. Circle quickly. Allow your enemy to see only where you were, never where you are. Fall on him quickly, and you double your strength.

"Now, with Famine," said Negassa, "famine is the easiest. You will leave here with as much grain as your mules and donkeys can carry. Keep it dry, and keep the mildew and rot out of it. Keep it as long as you can. Get as much food from somewhere else as you can. In Assella, the army will provide you with meat. Take whatever you can get. Emperor Menelik has decreed that the army cannot live off the land any more, but there will be opportunities. Maybe a chicken will be running loose and you will not know where to return her. Maybe a village will need protection from shiftas. You are strong. Trade for food. A good source of food is your enemy, but make sure he is dead or has retreated before you go through his goods. Here you must be alert to unseen danger before being quick. Sometimes your enemy will have things others might want. Take those things to trade for food. Do not take rifles from dead enemies. You can't eat a rifle, and you can't shoot two at once. It will only drag you down. Are all your men protected against the smallpox?"

"I know seven of us are," said Bedane. "I am not sure of the other three. They seem not to want to talk about it."

"Aha!" exclaimed Negassa. "A sure sign that they have not been cut. They are frightened. Be sure they are cut before they leave Bekoji. If they do not do it, leave them behind and take three others. I say this because if they will not do it, they are cowards. They will not look Death in the face. If they will not sit still for a little fever, what will they do against bullets on the battlefield? They will run. I know that.

"Two, if you take them, they will die. It would be the same as if you had started with seven. Look at how the pox has ravaged our land! And you can prevent it. You cannot prevent the lung diseases, or the bloody flux, or the diseases that burn the tongue and the throat or the leprosy that takes your arms and legs and nose. Only God can prevent those. But *you* can prevent the smallpox. God has shown us how to do that."

"But there is no inoculant in Bekoji, or anywhere around," protested Bedane.

"Waugh! It is war. You do not need to look for it. It will come to you. Believe me, every time there is war, the diseases will ride with you. No inoculant? Here is what you do. Find a debtera. They are trained in this."

"Mamo says his priest says that the vaccine is against the will of God; that only God says when we die, and nothing can affect that."

"Oh," said Negassa, "so it is Mamo who will not...ah, but he is one of your best, isn't he? God save us from ignorant priests! Here is what you must do. Introduce Mamo to another priest; one who says inoculation is all right. Then, find a debtera. The debtera will find a person with smallpox. It must be a person of good family. It must be a child, without any other diseases. And the debtera must be well-versed in the procedure. I have seen it done. The debtera has a clean half-eggshell, and a clean, sharp knife. First he scrapes the pus out of the sick person's sores, and places it in the egg. Then he adds some honey to it, and mixes it a bit.

"Now, then he cuts the arm of the person to be inoculated, and places some of the pus and honey in the cut, and seals it. That is how it is done."

The day dawned bright and crisp. The night before had been cold enough to create ice in the standing water in the fields. A mist hung low over the Field of Games at Bekoji. It gradually disintegrated and rose in wisps as the sun came up over the knife-edged ridge of Encuolo. Through the mist came the far-off sounds of horses' hooves. The bleating of sheep and goats, the lowing of a full cow, the trilling of thousands of birds—the sounds of a countryside waking filled the air.

Today was different from most days. Today would be the gathering of the cavalry battalions of Bekoji and Meraro and Robi. Together they would gather on this field, receive their orders, decide their line of march, untangle their goods, decipher their marching orders, and spend the night. Tomorrow, in the light of dawn, they would ride in their hundreds out of town, to the north, finding on their way the Horse of Lemu and Sagure awaiting them. From the west across the Dida Plateau would come the companies of Gunguma and Moto. Out of the mountains to the east, from Galama and Ticho and Siltana would come the Horse from those wide valleys. All would converge on Assella, and there they would meet the mounted battalions of northern Arusi. Taken all together, two thousand cavalrymen would ride out of Assella to the north, fully prepared and equipped. The Shoa Oromo would ride once more, dealing terror and death to their enemies as they had done for three hundred years. But this time, they would shoulder Remingtons.

As the sun rose higher in the sky, toward the third hour of the day, the first arrivals came onto the field. They were the staff of the Kanyazmach, and they divided the field into three parts, one part for each battalion.

Then the meto aleka of each battalion divided his land into camping areas for his soldiers. He assigned picketing places for their horses, areas for their camp followers, spaces for the mules and donkeys and chickens, a supply depot, a *shint* area, and a spot for a row of tents.

The tents were reserved for higher officers and the sick. Everyone else slept outside, wrapped in their gabis, which doubled as blankets. True, the nights were cold enough to freeze water, but Ethiopian hides are as thick as the soles of their feet, and the men slept well.

The campaigners began to assemble. There were three hundred soldiers and four hundred and fifty camp followers—servants, wives, girlfriends, blacksmiths, cobblers, sutlers, beggars, adventurers, and people seeking positions (the ones Negassa warned Bedane about). Add the clergy, blessing, blessing, talking, chanting, drumming, and blessing. Add the families saying their goodbyes, bringing last-minute goods. Add the horses, mules, donkeys, sheep, goats, and cows. Add the chickens. Add a frightened armadillo trying to escape all of this hubbub on what used to be his territory. Is this a whirlwind of activity, or what? Is there a silent center to this wild activity?

There is.

In a large battle tent stood the Kanyasmach, talking quietly, surrounded by his three meto alekas and by their lieutenants, their hamsa alekas.

In a little while, the alekas departed to speak to their squadron leaders. From the tenth to the eleventh hours, there would be a review. All cavalrymen must present themselves and their chargers, ready for battle, for inspection by the Kanyasmach and the alekas. Each soldier would be responsible for seeing that his servants, followers, and animals were also present, ready for the march. Would that be enough to keep the troops busy for the day? Would that cause some raised voices in the ranks? Oh, yes. Better now than later.

Would that leave enough time for anyone to think of anything else? Of course. On a far-off part of the field, two men met and spoke.

"I have spoken to Mamo and the other two," said Debtera Markos to Negassa Merga. "They will abide by Bedane's direction. They will take the smallpox in Assella. There will be enough time there in case they get sick and have to rest. And surely there will be enough smallpox there for the proper inoculation."

"Thank God," said Negassa.

"Now," said Markos, "I have done you a favor."

"That is true," replied Negassa. "You have strengthened my son's life by a third."

"So I ask a favor of you," said Markos, quietly.

The two men walked slowly side by side: Markos heavily, parting the way with his cross-topped staff; Negassa treading lightly, still with the spring of the warrior in his step.

"I ask for a year of the life of your second son," said Markos. He stopped and waited for an answer.

There was no answer. Negassa simply stopped and looked at him.

"Will you put him under my protection for a year?" asked the debtera.

"What would you have him do?" blurted out Negassa.

Debtera Markos breathed deeply and answered quietly, "He will be under the protection of the Church."

"What would you have him do?" asked Negassa, sternly.

Markos was ready for this. He had realized early, when coming into this land, that these people, the Oromo, had no subservience in them. They believed in honor and bravery and fealty, but unlike so many other peoples of this Empire, there was no sense of bowing to the will of others. This was the pride which had kept them strong.

"A friend of mine comes from Ba'le next week," he said. "He is a great priest; a powerful priest. He needs a helper."

"You ask for Chala to be his servant?" said Negassa. He could hardly keep from smiling. He knew his son well; knew the strength of his backbone. People who tried to make Chala a servant would be well advised to search elsewhere was Negassa's thought.

"My friend must ride to the north," said Markos. "He goes to the Court of Menelik. He will be among the clergy who accompany the Emperor and the Empress. He will pray for them, and protect them. He is a very strong priest."

Negassa simply stared and said, "He is one of those supplicants to the Court who follow the nobles around like dogs begging for a piece of injera? My son is to be a servant to a dog?"

"No," said Markos. "I have said, my friend is a very powerful priest."

"By the glory of Christ and his Virgin Mother," said Negassa, "what you say had better be truthful, Reverend Father, because you are frightening me. You are talking about the future of my family, and the possible destruction of it."

"I know how you have suffered," said Markos quietly. "Moreover, I know how many of your children are buried in the graveyard. I know that your stalwart eldest son is now going to test his life against the steel and thunder of the Ferengi. But I tell you, Negassa, I tell you: my friend is a great man, a great priest. And I tell you that your son Chala is a very unusual son. Now, he is not big enough to fight, and not small enough to tend the animals, and he worries a lot about who and what he is and what he is to do with his life. Well, I tell you, my friend Negassa, that a lot of the saints were like that, too. Questioning. Questioning. Your son Chala questioned early. He is very bright."

"Not as bright as his cousin Nagara," said Negassa, "as you have told him time after time."

"Faugh!" said Markos. "There is no comparison. Nagara is bright; quick. Yes, that is true. But Chala has the deep understanding. With time, it will come out, and shine like a star or a jewel. I tell Chala that Nagara is swifter merely to keep him on course."

"Who is this priest?" said Negassa.

"His name is Haile Mikael Tesfaye."

"'The Power of Michael, Son of Hope,'" said Negassa. "A strong name. What is his position?"

"He is the Bishop of Ba'le Provence," said Markos.

Negassa almost gasped. "I am astounded!" he said, drawing in his breath. "You know the bishop of Ba'le Province?"

"We studied together," said Markos. "We are friends from long ago."

Negassa looked at the horizon of trees for a long time. "You are a strange debtera indeed," he said to Markos, "who makes friends of bishops."

Markos smiled. "He was brilliant. First in the class. First in many classes. I was not." The priest lifted up his hands and looked up at the sky. "God gives us to do what we are intended to do," he said, and waited.

"What would Chala do for the bishop?" asked Negassa.

"Take care of his personal needs," said Markos, with a shrug. "Buy his food. Arrange his lodgings on the march. Hold his horse at the palace. The usual things. Be his defender from the mobs. Beat off the beggars with a stick when they get too thick around him. You know how it is up there."

"He would be the one who runs before the bishop's horse, clearing the way," mused Negassa, not liking much of what he was hearing.

"I know what you're thinking, friend Negassa," said Markos. "That Chala would not do servant's work. Do not worry. No, Chala will not run before the horse. He will have his own horse. He will ride at the side of the bishop. Well, slightly behind, of course, but close enough to learn a lot from my friend." Markos paused, and brightened. "And in the countryside," he added, "they would ride side by side, I am sure. Haile Mikael is not one to make a lot of show and demand subservience and that sort of thing. Except in public, of course, to protect his reputation. That sort of thing is sometimes required in the circles in which a bishop rides. But in his dealings with people on an ordinary basis? Ah," said Markos, "he is too close to God to partake of vanity and all that foolishness that comes along with it. He is a good man."

"Why Chala?" asked Negassa.

"Bishop Haile Mikael asked me to find someone. He wanted no one from Ba'le. He wanted someone he does not know; someone who is not a fawner, who will not fall all over him kissing his hand and his feet and the hem of his garment. A good, bright, intelligent boy, he said. Someone with promise. Any choice he could make in Ba'le would be mired in politics. Terrible. So he chose to ask me to find someone. I think Chala would be best."

"You think Chala will become a priest?" asked Negassa.

"I don't know," said Markos. "I do think he would be a good one, if that is what he chooses."

Negassa thought. It was something that he had never thought of before. A priest in the family. So many of them were scamps or scoundrels, and they always seemed to side with the nobles over the farmer. But some of them were truly good men, like Markos here. Negassa believed Markos to be a good man. Likewise, the chief priest of the Church of Saint George, Gebre Medhin Teshome, was a good sort, looking out for his flock. A good shepherd. But this business of the bishop, now—that sent a cold chill up Negassa's spine.

"Markos," he said, "two things trouble me. One, Chala has never been away from home before. That is bad enough. If these were peaceful times, that would be one thing. But these are not peaceful times. And you know as well as I do that being near the Emperor is the surest way to meet danger that you can find. Look at our history. Emperor Tewodros—Theodore the Great—dead, a suicide, after his defeat by the British at Magdala. Emperor Yohannes, dead from a stray bullet after a victory at Galabat over the Dervishes. Now it is the turn of Emperor Menelik to put himself under the cannon of the Ferengi. Who knows what will happen? And if the Ferengis and their askaris break through and go for Menelik, there will be your friend the bishop standing there with all of his brethren, eyes and arms lifted to the heavens, and there will be my son Chala, wondering which way to turn and wondering where his spear is."

"Let him bring his spear," said Markos.

"What will I do if my sons do not come back?" said Negassa. "What will I do with all my lands that I fought so hard for? My reward—a lot of land and no sons. What good is that? What would I do?"

"God would tell you what to do," said Markos.

"I will have to think about this, Reverend Father," said Negassa. "With one hand, you have helped me to preserve my son Bedane's life. With the other, you would have me place both my sons in danger. What am I to do? I will need time to think about this."

"That is all I ask," said Markos.

"When does the Bishop arrive?"

"One week from today, God willing," said Markos. "Take time to think, brother Negassa. But let me know soon. I hope you say yes. It could be a great opportunity for Chala."

Negassa sighed. "By the Power of the Trinity!" he said, "I wonder what Tsehai will think of this!"

"No no no no no!" said Tsehai. "He cannot do this. Markos cannot ask this of us."

There was a stream at the edge of the Field of Games that had for thousands of years cut its way into the earth and by now had made a deep and wide ravine, sheltered from the wind and fertile enough for large trees to grow. This stream had been set aside for drinking water for the gathering, and it was there that Negassa had taken Tsehai. They went down the stream a bit from where the women of the encampment scooped gourds of water into large earthenware pots, and they walked until they found a shady glen where they could have privacy, surrounded by the silence and the huge trees. It was there that Negassa told Tsehai about his talk with Debtera Markos.

"It is too much, Negassa," Tsehai said. "He asks too much of us. Are we to be left only with the child in my belly, about whom we know nothing? Three are already taken from us. Are we to lose two more? It is bad enough that Bedane goes now, as he must, but Chala is not yet of age. Who will help you in the fields? Who will supervise the farm?"

"I have been all over this in my mind," replied Negassa. "I am not telling you that this must be. It is like a bolt of lightning in my head. It is just there."

"Who is this priest, anyway?" said Tsehai. "This bishop? What kind of bishop is he? Why does he ride alone? Where are his servants? His slaves?"

"I did not ask," said Negassa, abashed. "I did not think to ask."

Tsehai was quiet for a long time. She pressed her palms together, in a gesture of prayer, and lowering her head, pressed her fingers against her forehead, her fingers touching the blue cross tattooed there. She stood silently in the green grass of the riverbank, the stream murmuring gently at her feet. Finally, she looked up at Negassa.

"I have heard," she said, "that to the north and to the west things are different than they are here. I am just a poor country woman, Negassa, but I have heard things. I know that over those hills there are many strong men, who have many servants and slaves from the wars. Why does the bishop travel alone? How can he stop a strong man from taking our son? Does he wish to make him a slave? Sell him to another? I have heard of such things happening. I cannot bear this, Negassa. My belly hurts now. I do not wish to harm the little one inside." Tsehai sat down on a high rock, breathing heavily. A light breeze moved through the branches of the trees.

"Negassa," she said, "this might be an honor, but I am so frightened. It might be the death of all of us. Who would give up such a good life as we have for something of little worth? For an honor?" She was silent.

Negassa said, "I owe Markos a favor, but nothing as big as what he asks of me. It is obvious to me that Markos owes the bishop a favor, or wants to curry favor with his old friend. For his own advancement, I suppose. And why not? What is wrong with that? But, Tsehai, I think there is more here than that. I think Markos really feels that there is an opportunity here for Chala."

Then both were silent. After a long time, both almost at the same second looked at each other and said, "We must meet with this bishop before we let Chala go." They said it almost as one person and they laughed.

"We must have the bishop to dinner," Tsehai continued. "Only then will we know what kind of a man he is. Only after that can we give permission."

"I will tell Markos that," said Negassa. "He will not like it. He will want it settled, so that if we decide no, he can find another boy."

"Then what is lost?" said Tsehai. "Only a sacrifice. And what is gained?"

"The safety of our son," said Negassa. "He is not yet a warrior, so this is a big thing. We are strong. The Shoa Oromo are strong, and we do not give away our children."

"But then," said Tsehai, "if Markos agrees to wait, it is a sign that he is truly interested in our son, and is considering his well-being as well as that of his friend."

"Yes," said Negassa. "If he agrees to wait, then we will be able to meet with this bishop, and find out what kind of a person he is. That is a good plan. That is a strong plan."

"Negassa," said Tsehai, slipping off the rock and taking him by the arm, "take me back to the field. It is getting late. We must be there to see Bedane form his squadron. I am happy now with what we have decided."

"I too am happy," said Negassa, and he took her by the arm.

Negassa and Tsehai walked across the Field of Games. In a few minutes it would be time for the formation of troops to be reviewed by the Kanyazmach. The soldiers were busy readying their mounts and checking their equipment. Negassa stopped beside a donkey and spoke quietly to the servant holding the animal, then took a large round package wrapped in hide off the beast's back.

Then Negassa and Tsehai walked to the area where Chala was helping Bedane adjust Star's harness. They stood watching the two boys work, and waited for them to finish. Around them, Bedane's soldiers stood talking or examining their equipment. It was the time of day when the wind went down and a calm settled over the land.

"Bedane," said Negassa. Bedane looked up and smiled.

"Well, Father," he said. "I think we are just about ready."

"That is good," said Negassa. "Now, I have something to give you."

Bedane was silent. Negassa opened the package of hide and pulled out a shield. It was a glorious shield, made of the finest black hippopotamus hide, and embossed with silver. Around the rim of the shield a silver pattern played, and the center of the shield was strong with silver. It shone in the afternoon sun. Negassa held out the shield to his son. "Take it," he said.

"I cannot take that, Father," said Bedane. "It is too good. It is too beautiful."

"Now this beautiful shield is yours," said Negassa. "It is time for you to carry it into battle."

Bedane's men stood around him in a wide circle. "Ah!" said Mamo, "it *is* beautiful, Bedane." And Wondimu said, "Take it, Bedane, and lead us with it. With such a shield, we cannot fail. It will bring us glory."

"I have not earned this shield," said Bedane.

"You will have to prove yourself worthy of it," replied Negassa. "I think you can do that." The father smiled.

"It is the shield of a tested warrior," said Bedane.

"It is yours to fill with deeds of valor," said Negassa. "Let those deeds sink into it, and with each deed it will grow stronger, and protect you. It is your shield against Death and against all the ills of war. Fill it with valiant deeds."

Bedane had never seen his father look so serious. He bowed deeply to him. Negassa handed him the shield.

"It is light," said Bedane.

"It is the work of the hippopotamus," said Negassa, laughing. "It is light to let him swim fast and surface fast, but it is strong to protect him from the lion and the crocodile. It cannot stop a bullet, but it can deflect one. And it will frighten any opponent in battle. Boys," he said, "don't forget that. They'll be frightened of you. Make sure they have reason to be scared."

Negassa paused just an instant and looked around. His eyes were gleaming. His memories of great battles in the west were welling up in his mind's eye. "All right," he said to the squadron, "Mount up. It is time for the review. The worst thing you can do is to be late. The Kanyazmach will skin you alive."

Throughout all this, Chala had been silent. As soon as his father had taken out the shield and presented it to his brother, his mind spoke to him with such force that he could only stand silently. "I want to go," said his mind. "I want to go. I have to go."

"What can I do with this rabble!" Babilla Wami was yelling to Aleka Bedasa. "Look at this garbage! They are not worthy to be fed to the hyenas! Look at this one. His spear tip falls off. Look at that one's servant—running sores all over. He will infect the whole camp, I tell you!"

The review was not going well, at least in Babilla's eyes, and he was furious. "Look at them!" he fumed. "They can't even line up in good order to show off for their folks. The Ferengi are going to laugh at them. They will aim for them with their cannon just to see them scatter."

Babilla was furious, and wheeled his horse up and down the line, screaming at the troopers. "Line up straight, you idiots! You dogs! Have you never been on a horse before? You shankalla! You baria! You slaves! May Menelik die before I go into battle with you at my back.

"Sons-of-bitches!" he muttered under his breath as he rode back to Bedasa. "Look at them, sir. What can I do? They will disgrace us."

"Stop whining, Babilla," said the Aleka, with a twinkle in his eye. "Just get them into a straight line for the Kanyazmach. They will be fine after you have trained them for two weeks."

Babilla scowled. "I have already trained them," he muttered through clenched teeth.

"You have gotten their attention, anyway," laughed Bedasa. "Go line them up; then we'll be ready for the review."

"Yes, sir!" said Babilla, and wheeled his horse back toward the Meraro battalion.

"Oh, God, here he comes again," thought a hundred minds in unison. The reputation of The Wild Warrior Of Kofele was being borne out. Babilla was the lieutenant of Meto Aleka Bedasa, and it was his duty to safeguard his Meto Aleka. The troopers had the impression that Babilla would kill them all in order to do his duty.

"I want those horses lined up straight!" bellowed Babilla. "I want their noses in a straight line, so I can shoot a rifle bullet down this line and not ping any of their nostrils. That's the least you can do for your Aleka, and for your Kanyazmach, and for your Emperor!"

Babilla stopped his horse and snorted. Incredibly, the line was really straight. Babilla's eyes gleamed with pleasure. "You sons-of-bitches!" he yelled. "I'll bet you don't even know who your fathers are!"

That was the worst insult you could hurl at a man in our country. Babilla glared at his troopers, daring any of them to meet his eyes. Muscles were bunched in their arms and stomachs, and you could feel a seething anger beginning to grow, but not one of the men raised his eyes. They were too new at this. They didn't know what was happening to them. This had never happened before. Even the strongest warriors among them—even people like Wondimu and Mamo—behaved like little puppies before the glare of the Wild Warrior's wrath. All any of them did was to keep his horse absolutely still.

Beyond the line of horsemen, behind their servants and animals and equipment, in the midst of the spectators, Negassa, out of politeness, drew the edge of his gabi across in front of his mouth and smiled. He watched his brother far across the field, sitting quietly on his horse, waiting patiently for Babilla to shape up the troops.

And although they were far off from each other, the eyes of Bedasa and Negassa met, and understood. Their eyes were grave and serious. They were proud of the soldiers; proud to see this disciplined line of horse. But they knew that there was much yet to be done. Babilla's job was to make these men as crazy as he was, and he had just begun. Their anger and their valor had to grow into fury and bravery in time for battle. These men all had strength. They all had skill in horsemanship and in the use of the spear. Now they needed instruction in fighting and the shooting of the rifle and living off the land. But before anything else, they had to be taught fury and bravery. Babilla would be an excellent teacher.

Negassa and Bedasa looked into each other's eyes, and each nodded almost imperceptibly. It was their farewell to each other.

CHAPTER 11

THE WAR DRUMS OF THE RAS

The next morning at the second hour of the day, the *nagarit*—the great war drums of Ras Gobena of Ba'le—boomed out in unison over the Field of Games. They sounded just once, and would continue to do so once every minute for the next thirty minutes. At the end of that time, the army would be packed and ready to go, all at attention, the troopers on horseback, their followers standing by the donkeys and mules, all of them ready to form up for the march to Assella.

At the twenty-sixth drumbeat, Bedane began to form up his squadron along an imaginary line pointed out in the dirt by Babilla with his spear. Other squadrons were forming at the same time, in the crispness of early morning under that cloudless blue sky.

At the twenty-eighth drumbeat, the line was formed, and the three hundred troopers of the battalions of Meraro, Bekoji, and Robi settled into their saddles. The line faced east. Meraro was on the right, Bekoji in the center, and Robi on the left.

At the twenty-ninth drumbeat, everyone became as silent and still as statues. Each trooper held his shield and best spears in his left hand and the reins of his horse in the right, and waited.

At the thirtieth drumbeat, the Kanyazmach, the two sons of Ras Gobena, and the three alekas trotted their horses out of the trees near the edge of Bekoji town and walked them slowly down the line of troops. They looked at every man and every horse. There was no way to tell what they thought.

When they reached the end of the line they wheeled their horses and trotted them to the center of the field, next to where the great drums were being slung into their harnesses between teams of powerful mules. Everyone strained and leaned forward just a bit to hear what the Kanyazmach had to say.

"Today," said the Kanyazmach, "we go to the north, to join our Emperor. We all know why we are going. Our land has been invaded by the Ferengi, and we must kill their soldiers and drive them out.

"It will be a long journey. You must all keep strong. The Emperor depends on it. You will train on the way, so that when the battle begins you will be ready.

"Today we will go as far as Lemu. We will camp just to the north of that town. The Lemu battalion will join us there tonight.

"Now you may not think that that is such a long trip. I am sure that many of you have walked or ridden there in a very short time. But listen to me, boys. This is your lesson for today. Today you will see what it takes to move an army from one place to another. Get wisdom from this day. Let us make this first day of ours a good one. Listen to your leaders and your alekas. Listen to their advice.

"Now listen to me. We depart now. Unfurl the flags. We depart in a column of fours, down the main road through town. Follow me now at a canter. I have spoken."

The Kanyazmach and the Ba'le nobles wheeled to the left, made a wide circle, and cantered their horses toward the road, followed by their staffs and flag bearers. The green flag of Arusi and the red flag of Ba'le streamed out together side by side.

The column turned toward the right and, describing a wide arc, followed their alekas into the road. When the troopers were all assembled in rank in the road, a signal was given, and the leading aleka, Bedasa Merga, began to ride at a walk, then at a trot, then at a canter. The troopers followed, urging their horses onward.

What a brave sight they made! As they rode through town past the cheering people, the troopers hardly looked at them but concentrated on their riding, concentrated on looking brave and skilled. The low rumble of their horses' hooves seemed to open the ground before them and sew it back up in back of them. They rode easily and slowly, feeling their power, finding strength they never knew they had, knowing the exhilaration of the centaur.

There was no lust for battle in them; no, not yet. There was just a wonderful feeling of power, and goodness, and strength of purpose, and youth.

Through the town they cantered, and on up the road to the north, the horses held tightly reined. The purposeful faces of the troopers looked straight ahead. Their dark skins glistened under their monkeyskin headdresses. On, up, and over the hill to the north they went, and disappeared, and the sound of the horses' hooves, like the sound of a roaring river, diminished in the distance, but never really ended. That sound is still there, faintly, to this day. It is in our memory, and now it is in yours, and it will never die.

That is what we say in our country.

And these were the warriors who followed Bedane Negassa to the north: there was Mamo Galata, who played in the horse games with Bedane. There was Wondimu Gemechu, always ready to smile or dance or sing an old song, who could throw a spear as far as anyone in the province. Egersa Regasa followed him, with his heart full of searching and his head full of knowledge of plants and herbs. Tula Urga, Dabale Ariti, and Shifaraw Merga—all strong, strong men from the plains of Meraro—gave the group a fearsome appearance. Shasho Megenasa, the sharpshooter, rode with eyes that gleamed for battle. Taffa Bulcha, sometimes laughing, sometimes brooding, sometimes writing songs in his head for Wondimu to sing, knew more about the country than anyone else, and could always tell exactly where he was, and where he should be going. And finally there was quick Ibbsa Biya, who could show up where you would least expect him, a long time before you thought anyone could be there. Ibbsa carried his bible with him and referred to it often. These, then, were the soldiers who followed Bedane Negassa into battle.

Making a fine appearance, the column rode north on the main track and then came down a decline to encounter its first obstacle—the ford of the Galema River. True, it was not much of an obstacle. It was simply a small stream, some thirty feet wide, and the stony bottom had been pounded very smooth by decades of travel over this spot.

The obstacle was more in its effect on the column than on anything else. The first horses went in and out fast, and on up the hill on the other side, but they kicked up water. This caused the second rank of horses to miss a beat, thus slowing them down just a bit, and so on and so on through ranks of horses, until those men coming up onto the southern bank were, if not holding their horses still, just walking them slowly, and watching the head of the column climb up the northern bank in some disarray.

It was an inexorable fact of nature. Bodies at speed, forced to slow, would force other bodies behind them to slow faster than the bodies in front. And thus it is that armies, if untrained, take longer to get to where they are going than anything else in the world and can be cut to pieces by a well-trained force skilled in quickness and surprise.

So this was a good lesson for all the soldiers, all of whom had galloped and splashed their horses individually across this stream for years. Now they knew more than they did before. In their minds they felt vulnerable, and they knew that in the future there would have to be outriders and scouts well ahead of the column to protect it, to be the eyes and ears of the column, as the column would be the eyes and ears of the Emperor.

This, then, would be the job of the meto alekas and the hamsa alekas—to make the column as vigilant as the cat, tense and coiled and ready to spring immediately to defend itself; to make it so savage that it could pounce on an enemy and slash and rip it to pieces before the enemy even knew the column was there. This is what they would learn at Assella.

Babilla Wami was at the top of the northern bank of the river, his horse off to one side. "Column of twos!" he was calling out as the horses came up to the crest. "Column of twos! Column of twos!" he called out over and over. "And keep the pace up. Keep them kicking."

So on into the day the column surged to the north.

At the fifth hour of the day the Kanyazmach called a halt next to a wide, smooth-running stream with green grass on its banks and great water-smoothed rocks in its courses. As the men sat on the banks or watered their horses, Babilla Wami approached Bedane and said, "Bedane, you will take your squadron and come with me. We ride ahead of the others and look for our campground for the night. The other hamsa alekas and their picked squadrons will ride with us, and together with the Kanyazmach we will decide on the camp."

"It is an honor," said Bedane, bowing delightedly.

"That's what you think," said Babilla. "You get to make all the mistakes and listen to all the complaints. That's all right. You will learn fast, ahead of the others. Gather your men and mount up."

It was a pleasant ride towards Lemu, for the most part through fields and large, sparsely situated trees that grew along the banks of the stream. The thirty-three men and horses enjoyed themselves here. This was a more manageable group than three hundred. They were not obliged to keep in line, either. Each horse and rider picked their own way along the trail and through the fields. They moved rapidly, but not in so much of a hurry. Twice they crossed the stream, clambering down one side, slipping up the other, some of the men leading their mounts, some riding carefully.

It was toward the ninth hour of the day that, north of the small village of Lemu, they came upon a wide open fallow field. This field had been chosen some days before by scouts. It was wide enough to form the camp, and was bordered by the brook, which formed the east and north sides of it. The brook here was bordered by thick stands of gnarled old trees.

Babilla Wami rode to the center of the field, where it rose just slightly into a little hillock. "Everyone down," he said, facing the troopers. "Three of you in each squad, hold the horses. Face them at me in a semi-circle. The rest of you, gather in front of them. Make sure everyone can see this piece of ground."

Babilla took his spear and drove it into the ground. There was a general milling around while everyone got the horses straight and took places where they could see the spear shaft.

"Now," said Babilla, "look at me." He stood with his hands on the shaft of his spear. "Where we are is where the Kanyazmach will pitch his tent and camp for the night. Look around. What do you see?"

The men looked. Although the hillock seemed low, from it you could see for miles in all directions.

"Listen, boys," said Babilla. "This may seem simple, but it is very important. The first duty of an army is to protect itself. Suppose we are not here at home in Arusi. Suppose instead we are off somewhere in the west, in Kaffa, for instance, in the middle of a war. What do we want? We want to be able to see an enemy coming at us no matter how he comes. Now what do you see here? Look around. From here, you can see for miles in any direction. There are some gullies and some hidden approaches. You will find them later and set guards on them. But for the most part, from here the Kanyazmach can see everything. It is ideal. From here, if danger comes, the Kanyazmach can direct us to where it is, and we can deal with it quickly. Look around. Then when you become a Kanyazmach, if you live long enough, you will know what kind of a place you will want to set up your camp."

Babilla paused, and the men looked around. The light breeze from the west blew against their faces, into their nostrils and along their necks. The world was still. Not even a vulture soared in the mid-afternoon sky. Babilla broke the silence.

"Now," he said, "You ones in front. Get down. Squat. Kneel. Whatever. Just make sure you can see this piece of bare ground." He drew his spear out of the earth, and used it like a giant pointer.

"Here is where the tent of the Kanyazmach will be placed," he said. "As you look at me, you are looking north. That is where we are going. That is our line of march. So, the opening of the Kanyazmach's tent will be placed toward the north, toward the direction of our line of march. Is that clear?"

Some of the men nodded.

"Good," said Babilla. "This may seem simple. This may seem stupid. But it is very important. Until you return to your tukul, this tent is the center of your world; the center of your life. You must understand what goes on here. You must understand the order of things. Without order, there is craziness and stupidity, and probably a slow death with your balls cut off and your guts wrapped around your neck. Do I have your attention?"

He had their attention. Battle in Ethiopia was very personal and very dangerous. They all knew that.

"Now," said Babilla, "the tent always opens in the direction of the march, which in our case is north. Around the tent are stationed the Kanyazmach's personal guards, more in front than in back. In back are kept his horses, the horses of his guards, his retinue, his guards' servants, donkeys, cows, whatever."

Babilla paused. Around the spot of earth where his spear had struck he drew a square. "Here is the tent," he said. "Here are the guards and the horses." He drew a circle around the square.

"Now," Babilla continued, "each night one man from each squad will report here, and supplement the Kanyazmach guard. Is that clear? So tonight, three of you will be here. Bedane, I appoint you to inform the other Meraro battalion squad leaders. See that it is done as soon as they are settled. The hamsas of Bekoji and Robi will do the same for the Bekoji and Robi battalions. I will inform the Lemu hamsa aleka when he arrives, and let him worry about them.

"For the rest of it," said Babilla, going back to his spear drawing, "watch carefully. Around the tent tonight there will be a larger circle. It will be made up of the Bekoji, Robi, and Lemu battalions. In front of the Bekoji battalion, at the front of the march, will be the Meraro battalion. Every night that we camp, a different battalion will take the forward position, and the forward battalion from the night before will drop back into the circle. Understood? It sounds complicated, but it isn't. All it takes is one word from the Kanyazmach each morning. If there is no word, the formation remains the same."

The three squads, after marking the site of the Kanyazmach's tent, broke into three groups and rode to their respective campgrounds. There, their hamsa alekas showed them what to do next. The Meraro squad stayed with Babilla.

"We," said Babilla, "the Meraro battalion, tonight are like a shield for the camp. So deploy yourselves like a shield, off to the left and the right. Where each of you stops, there must be made room for a squadron of ten, their fires, their tents, their animals and their servants. The line must be wide enough to shield the rest of the camp, but not so wide that you are too thin to defend it. Now, go out to the left and the right, and stop where I tell you. When you get to the right places, after I check them, stay there. Each of you, for a while, think of yourself as a squad leader, and decide where you will place your fires, tents, servants, animals, and guards. Especially the guards. Then I will come by and inspect your work and tell you how stupid you are. Go now, form the shield. Bedane, you stay here in the center, with me. We will move just to the right of center."

When the other riders had moved off, Babilla said, "Bedane, what I say to you now is most important. I will be quick, and we will review this later."

Bedane looked at Hamsa Aleka Babilla intently.

"You have a good, strong squadron, Bedane, but they will be nothing but rabble unless they can all act with authority. Here is how you will give them authority: you will appoint yourself an assistant squad leader. You will appoint two men to be in charge of the food; two in charge of the other supplies. Another will become leader of the guards, and will assign them each night. He will have an assistant. Another will be in charge of keeping the men well. Another with a good fast horse will be the courier. If there are other assignments, you can pour them on your men like hot tea into a glass. They won't like it, but they will see that it must be done."

"Here is how you will do this: the men that you assign to be in charge of the food must be good, strong men. They must have a sense of humor and a sense of justice: a sense of humor because everyone will think at first that you have assigned them to be cooks, and they will laugh at them; a sense of justice because it is they who will be responsible for finding the food and distributing it. They must be men who can be ruthless. They must be good scavengers. They must be trustworthy because they will control everyone's food.

"That is what you must decide: who can do that.

"Now, your assistant. He must be the best of them, the one who can lead them if something happens to you. One or the other of you must always be in camp. If you are not in camp, he leads, and speaks for you. If you are both in camp, you, of course, lead.

"You must choose wisely and well. The ones who are in charge of supplies must be ones who will see that nothing is forgotten. They must want to accumulate things—bullets, for instance. They must be men who can remember every piece of equipment everyone owns. You must be well-equipped. At the same time, you must not be overburdened. They must make sense.

"The leader of the guards must want to fight. He must have courage, and through his example he must give courage to others. But you must control him.

"The one who heals is very important. He heals not only bodies, but minds. You have no idea what it is like to be in a strange land, among strange people, people who could turn on you with hatred at a moment's notice. You have no idea of the fear that can cause in a man. In a squad. In an entire army. And when that fear begins to work—waugh! It is not pretty, believe me. It is not pretty at all.

"Your courier will be your lifeline to headquarters. He must be one who can speak quickly and with great accuracy. If he comes back from headquarters and says, "The Kanyazmach said to charge straight ahead," when the Kanyazmach actually said, "Charge to the right!" he can get your whole squad killed in less time than it takes to blink. Wouldn't that be nice? Above all, he must be someone who is comfortable with the truth, even if he hates the truth he has to tell.

"Now you yourself: through training your men in such a fine manner, you should leave yourself nothing to do. Nothing to do but think, and look ahead. To see what is coming down the road to you. And what is coming up on the road you are traveling. Your mind must be out in front of everything. When you do this, you will be successful. And your first duty is toward your men. Your warriors. You must keep them well, and safe, and ready to fight. Then when the fight comes, they will reward you by keeping you safe, and selling their lives as dearly as possible. You will be their king, in a small way. You will have a strong band, and you will make them stronger, and they will give their strength to you. That is how it works.

"Bedane, listen well. This may seem strange coming from a man who is known as The Wild Warrior Of Kofele, but the reason I can be a wild warrior is because I know I have you and your men, all the squadron leaders and their men, behind me.

"See how it works. In this Army of the Right Hand, I am the leader of the guards. Meto Aleka Bedasa is the leader of my squad. I train you so that he can look afar off and be aware of what is coming down the road. That way, he can protect us. At the same time, the Meto Aleka is a leader of the guards for the Kanyazmach, and the Kanyazmach for the Ras, and the Ras for the Prince, and the Prince for the Emperor, and the Emperor for the Land. Do you see how it works?"

Bedane was overwhelmed by the number and speed of Babilla's words. "It is complicated," he said. "You give so much so quickly."

"It is not something to be learned in an hour," said Babilla, "but tell me: do you understand what you are to do with your squad?"

"Yes," said Bedane.

"That is enough for now," said Babilla. "The rest, the business about the rases and kings and the Emperor and the Land—well, what it all means is that you protect the Emperor, who protects the Land, and you do that best by training your squad well. 'A smart farmer is worth ten foolish princes.' Do you understand?"

"I do," said Bedane.

"That is good," replied Babilla with a smile, "because in a sense you will be my assistant hamsa aleka. Your first assignment will be this afternoon. When they come up, you will gather all the other squad leaders, and tell them how to train their squads, just as I have told you. Then, after they have appointed their assistants, you will gather them together again and bring them, with their shields and spears, on foot to the tent of the Kanyazmach. You squad leaders will be his guards for the night. Then we will see what kind of assistants you have appointed, when they are thrown so quickly on their own. Ha! Now, do you have any questions?"

"Where do I place my guards?"

"Normally, you would place two together, so one could watch while the other sleeps. But for tonight," said Babilla, pointing, "put them apart, one on this side, one on the other side of the stream. No rifles. Spears and shields only. No noise. Just reporting."

"Where do they relieve themselves?"

Babilla squinted. "In that patch of trees. Don't let them go all over. Tell them that patch of trees, and to watch their step when they go in there." Babilla laughed.

"It's pretty close to the river," said Bedane.

"If you've got some birdbrain who doesn't know enough to keep his shit out of the river, I guess he'll have to drink his shit in the morning. If anybody's that stupid, he shouldn't be here. But you're right. Tell them no pissing in the stream. And tell your servants that no animals are allowed near the stream until we have drawn all the water we need in the morning.

"That should cover it. Let's go see how your fellows are doing. And watch them. See which ones you think are the best leaders. It doesn't just go up and down in your squad. It goes back and forth among squads. You, as senior squadron leader of the Meraro battalion, will choose a first assistant and second assistant from among the other squad leaders."

"This sounds *very* complicated," said Bedane.

"It is not," said Babilla Wami. "It is simple. I have asked you to do three things: instruct your squad; instruct your fellow squadron leaders; observe your fellow squadron leaders. As for the last, this is the reason: if something happens to you, I want to know who I can rely on. I want you to tell me who that is. Understood?"

"Understood," said Bedane. As he and Babilla rode to observe the positions of his men, Bedane felt good. He felt strong. Babilla's words had filled him with knowledge. They would help make him a good leader.

Bedane made his choices as follows:

As his assistant he chose Mamo Galata, for his steadiness and solidness and the no-nonsense way he had of staring at people out of glowering eyes set in that dark head. People would follow the orders of such a man.

In charge of supplies, he appointed Wondimu Gemechu and Shifaraw Merga. Wondimu was always worrying about the quantity of grain his large, extended family would have for the winter and Shifaraw was of a like mind about horses, donkeys, and cattle. They were worriers, Bedane reasoned, so they might as well have something to worry about.

Tula Urga and Dabale Ariti he placed in charge of food. He did this with some trepidation because he felt that both of them might be too good for what they might have to do. He would speak to them about that.

Egersa Regasa was named *hakim*, in charge of the health of the warriors, their servants, and all the animals.

Shasho Megenasa was named co-leader of the guards. He would use some of his energy in setting up the rotation of guards.

Taffa Bulcha was named co-leader of the guards, to leaven the decisions of the hot-blooded Shasho. He was also admonished to learn the history of the campaign, and to set it down later when he got the chance.

Ibbsa Biya was named courier. He was quick as lightning, with a keen mind. He always carried with him a copy of the Book that he had gotten somehow. He was truthful to a fault. This quality, thought Bedane, would bring much good information to him.

To Mamo, Bedane said, "My friend, I would trust you with my life. Be sure you are fair with your decisions. Be sure the men carry out your orders. Be sure they are fair with others. Tonight, you are in charge. Review the rotation of the guards with Shasho, and make sure everything is in order for the march tomorrow."

To Wondimu and Shifaraw he said, "Especially be sure that every morning, everything is ready to go by the first hour. It must look like it is new equipment. Be sure the servants pack it carefully."

To Tula and Dabale he said, "A great deal of the country we must go through is poor, and without much food. You must find food for us, and keep us strong. Do not forget: you owe your allegiance to us first—to your squadron mates. You must get us home alive. When you are dealing with others in obtaining food, be just if you can, but do not let your better natures allow you to be weak. Be strong, and be sure to keep us strong."

To Egersa he said, "Egersa, my friend, I feel myself very lucky to have you with us. I think you are the best doctor in the province, if not the Empire. Keep us strong, and look for new weeds and potions on the way."

To Shasho he said, "Shasho, your position requires that you be just. On a long ride like this, some anger may develop between the best of friends. See that you do not assign those who are temporarily angry with each other to guard duty together. And see that the duty is always fair, so that no one bears you or me a grudge. That can hurt us. Be sure that it doesn't happen."

To Taffa he said, "Taffa, you know how hot-headed Shasho can be. You must always be there for the guards, to be sure things are going right for them. Counsel them wisely. They will come to you with their problems. I know this. You are the one who will hold them together."

And finally to Ibbsa he said, "Ibbsa, you have the fastest and keenest and most accurate mind I know. You must tell me *exactly* what people say. Do not tell me what you think until I ask you. I will ask you, but first—tell me just what has been said. Peoples' minds are different. Sometimes it is hard to understand their reasoning, but we must listen to them to understand. Be quick as lightning, and always carry your spear."

And to himself, Bedane said, "I think I have the best squadron in the entire army. Thank you, Father, and Uncle Bedasa, for training me to choose well."

CHAPTER 12

THE GREAT BASHAW

The huge tent of the Kanyazmach was the center of a mass of swirling activity. It was the eleventh hour of the day when Bedane and the other Meraro squadron leaders arrived to begin their guard duty. The Kanyazmach's personal guards had developed a perimeter, but with the comings and goings of untrained guard units, horses, servants, donkeys, mules, officers, hangers-on, local dignitaries from Lemu, couriers, priests, and local villagers anxious to sell their wares to all of these, the scene appeared to be the dream of a whirling dervish.

Bedane searched for someone in authority able to direct him to his post. Near the opening of the tent, he approached the Aleka of the Bekoji battalion, Merga Gebre Meskal, and asked what he was to do.

"It is simple," said Aleka Merga.

There were those words again. Now every time he heard those words, Bedane became automatically alert. This 'simple' business seemed to be the watchword of every officer in the army.

"It is simple," repeated Aleka Merga. "You take your formation around the tent in the same position that your battalion has taken in the field. Except that it is, in your case, reversed."

"Reversed," said Bedane, with a quizzical look on his face.

"Reversed," said the aleka. "Since your battalion is out in front tonight, you have the honor of being closest in to the tent. So you see where my lads from Bekoji are? Out in front, there? Well, you will stand between them and the tent here, midway between the Bekoji guards and the Kanyazmach's personal guards. Simple," he said again. And with that, Aleka Merga turned and strode into the tent, from the interior of which issued forth a babble of voices.

"And what are we to do?" asked Gamtessa Lami, another of the Meraro squad leaders. "Stand around and look at things?"

"No, idiot," came a voice from inside the tent. It was Babilla Wami. "You are a special guard of honor tonight. Stand up straight, look like you know what you are doing, and stay out of the way. Sir, what can I do with these fools?" The voice trailed off, and was gone.

"He is everywhere," said Banda Luka, another squad leader. They all laughed.

They placed themselves in a circle outside the tent, and talking, decided that the best thing they could do in case of an emergency was to stay together and go to where they were most needed.

That is where they were when the procession approached.

They had a good view of it as it came across the field from the direction of Lemu. Men on horse and foot, cattle being driven, the drivers shouting at the long-horned cows, the men on foot in front yelling at everyone to get out of the way of the fast-moving procession, to get out of the way of the Bashaw.

The men on horseback clustered about one man seated on a large mule in the center of the melee. They constantly bowed toward him as the caravan made its way across the far field toward the tent.

Suddenly, they were there, approaching the tent, the cattle being driven past it; the men on foot, full of importance, yelling out "Make way! Make way for the Bashaw! Make way for the great Bashaw Indelibu! Bashaw Indelibu comes to greet Kanyazmach Didda! Make way for the Bashaw!"

Attracted by the noise, and warned by shouts from the guards, the Kanyazmach and his officers appeared in the doorway of the tent, summoned, as it were, by the presence of some special being of immense greatness. As the mule bearing Bashaw Indelibu was led to the front of the tent, all the officers—the meto alekas, the hamsa alekas, the Kanyazmach himself, even the sons of the great Ras Gobena of Bale—all of them bowed low, and with his body still bent low in supplication, the Kanyazmach thundered out in his great, strong voice, "A thousand greetings from your servants, oh great and honorable Bashaw Indelibu! We are honored by your visit! Now we know we are on the right path. Welcome to our camp. A thousand welcomes to my tent."

The Bashaw was old—venerably old. In a land where the average lifespan was thirty-eight, the Bashaw was seventy-two. And, he was a most remarkable shimagele. He had not chosen to retire to his tukul and keep busy shooing the chickens away from the door. He was too busy for that. He had all he could do to keep his retainers and servants and local officials from fawning over him all day long, from rushing to kiss his feet and grasp his ankles as they asked for blessings and favors and money. For some years past, he had taken to kicking at them when they did that. But lately, he had not even the strength to kick them. So he sat quietly on his stool, accepting their adulation and praise, keeping in contact with the court, and muttering to himself.

Now he had roused himself, had ordered his minions to place him on his mule, had set off across the plateau to intercept the warriors going to the fight.

Bashaw Indelibu was a young man of eighteen in 1842 when he had been given the honor of joining the guard of the young King of Shoa, Sahle Selassie, at his palace at the old mountain fastness of Ankober.

He was twenty-eight when the Empire had witnessed the rise of Ras Kassa of Gojjam to power. At thirty, he was among the retinue of nobles and retainers who had journeyed north to see Ras Kassa crowned as Emperor Theodore II.

In 1862, he was already old, a veteran of the Court of Shoa, when he was made Bashaw—leader of the riflemen. The great race for power among the kings and rases of the Empire had begun in earnest. Sahle Selassie was importing as many rifles as he could. Indelibu trained the King's soldiers as fast as he could. It was also in this year of 1862 that he, with the rest of the court, learned of the death of Theodore's beautiful wife, Tewabech, and of the murders of the Emperor's English advisors Plowden and Bell.

In 1865, at the age of forty-one, he accompanied the grandson of the King to Theodore's fortress of Magdala, in Wollo Province. Menelik, grandson of Sahle Selassie, inheritor of the Shoan throne, was to be in attendance at Theodore's court whether he liked it or not. It was also in that year that Indelibu heard the rumors that Theodore had become unhinged.

In 1866, Theodore took prisoner the English clerics and workers living in Ethiopia. He did this because he felt slighted by Queen Victoria and the British Foreign Office.

It was in 1868 that the British army under Sir Robert Napier stormed the Magdala fortress and released the prisoners. Theodore refused to surrender, preferring death. One week before that battle, Indelibu had led a party of Shoans into Magdala and spirited Menelik away, back to his homeland.

In 1876, fighting for Emperor Yohannes, this same Bashaw Indelibu led a rifle attack on the Egyptians at Gundet.

In 1889, he was an advisor to Emperor Yohannes at Metemma, and was within twenty paces of the Emperor when, the battle against the Dervishes won, Yohannes was struck down by a stray bullet. Indelibu sent his lieutenants galloping across the countryside with the news to Menelik, back at Ankober. Menelik was strong, and ready, and took the throne.

In 1890, with Menelik secure on the throne of Ethiopia, Indelibu retired to the estates newly granted to him in Arusi and helped to seize that province, once and for all, for the Empire.

Now he was a legend.

Now he looked down at them all from the great height of his Imperial mule. His unclouded eyes glittered sharply down at the officers and men over his long hooked nose. He looked like a great old hawk or eagle.

"I have come to do the bidding of my King, my Emperor," he said. "I cannot go with you this time. I am no longer strong. I am weak. But I am rich. Here, take these cattle. Take them with you. The longer you have these to eat, the less you will be hungry when you enter the kingdoms of the north. Go, all of you, and may all of you come back. My spirit goes with you."

"Bashaw Indelibu," said the Kanyazmach softly, "we are honored. You have given us a most useful and beautiful gift. But come; come into the tent, and take some coffee with us."

"What?" said Indelibu. "You'll have to speak up, son."

There was general laughter among the troops. The Kanyazmach reverted to his original tone of voice and shouted, "Would you like to come into the tent for a cup of coffee?"

"I would certainly like to do that," said Indelibu, "but if I got down off this mule it would take your whole army to put me back in the saddle, and I would be yelling with pain all the way. You have no idea of the pains of old age. No, I will stay here on this mule. He is an exceedingly gentle mule. Sometimes when I ride him, I dream that I am on a boat upon the sea."

The Bashaw smiled and pulled his gabi and his black highland burnoose closer about him. His head appeared swathed in cloth. Only his piercing eyes and hawk nose, his high cheekbones and strong jaw, appeared out of the warm clothing.

"Servants! Servants!" called the Kanyazmach, clapping his hands. "Some coffee for the Bashaw! Where are your manners? Lift it up to him."

Servants appeared out of the tent with the paraphernalia of coffee-making, and soon a steaming hot glass of coffee was handed up to the Bashaw.

"Ah!" said the Bashaw, cupping the glass in his hard old hands. "This is good. The warmth alone eases my pain." He drank, and drank again. The coffee, sweetened with honey, seemed to appeal to him, and gave him some strength. "This is good," he said again, and handed the empty glass back to the servants. "Now I must go," he said, setting off another round of bowing from the officers. "Do not forget: my spirit goes with you."

And with that, he turned the mule around and moved off toward the small town of Lemu, heading back to his compound in the far hills. From there, he and his men would guard this portion of the valley until the battalions returned. They would keep it safe from shiftas, and make sure the local officials did their duty correctly.

The Bashaw was the eye of the Emperor in this land. His word was law. He reported only to the Ras, when he felt it was necessary to do so, and to the Emperor himself.

His spirit would be with them, he had said. His spirit was a great one, and threw a great white cloud of courage over all of them. They would come back if only to show the Bashaw that they could.

That night there was a great feast. Great iron pots were hoisted off donkeys. Great fires were built. Groups of men held cows still against their wills, and certain men, trained in the ways of the Book and the Law, slit the necks of those cows in the way prescribed by the Book.

The cattle were cut up and cooked in many ways. Parts of them were eaten raw, with pepper. The men of the army and all their servants gorged themselves that night and wished for some tej or tella to drink. But even without the drink, it was a great feast.

Bedane and the other young soldiers could not believe it. They had never seen feasting like this.

Bashaw Indelibu's cattle would last for many nights. In fact, the biggest problem would be when to eat them and when to keep them alive. This is the kind of problem any man likes.

That night, happiness reigned in the camp of the Kanyazmach. And across the land, where the people understood that the army was well-fed and happy, there was also happiness, and relief.

That night, the whole world was thankful for the Bashaw's gift of cattle and praised the Bashaw to the skies. For the first time, an army roaming across the land did not behave like locusts, eating everyone in its path out of house and home.

And the army itself hoped for many Bashaws along the way, to help speed it along to the battle. Soon it would find out how few Bashaw Indelibus there were in this world, especially when you were far away from home, in a strange land filled with fearful people.

In the morning, the army awoke slowly. It had feasted too well the night before, and was logy in its getting up and getting started.

When the first light of dawn came and the Meraro squadron leaders were relieved of their headquarters duty, Bedane went back to his camp and found everyone still asleep on the ground. Only Egersa Regasa, assigned to tent duty for the night, was in one of the tents. He, too, was asleep on the ground, his gabi wrapped around his head and down the length of his body. His legs and feet stuck out at the end.

Bedane looked at Egersa's tough feet. Those Ethiopian feet could carry a man for miles; for days. Indeed, they had to carry him for his entire life. They could carry him through broken glass, or across a field of desert lava, or through a fire. They could carry him through three months of the rainy season without rotting away in the thick mud of the highland winter. In old people, the feet were so large and calloused and extended that they resembled huge hoes or shovels, covered with cracks from being too big and too old, but still carrying their owners on, slower and slower, until they were finally no longer needed, and stopped, along with the rest of the person's body.

Bedane smiled at Egersa's feet, and he turned and walked away into the silent silver dawn. He went past the fires that still sent trickles of thin smoke into the skies, and past all the white lumps of the gabi-coated bodies of his sleeping men. He went out of camp, toward the river, searching for Taffa Bulcha and Shasho Megenasa who, as guard leaders, felt they should be out in front the first night, at least.

Bedane came across Taffa sitting propped up against the trunk of a large tree by the side of the river. Taffa was silent as Bedane approached and squatted down next to him.

"Good morning, Taffa," said Bedane. "And what have you learned this night?"

"I have learned many things," replied Taffa quietly. "I have learned that it feels good to know what is at your back. I did that right, choosing this tree to sit against. I have learned that a long silent night opens up wide spaces in the mind, and that some of those spaces are filled with sun-filled skies and green grass and pretty girls, and some are filled with lions and devils and sorcerers and hyenas and snakes. I have learned that while it is pleasant to sit by the side of a stream, the sound of the stream takes away your hearing and puts you to sleep. I will never do that again— I mean, choose to take guard duty by a stream. If something happened to Shasho across the river, I would never know it. If he were overpowered, and an enemy came upon the camp, I would have no knowledge of it until they were upon me. Of what use is that? But I have also learned that a river is an open space, and on all but the darkest moonless nights an open space is like daylight to someone who cares to look. That is most useful knowledge. One other thing I have learned: our camp is too loud. If an enemy attacked at night, it would attack silently, on foot, with stealth, and conquer simply by thrusting their spears in the direction of the cackling of our brothers."

"They are that loud?" asked Bedane.

"They sound like a tribe of baboons," replied Taffa, smirking. "They should be told to keep their howling and laughing to themselves, until daylight at least."

"This is very useful," said Bedane.

"If they all keep quiet, we will all live longer," mused Taffa. "Let others cackle and die young. We should be as silent as the night."

Bedane found Shasho standing by a grove of mixed trees at the near edge of a wide field. Having had such good luck with his question to Taffa, Bedane decided to ask it again of Shasho.

"What have I learned?" asked Shasho in return. "I have learned that this is a great field for hunting dik-diks. There are seven of them right now within twenty feet of us. I will remember that when we return. They are always a good dinner. Also, there is a huge armadillo in there. His burrow is on the far side, and he looks as big as a rhino, at least at night. If an enemy started across this field, I could pick off a half-dozen of them before they knew I was here, and be off to tell you what was going on while the rest of them were still scattering for cover. This is easy. May all our positions be picked with such care."

"Be sure all our men know what you know," said Bedane. "And fill them with your spirit and your knowledge."

Bedane left Shasho and, circling around, went back toward the river by a different route. Soon he found himself in a grove of trees set in a small ravine. A small spring gushed out of the side of the ravine in a dozen places, seeped down, pooled, and began to run toward the larger stream in the distance.

The trees here grew along the sides of the ravine, and formed a canopy that sheltered the stream's birthplace. Bedane sensed that he was alone here, and he was happy for that. He needed some time alone, away from the others. It was a gift, granted to him to make the best of this time.

He used this time to think. He thought of the duties of the day coming up, what he had to do, what he had to teach, what he had to learn. And when he had all that settled in his mind, he realized exactly what a great gift this was, this gift of solitude and time. He would do this again, every chance he got. He would become strong through this.

When he had finished thinking, Bedane looked around. The trees that formed the canopy were old and gnarled, with great twisting branches that went this way and that. One tree in particular overhung the stream, and had many prominent branches that were within easy reach. As the sun came closer up toward the sky, and the light became brighter, Bedane saw that these branches were covered with brightly-colored pieces of string and yarn. From some of those pieces of string hung little brass bells. The strings and bells hung motionless in the still predawn air. There were dozens of them. Bedane had unwittingly wandered into a sacred place, a place where the people of the old religion worshiped.

But it was not a strange place to him. Bedane was a Christian, and the Shoa Oromo were either Christian or Muslim, but here in Arusi, especially in the mountain valleys to the east and the west, there were Oromos who were not of Christ or Allah, but of the old gods.

And they were good people, not worshipers of the devil as the Amhara priests contended. They were good people who worshiped the gods and the earth in their own ways, the ways of the ancient religion. And Bedane knew these people were good, because some of them were his relatives. He knew them, and he knew of their goodness.

So this altar of nature did not make Bedane uneasy. Instead, it filled him with peace. There were many little places like this, all over Arusi. There were as many of these little woodland altars as there were Christian priests and Muslim mullahs combined.

Bedane worked the edge of his gabi until he had loosened the outermost strand of cotton. He stripped that thread from the garment, then carefully knotted the hem of the gabi up again. Then he took the loosened string and tied it to a small twig that sprouted from the larger branch and with his thumb and index finger gently pulled it straight, so that it hung down motionless in the early morning air.

"God of The Tree," said Bedane silently, "send my prayer up to Waaqa, the God of The Sky, to the God of Gods, the God of my ancestors, and to all the other Gods who watch over us and protect us. May our march be quick, our victory strong, our return swift. May our families prosper while we are gone, so that when we return our greetings will be full of joy and our futures full of happiness." And having prayed that, Bedane felt good.

And as he looked down after his prayer, his eyes looked into the pool of water that came from the spring, and a shadow warrior looked back at him out of the quiet waters.

Bedane smiled; so did the shadow.

Bedane bent toward the water; the shadow rose to meet him.

Bedane knelt by the edge of the pool, shield in his left hand, spear in his right, and gazed intently into the pool in the growing light. The water warrior gazed back, spear held in his left hand, shield in his right.

Bedane gazed, and examined the reflection. He saw a young warrior in his prime. He saw the roundness of the shield; the sharp point of the spear; but mainly he saw the face. It was a good face, long rather than square, with an aquiline nose that would become handsomely hooked with age. He saw a high forehead and distinctive eyebrows. And he saw the eyes. They were keen and bright and alert. Thus will all young warriors always look, before the battle.

CHAPTER 14

THE PLAINS OF SAGURE

The encampment, though waking late, was ready to go by the third hour of the morning. The great war drums sounded once again, the columns formed and wheeled down the road, and the servants and hangers-on scurried about, breaking down tents, loading up the pack animals, and lumbering out onto the trail behind the fast-traveling cavalry. In the space of a few minutes the horses had put them out of sight; their riders had put them out of mind.

At the fifth hour of the day, the column emerged from a small wood onto the southeast corner of a huge field. The leaders wheeled the column to the west, along the edge of the field, until all four battalions were formed in a long column of twos. Then, without warning, the Kanyazmach bellowed:

"Column! Wheel to the right! Form a single line. Colors forward. Listen to me, boys. Enemy troops have been sighted. They are in that hedgerow across the field. Are you ready? Charge!"

And with that, Kanyazmach Didda Bokku spurred his horse and galloped out across the field. Like a magnet, he drew the alekas and the hamsalekas and the troopers along behind him until they were all at a gallop, four hundred strong, across that field.

Now the horses, given their head, surged forward in a long thundering line, and the troopers let them go and unlimbered spears and shields and readied themselves for the fight. What a sight they were. Fearsome. On they went. Hedgerows and ditches came up ahead, the horses jumping them as though they carried nothing on their backs but the wind. Horses swerved past branches and soared over bushes and tore along as if the very day depended on it. And their riders grew wilder and wilder, shouting and yelling, urging the horses on faster and faster, until suddenly they were in the trees on the far side of the field, the formations broken, the horses galloping this way and that. The riders, searching for enemies, broke through the cover of trees into another field beyond. There they saw the Kanyazmach and his alekas, mounted, facing them.

"Down off those horses!" yelled the Kanyazmach. "Down! Down! Some of you hold the horses. The rest, follow me. Those scurvy dogs of cowards have retreated! They are on that hill. Your horses cannot go there. Follow me on foot. Take that hill! Kill them!"

The leader was off his horse and running toward the hill.

"Assign three from each squad to the horses!" screamed Babilla Wami. "The rest, follow me. Keep in your squads."

"Tula, Shasho, Taffa, to the horses," yelled Bedane. "The rest of you follow me!"

All of a sudden the cavalry battalions had transformed into wild infantry, scampering faster than tribes of baboons toward the far hill. Oh, they were fast. They were so fast. In my country they are all lean and hard, with muscles as hard as bone, and fast, as fast as cheetahs.

"Come! Come!" yelled the Kanyazmach, but they were already overtaking him, some already far ahead of him, all with the single goal in mind—to get to the top of that hill first and kill whatever was there.

What was there, halfway up the hill, was a herd of a half-dozen antelopes, and they galloped away over the crest. That was all there was. There was no enemy, but by the time the warriors realized that, the charge had been transformed into a footrace, with the hilltop the finish line. A squad from Bekoji reached there first, and stood jumping up and down, spearing imaginary enemies.

"This is good! This is good!" yelled the Kanyazmach, clambering to the top of the hill. "The best parts of the beef tonight to the squad from Bekoji. But boys, boys, you have a lot to learn. Look how far away the horses are. They should have been walked closer. And you are all looking at me. Some of you should be looking outward, always. See what is happening? The enemy has gone to the far side of the hill, split in two, and now they are coming round the bottom of the hill between you and your horses. They are going to spear your friends down there and steal your horses. Won't that be a sight! What will you do then?" Some of the men began to charge back down the hill.

The Kanyazmach paused and let out a deep breath. "Listen, boys," he said. "That was a good charge, and you did well in the trees. You did things you could never guess you would be asked to do, and you did them with the speed of hungry cheetahs. But listen. In war, things happen so fast! You must always be swift, but you must also always listen to your leaders. You must always see everything, and you must always kill your enemy. Don't let him escape, and don't stand around cutting him up. Leave that for others. It is meaningless. You leave yourself open to Death when you do that.

"But you are good lads. You are true warriors! Now you will start to learn what it means to become soldiers.

"Listen. Two years ago I led ten battalions against the armies of Kaffa. They were the best battalions I had ever led, and I think perhaps you are even better. And some of *them* are still alive!"

The Kanyazmach bent double with laughter, then suddenly raised up his head and laughed to the sky.

"Now let's go on," he finally said. "Sagure tonight, then Assella in two more. Then the work begins. Then you will learn to shoot, and fight, and march, and run, and kill in so many ways that you cannot count them. But remember, through all this, before anything else: you are Oromo warriors. You are the Galla! The Outsiders. They fear you. They fear the very talk of you! You are the worst nightmare they have ever had. They think you are all crazy. All wild beasts. Be sure you live up to your reputation. Because if you don't, I will kill you myself with my bare hands! I swear to God, may He witness these words!" The Kanyazmach's lionhair headdress shook in his anger and wrath.

"Come now, on to Assella! On to the north! Death to the Ferengi and anyone else who would harm our great King Menelik!"

"On to Assella!" shouted the warriors, brandishing their spears.

The Kanyazmach lifted his arms, quieting them. "And don't forget to pick up your horses on the way," he said, grinning a wicked grin.

The Kanyazmach was a very happy man. With these boys, he could kill anything.

PART III

A MAN OF GOD

CHAPTER 15

ABBA HAILE MIKAEL TESFAYE

At the fourth hour of the morning, on the Wednesday of the week following the departure of the troops, Negassa heard the hoofbeats of a single horse walking slowly toward his compound, and as a sign of respect toward his expected guest he walked out of his tukul and prepared to greet him.

The horse and rider came into the compound slowly as if to preserve the quietness and dignity of the place.

Looking up, Negassa saw a tall, spare man with striking angular features and dressed in clerical garb sitting relaxed upon a big chestnut gelding. The priest's hands held a beautifully-worked silver cross. Before any other greeting, Negassa walked silently across the compound yard to where the priest sat with an air of reverence, the cross extended. Negassa kissed the proffered cross, and only then did he say: "Welcome, Your Eminence. We have been awaiting you."

The priest smiled a kindly smile and said in a soft voice, "You do not have to call me Eminence, Negassa Merga. I am not yet the Abuna." With that, Abba Haile Mikael slid lightly off the horse and, taking a deep breath, stood before Negassa in all the grand simplicity of a true man of God. Over his white tunic and pants there hung the full-length black clerical cloak. On his head was the white turban of the priesthood, and on his feet were the flimsy black shoes preferred by the clerics of the day. The cross had disappeared somewhere into the folds of the tunic. It would reappear as if by magic at any given moment, when someone new came upon the scene and needed to kiss it.

"Welcome to my humble house," said Negassa. "I hope you are able to come in and spend some time with us. We would be honored."

The priest fixed Negassa with bright, piercing eyes that held the lilt of a smile in them. "It is I who would be honored," he said, "to be invited into the home of such a distinguished soldier."

They exchanged mutual bows; Negassa's deeper than Haile Mikael's, as befitting his acknowledgment of the priest's superior position. They entered the home, the priest first, and Negassa motioned his guest to sit in the place of honor. Fresh straw had been strewn over the floor in anticipation of the visit, and a three-legged wooden stool, carved from a single piece of Kaffa wood and borrowed from a neighbor, was ready for the honored guest to sit upon. Negassa and Tsehai would sit on lower stools, fashioned locally.

The priest and the soldier sat. Tsehai entered the room, bringing a bowl of water and a towel from the kitchen. Not looking up at the priest, she knelt and began to wash the Bishop's feet. Haile Mikael protested. "This is not necessary," he said. "I have not come far, and I have not been walking."

"It is the custom," said Tsehai softly, "and it is a good custom. I do this willingly."

"I accept your gift of hospitality," said Haile Mikael, "and I bless you for it." He extended his hand in blessing over Tsehai's head.

When Tsehai rose and went back to the kitchen, the Bishop noted the tattoo of the cross on Tsehai's forehead and said to Negassa, "I see that your wife carries the Sign of the Cross."

"My family has always been Christian," said Negassa, "as far back as I can remember, Reverend Father."

"And how far is that?" asked Haile Mikael quietly.

"In my great-grandfather's time, I am sure of," said Negassa. "Beyond that, it is said that we always served the Christian king, even back to the time when we first came into the land."

"Almost back to the time of Mohammed Gran," mused Haile Mikael.

"Not quite that far back," said Negassa, grinning.

Mohammed Gran had come sweeping up from the deserts of the east. The year was 1520, and the Muslim fanatic had pillaged and burned all across the highland kingdoms. After twenty years he was finally killed, but by then the riches of Ethiopia—the gold, the silver, the old books—all were gone. Emperor Galawedos, with the help of Portuguese allies, began to rebuild, but there was much to do, and centuries passed before the Empire recovered. Both men knew the story well.

Tsehai returned with the coffee, bowing to the priest as he took his cup from the tray. She stood before him, not knowing quite what to do, and Haile Mikael said to her, "Sit, Waizero Tsehai. You do not need to be so formal with me, although I appreciate it. I come to you today not as a representative of the Lord, but as a supplicant, begging a worthy favor of you. Please, sit.”

Tsehai sat, and for a while the three of them sipped their coffee in silence. Finally, the priest said, “This is good coffee.”

“It is from Kaffa,” said Negassa, with some pride.

“Ah, yes,” said Haile Mikael. “From Kaffa. Some of your boys have been over that way recently, haven’t they? That will be a boon, when that savage kingdom finally falls to the Empire.”

“But it has already fallen,” said Negassa, puzzled by the bishop’s lack of knowledge. “That is how we have this coffee, and the stool you are sitting on, Reverend Father.”

“They are up again,” said Haile Mikael. “As soon as they heard of Menelik’s proclamation, the remnants of the Kaffa nobility allied themselves with Bonga, and the two kingdoms are forming an army. It is foolish, of course. As soon as Menelik finishes with the Ferengi, we will be on them. But their belief, as always, is that they can expect arms from the Sudan and alliance with the sultanates of the Danakil and Somali deserts. They do not understand the power of Menelik any more than do the Ferengi understand it; nor do they understand our alliance with you and Ras Gobena. Nor do they understand geography,” said the priest, with an indignant snort.

“Geography?” asked Negassa. “I do not understand this word.”

“The science of measuring the land,” said Haile Mikael.

“Ah! Acreage, and the like,” said Negassa.

“Exactly,” said the priest. “And how it is we now stand between them and their old allies. What they do understand is that we have snapped many of their old trade routes. *That* they understand quite well. But enough of them,” said the priest. Once again he was silent, and seemed to gaze down his long nose and out into space somewhere, as if he were suddenly somewhere far away. The wars with Kaffa were a long-standing fact of life, and worth just so much talk, and no more.

After a long silence, Haile Mikael said, “I have come to you today because I have need of an assistant. Not a slave, not a porter, not a servant, but an assistant. Someone who is both quick and wise, who has both of those kinds of wit about him; and who is also young and in good health and full of energy. My old friend Markos assures me that your young son Chala is such a person. Now, let me answer a question I am sure you have—why I did not choose someone from Ba’le Province, because it is certainly true that I had thousands to choose from there.

“It is simple. I am well-known in Ba’le. There, I am in the midst of politics, although the great God above knows I do not wish to be. Any choice I make in Ba’le carries the smell of politics about it, and I cannot have that. For any boy I chose, I would create pride in him and in his family. There would be bad blood and jealousy and envy created in the society. That must not be. We must be united, not quarreling."

The priest's eyes became very sad, and he said, "For this is a war like no other war. This is the most important war since that against Mohammed Gran three hundred and fifty years ago. Here is the importance of it."

Haile Mikael held his hands out in front of him with the palms up. "There are two things in this world," he said. "These are the Church and the State. The State protects the Church on Earth, and the Church watches over the spiritual well-being of the State. Thus it is. Together, these two balance each other and raise up the population, through the intercession of our Lord Jesus Christ, to be worthy of uniting in the next world with the Creator of the Universe, the Father of us all.

"I am called to help in this war through prayer. I must be at the battle to pray. The Church must do its part to insure the victory of the State. I must have someone who can help me reach there. He must have his own horse. It is a long way. Can your son help me?"

The priest ceased his quiet, earnest speech. Silence descended in the cool tukul. Negassa and Tsehai pondered his words. Finally, Negassa cleared his throat and said,

"Abba Haile Mikael, in the army it is the duty of the soldier to report to his officer with absolute truth everything he sees, everything he knows. I will consider you as my officer now, and report to you. I must tell you, when Debtera Markos told us of your request, we were alarmed. We didn't know what to do. This is the reason: the last half-dozen years have been hard on us. True, we look prosperous now, but we really are not. Much has been taken from us. Our most precious gifts have been taken. A son and two daughters have been taken before us into Heaven. The diseases. The cholera. Now just last week our eldest son left for the battle. He is good, and keen to fight. He is a leader, so he will be in the front and he, too, may very well be taken.

"Now Tsehai is with child again, and that is good, but you know how uncertain that is." Negassa paused, and sighed. "So that leaves us with only Chala. We thought he was safe; too young to fight. But now that may not be so. You may change all that. Your Eminence, he may be the only one of our family to carry on our family into the next generation. Now you want him, to carry him off to who knows where, to find who knows what destiny. This frightens us, and saddens us. Of what use is all our work if we cannot give the rewards of it to our sons? And what are we to do if our sons are taken from us? Who will help us in our old age? Shall we wander the land, begging? Ah! I have seen enough of that in my travels, and I would not wish it on Satan himself. Better to be eaten by hyenas."

There was silence. Haile Mikael sat quietly and tugged gently at his beard. After a long while, the priest spoke. His voice was low, and his words were chosen with care and came with earnest thought.

"I cannot feel the way you do, Negassa and Tsehai," he said, "because I do not have children, but I think I can understand something of what you say. Now in return, I could say that God determines our destinies, and that we should all cooperate with God's plan. Thus, Chala should be allowed to follow this destiny. If I were advising someone, I might say that. But I am not advising someone." The priest sighed. "I am arguing from the reasoning of a man who needs a helper to get from one place to another. Therefore, my reasoning is not pure. I argue from self-interest, and not in the interest of Chala, your son."

"And we argue from our interests and our hopes," said Negassa, with a wry smile. "We argue as though he is a goatskin of grain."

"But we argue from wanting the best for him, also. We argue for what we believe will be the best for his future. That is what parents do," said Tsehai.

"And you are right to do so," said Haile Mikael.

Negassa took a sip of coffee and said grinning, "We all agree on one thing. We all agree that he is a goatskin of grain."

"That is very true, Ato Negassa," said Haile Mikael, and his eyes suddenly lit up. "There is great truth in what you say." The priest became animated. "Hear me," he said, "Chala is *exactly* like a goatskin of grain. Soon that goatskin will split open. How many kernels of grain shall spill from him in his lifetime? Thousands! What are those kernels? His thoughts; his deeds. Everything that is in him will come out, and in the end, the angels will write down the thoughts and deeds of his life in the Book of Judgments.

"So you may have your wants, and I may have mine, but of what use are they to Chala? Will they help him fulfill his destiny? There is another person to consult here. Just, let us find out what Chala believes he wants!"

"You mean we should invite the goatskin of grain himself to meet with us?" asked Negassa.

"Exactly," said the priest. "Not to allow him to decide by himself; but for us to listen to him and see what he says and what he wants."

"He doesn't know what he wants. He is too young to know," said Negassa. "He is at that age. And I am fearful of your plan, Reverend Father." Negassa glanced at Tsehai, and continued, "I am fearful because I know what I would do if I were his age and a chance for adventure like this were offered to me. Lions could not keep me away. That is how *I* would feel."

"Hmmm," said Haile Mikael. "So you do not wish to ask him?"

Negassa sighed. "He is my last son," he said. "But let us ask," he added.

"Oh, no, please," said Tsehai.

"We must allow this," said Negassa. "Let us see what he will say."

Tsehai buried her face in her hands. "You know what he will say," she whispered.

"Chala!" yelled Negassa. "Chala! Get in here!"

Chala had been waiting fearfully across the compound, and now he walked tentatively across the yard and poked his head into the doorway. All he knew was that this serious-looking stranger was visiting and that he himself was the reason. His father had told him to be well-washed and well-dressed and to be sure to be ready when he called, and that was all he knew.

He suspected a bit, though. There had been too many hurried, alarmed conversations between his mother and father lately, and a lot of bother about cleaning the house and collecting furniture and being sure the coffee was of the best in order to greet this enigmatic honored stranger who was here for this mysterious meeting.

Chala entered the tukul and bowed deeply to the stranger, who offered his cross to be kissed. Chala did so without thinking about it; and assumed a posture of humility and attentiveness.

"Chala," said Negassa, "this is Abba Haile Mikael Tesfaye. He is an old friend of Debtera Marcos, your teacher, and he is the Bishop of Ba'le Province."

Startled, Chala looked at his father and then automatically turned again toward Haile Mikael, bowed deeply and quickly three times, and then knelt before the bishop, his forehead touching the earthen floor of the room. There he stayed as still as a stone, prostrate before the great bishop, and chattering off prayers as quickly as he could think of them.

"Chala! Chala! Get up!" said Haile Mikael quietly but firmly. "Thank you, but this is not necessary. Please. I do not need this, and I do not want this."

The bishop leaned down from his stool and took Chala gently by the arm and raised him up. Chala came to a kneeling position. "I...I..." he said.

"Chala!" said the bishop, pulling him up to his feet, "Chala, I hear you can ride like the wind, and read and write, and that you have an excellent memory and that when you are given a task to do, you do it quickly and you do it well and that you finish your task."

Chala looked up at the bishop. Haile Mikael was smiling. Chala said nothing. There was nothing to say. In Chala's world, if you met a bishop, you went flat on your face and began to chant prayers. Meeting a bishop was almost like meeting a ras or a prince or the Emperor Himself.

But this was a very strange bishop. This bishop was laughing, not stern and scowling like the pictures of bishops Chala had seen.

"Now, Chala," this strange bishop was saying, "I want to talk seriously to you, and I want you to think over most seriously what I am going to say." Chala nodded, and the bishop proceeded. "I need a helper, Chala. I need a guide. I need an assistant. Now, Debtera Marcos has told me that you can be that guide, if you wish. But only if you wish. That is the important thing.

"Now, your parents are afraid for you. They see danger in your coming with me. That is natural. So they are afraid to say that you should come with me. And I, *I* need a guide and a helper. I have been told that you are good at this. So I would like you to come. But we need to know what *you* think. What do you think, Chala?" Haile Mikael stopped and looked at Chala, and his face bore a look of concern.

Chala's eyes were gleaming. "Where are we going?" he asked.

"Ah!" said Negassa. He shrugged his shoulders and glanced at Tsehai. A tear dropped from Tsehai's eye. Haile Mikael gazed at them both with eyes filled with longing and seriousness.

"I will take care of him," he said. "And he will take care of me."

Then Haile Mikael turned to Chala and said, "If you wish, but only if you wish, you will come with me. You will not be my servant. You will be my companion. You will ride your own horse. You will bring your own spear. You will have your writing implements, and parchment, and paper. We will be given food and shelter along the way. You will return here, safe, after all of this is over. If you do not, your parents understand that you have fallen in the service of the Almighty God, of Jesus Christ and His Holy Mother Mariam and all the Saints, and in the service as well of the Emperor, Menelik the Great, Emperor of All the Ethiopias."

"But where do we go?" whispered Chala.

"We go to Addis Ababa, to the palace of Emperor Menelik. We go to the castle of the Abuna, Mattewos, and to the monastery of the Ichegie, master of all the monks of Ethiopia. Then we go north, to join the armies of Menelik. We will pray for them and offer our guidance to them. Chala, there is a great battle coming, and we must win that battle. There are forces coming to destroy our Empire, and if the Empire is destroyed, there will be no safe haven for the Church. Who then will praise God in the way He should be praised? What will be the fate of the helpless people of God? They will be left to the will of the four winds of the earth and the four horsemen of Hell. There will be plagues and death and torture and destruction such as no man living has ever seen. From all directions the infidels will sweep in upon us, and that will be an end to us, and of all the prayers to Heaven that go up from us to God and His Saints each day." Haile Mikael paused, then spoke again, this time very quietly. "That is where we go, Chala. We go to save the Empire and to fight for God. Will you come?"

There was a stillness in the room.

"If it is my parents' wish," said Chala, "then I will go."

Negassa emptied the few remaining drops of coffee onto the ground. "It is the wish of your parents," he said grimly. "But it does not make us happy. What will make us happy is to see you again, here in this house. Son, be sure you take care of yourself."

Tsehai ran from the room, crying. That night, there was wailing from the tukul of Negassa and Tsehai, as if Death had come down to visit them once more. And Death, though far off, perked up his ears, and grinned with satisfaction.

CHAPTER 16

EMPIRE

Bishop Haile Mikael had gone on ahead to Bekoji that night, to spend the evening with Debtera Marcos and the priests of St. George's Church.

Early the next morning, Chala prepared to ride out of his parents' compound on his night-black horse Eagle. Eagle was a young horse, small and quick and sure-footed. Like Chala, he was an excellent find for the bishop, and would serve him well.

Chala carried his spear, and in the same way Negassa had given a shield to Bedane, so too he had given a shield to Chala. But it was not a war shield like Bedane's. It was smaller and lighter, and Chala wondered what it would be good for.

"You will find out when you get to the city," said Negassa, grinning. "There is much to see there. Maybe some of it, you will not wish to see. Some of it, maybe you will want to hide from behind that shield. And maybe it is a good one for pushing away things you do not like. At any rate, it will prove useful."

Chala kissed his father on both cheeks, and turned toward Tsehai. Then he did something he had not done since he was a little boy. He embraced his mother, and clung to her hard. She returned his embrace, and held him to her, rocking him back and forth like he was a baby, and stroking his hair.

"I don't care what the Bishop tells you," said Tsehai, holding him. "Before you do anything, you *think*. Think of what will happen if you do what he says. Think if it will be good for the Bishop and good for others. But *first*, think if it will be good for yourself. And don't be in awe of anyone that you meet. You are of good stock. You are our son. You are an Oromo, and a warrior."

The last sound Chala heard as he rode Eagle out of the compound was his mother's voice, trilling the ancient joyful chant of triumph for the departing warrior.

Truly, all their lives had changed with the speed of lightning in one short month. How strange life is! You can never tell what will happen next. That is the way of the world.

From Bekoji, tracks lead north and south, east and west. There are main stems to Assella in the north and Goba on the Wabi Shibelle in the south.

Chala and Haile Mikael took the main track north, but soon after crossing the Katari River they took a less-traveled track that led northwest over the Dida Plateau and headed over rolling meadows and through small forests towards the escarpment. Before reaching the cliffs the path led through several villages and settlements. It was a long way.

The main track had had six trails side by side. It was a superhighway of a track, enough for large parties to pass each other easily. This smaller track had only two trails, but there were far fewer travelers, and Haile Mikael motioned Chala to bring Eagle up abreast of his horse instead of trailing behind.

"You are not a lackey," said the Bishop. "You are my companion. See that you think of yourself as such, and see that you comport yourself in a fitting manner."

"Yes, Reverend Eminence," said Chala, bowing in the saddle.

"And stop calling me Reverend Eminence and Regal Sunlord and Posturing Lunatic," said the Bishop. "There are too many syllables, and more important, there are too many people who want to kiss crosses. We need to travel fast. As far as anybody is concerned, I am a poor country priest and you are...you are...my acolyte? No. My deacon? No. Here," he said, reaching into his saddlebag, "Wear this." Mikael drew from the bag a priest's turban cloth, and handed it to Chala.

"But this is a priest's cloth!" exclaimed Chala.

"Not if you are not a priest," said Haile Mikael.

"But they will think I am a priest," said Chala.

"Nonsense," said the Bishop. "Not if they look at you. Not if they look at the rest of your clothes."

"Then will not this cloth look foolish?" asked Chala.

"Not by the time we are finished with this," snorted Haile Mikael. "By the time we are finished with this, you would not believe what will look foolish and what will seem grand. For now, Chala, just put it on. We will see what happens with it."

So Chala wrapped the holy turban around his head, and it felt good, and he smiled.

"Ride ahead of me and clear the way," said Bishop Haile Mikael. "You will have to get used to that."

Twenty minutes later, the Bishop shouted to Chala, "Get back here and don't ride in front of me again until we get rid of that chicken! It's driving me crazy! It's making me sick!"

Ah! The chicken! The merchant had given it to the bishop at the Bekoji market as Haile Mikael and Chala were riding out of town, beseeching Haile Mikael all the while to intercede for him for some infringement which the poor merchant was certain could never be forgiven by any God in any universe.

The bishop thanked the merchant and blessed him, and handed the chicken to Chala, who tied it to his saddle in back of him.

The chicken was having a bad time of it. It was bouncing around on Eagle's back as the horse trotted on. It was no life for a chicken, or anything else.

"What shall we do with it?" asked Chala, looking behind him at the panting chicken.

"Eat it. This evening, I hope," said the Bishop. "We will hand our host a good surprise. Whoever it is will not expect a gift of this size from travelers. It will serve us well. But meanwhile, the poor chicken..."

At noon, the travelers stopped for a bite of bread beneath the shade of a few trees that grew along the side of the path. They left their horses to graze alongside the road. Chala retrieved a huge, round, thick, circular loaf of bread from his saddlebag. It looked like a gigantic moon fallen out of the sky. He cut off a piece of it and offered it to the Bishop. Haile Mikael nodded his approval, said a quiet but heartfelt prayer over the feast, and motioned for Chala to cut a piece for himself.

"That is a huge loaf of bread," said the Bishop. "Do you think it will take us all the way to the battle?"

"It will take us a long way," said Chala, slicing away. "I have seen five boys live for five days on nothing more than a loaf this size."

"That *is* a lot of bread," said the Bishop. "It will make a lot of midday lunches for us."

"It will last us over a month," said Chala.

"If the rain or the maggots don't get it," laughed Haile Mikael. "Perhaps we should share it along the way; trade it for something. Don't forget: we know it lasts for a week. But how much longer can it last?"

Chala thought for a minute. "That is true," he said. "There is more than one way to measure something."

"Ah!" said the Bishop, raising his index finger and looking pleased.

They rode side by side along the trail, trending northwest all the way. They passed several small sleepy-looking villages and many miles of fields and tukuls. Once they entered a cool forest—it was hot for a day in Meskarem—and hanging in the trees were man-made beehives, with swarms of bees going about their business of collecting from the flowers in the fields that bordered the forest. They were collecting nectar from the Meskal daisies. It would be a good year for honey.

Though the ride was pleasant enough, it began to be wearisome toward mid-afternoon. Chala was almost asleep in his saddle when he heard Haile Mikael clear his throat.

"Once upon a time," began the Bishop, and Chala looked up.

"Aha!" said Haile Mikael, "I thought that would get you. Everyone loves a good tale, right?"

"Of course," said Chala, for tales in our country were as common as the days were long. It was how we kept ourselves amused.

"Very well, then," said the Bishop. "Listen carefully," and he began again. "Once upon a time, a man was going from Siltana to Bekoji. As he approached that wild area near the base of Mount Encuolo, he was attacked by shiftas, who wounded him and stole all his clothes and left him lying by the roadside half-dead.

"After a while, a priest came along the road. But when he saw the wounded man he crossed into the field, pretended that he had seen nothing, and went on his way, putting the wounded man completely out of his mind.

"After a short time another man came along the road. He was a trader, and quite rich. He also passed by because he was in a hurry to purchase some goods in Assella. He did not want to be delayed.

"The third to come along was the enemy of the wounded man, but when he saw him lying there he was very sorry for him. He quickly tore up some of his own clothes, poured oil into the man's wounds, and then bound them up. Putting the man on his own donkey he took him to the nearest house, and asked the people there to look after him. And he left them money to pay for anything they might have to buy for him.

"Which one was the good neighbor?" said Haile Mikael, ending his parable.

"Why, the enemy of the wounded man," said Chala. "Everyone knows that. But I never knew that happened right near Bekoji. Is that true?"

"What difference does it make?" asked Haile Mikael. "It is good to tell a story that way, because it takes the story out of the air and puts it into your heart. You see, Chala, it does not make any difference where the man was attacked. He was attacked here on earth, and it is here on earth that we must be our brothers' keepers. And all men are brothers. It is so sad when brothers quarrel." Haile Mikael sighed, and stopped talking.

"And yet," said Chala, "we are on our way to a battle, to pray that our soldiers can kill as many Ferengi brothers as possible."

Haile Mikael reined in his horse and looked down at Chala. "Oh, no. No. We do not go to pray for that. We go to pray that our Empire survives. You see, Chala, if our armies are defeated by the Ferengi, the infidels will sweep into our country. Already they are arming and preparing. From south, east, and west they will come, and the Ferengis, who think they are going to conquer a beautiful land, will find a land of desolation and death, a land of kaffirs and dervishes and Mahdists, all of them crazed by the Devil himself and out for blood and death. We cannot allow that to happen. We must preserve our Empire, because our Empire is especially pleasing to God. Our prayers go up to Him from so many souls every morning, noon, and night.

"It is strange," continued, the Bishop. "The Ferengi, as fellow Christians, should be helping us, like they did in the past. Instead, they are trying to steal our land. I must conclude that they are not true Christians. Regardless of our differences, we all believe in Christ. But these men seem to care only about taking our land. It must be that where they come from the land is very scarce and poor. It is strange."

Haile Mikael smiled a puzzled smile. "But if we sit here wondering we will not get anywhere. Innihid! Let's go. The horses still have some good miles in them today."

They let their horses trot ahead at their own pace and continued down the track until, coming up over a gentle rise, they saw a small village in the plain below.

"That would be Geddeb," said Chala.

The priest and the boy looked down at the small town, and Haile Mikael said, "Now, Chala, here is the first big thing you can do for me. Go down to the village and find a good house for us for the night. I will stay here, and follow you in about half an hour. It is time for me to say my daily afternoon prayers, and this looks like a good place for it. It is so silent here."

"I go," said Chala, "and when I find a place, what should I do? Wait for you there, or come back along the trail?"

"Meet me at the entrance to the village," said Haile Mikael.

"I will get a good house," said Chala.

"I am confident that you will," replied the Bishop. "Oh, and Chala," he said, holding up the boy for just a second more, "when you talk to anyone about me, why don't you just call me Father Haile, eh? That will be good enough."

"Yes, Father Haile," said Chala. He smiled, and spurred Eagle with his bare heels, sending the horse down the easy slope to the town.

CHAPTER 17
THE MEDITATION OF
HAILE MIKAEL TESFAYE

Haile Mikael stood alone upon the gently sloping hillside. He watched Chala ride off toward the small town, really no more than a collection of farms, in the distance. He looked then toward a more distant range of mountains in the west. That would be the region of Kuarta, and far beyond that was the kingdom of the Gurages.

Leaving his horse to graze at will, Haile Mikael drew a thick book out from under the folds of his cloak. It was bound in black leather, cracked now from years of use. It was his book of daily prayer, and it was one of his most prized possessions.

He said a small opening prayer, and thumbed the book open to the prayer of the day. It was not a prayer, really. It was an instruction. "Say your daily afternoon prayer," it said in Geez, "and meditate upon Christ in the desert."

"And what did you go out into the desert to see? A reed shaken by the wind?" Haile Mikael thought, and smiled to himself. He had opened his meditation by having the wrong line of scripture pop into his head. "Lift up your heart," said something within him. Was it his heart or his mind that said that? "I have lifted it up to the Lord," said Haile Mikael in reply.

The priest gazed out over the grassland. He was all alone. The wind blew through the grasses and sent the reeds shirring against each other. The only other sound was the crunching of grass and an occasional snort as his horse ate his fill of the new green grass. "Surely," thought Haile Mikael, "if the Lord wished me to meditate upon the desert, He could not have placed me in a better place. Surely this is a desert place, devoid of all distractions. Surely this is as good a desert as any. Here there are no others to distract me.

Only I can distract myself, I and Satan." Haile Mikael sat down in the dry grass, facing west, and closed his eyes. Only the wind kept him company.

"And surely," he said, "here comes Satan, intruding upon my thoughts of Christ in the desert. Well, was it not like that for Christ Himself? When the Spirit drove Him out into the desert to fast for forty days and forty nights, was He not bedeviled by the Devil himself all that time? Did not Satan take Him up to the pinnacle of the temple and tell Him to cast Himself down, and say that a host of heavenly angels would catch him before he hit the ground? Did not Satan take him up to the highest mountain peak and show Him all the kingdoms of the earth and say that all those kingdoms would be his if only He knelt down and worshiped Satan?

"And what did Christ go out into the desert to see? A reed shaken by the wind? Ah! He went to see His own soul. 'My soul doth magnify the Lord' said Miriam. Those souls were the greatest of souls, the immense souls of God Himself and that of His Mother. Compared to ordinary souls, they were.....like the whole earth compared to grains of sand? They were.... infinite? But if they were infinite, encompassing all space and time, were they then souls? And what space and time was left for other souls?

"It is not for me to speculate," said Haile Mikael to his inner voice. "It is for me to meditate upon Christ in the desert. I must go back to the desert. Satan, begone. Do not tempt me to stray into the realm of speculation. That is the temptation you tempted Christ with. What if? What if? Now I see one lesson of Christ among many. Go into the desert and look for the reed blown by the wind. Do not give yourself to Satan even for all the kingdoms of the world, for the kingdoms of the world are as nothing compared to one reed shaken by the wind but still alive and growing, if only just. With no water, with no companions, it grows, because the Lord has breathed life and a soul into it and commanded it to grow.

"That is how we are. That is how we are sometimes," thought Haile Mikael. "We are each alone upon the earth, struggling and striving like the reed, reaching up to what we think is God, but knowing as little about God as that reed knows about God. Still, it is our duty, and the life of our soul, to reach toward Him, to struggle toward Him. All else is vanity. All the kingdoms, all the angels, all the things that we create—all of this is as nothing compared to one reed reaching up to God. But I keep leaving the desert. Lord, bring me back to the desert. Let me look upon that one reed. How can I do this? The world of the Devil keeps breaking in."

Haile Mikael opened his eyes. Before him the vast plains stretched away, and beyond them the mountains. The world was so huge it was frightening. It was impossible to contemplate. And then, even as he watched, something miraculous happened. That whole huge world in front of him lifted from its place and seemed to float into the sky. He sat in awe and watched it. Up it went, into the sky, as if God Himself were toying with it. "Ah!" said Haile Mikael, and he thought, "God has given me a plan." And he closed his eyes again.

Haile Mikael's plan was this: even as God had uprooted the world in front of him and sent it sailing, even so would Haile Mikael uproot himself from this world and send his soul sailing back to Christ in the desert, nineteen hundred years ago! It could be done. He could feel himself doing it. His soul was sailing back in time, and the rest of him, corporeal and spiritual, was following. He could feel the weight of sadness lift from him, the sadness of the world that had pressed down on it for nineteen hundred years, growing and growing as more sins were committed, more injustices were done, more good people were led astray through their own weaknesses and the temptations of the flesh and of the world.

Now he was leaving all of this sadness and flying back to Christ. It was as though he had sprouted wings, like the angels. He was flying back to Christ.

Now before him was the desert. All around him were the colors of the desert—the reds, the oranges, the purples of the shadows thrown upon the great rock walls of the endless canyons. The yellows of the sands.

Haile Mikael walked down a silent canyon. His feet slid in the sand, so the going was hard, but he kept going. All of a sudden, he came around a wall of rock and there, seated in a small sheltered declivity in the valley of sand, was Christ.

Jesus was looking down at something in the sand. He seemed to be smiling. Haile Mikael walked closer. Jesus looked up and smiled at him, and that smile was softly radiant.

"God be with you," said Jesus.

"And may God be with You also," stammered Haile Mikael.

"And what have you come out into the desert to see?" asked Jesus. "A reed shaken by the wind?" Jesus smiled. "Come, sit with Me," said the Christ.

Haile Mikael sat.

"Look," said Jesus. He gestured with his hand. Haile Mikael saw that Christ's hands bore no scars. So this must have been before the crucifixion, thought Haile Mikael to himself with a start. But of course. This was in the desert, before His ministry began.

"No. Not my hand," said Jesus. "Look. Look here," and he pointed to the desert floor.

There was a reed.

It was a single reed, dry and fragile, the color of the sand itself. Two dried leaves grew from the stalk, and it blew in the gentle hot wind of the desert.

"Welcome to My home," said the Lord.

Haile Mikael stared at the reed. So his first thought had been the right one after all. Even if it had come from a different scripture, it had brought him here to Christ. Haile Mikael sat silently and looked intently at his Lord.

"Thank you, my Lord," he said reverently.

They sat there for a while together. Haile Mikael had no comprehension of the time. It could have been years. It could have been seconds. It could have been an eternity.

Finally, Jesus laughed. "Have you no questions?" he asked.

"No questions," said Haile Mikael.

"Good," said Jesus. "But questions will come," he warned.

"I know," said Haile Mikael.

"But not now?" asked Christ.

"Not now," said Haile Mikael. "It is enough just to sit with you."

"I am happy about that," said Christ. "But when you leave Me, think of the reed. That is your salvation."

"I know," said Haile Mikael.

"You must find out who first told you about the reed," said Christ. "You must thank that person."

"How?" said Haile Mikael.

"I don't know," said Christ. "It is for you to do, not for Me. But it would be a nice thing to do."

Haile Mikael looked up.

Christ had a twinkle in His eye.

Then Christ laughed again, throwing His head back.

Haile Mikael broke into a smile, and then suddenly he too was laughing. Laughing with Christ!

"Isn't this wonderful!" said Christ. "The two of us can sit in the desert and meditate upon a reed, and be happy, and laugh, and learn all sorts of things."

"Ah!" exclaimed Haile Mikael. "I can learn, but You already know all."

"Oh?" asked Christ, amused. "Who told you that?"

"Ah....oh," said Haile Mikael. "Oh. Forgive me, Lord. Who am I to presume to tell You what You know or don't know?" Haile Mikael was mortified, and he knelt before Christ, pressing his head into the sand.

"Faithful servant," said Jesus, "Do not be sad. Do not be afraid. At least you know that you presume. I have had to listen to thousands who tell Me who I Am and what I know. They tell Me what the universe is. They tell Me how I built it. None of them know, but they think they do. They presume. But you, Haile Mikael, you do not presume. You are content to sit with Me and look at a reed. I like that. Look at that reed, and the colors of the sand and the rocks. And then look at Me."

Haile Mikael did as he was bidden. When he looked at Christ, Christ said, "Was it not easy to find Me once you found the key?"

"Yes, my Lord," said Haile Mikael, bowing his head.

"Go, then," said Christ. "Think of Me always, and when you have found a good way to do it, give the key to My people."

"I shall do my best to do Your bidding," said Haile Mikael.

"Good. Now go, Haile Mikael. You have been set upon My Earth to help My people. Feed My lambs. Feed My sheep."

Haile Mikael looked up. Jesus was gone and Haile Mikael was alone, kneeling upon the yellow sand in the bottom of that fabulous red-rocked canyon of purple shadows. But he did not feel alone. He felt a vast peace settle over him and warm him to the very essence of his soul.

And then everything was gone. Everything: sand, canyon, colors, reed—everything.

Haile Mikael opened his eyes. He was sitting in the grass on the hill overlooking that small Oromo settlement on the Arusi Plateau. The priest took a deep breath and rubbed his face with his hands. He was overjoyed. Never before had he found that desert. Never before had Christ sat and spoken with him.

Haile Mikael was exhausted. He rose to his feet and looked to the west. Everything was in place. He walked slowly across the grassland toward his horse.

Everything had gone, except the Peace.

Chala was waiting for the bishop just outside of the little town. "You spent a long time at prayer, Father," he said.

"Why, yes I did," said the bishop. "See, then, what you have done for me. If I had been alone I never would have been able to do that. It was good prayer, too. Someday I may tell you about it. But tell me, Chala, what are we doing this night? What have you found?"

Chala said smiling, "I have found us a good place for the night, Father," and as they rode into town he told the bishop this:

"I met a man in the street, and I asked him if anyone might be willing to have a priest and his assistant stay the night. The man looked at the chicken tied onto the saddle and said, 'Well, son, I assume you are the assistant, because you look just a trifle young to be a priest, but if you want to bring that chicken with you and throw it into the pot, why don't you come to my house tonight?' so I went to his house and looked at it, and it looked good, so that is the place I found."

"So," said Haile Mikael, "is this man a merchant or a farmer?"

"A merchant," said Chala. "A transporter of goods. He has some mules. He is a Gurage."

"A Gurage," said Haile Mikael. "A hard worker, no doubt. A smart businessman."

"They have a reputation for that," said Chala. "Some of them work for my father. They are hard workers, and save their money."

"And make good bargains," said Haile Mikael. "A whole chicken for one night's stay. That is a very good bargain for this Gurage, Chala. And what was this gentleman's name?"

"Oh. I am sorry, Father. His name is Gata. Ato Gata."

"So," said Haile Mikael, smiling, "Ato Gata is a good bargainer."

"Well, Father," said Chala intently, "I thought it would be good for us, too. Breakfast is included, and a chicken lunch for tomorrow's journey."

"But tomorrow is a fast day," said Haile Mikael.

Chala had forgotten completely about that. "Oh, no!" he said. He was ashamed. "I am sorry, Father," he said. "But perhaps we can get something else from them. There will be plenty of food."

"A peasant with plenty of food?" asked Haile Mikael. "That *is* unusual."

"There is a wedding," said Chala, brightening.

"A Gurage wedding," said the bishop. "Well, that does make a difference. There *will* be plenty of food, and entertainment, too. Or *we* will be the entertainment. What do you think?"

"He thinks you are a simple country priest," said Chala. "There should not be too many demands on you. Besides," he added, "the Gurages around here all worship trees. They should not bother you too much."

"Ah!" laughed the bishop. "Pagans! Good. I should be able to get away with only a few blessings, then. That is good, because I am tired. Look, Chala. The day has become converted into night."

It was one of the poorest houses in a village of poor houses. Chala and Bishop Haile Mikael entered the low door and were greeted by the owner of the house, who smiled and bowed and said, "Welcome, Father, to my house, and thank you for your gift. It is much appreciated by me, by my daughter, and by my new son-in-law. They will make good use of it. Please, be seated."

The man gestured for them to enter the main room, and there they joined a goodly number of guests who had already arrived. They sat among the others, all of them on the one side of the room, facing the center. On the other side sat the bride and groom, facing them. The bride was radiant; the groom seemed perplexed. Next to the new couple was a huge, fluffed-up pile of chicken feathers.

The wedding had been celebrated the previous Saturday. The feast had gone on since then. Now according to the custom of the Gurage, everyone who came to the feast brought a chicken. As they came in, all the chickens were slaughtered and plucked, and their feathers heaped up in a huge heap in the main room of the house. At the end of the feast, which would last until Saturday came 'round again, all the chicken feathers would be scooped up in a big cotton sheet, sewed in, and presented to the newlyweds. That would become their bed. The larger the feast, the fluffier the bed, and in the bed would be all the happy memories of all the people who had attended the feast.

This feast was producing a prodigious bed. There were not all that many Gurages in this district, it being mainly an Oromo land, but all those who lived anywhere near this village felt compelled to come, simply because of their small numbers. There was, therefore, really good attendance, which was buttressed by the additional appearance of the Oromo neighbors of this family, who liked them a lot. So it was a good turn-out.

The guests sat and talked quietly. There was a good feeling here in this house, with people quietly talking and laughing. Every so often, a guest would make a joke or ask a question of the couple, who would smile with embarrassment and pleasure, and answer as best they could. It was as if everyone in this room were a part of the same large family—a family that, quietly and with a lot of love, put its arms around the couple and gently welcomed them into adulthood.

And the food was good, too! Of course, there was Haile Mikael's chicken stewing in a pot, but there were other things in that pot also, like hard-boiled eggs and potatoes and berbere pepper and cabbage and onions and butter, so that it was very good. And besides that, there was the traditional Gurage food – things like kocho, a food extracted out of the false banana plant; and kitfo, gomen kitfo, and ayib. With all that, it was a substantial feast.

And what local notables there were had come, too. The chicka shum of the village was there, and noticed Chala and the priest, and nodded to them. After a while, he came over to where they were sitting, bowed, and sat next to them. "I beg your blessing, Father," he said. Haile Mikael took out his cross and the shum kissed it.

"Where do you travel?" he asked.

"To the north," said Haile Mikael. "To the battle. To pray. For our Emperor and Empress, and for our people."

"Ah!" said the shum. "That is a good thing. I wish I could go with you, but I am getting old, and my old wounds hurt. But who is this?" he asked, nodding toward Chala.

"This is my guide," said Haile Mikael. "He is named Chala Negassa, and he is the son of a friend of a friend of mine. He is from south of here, from near Meraro. Do you recognize him?"

"He has a good name," said the shum, seeming to weigh his thoughts. "If he is who I think he is, he is the son of Negassa Merga, elder brother to Bedasa Merga, a great warrior. A family of great warriors. If he is *that* Chala Negassa, you have obtained an excellent guide, Father."

Chala sat silently, pleased by the recognition.

"Father," said the shum, "if this feast goes on too long tonight, or gets too loud, and if you wish your rest, you are welcome to stay at my home tonight. It would be an honor for me and my family."

Chala looked up and became alert. This was an odd thing for a shum to say to a country priest, but it was the way the shum spoke that startled

Chala. He spoke the way people spoke when talking with a person in a position vastly superior to their own. There was an automatic deference; a recognition of great power and position. It contained none of the petulance and petty bullying seen so much in so many of the local officials. And what Haile Mikael said next amazed Chala.

"Do not blame Chala for not seeking you out," said Haile Mikael. "I told him that I wanted to travel as quietly as possible."

"I know that is your wish," said the shum. "Just know that if you need anything, I am here to serve you. My house is at the other end of the village, up on the hill, on the right. If you need anything, I am there."

"I thank you, my friend," said Haile Mikael. "I appreciate your words." he held out his cross again, and the shum kissed it.

Chala looked at the two men. All of this had been said very quietly. No one else had heard. All the others were listening to the banter between the bridegroom and one of the guests. But it was obvious to Chala that something had happened here. The shum obviously looked upon Chala's Father Haile with a respect that bordered on awe. What kind of man was his Bishop, anyway? What power had he, what position, that this local shum would seek him out to offer his service? How did he know, in the first place, who Father Haile was?

Nothing more was said between the two men. The shum sat with the priest for another hour. They smiled and laughed and joked with the others. At the proper time, the shum left. The father of the bride led Haile Mikael and Chala to another room. This was the family's room. It was a great honor to be allowed to sleep here. Usually a guest would be allowed to sleep only in the outer room, never here.

"Well, Chala," said Haile Mikael with a wry smile, "I see my reputation precedes me. This is the kind of thing I was talking about. In this country, I am never alone. Well, pretty soon we should be among so many bishops and abunas and ichegies that we become lost in the crowd, thanks be to God. That will be a relief."

"But, Father," said Chala, "How did he know?"

Haile Mikael smiled. "It is the Empire, Chala, my son. The Empire is like a great river. It runs deep. If you are in it, you are in it. As you swim down the river, water rushes by you, and brings news of you to others further on. This is not bad, nor is it good. It just is. Now let us say our prayers and go to sleep."

The night was pleasant enough. Two or three times they were awakened by the happy singing of the guests, or a laugh or two, but long before dawn the whole house slept.

In the morning, Chala and Haile Mikael said farewell to their host, who supplied them with a porridge made from the ensete—the false banana plant. Now ensete was no substitute for chicken, but as Haile Mikael had noted, it was a fast day anyway, and this would be a good lunch. Besides, said Haile Mikael, they were going to have a great dinner; probably of a kind that Chala had never had before.

They continued their journey toward the northwest, until at noon they came to the crest of a small hill. There, they dismounted. Stretching out below them was a wide, wide valley. The floor of the valley was five thousand feet below, and almost straight down. It was thirty miles across to where the cliffs went straight up again at the western edge. And in the bottom of that vast valley were four great lakes, stretching from north to south. From the north, the names of those lakes were Lake Zwai, Lake Langano, Lake Abijiata, and Lake Shala. From where they stood on the rim of the cliff, Chala and Haile Mikael could just see the northern edge of Lake Zwai. They could see the whole of Lake Langano below them, and all of Lake Abijiata. They could see nothing of Lake Shala, far off in the south, but Haile Mikael assured Chala that it was there.

"I have seen it," said Chala. "When we would ride from Meraro just north of the Western Mountain, we could see it from the rim there."

"So, that is good," said Haile Mikael. "You know where you are, then."

"I know where I am, Father Haile. But where are we going?"

The Bishop pointed down into the valley. "Tonight we will stay at Lake Zwai," he said, "then we will go on to....." The priest's voice trailed off as he looked at Chala. "What's wrong, son? What's the matter?" he asked. "Are you sick?"

Chala's teeth were suddenly chattering and his eyes looked glazed. "I am afraid," he said.

"Of what?" asked Haile Mikael.

"Of the diseases," said Chala. "We know there are bad sicknesses down there. And there are other things....."

"Yes?"

"Tell me, Father, are you truly a priest of God?"

"Truly I am, Chala."

"You would not be false to me?"

"Certainly not. What kind of a question is that?" asked Haile Mikael, becoming more alarmed by the second.

"Zars," said Chala, hoarsely. "Zars. Budas. That valley is alive with them! Why do we go there?" he fairly shouted at the priest. Haile Mikael looked at Chala in confusion, then took a deep breath and smiled to himself. So the stories were still alive, he thought, and still very powerful. Look what they had done to this level-headed boy. Turned him into a sniveling idiot in the space of seconds. Well, this could be overcome.

"Chala," said the Bishop, "where we are going there are no zars. No evil spirits. And no one there is a buda. No one will give you the evil eye. Look. Look at Lake Zwai. Do you see the islands in the middle of it? Do you see the biggest one? The highest one? That is where we are going...."

"That is where they all come from!" Chala shrieked. "That is the home of the zars! That is the house of Satan!" Chala backed away from the priest and put his back against a rock wall.

Haile Mikael's first thought was that the stories had worked too well. Well, there was nothing to do but to tell the truth. He took his cross from beneath his cloak, and holding it high, he said, "Listen, Chala. Wherever we go, Christ will go with us. He will protect us. You must believe that, or you are of no use to me or to yourself. He is with us all of our days, even to the ending of the world. Look at the cross. It will go before us, and the light of its grace shall light our path. No evil spirits will dare to harm us. If they show themselves, the cross will destroy them, and they will go howling away into the darkness of the night created by their own degenerate, evil souls. They can do nothing against us.

"Now listen. Come and sit and listen," he said soothingly. He motioned Chala to the side of the trail, and both sat there, face to face, but separated by a good distance. Chala saw to that.

"There are no zars there. No budas. No sorcerers or masters of evil. This is what is there: there is a monastery on that island, and a few thousand people live there. Some of them are monks. Some of them are farmers and fishermen. These people are called the Lati. Have you ever heard of them?"

Chala shook his head.

"Well," continued the priest, "the Lati came here long ago, during the time of the troubles. It was when Mohammed Gran came up out of the desert and laid waste so much of our beautiful land. So fast he came, and so vicious he was! He killed so many people. Our armies could not stop him. He burned churches and monasteries, and killed and killed and burned and slaughtered. King Lebna Dengel tried to stop him, but Gran kept chasing him all over the countryside. It was awful. It was like the end of the world. And everywhere he went, Gran stole. Chala, believe me when I say that at that time our land was one of riches. The kings and nobles, and many of the people, were rich. The churches and monasteries were especially rich." Haile Mikael turned pensive. "Perhaps," he said, "perhaps Gran was sent because the Church was too rich. Perhaps God sent Gran to show us that we were supposed to be not so rich. I don't know. Anyway, everywhere he went, he stole the silver and gold from the churches and monasteries. He destroyed the vestments and paintings. But worse than that, he desecrated and burned the holy books and scrolls. People became fearful not only that he would wipe them out, but that he would also wipe out all traces of their religion. Indeed, all people that he caught who would not convert to Islam, he killed. He killed all the priests and monks wherever he found them. People were so afraid, Chala! A terror gripped the land.

"It was in the middle of that troubled time that some people decided that they must save the treasures of the Church, and by treasures I do not mean mere silver and gold and precious stones, of which there was an abundance. By treasures I mean the sacred books and scrolls and writings of the Church—those writings that go back through centuries of time, back all the way to the Christ.

"So in the Year of our Lord 1530, when Gran was at the height of his power, people of the land between Lake Tana and Debre Tabor, under the leadership of the holy Abba Lati, all of them with their families—all left Lake Tana for a hideaway somewhere in the south. There it is below us, Chala.

"They came here. They came with soldiers led by a renowned knight named Birru, and with monks of Debre Libanos, and with fishermen of Lake Tana who knew how to make reed boats. They brought the reeds from Lake Tana, the ancient papyrus reeds, and planted them along the shores of Lake Zwai.

"Here they were safe. Here they built a monastery and a town. They called themselves 'The People of Lati'. But still they were fearful. They were few in numbers. They were at the very edge of the ancient Empire. There were many angry tribes about. So they devised a plan. They made it seem to those people around them that they were sorcerers, and kept the home of the zars, and could do the evil eye."

Chala blinked.

"The Lati had some other allies, also. There are in Lake Zwai crocodiles and hippopotamuses. There are diseases around the shores of the lake. It is very easy to die there if you don't know what you are doing.

"So the people of Lati told as many people as possible about the zars and the budas, and between the stories and the dangerous animals people left them alone. But I did not know how great was the power of the Lati until just now." Haile Mikael smiled. "It seems that the Lati have done very well as Protectors of the Faith. I hope you come with me, Chala, and meet them. You will see things you have never seen before. Oh, and Chala, if there are any spirits among the Lati at all, they are good spirits. They are angels. And there might be some archangels visiting as well. Will you come with me?"

Chala sat with his head in his hands. He could not speak.

"Then at least have lunch with me," said Haile Mikael. He retrieved the wooden container of ensete porridge from the horse's back, opened it, and brought it to Chala. With it he brought two wooden spoons, and handed one of them to the boy. They ate silently, taking turns dishing porridge out of the bowl. When it was finished, Haile Mikael said, "So, then, Chala. What have you decided?"

Chala stood up and walked to the edge of the cliff and looked over into the valley with its vast blue lakes. The sun was still high in the sky. He looked at the five islands of Lake Zwai. He looked especially at the largest one. Then he turned slowly toward Haile Mikael and said:

"An evil spirit cannot touch the Cross. This I know. And my teacher, Debtera Markos, says you are a great priest—a man of God." He paused and the priest waited. "But you say things that I do not understand. All my life I have heard people talk about the powerful evil spirits of Lake Zwai. Can they all be wrong? Can they all be so foolish? My mind strains to believe you, but what you say changes what I believe. Because they all say it, you know. 'Beware the evil of Lake Zwai. Beware the buda; beware the zar. Beware. Satan lives there. Never go there.' They all say it, Father. All of them—Christians, Mohammedans, the people who believe in the tree gods and the sky god. Are they all fools?" Chala fell silent.

"They are not fools," said the priest. "There are evil spirits. There are people who can perhaps send evil your way with a look, if you are unprepared for them. There is, certainly, Satan. That monster lurks in wait for us all. So they are wise to be fearful. Where they are wrong is in thinking that evil comes from those islands. Chala, evil comes not from islands, nor from any other places or peoples. It comes from Satan and his legions of evil angels, and from the hearts of men when they are corrupted by Satan and his followers. The world is not evil, Chala, but there is great evil in the world, and that evil is what men do to each other when they are led astray. Christ saves us from that evil, and cleanses us from evil when it enters us, and lets us move away from it and towards Him. Truly, Christ is our salvation."

"I will go with you," said Chala, "but I am afraid."

"It is well to be afraid," replied Haile Mikael, "but for now look at that island in the lake. The largest island. That is where we are going. The name of that island is Debre Sion—Mount Zion. Can any place with such a name harbor evil spirits?" And Haile Mikael made the Sign of the Cross.

The trek down the trail was long and hard. The path followed a fault created eons ago when the Great Rift Valley was new. It moved at a diagonal down the great cliff wall. It was not so steep, but it was treacherous, with falling rock and places that narrowed down so that sure-footed mules would have been better to have than even the best of horses. The two travelers and their mounts were hot, tired, and thirsty by the time they arrived at the bottom of the cliffs.

Still there was the ride to the lake, some seven miles away through the dense valley forest. Those seven miles were filled with small Oromo villages, one about every mile-and-a-half or so, and that gave Chala some comfort. But these Oromo spoke in a different way from the Shoa Oromo of the plateau. They had a different accent, and Chala found it strange. It fascinated him, and so did the fact that these Oromo relatives of his lived in a lush forest. He was not used to that. He had never even thought about any of his people living anywhere but on the great plateau. Still, finding these people here made him feel that he wasn't that far away from home.

Truly, he was not. He was only a two-and-a-half-day ride from home. But that ride had been in a straight line. It is strange, is it not, how far a straight line will take you? A straight line will take you far, far away.

When they had nearly arrived at the lake, they came upon a clearing on a hill. It was hotter here; steamy, in fact. No longer were there the cool, gentle breezes of the high plateau.

And the birds! Here in the forest there were so many birds. On the plateau there were the great black and white ravens, and the eagles, and always, of course, the vultures. There were a few hummers and jays, too. But here! Here there were all kinds of birds flitting through the forest: bright little things of blue and red and yellow and green, and so many of them.

And monkeys! Chala had never seen a monkey. True, one of the merchants of Bekoji kept an old baboon as a pet, chained up in the front yard. But monkeys were different. If they had ever been on the plateau, they were all gone now. They must have all come here! Chala could hear them constantly, howling and yowling their way high up in the trees. Once he caught sight of a tribe of them before they quickly soared into a mass of branches.

Truly there was a magic at work here, regardless of what Father Haile had said. This was a magic forest, and Chala was delighted with it.

Now suddenly, within this clearing, all of that was gone. For from the clearing, they could look down a hill some five hundred feet high, and across to the lake. Directly across from them was the island of Debre Sion, and on the lake itself were some things that again Chala had never seen before. Upon the lake were boats.

True, they were small boats. They were made of reeds, and they were only big enough to carry one man, but still, there they were. They were so light and small that they could be paddled with sticks, and they flitted over the lake's surface like giant yellow water beetles.

The clearing contained a small hut and a corral. In front of the hut was a large pile of wood waiting to be lit. Two men stood by the doorway to the hut, waiting for them. They had heard the sound of them moving through the forest.

"Welcome, Your Grace," said one of the men. Both of them bowed low, and the usual long Ethiopian greetings began. Chala did not understand the words of these men. This was a language he had never heard before, although the bishop seemed to understand it perfectly. Chala listened carefully as Haile Mikael spoke with the men.

When the conversation ended, the Bishop turned to Chala and said, "These men are of the Lati. They will watch over our horses while we are on the island. They will feed and water them, and keep a fire. There will be enough smoke so that the insects and wild animals stay away. You need not worry about Eagle. Even here in the lowlands horses can be protected for a short while. And here, they are five hundred feet above the marshes. They will be safe."

"Do the Lati do this for all their visitors?" asked Chala.

"There are not that many visitors," said Haile Mikael, smiling.

On their walk down to the lake, Chala asked, "What is that language you were speaking?"

"You know that language, Chala," said the Bishop. "You have heard it many times, at your Church of St. George. It is the ancient tongue—the sacred tongue. It is Ge-ez. All the church services are said in it. But here, there are differences, so that you don't recognize it. Here on Debre Sion they speak it every day, to make sure that they don't forget it. Because they use it all the time, it has changed somewhat. No longer is it the Ge-ez that they brought with them when they came here over three hundred years ago. Don't worry, they speak Amharic also, although again with a strange accent. But you'll get used to it."

At the edge of the lake, there were two more men standing next to a boat made of reeds. But this boat was much larger than the little skimmers Chala had seen from the hill. This boat could carry many people. The men bowed to the bishop, and Haile Mikael and Chala got on board and sat. The men began to paddle the boat toward the island, two miles distant. Chala looked about him in awe.

"Just like the Apostles, isn't it, Chala?" said Haile Mikael. "But they didn't have to worry about hippos or crocodiles, just sudden storms."

Chala looked around. He was surrounded by more water than he had ever seen in his life. That water was filled with wild beasts that wanted to eat him, and the air was filled with deadly diseases that wanted to kill him. Why would anyone want to live in a place like this? Truly, the fear of Mohammed the Left-Handed must have been a fierce fear. And here we are again, thought Chala, with a new bunch of lowlanders trying to kill us all. What kind of a world is this, thought Chala, that keeps trying to kill us?

And yet, it was a pleasant day. Through the lake's haze, the sky was blue above, and the sound of the waves lapping against the sides of the boat was pleasant. Chala felt himself becoming drowsy even as he sat there.

"Can I paddle, Father?" he asked.

One of the men gave Chala his long sweep pole. There was no paddle end to it, but the boat was so light that two men sitting on opposite sides of the boat and sweeping the water with these poles could propel the boat quickly.

A few of the smaller one-man boats were in sight. All of them appeared to be heading for the island. It was nearly the end of the day.

As they drew closer to Debre Sion, Chala could see the low-lying marshy areas of the island. These marshes were filled with the reeds that made these boats. Papyrus. It was ancient, and long ago, said Haile Mikael, men used to write on the insides of papyrus, long before parchment was used.

Beyond the marshes, great trees rose in a dense forest that grew up the slopes of the island. Now Chala could hear the howls of monkeys and the calls of the small tropical birds. They were all over the place. The air here seemed thick, and filled your lungs like some kind of heavy thing. It was good to breathe it. There was a rich smell to it.

The boat headed toward what seemed to be a special landing place. There was a group of men standing there, waiting for them. They bowed low to the Bishop, greeting him profusely and with real feeling. They obviously liked this tall, thin, smiling man. More, they seemed to revere him, and not just because he was a bishop.

Haile Mikael brought Chala forward, placing his hand on the boy's shoulder and introducing him. "These are the Keepers of the Faith, Chala," he said. "Some are monks, some are priests, some are warriors, and some are fishermen and farmers. All of them are the Keepers of the Faith." Chala could hear the warmth and respect in the Bishop's voice as he spoke about these men, and that made Chala feel good. The Bishop was very much at home here.

Deferring to the Bishop, and letting him lead the way, the group walked through the forest and up the hill to a small village. Like the clearing on the opposite side of the lake, it was high up, at about five hundred feet above the lake, and it was just above the great forest. Beyond the village there were cleared fields full of grain. The air was brisker here, though still warm, and Chala could see many small gardens near the village houses. Each garden contained beautiful vegetables. It was a fertile place.

As the sun was setting, the group approached a tukul larger than the rest. This was again a new thing for Chala, for this tukul, and all the other houses in the village, had stone walls. The walls were about four feet high, and then the wooden framework rose from there, and high above, the ceiling rose like a beehive, supported by spokes of strong wood, so that it looked like the inside of an umbrella.

Inside the house was one large room, with a door at the opposite side that led into another, smaller round house. Indeed, this was the community gathering place. It was a meeting room, a tavern, an eating place, all in one. Gathered there were a great number of guests. They were the village elders and the important men of the community.

Haile Mikael and Chala were led to carved wooden stools set in a place of honor. They sat, and a servant brought water for washing. More servers approached. Two carried a *mesob*, a wicker table covered with a high wicker conical top, which they set down before the bishop. A third server lifted the top to reveal a glorious dinner. At the bottom were rolls of injera, rolled out flat. On top of the bread were vegetables, and a pile of dark brown berbere (pepper), and pieces of fried fish. Chala had never had fish of any kind. It smelled strange, but good.

"I told you we would have a wonderful meal tonight," said Haile Mikael. "Although it is a fast day, and meat of course is not allowed, fish is, so we will eat our fill of fish, as fish was blessed by the Lord Himself," and saying this to Chala, Bishop Haile Mikael raised his hands in the sign of the blessing, and gave thanks to the Lord for this wondrous feast, as he called it. He then blessed the meal, and the people assembled in the house, and all those who lived on this island and safeguarded the ancient faith. He invoked God's blessing and that of all the angels and the saints on the people of Ethiopia, and on all good people of the earth, and finally upon the Emperor and the Empress, who were in great need of His blessings right now, he said. He blessed the fields and the animals and finished by blessing the clouds that brought the prosperous rains of the past three months.

"We thank You, Lord, for the bounty of Your earth," the bishop ended, and thought to himself of the reed shaking in the wind. Then the food was brought out for everyone, and all assembled fell to and ate. Tej was brought, and the place was merry. There was cabbage and kolo, and beans and potato, and the fish. Chala liked the fish. It was different from any meat that he had ever tasted before, and it filled him well. Chala was beginning to think that the people of Debre Sion, be they angels or devils, were very lucky angels or devils indeed.

When the meal was over, Bishop Haile Mikael rose and distributed a final blessing. Then he announced that he would remain this night and the next night and asked the elders that someone be assigned to bring the horses around from the east to the west side of the lake. That done, he turned to go.

Upon his turning, the bishop looked directly upon a younger man who had silently appeared and now stood near him and said, "Your Grace, I would be honored to accompany you to the monastery."

"Birru!" exclaimed Haile Mikael. "Birru! It is you! I had wondered where you were, old friend."

"I am sorry I could not be with you until now," said Birru Goshu, smiling broadly. "Duties. I am now the Shum of Debre Sion."

"Ah!" said Haile Mikael, truly delighted. "My congratulations, good friend."

"May I accompany you?"

"But of course. I would be honored."

"It is I who would be honored, Your Grace. Is there anything special that you require?" asked Birru.

"Simply the usual provisions," said the bishop.

Outside, Birru had torches brought, and he and half-a-dozen other men walked with Haile Mikael and Chala up to the monastery at the top of the hill. There, instead of entering the large building, they went directly to a smaller house next to it and entered.

This was a square house. Inside, it was divided into a large front room and four smaller rooms. Doorways led directly to those smaller rooms from the back wall of the common room. In the common room was a table with lit candles on it. A colobus monkey skin stretched across it. Several stools were scattered about, and one massive old chair draped with hides was planted close to the table. The floor was covered with new straw.

"Please be seated, Your Grace," said Birru Goshu, bowing and indicating the chair.

Haile Mikael returned the bow and sat. A young boy of about nine or ten approached with a basin and towel. He knelt before the bishop, removed Haile Mikael's shoes, and began to wash his feet.

When the boy finished, he disappeared quickly with his basin, Haile Mikael throwing a quick, whispered blessing after him.

"Will you need anything else this evening, Your Grace?" asked Birru.

"Leave an extra torch or two, if you would be so kind," said Haile Mikael with a twinkle in his eye, "just in case my traveling companion wishes to go exploring before daybreak."

"Indet?" said Chala, under his breath. He had no thought of going out in the night air with all those zars and budas around. Some fright still showed in his eyes, even with all the good food in his stomach.

"It will be done," said Birru.

"Melkam," said the bishop. "It is well. May the peace of the Lord be always with you."

"And also with you," said Birru. He bowed and went out the door.

For a while, there was silence in the room, as they listened to the steps of the departing men. Then Haile Mikael cleared his throat and said, "The first order of business, Chala, is for you to pick your room for the night." The bishop gestured toward the back wall. Four doors stood open, and there was blackness beyond.

"My own room?" said Chala, almost whispering. He had never heard of such a thing.

"Of course," said the bishop. "Take a look at them. I favor the one on the right, although they are all pretty much the same."

Chala took a candle from the table and looked into the rooms. It was as the bishop had said. They were all the same, except that the one to the south and the one to the north each had an extra window in the north and south walls. Otherwise, each room was the same: rectangular, about eight feet wide and twelve feet long. Each contained a bed and a stool. The bed was low, about a foot off the ground, made of a wooden framework of sticks. Criss-crossed over the frame was a latticework of inch-thick strips of hide. Folded on each bed was a rough woolen blanket.

Chala had seen beds like these before. They were like the beds used by the very old and the very rich in his country. Chala had never slept on a bed.

And the window: it was not just a hole. There was a wooden shutter over it. Chala touched the shutter with the palm of his hand. It was thick. He could tell. He dared not push it open. He might damage it, and that frightened him. He returned to the common room.

"If I can have a candle," he said to Haile Mikael, "I will take the room third from the south." It was one of the interior rooms, but removed from the bishop's room of choice. The last thing he wanted was to infringe on the bishop's privacy.

"A good choice," said the bishop. "Perhaps at some time a saint slept there. And of course you can have a candle. But if you couldn't, what would you do? Sleep on the table?" The bishop laughed, delighted.

"On the floor, over there in the corner," said Chala.

"Aha! Where the zars couldn't get you, eh?" said the bishop. "It would be a bad night's sleep, I am sure. It's a good thing we have an extra candle." Suddenly, Haile Mikael said, "Listen!" and he startled Chala.

Chala jumped. "What! Indet! " he shouted.

"Can't you hear it?" said the bishop. "The singing?"

Through the still night came high voices over the air. It sounded like wailing.

"Come," commanded the bishop, grabbing Chala by the hand. The two were out the door into the dark night before Chala could think.

"This way," said Haile Mikael, pulling Chala. "Don't worry," he said softly. "There are no hyenas on the island. It is safe. Come over here."

They stumbled through the dark for about a dozen paces, and reached the spot where the rocky path descended to the village. There they stood in the dark.

"Listen," said the bishop.

Chala strained to hear.

Far below, in the dark village, women were singing. They sang in a way that was so strange, so magical, that in the still, starry night, it seemed like ghosts were laughing.

"You must go and listen to them," whispered Haile Mikael. "You may never hear music like this again. Come, let's get a torch."

Before Chala could respond, the bishop was halfway back to the house. Chala could hear him pad lightly across the stones. There was the sound of the door opening and before Chala could get back to the house Haile Mikael was coming out the door with a torch held high.

Chala scrambled after Haile Mikael. The bishop was bounding down the boulders that served as a path between the monastery and the town. As they entered the town, the path narrowed until they walked in what was little more than an alley between stone-walled homes. The stone gave forth a coolness in the moist night air.

They approached the meeting house. Still the music came from the interior. Haile Mikael handed Chala the torch and said, "Now go, and enjoy yourself."

"You are not coming?" asked Chala, startled.

"If they did not know me, I would. This is beautiful music. It is at least 350 years old, Chala. They still sing it here as in olden days. Ah, I wish I could come with you. But if I stepped through that door, they would become embarrassed and start singing sacred music. This is not sacred music. Enjoy yourself. I will wait here for you." And saying this, the bishop melted into the shadows. "Do not worry," he said out of the darkness. "I will be here when you come out."

Chala stood before the door of the meeting house. Stubbing out the torch, he drew his gabi over his head and across his face, leaving only the eyes visible. Then he pushed the door open and entered. Not one head turned toward him. He sidled along the wall and pressed himself against it. From there he watched.

At the far side of the hall, six young women in shimmering white dresses danced in a line illuminated by flickering torchlight. They accompanied themselves by clapping hands in a slow cadence. They were beautiful, and so were their voices. Each voice was strong, but soft. The women danced a graceful dance, and their dresses and eyes caught the light. They wore gold bracelets and earrings and necklaces. What a glorious sight they were. Chala looked at one girl in particular. She saw his eyes, and hers dropped demurely. But twice during the song she looked up at him, and her eyes flashed.

The dance ended; the audience applauded. Chala noticed that there were some women in the audience. This was different. This was not some tej-bet in some poor village where the girls sang first and went into the back with the men later. There was something else going on here.

The next thing that happened were the drums. Two men sat rumbling out a staccato rhythm on the drums, and they smiled broadly as they pounded the goatskin drumheads. Men rose from the audience and picked out girls, and there was laughter and comments thrown back and forth. The men and women on the stage chose partners, and a wonderful dance began.

The couples faced each other and began by swaying to the rhythm of the drums. From somewhere in the shadows a man began to sing. The audience clapped. Gradually at first, the dancers began to move their shoulders. They swayed and moved their shoulders, nothing more. Then you could see that their shoulders moved more rapidly. The movements became more intense. The legs moved. Bodies moved. Men circled their partners. Women drew their shammas across their faces, flirting. Through the thinly woven cotton, you could see their smiles. The singer was leading the audience now; all were singing the chorus of a song. This dance they danced was a dance of the northern mountains. Ah, the beauty of it! thought Chala, who realized that he was clapping along with the rest. Ah, how beautiful it was! Ah, how beautiful these women were! Ah, how beautiful that one with the flashing eyes...

The music and the dance came crashing to an end. The audience kept applauding wildly. The dancers joined hands and bowed to the audience.

A tall, beautiful dancer did not bow, but stood to the side of the stage, waiting. Her name was Meheret—Mercy—and she was willowy in her flowing gown. She stood like a statue, waiting for silence.

And silence came. As the exhilaration of the dance subsided and the stage cleared, face after face turned toward her, and whispers of "Meheret waits," "Meheret speaks," filled the room, and silence came. The room waited for Meheret to speak.

"This year," said Meheret, and somehow her voice was low and powerful at the same time, "This year the Lament will be sung by Almaz Birru. She will accompany herself on the begena."

It was the young girl with the flashing eyes—Almaz—who walked to the center of the stage. She sat on a stool and a musician handed her an ancient harp. It had eight strings and they were strung from a sound box between two horns of wood. She sat and waited until there was absolute silence. She did not look at Chala or anyone else. Her eyes were fixed in space, and her fingers rested on the strings of the harp.

Then she began to play, and finally she sang. She sang in a voice of thin silver, with so much sorrow that it was unbearable, and the melancholy of the strings matched the melancholy of her heart. And this is what she sang:

> "When sorrow penetrates the heart of man,
> It is the moon who comes to shine on him.
> Lest you should see the sorrow that is mine,
> Oh that the darkness might be more profound!
> My grief will never end;
> My lamp sheds its last rays, and is extinct,
> And oh! the land of Semien is so far!"

When Chala emerged from the meeting hall, his flickering torch held high, he was overwhelmed and frightened by the immensity of the night.

But his fear was not allowed to grow into the monster it might have become, for Haile Mikael stepped from the shadows, smiling and laughing quietly.

"Come," he said, "it is late." He took the torch from Chala's hand and went scampering up the stone stairs to the top of the hill. Chala followed quickly, unwilling to fall behind and be swallowed up by the dark.

They gained the hilltop and once more entered the monastery's little guest house. There, they lit candles from the torch, and Haile Mikael sat in the Bishop's Chair. There was no question of sleep. Chala was wide awake, pacing back and forth.

"So, what do you think?" said the bishop, with that twinkle in his eye that Chala was beginning to know so well by now.

"I don't know what to think," said Chala. "It was so beautiful. But it was strange. The language—it was Amharic, was it not? But different. I could hardly understand it."

"It was ancient Amharic," said Haile Mikael, "spoken as it was centuries ago, and far away from here. It has not changed much here on the island."

"Where is the Land of Semien?" asked Chala.

"Far to the north," said the bishop. "Or did you mean to say 'Who is that girl?'"

Chala grinned, embarrassed. He was startled by what the bishop had been able to see in his mind. "She was beautiful," he said.

"Ah!" said Haile Mikael. "You are in love. Is it reciprocated?"

"How can I know?" answered Chala, delighted. "I do not know if she even saw me."

"Well, you can find out tomorrow, I suppose," said the bishop. "Although there is much to do, there will probably be some time to inquire about the girl."

"Almaz," said Chala.

"A pretty name," said Haile Mikael. "Diamond. Yes, a very pretty one, too, from what I could see when I peeked in the window."

"She was so sad," said Chala.

"It is a deep sadness," said the bishop, "the sadness for a lost home so far away. Well, to sleep." Haile Mikael yawned. Then he rose and went to his room. At the doorway he turned and said, "Good night, Chala. The peace of the Lord be always with you."

"And also with you," said Chala. He took his candle and looked into his little room. The light from the candle caused frightening shadows on the walls and ceiling—shadows that darted and swayed and thumped across the room. So before those shadows could turn into anything monstrous, Chala got to the side of the bed, pulled the blanket around him, and blew out the candle.

There was silence. It was very peaceful.

And all through the night, as much as he had fear of zar and buda, those strange creatures of mayhem and destruction never entered his mind. All through the night, no matter how hard Chala tried to be afraid, he could not be. Somehow, he just kept dreaming about stars. There were thousands of them, and they flashed like diamonds in the night.

CHAPTER 21

DEBRE SION

Chala awoke with the first crow of the rooster. Darkness surrounded him still, but in the dimness he saw lines of light against the wall. It was the dawn trying to come through the window shutter, and the soft light penetrated along the outlines of the heavy wooden slabs.

This morning felt strangely warm, he thought. He was used to waking in the cold. Here, it was easy to get out of bed. And somehow, now it was easier to try to open the window. It must have been that somehow Chala had become more familiar with his surroundings even as he slept. Whatever the reason, he felt no fear in padding across the room toward the light and pushing the shutter open.

Before his eyes lay a scene that could have been millions of years old. He looked east across the lake. The lake was black except for a reflected shimmer on its surface. Beyond the lake, the escarpment rose in its pure blackness for thousands of feet. Above it, the sky was just beginning to glow with that strange translucence that is the first light before dawn. All was still. The brightest of the stars still shone in the sky, but one by one they were slowly winking out.

"Just as it should be," Chala thought. He breathed deep of the cool, pleasant air of the dawn and stuck his head out of the window and looked south along the lake. The valley stretched forever on, and seemed never to end. "Surely," thought Chala, "Surely this is a magic place, full of good magic and heavenly spirits. I have never felt so much at peace. Now I know that however hard the journey becomes for me in the future, I will always have this place, and my home, and last night and this morning, and I am rich with that, and it will be with me all my days. What a story I will have to tell my friends."

And thinking all of this, Chala closed the window and walked to the other end of the room, where he opened the door and went out into the main room of the hostel.

Haile Mikael's door was ajar. On the table were two cups. One was empty. The other was full of lukewarm coffee. Chala drank, and wondered how early the priest had been awake, and where he was now. He went to the door, opened it, and peered out through the dawn light.

From across the plaza, from the church, came the sounds of priests chanting. The dawn mass had begun. After relieving himself in the small outhouse north of the hostel building, Chala hurried across the stone plaza and into the church.

At this stage of his life he was allowed only into the second circle of the church. The mass was being celebrated in the third circle, the innermost sanctuary which surrounded the Holy of Holies, where the Ark was kept. A fleeting thought entered Chala's mind. Could this be the place where the real Ark was kept? No. He put that thought to rest almost immediately. He knew, he had been taught all his life, that if the Ark were anywhere, it was most surely hidden in the cathedral at Axum. 'Ay!' thought Chala. 'We are going up there. Will I have a chance to see Axum?' Then he remembered that he was at Mass, and he should be saying his prayers. So he let the thoughts of Axum and the Ark go and concentrated on his prayers. He prayed to be allowed to go to Axum and see the Ark.

At the end of the mass the priests, led by Haile Mikael, came out of the sanctuary. Haile Mikael saw Chala standing in the shadows and smiled and, putting his arm around the boy's shoulders, walked him out of the church into the early morning sunlight.

Outside, he introduced Chala to the other priests and then said, "Chala, you are welcome to join us for breakfast. There is a table around the other side of the church. But first, will you bring me my cloak? I should have it for this breakfast."

"Of course, Your Excellency," said Chala.

When Chala had gone, an elder priest said to Haile Mikael, "Reverend Bishop, a word with you in private?"

"Of course," said Haile Mikael, and the two priests walked toward the edge of the hillside away from the others.

When the rest of the priests were out of earshot, the elder priest said, "Reverend Bishop, I will not waste any time. I will come right to the point. We will be speaking of important matters. Can the boy be trusted?"

"I believe he can," said Haile Mikael, taken aback. He thought, and then said, "Here are my reasons for saying that. He comes from our friend Markos of Bekoji. Markos has been his teacher for years and recommended this one out of all of his students. His family is a good one. Grandfather, father, uncle, brother—all are warriors of the Shoan kingdom. Chala's soul, too, is growing rapidly by the day. It is a good time of life for him. He is loyal and intelligent, and there is love in his heart for the nation. He will not betray us."

"Even if he is tortured, Reverend Bishop?"

Haile Mikael paused a moment in thought. Then he said, "Where we are going, if he is tortured, they will torture him to find out the strength of Menelik's army, not for the location of the Sacred Word. He will die with the knowledge of our secrets unrevealed."

Haile Mikael rolled his tongue around inside his mouth as he thought. Then he continued, "As for after, who knows what will happen? Only God. I understand your fear, Father Bekele. He is an Oromo—an outsider—but remember, so is Menelik's great general, Dejazmach Balcha. The times are changing, and one good Oromo is better than a hundred corrupt Amharas. No, I am very sure that Chala will not betray us. He is a good lad."

"Pardon me, Reverend Bishop," said Father Bekele. "I did not mean to question your judgment. But I had to ask. When fear drives a nation, as in these perilous times, anything can happen. I had to ask."

"It was your duty to ask, Father," said Haile Mikael, "and I am glad you did so. It is awful to have doubts hanging about. It sullies the very air. You have to do everything in your power to safeguard the Book."

Father Bekele sighed and said, "He is a good lad, if everything you say is true. He is likable and seems quick and intelligent. He will serve you well."

"If he keeps the crowds off me, I will be satisfied," said Haile Mikael, grinning. "Honestly, Father, you have no idea what it is like in the cities. And I think he will do much more than that for me. However, I do not take your warning lightly. I will test him many times along the way. I have seen how he is so far. He has courage and honor, and he likes this world of ours."

"Then Markos has chosen well for you," said Bekele.

"Shall we join the others?" suggested Haile Mikael.

The old priest nodded his assent.

When Chala, carrying the bishop's cloak, came around the side of the church, he saw that there was a large table, big enough for a dozen people to sit at six to a side, set out in the open air. It was under a thatched roof that was held up by four slim corner posts. The view from the table looked out over the lake to the valley and mountains beyond. Around the table were seated some ten priests, Haile Mikael among them. On the table were piled baskets of morning breakfast rolls.

The bishop gestured to Chala to sit on the bench beside him. Chala stood still, with wide eyes.

One of the priests laughed and said, "He cannot believe it." Other priests laughed, and Chala looked up to see all of them smiling at him.

"Break bread with us, Chala," said the Bishop. "You will find us generally a pleasant crew and nothing to be frightened of. Usually," he concluded, to some more quiet laughs.

And so Chala joined the priests, and bread and coffee was set in front of him, and a majestic-looking elder priest pushed a common bowl of honey closer to him, and the priests went back to talking among themselves. They talked mostly about Haile Mikael's coming northern travels, and the bishop spoke mostly about the beauty of their island and its importance to the Church and to the Empire.

"You may envy me my journey," he said, "but it is not entirely pleasant, I can assure you. It is sometimes frightening, and what this lad and I will encounter during the next few months I cannot dare to say. If the enemy is defeated, all well and good, to the glory of God who protects us. But if the enemy defeats us—and it is a very strong enemy—you will have to be prepared to safeguard the writings, because the world is changing and you are no longer so far away from everything. The enemy, if successful, will be here among you, right on this island. The heritage must be made safe."

"We have always taken precautions, Reverend Bishop," said the elder priest, "and recently we have made greater efforts to copy the writings. Six of us here now are scribes, and we copy like the devil, if you'll excuse the expression."

It was Haile Mikael's turn to smile. Chala didn't know what to do. Did priests talk like this? Well, Markos did, sometimes, especially when students exasperated him. It was probably all right.

"We not only have the traditional hiding places for the originals," the older priest went on, "but we have scouted out additional places. And we have obtained a new kind of wooden box. These boxes keep moisture away from the parchment better than anything we have seen before this, and that is a big help.

"Also," he continued, "as I said, we copy fast and accurately, and almost constantly. It is not easy. Sometimes after a long day the words seem to lose their meaning and appear to be merely marks on paper. But we persevere, and we check each others' work. It is our duty to God and to the Empire which protects His Holy Word.

"And we have taken other precautions. If an enemy sets foot on this island, he will find few priests. He will find a few more fishermen or farmers, all of whom will appear to be great fools. The priests he finds will know nothing of any hiding places." The old priest was silent.

"And the enemy will not question them," said Haile Mikael. "They will just kill them for sport, if that is their whim. If they torture them, they will find out nothing. Are there others who will know, in case it appears that the knowledge will be lost?"

"The usual ones," said the old priest.

"This is a good plan," said Haile Mikael. "It is strong. If the rest of the Empire has prepared as well as you, my brothers, we are well-prepared indeed. I can leave here feeling greatly at ease, for now at least. I thank you, my brothers, for this great gift of your diligence."

The breakfast ended on a note of satisfaction. Bishop Haile Mikael rose, threw his cape over his shoulders, and while the priests bowed their heads in silence, he delivered a prayer of thanks to the Lord.

"Now may I see the writings?" asked the bishop.

Outside of the library building, Haile Mikael beckoned Chala to accompany him, and the bishop and the boy went inside with Father Bekele. The library was one large room. There were many windows on three sides for light, and a group of tables, desks, and chairs filled the center. Alongside one wall was built a desk that would be just the right height for a man standing to work at, and below the top of the desk were cubby holes that extended from desk top nearly to the ground. They looked like a honeycomb, and they were stuffed with parchments and scrolls. On top of the desk lay more scrolls and books, and Haile Mikael went quickly to the desk and laid his hands on some of the works.

"See, Chala," he said. "These are some of the most precious jewels the Empire possesses. What is here is so much more valuable than gold. What is gold compared to these, the writings and instructions of the Lord? Look at this one." Haile Mikael struggled with a thick book of parchment four inches thick and two feet high. "It is the Kebra Negast: The Glory of the Kings. This is the history of the kings of Israel and of Ethiopia. It tells how Makeda of Axum and Solomon the Wise of Israel had a son who was named Menelik and became the first king of our nation. You know that story. Here is the book of that story." Haile Mikael opened the book in the middle, and Chala gasped. Never had he seen such beauty. The writing was beautiful in itself, but it was surrounded by even more beautiful paintings in gold and red and green and all the other colors. There were pictures of saints and angels and devils and happenings from the Bible tumbling all over each other. As Haile Mikael kept leafing through the volume, Chala saw that page after page was like this.

"Here is another one," said the bishop, pointing to an equally thick and high book. "This is the Fetha Negast—the Law of the Kings—by which we are all governed even to this day." He pointed to other, smaller books and scrolls. "Here," he said, "Here is the Book of Job, and the Book of Daniel, and here are the Songs of David. Here is the Song of Songs. Here are the writings of Moses, and the story of the Garden of Eden—the Book of Adam—and the writings of Paul and John. It goes on and on. It is our Faith, Chala. It is the writing down of our Faith. This is the center of it, and this is what the Empire exists for: to preserve the Faith. And the Faith sustains the Empire, and brings the people of the Empire to Heaven, to God. Against all the wiles of Satan and his zars, the Faith brings the People of the Faith to God."

The bishop paused. His eyes were intense and bright. "Look at this one!" he said, excited. "This is my favorite. It is the Book of Enoch. Some call it The Book of Jubilees. In it, Enoch describes Heaven, and who is there, and where in Heaven they are. And believe me, there are some surprises. Here. Look at it."

Haile Mikael thrust the small book bound in leather toward a startled Chala. Then gently he placed it into the boy's hands. It was only about five by seven inches, but it was very thick. Its parchment pages were very much yellowed along the edges, and somewhat brittle, so that they had to be handled carefully. But what was on those pages! Such beautiful paintings Chala had never seen before. They were all the colors of the rainbow, and they showed angels and devils and humans in such detail that they looked alive. Shades of color shaded into other shades, and the proportions of the figures were absolutely perfect.

"It is nearly three hundred years old," said Haile Mikael. "Such beauty, and so ancient. And yet it is only a representation of a story written so long ago that the time is almost incomprehensible to us. But, if you read this book, you will see that they lived then very much as we do today. More important, they thought then as we think today. Not that much has changed, Chala, except that we have talking wires and engines that run on steel rails, as you may see when we arrive in the city. But this creature that the Lord has created lives very much now as he has lived for as long as we can know about. Honor your God, Chala. In you He has created a very wonderful creature indeed. You owe Him a lot. You owe Him your very soul, and that is a very beautiful creation. You are holy, as are we all, and we must always strive to recognize that holiness in ourselves and in all others."

Chala stood silently, looking at the book, letting all this beauty fall into his mind through his eyes. But while he saw with his eyes, Chala was looking inward, into himself. The words of the bishop had opened something in him, so that he was able to look and see things he had never known before; had never thought of before. Haile Mikael's words had given him the power to see his soul, and as he stood here on this island, surrounded by these soft, warm breezes so unlike the winds of the highlands, he looked inside, and saw the future and the universe. A feeling came over him like he had never felt before. It was a feeling of peace, and rightness, and warmth. He heard the song of birds outside the window, and he was one with the earth, and at peace with his God.

Father Bekele stood to the side and furtively watched the bishop and the boy. What a picture they made, he thought. The bishop with the light of holiness streaming from his eyes, and the boy growing like a tree right before him. If this bishop could reach all the people like he had reached this boy—ah, but that is what this bishop did. That is why he was a bishop, even though he was so young. If everyone could see this world as the bishop could see it, the Kingdom of God would be at hand, thought Father Bekele. The world would stretch out its hands to God, even as God stretched out His hands to the world. What would it take to have the world do that? thought the priest. Why must we be so misunderstanding of the Lord?

And around them all, the gentle breezes of mid-morning blew. The birds sang, and the beauty of the world was infinite....

When the study of the books was finished, Chala and the bishop stepped outside and took their leave of Father Bekele.

"We will return for dinner, Father," said Haile Mikael, "and I think we may be bringing some of it with us. If I remember the people of your island correctly, I will bet that we come back staggering under the weight of their gifts."

"That may very well be, Your Grace," said Bekele, "but try to discourage them, please. We have plenty here."

Once again, Haile Mikael and Chala walked down the stone path to the town. It was easier in the daylight. It was fun for Chala to look down at the town, to see its twisting streets and the houses, one against another, rising up out of the ground like a collection of stone mushrooms with tawny tops.

"Where are we going, Father Haile?" he asked.

"Why, just visiting, Chala," said the bishop. "Didn't you ever go just visiting?"

"Surely, Father," replied Chala. "We visit a lot in our country. It's fun."

"Just!" said the bishop. "That is what we are doing. I have a lot of good friends here. I'll introduce you to them, and we will take this time to enjoy ourselves. Our journey will very seldom be as pleasant as this. Let's use this day to gather strength. We will need it. See over there," he said, pointing out over the south side of the lake. "Right now, probably, they are bringing our horses around to the western side of the lake. We will take the boat there tomorrow, and be off again. For now, just breathe deep and enjoy yourself."

And so the two went jumping down the path with light steps and lighter hearts. The bishop was fast on his feet, and Chala was fast as only a tough young kid of fourteen can be fast. Down the path they went, galumphing into the town, laughing all the way.

"Surely," thought Chala, "this is a very strange bishop, but if this is what I am in for on this journey, that's all right with me."

It was the kind of bright, clear morning when walls glistened with water left by the heavy morning dew. It was mid-morning, but it seemed earlier. There was still a freshness to the day.

Haile Mikael and Chala strolled into the market area of the town. The bishop was constantly approached by people who wished to speak to him, or kiss his cross, or give him gifts. The gifts—fruit, bread, grain, and the like—went into a sack that Chala carried with him. The bishop seemed to enjoy this attention, and later, when Chala mentioned that, Haile Mikael said, "I do enjoy it. It is *what* they want that I like. These are old friends, and they want to say hello and see that I am all right. That is easy to take. This is a small place, Chala, and that is what a small place is like. What is difficult is a large place, where they don't know who you are, but they can see *what* you are. In that case, they want different things. They want a piece of what they think you are. They want help at any cost. You will see what I mean. It is almost intolerable to me. I suppose that is a failing in my nature, something the Lord wants me to work on, but still it remains difficult. I am not perfect. No one is."

But meanwhile, the Bishop of Ba'le walked among these old friends and talked with them and was happy.

And so was Chala.

After they had walked about the town for a while, Haile Mikael walked down a lane that wandered through the fields and groves to the south of the village. On either side of the lane tree-lined fields stretched away. They were smaller than the fields Chala was used to, for land was limited on this island, and so had to be husbanded more carefully. Great care was taken to use every inch of ground and use it over and over again.

Down the lane they roamed. Haile Mikael took his time, but he seemed to know just where he was going.

With the smaller fields, the houses were closer than in the usual spread-out farming community. Chala noticed, too, that there were fewer domestic animals here. Occasionally on the path they would meet a person coming the other way. Sometimes it was a farmer, or a woman carrying water. Once it was a pretty young girl. Chala noticed her, and there was a leap of joy in his heart, something that he had never felt before.

For the girl coming down the lane was Almaz—the girl who had sung the Lament the night before. Chala had not hoped to see her again. As they approached her, she stopped, and averted her eyes and bowed graciously. Haile Mikael stopped. "Good day to you, young lady," he said. "Who are you, and how are you today?"

"I am well, Your Grace," she answered in a voice just above a whisper. "My name is Almaz, and I am the daughter of Birru."

"Ah!" said the bishop. "Just as I thought. Your father and mother have produced a beautiful daughter. But you are mistaken about me. I am not Your Grace. I am Father Haile."

Chala looked at the bishop. Haile Mikael had that strange quirky smile on his face again.

Almaz looked up, and her eyes seemed to be laughing, they sparkled so much. "I know who you are, Your Grace. I saw you yesterday, when you arrived."

"Ah!" said Haile Mikael. "So you know who I am. But do you *know* who I am?"

"You are the Bishop of Ba'le Province," she answered.

"No. No, I am not," said Haile Mikael. "I am, to you, Waizerit Almaz Birru, simply Father Haile. Is that all right?"

Almaz's breath came in a gasp. "It is an honor, Your Grace. I am not worthy."

"Yes, you are," said the bishop, "and if you call me Your Grace once again, I will tell your father. He will punish you. He will keep you from your breakfast tomorrow morning."

Almaz began to giggle.

"Where is your father, by the way," asked Father Haile. "I wish to speak with him."

"He is at the house, just around the next bend, Your..."

"Ah?"

"Father Haile."

"Just," said the priest. "Almaz Birru, may you always call me Father Haile. If you would do that, I would be most happy. Can you lead us to your father, or.....oh, but where were you off to?"

"To the market, Father, to buy spices," said Almaz, smiling. "But I would be honored to lead you to my father."

"Ah, but would I incur the wrath of your mother, who has sent you on this errand?" asked the priest.

"Oh, no, Father," said Almaz. "On the contrary, she would be most pleased and honored. As long as I have the spices in time for supper, I will be fine."

"Well, then," said Haile Mikael, "let us go then and search for your father. Oh, but I am being most rude, Waizerit Almaz. I have not introduced you to my traveling companion, Ato Chala."

Almaz looked at Chala and smiled and bowed. But Chala was not looking at her at all. He was looking at the bishop's face. At the sound of the words Ato and Chala together, the boy was so startled that both he and his mind had jumped.

You see, in our country, Ato means Mister, or Sir, and Chala had never heard himself called that before. And secondly, and much more important in Chala's society, to be introduced to a girl like this was almost unheard of. It just didn't happen. Especially when you were introduced by a bishop. So this was very unusual indeed.

But Chala was beginning to get used to unusual things, and when he saw that the bishop was thoroughly enjoying this situation and, as he thought, having a good silent laugh about it, he brought his eyes down again and looked at the girl.

And then suddenly, he felt proud, and bowed to her. "My name is Chala, son of Negassa," he said. "I am of the Shoa Oromo of Arusi, and my home is up there." He gestured toward the top of the far cliffs. Almaz turned and glanced up at the heights, and Chala thought the profile of her face was beautiful.

"Well, let us walk together, then," said Father Haile. And they strolled down the path together in the direction of Birru Goshu's house.

"I am honored, Your Grace!" exclaimed Birru Goshu, jumping up from his stool. The stool sat in front of the door to Birru's house. Haile Mikael and his two young companions entered the yard of the house, a small space bordered by the wall of the lane. To left and right, there were plantations of false banana, their fronds reaching high up into the sky. Beyond that were larger trees. In all, it gave the effect of a glade in the middle of a deep forest, although the field of grain across the road proclaimed that they were deep in the middle of farming country.

In the cool green of the glade, Birru Goshu advanced toward the bishop, bowing low. The bishop offered his cross, and Birru kissed it.

"I am Father Haile to my friends," said the bishop. "Especially to my old friends, old friend. And as your daughter already calls me Father Haile, Shum Birru, it would be unseemly if you did not also address me in that friendly fashion."

Birru Goshu looked at his daughter. She grinned at him. He looked back at the bishop.

"I came to thank you for your hospitality of last night," said Haile Mikael quietly, "and also to talk to you of other business. Including your appointment as shum, of which I was unaware. Congratulations. Twelve years is a long time."

"Please sit and take coffee with us," said Birru, clapping his hands. Almaz's mother appeared in the doorway of the house, and froze, her mouth open. It is not every day that a bishop appears in your front yard.

"Well, I *will* take coffee with you," said Haile Mikael. "It is delightful here, Shum Birru. What a nice spot you have selected for your house."

"Thank you, Your Grace," said Birru. "Allow me to introduce my wife, Aster. Do you remember her?"

"How could I not?" said Haile Mikael, smiling. "She is as young and beautiful as the last time I saw her. How are you, Weizero Aster?"

Aster bowed, but her mind was darting about in many places. Why hadn't Birru warned her? Where was another stool? Where were the servants? Was there any coffee? When was she going to kill Birru for letting this situation develop? Her eyes fell upon Almaz standing next to the bishop, and her wrath was about to descend on her daughter when the bishop said,

"Please forgive me, madam, for just showing up like this, but I had no choice. I have only a little time, and I needed to speak with you and your husband before I left."

"Oh!" said Aster. "Oh, dear!" And that was all she said, for what do you say to a bishop who has just dropped out of thin air and is standing, smiling, in front of you? Yes, that was all she said, but it was not all she thought. Foremost among her thoughts was what she was going to do to Birru after their guest had gone.

So soon they were seated in the dooryard of the home—Haile Mikael, Birru, and Aster. They sat and sipped coffee in the cool morning air, and when it was appropriate, Haile Mikael spoke.

"Your house is admirable, Weizero Aster," he said. "It is beautifully kept. I can see that you care for it with great attention, and that you are a superior housekeeper."

"It is in terrible condition, Your Eminence," said Aster. "If I had but known that you were coming..."

"It is in fine condition, Weizero Aster," said the priest, "and again, I apologize for my sudden visit. But we have other things to talk about, do we not? I must know how the people of the island feel about the upcoming struggle. I already know what the priests intend to do, but what about you?"

"We are ready, Father Haile," said Birru with a quiet smile. "We send one hundred foot soldiers to the battle, but a goodly number of us will stay and safeguard the monastery and the ancient works. I wish I could go! But as you know, it is my duty to stay here. My second-in-command, Galawedos

Tekle Giorgis, will go in my name. And I offer you, Father, twelve strong men to act as your escort. They are fleet-footed warriors, and can easily keep up with your horses."

"A thousand thanks to you, Shum Birru," said Haile Mikael, "but I do not need your men. Chala will suffice for my escort. But I do detect a strange discrepancy in your statements, Shum Birru. I do not understand. You send troops. You assign escorts. These are not the prerogatives of a shum. What is it that you are not telling me? Have you attained yet another title? A balambaras, perhaps?"

"He is a grazmach," Aster broke in, beaming with pride.

"Indet?" said Haile Mikael. "A grazmach? A leader of the left wing? I did not know! My congratulations, sir, and I am pleased to make your acquaintance, Grazmach Birru Goshu of Debre Sion, Defender of the Faith."

Haile Mikael laughed with pleasure at the good fortune of his friend, and Aster said, "He is so modest. He could have a place at court, if he wished..."

"I do not wish," broke in Birru, strongly. "I prefer to stay here. Why go to a place full of lies and deceit and squalor and disease and people squabbling among themselves to gain an advantage? Of what use is that? Here my work is to defend my country and the old regime. That is important. That is important to me, and to the nation."

"Ah, Birru, my brother," said Haile Mikael, "it is important to me also, because I myself feel the same. But you are luckier than I. I thought Ba'le would be far enough away, but it was not. Intrigue abounds even there. It is not that far from Harar, you know. But you, Birru—here we sit in front of your pleasant house, right by your beautiful garden, across from your fertile field. And here you are surrounded by your wonderful family. What a pleasant life you have found!"

Away from the house, by the side of the garden, there grew a grove of ensete, the false banana plant. The great green fronds of the plant stretched high into the sky, and in the deep sunlit green of this beautiful space walked Chala and Almaz.

"I thought only the Gurage grew this plant," said Chala. "But you are not Gurage."

"No," said Almaz. "We are Amhara, the old Amhara of the north. And you are of the wild Galla of the south," she said, teasing. "The fierce wild warriors."

"We call ourselves the Oromo, the People," said Chala quietly. He was enchanted by this place, and even more enchanted with this girl with the flashing eyes who teased him. "Only you Amhara call us Galla."

"Galla, yes," she said. "Outsiders. The old people say that you came out of nowhere, riding your horses up from the south and killing everything in sight. It was all we could do to stop you. Where did you come from, anyway?"

"*Our* old people say many things," said Chala. "Some say we came from far to the south, where the Great White Mountain is."

"That is where *we* say King Solomon's mines are," said Almaz. "The Emperor says that in the very old days that was the border of Ethiopia. How far is that, Chala?"

"I do not know," said Chala. "But some of our old ones say that we came from even further than that, from across the sea. They say that we came from boats that came to the coast where the Somali people live; that we came from very far away."

"The sea," said Almaz, musing. "I wonder what it is like."

"Bigger even than this lake," said Chala. "They say it is green, and full of sand, like the desert."

"In the north, our people say that the sea is red," said Almaz.

Chala thought a while, and then said, "They must be different seas."

They were silent then, because Almaz had had the same thought at the same time, and so there was nothing left to say. In her mind, Almaz had no wish to contradict Chala, and for his part, Chala felt the same. So they had found a puzzle, and perhaps someday they could solve it together.

"I would like to see those seas someday," said Almaz, "*and* the Great White Mountain." She looked off into the forest of ensete, and lowered her eyes.

Chala did not say "Someday I will take you there." He was too young and too shy to say that. But he thought it, and he wanted to say it, and he looked at Almaz with a look that said what his voice could not say.

Almaz was looking away from him, but somehow she could feel what he could not say, and a shudder of fear and pleasure and hope and excitement flew like a sharp spring breeze through her body.

They stood there silently for a time together, and then Chala swallowed. His throat was dry. "So if you are not Gurage," he said, "why do you grow ensete?"

Almaz looked at him and smiled. She rubbed a great waxy green leaf between her hands. "Because it tastes good," she said. She laughed, and to Chala, her laughter was like stars.

CHAPTER 24

HAILE MIKAEL'S VISION

Haile Mikael was exasperated. He could just not concentrate. He had chosen for his meditation site a cliff high up on the hill near the monastery—a cliff that looked south over the fields of the island and commanded a glorious view of the great valley. Thirty miles apart, the five thousand foot high cliffs marched along opposite each other into the south. And in the valley itself, the chain of lakes flowed along in the same direction. All was green and blue and the air was soft. It was a glorious sunny day, and the monkeys and birds called to each other in the forests. It was perfect for concentration, but Haile Mikael could not concentrate.

Haile Mikael's book of daily prayer today said that he should meditate on the fall of Adam and Eve and their expulsion from the Garden of Eden. But every time he tried to do that, Adam and Eve got lost. He started thinking only of Eden. Then he would look up and wonder how Eden compared to this verdant valley. There was a peace here which he could seldom find anywhere. Then he asked: is *this* Eden? Could this island itself be Eden? Stranger things had happened.

Then he began to see the lake populated by arks, Noah's among them, and then he thought of The Ark, Solomon's Ark, the Ark of the Covenant of Israel. The Ark stolen, no, taken, as allowed by God to happen—the Ark taken by Menelik I of Ethiopia, first-born son of Solomon and Makeda of Axum and Sheba. Then Haile Mikael smiled, and let his mind go and rest in that wonderful legend of the seduction of Sheba by Solomon.

He remembered the story well: how Sheba had learned of the wisdom of Solomon, and resolved to meet with that monarch so that she might learn wisdom from him. And so she travelled from Axum down to Jerusalem with a caravan of five hundred camels, all bearing gold and silver and jewels to Solomon as gifts. And when Sheba had arrived in Jerusalem, she was welcomed by Solomon with rich clothing, and spices, and a crown of gold, and he gave her a grand apartment in his palace, and rooms for all her servants and retainers as well. And he treated her as his equal, for that is what she was.

And when Sheba had been with Solomon for many days, the king gave her a great feast; and that night, after the feast, the King and Queen slept together, and Sheba conceived. And on her journey back to Axum, in a small town on the border of Ethiopia and Nubia, she gave birth to a son, and she named the boy Menelik.

Now when Menelik was twenty-one years of age, Sheba sent the prince back to Solomon, who recognized him as his first-born son. And Solomon blessed Menelik, and gave him the first-born sons of the nobles of the Twelve Tribes of Israel to be his nobles, and sent him on his way.

And on the night that Menelik departed from Jerusalem, Solomon had a terrifying dream. In his dream, the sun rose up over Israel as usual. But at mid-day, it quit its place in the sky over Israel and fled to the south, where it shone over the land of Ethiopia forever—even to the end of days.

Then Solomon, in a panic, awoke from his dream and leaped from his bed and ran to the temple. Into the Holy of Holies he ran, and behold! The Ark of the Covenant was gone! It was stolen! The Covenant which had guided Israel forever, the Covenant between the Lord and the people of Israel, had vanished!

And so Menelik and his noblemen, having stolen the Ark, took the Ark of the Covenant and went down into Africa, to Ethiopia, carrying the Ark with them. They carried it to the holy city of Axum: Sheba's city; Menelik's city.

"Where the Ark still resides," thought Haile Mikael, and he smiled. "Lucky Solomon," he thought, "to have such a beautiful woman as our Queen Makeda." And then he stopped thinking, for from somewhere deep down within him images like winged fish swarmed up from the dark depths into his seething mind, and he thought, "Makeda. Makeda. I see her. I see her breasts....rising...falling....rising....falling...."

"Aiyee!" shouted Haile Mikael, jumping up from his rocky seat on the cliffs. "Yeoww! Aiyee! What have I done?" For his meditation had turned into a lustful dream of a beautiful queen long dead, and what could this be? What could this mean?

Haile Mikael let out his breath and blew out his cheeks. His eyes bulged, and he swirled his priestly garments about him as if he had been attacked by a swarm of bees. "My God," he said to himself. "It must be this air. It must be this island. I am not used to this. It is so gentle here, and so kind. But my God, what kind of dream is this, right in the middle of my meditation? What does this mean?"

Haile Mikael was a celibate and had been for over twenty years. But he had not always been celibate. When a man entered the Church in Ethiopia, he had to make a choice. He could marry, if he wished, before he became a priest. In that case, he would remain married and keep on with his familial duties, adding priestly duties to them. But since family duties do take energy and time, most of the married priests concentrated on chores at the parish level. Many of them became debteras, and lived a reasonably holy and stable life in their communities.

But if a man chose not to marry before his ordination and was ordained a priest without having a wife and family, then he would always remain single and celibate. He would be as celibate as the most brittle and dried up old husk of a monk. But his life, unencumbered by any other duties, would open before him like a grand series of lighted rooms. First he would become a debtera, then a master of the books, then a master scribe. After that he would become proficient in poetry, then in the ancient chants. He would study philosophy, and the mysteries. Finally he would emulate Christ and dwell on the glories of creation and the universal law and reasoning. Beyond the usual priestly training he would spend a dozen years in learning. After those incredibly arduous and difficult years, he would then, and only then, have attained the ability to become an important leader of the Church. Then the world would turn bright for him, and with any luck and sanctity he would be able to shed Christ's light and grace over a wide flock.

That was the position Haile Mikael was in—recognized at a relatively young age as a wise and respected leader of his Church; a bishop, created as such at an age when most men were still looking about them and wondering what on earth they were doing here.

So Haile Mikael was brilliant, and faithful, and strong. And celibate.

But he was not a virgin. For in the years before his calling to the Church, growing up as a young man, he had sampled intrigues with an interesting number of beautiful young girls. It was allowed. They were the tej-beyt girls—the bar girls—of the larger cities and towns. Haile Mikael, like most young men, had drunk his fill of their beauty. A man was expected to be knowledgeable about such things, and to dip his body in such gracious pleasures. And Haile Mikael had done so with delight.

So he knew what it was that he was giving up. And he knew that if he did not marry he would be expected to become one of the exalted ones— one of the celibates. And he made his decision: to give up these certain pleasures for unknown ones that were only hinted at, but which, he had come to fervently believe, Christ had in mind for him.

So for over twenty years he had given up women, and fornication, and even thoughts about all of that, and here, all of a sudden, in this beautiful place, the Mother of His Country was dancing in his head, naked in a moonlit night, her breasts rising and falling, rising and falling, in the darkness of a palace hall under a full moon, her body quivering with apprehension and desire.

"What! Have you gone crazy?" muttered Haile Mikael to himself, pacing up and down the rocks of the cliffs. "Are you mad?" And instead of the vision of the beautiful woman, he tried to concentrate on his prayers. But he could not. Makeda, Queen of Sheba, was powerful. Haile Mikael was not the first man to find that out. No, Solomon was the first to find that out, a long time ago.

Let us leave Haile Mikael for a while, sitting on his rock and holding his head in his hands. He is finding out once again that he is human. It is the first time that he has had the chance to do that in a long while.

It was a peaceful evening. Haile Mikael, finally quieted, and indeed humbled, descended from his rocks and dined with the monks and priests of Lake Zwai. Chala ceased his explorations and joined them. Later that night there was a solemn and heartfelt farewell to Grazmach Birru and Weizero Aster. Almaz was nowhere to be seen, and that hurt the heart of Chala, whose head was spinning with the fragrance of first love.

And very late that night, long after everyone else on the island had gone to sleep, the figure of Haile Mikael, Bishop of Ba'le Province, lay prostrate on the rude library floor at the monastery of Lake Zwai. Haile Mikael was deep in prayer. In his prayer, he asked saints and angels, the Christ and His Mother, the Holy Spirit, the Godhead Himself, for protection for this holy island of true Christendom: protection against the enemy, be it heathen, devil, or benighted Roman.

Chala lay deep in sleep. He dreamed of journeys, of horses, of clean, warm beds. And he dreamed of Almaz, and when he dreamed of her, every time he dreamed, she turned into stars. And Chala dreamed those peaceful dreams all night long, and the night was filled with stars.

The next day was a day of travel for Bishop Haile Mikael and his aide Chala Negassa. They rose early and looked at the serene lake and the quiet shadows of the cliffs. A few early morning birds darted through the warm air over the island.

Haile Mikael said a simple mass. There was a plain breakfast of good bread, honey, and coffee with the clergy, then the trek down to the water's edge where the reed boat waited to take them to the western side of the lake.

The ride across the lake was like a journey across a painting, it was so still. By the third hour of the day they were across, onto their horses, and riding to the north along the shore of the lake. Gradually the trail wended its way upward, away from the lake, ever upward. The forest became less dense, and gradually the land stretched upward like a bony finger, becoming a ridge beckoning to the north.

In the evening, they begged a place for the night at a poor village along the road. In the morning, they were off again as soon as possible, heading toward the immense volcano called Zukquala.

They crossed the Awash River, which at this time of the year flowed gently, calmed down from the raging torrents of the rainy season. It was an easy crossing. Once past the river, instead of following the main track toward Addis Ababa, they turned off on a scruffy path that led in zigs and zags up the side of the mountain. After a while they dismounted and led their horses, saving them. It was not until mid-afternoon that they arrived at the monastery.

The monastery of Zukquala had been built centuries ago near the summit of the mountain, almost at the rim of the caldera. It was situated at about 12,000 feet, high on the northeast side of the mountain, and it overlooked a lake formed in the mouth of the volcano eons before there was anyone to even think about building anything on the mountain. It was not a classic monastery as monasteries go, it being little more than a group of huts surrounding a small church. It was not a place where you went to study classic architecture. It was a place where you went to study God, and for that it was admirably suited. It almost blended right into the mountainside, and mountain and monastery became one in the tan tones of earth and rock. Above all, the eight-pointed cross of the church, enlivened with bleached white ostrich eggs fixed to the points, soared into a sky so blue at this high altitude that you would think that you could fall into that sky and keep falling upward until you arrived at God.

And below, the land of Ethiopia stretched out in every direction, stretching out its hands to God.

So late in the day that it was almost evening, Chala stood on a clifftop at the edge of the monastery grounds, silently surveying the wide, wide earth. He felt a hollowness in his chest. The earth was so large. The journey was so long, and who could tell what might await around every bend, across every brow of every hill? He took a deep breath, and stared into the distance.

A bony hand gripped Chala's shoulder from behind. The boy jumped, whirled, and beheld a frightening vision. An old man with wild eyes and lice-ridden hair stood leaning on a staff, glaring at him. The old man exhaled, leaving a cloud of rotten breath in the air. Chala gagged, and even with all the politeness of his upbringing it was all he could do not to run away. As it was, he took a step back, and the vision laughed.

"For where *you* are going, you are going to need protection," it said.

"Who are you?" asked Chala, scarcely above a whisper.

"I have fashioned protection for you," said the vision. "Look."

From beneath his ragged garments, the old man took out a small circular leather case, scarcely thicker than Chala's little finger, and about half as long. He fiddled with the case, and from it he extracted a small scroll, which he unraveled.

It was beautiful. The small painting, done in brilliant colors of red, orange, and black, showed nine angels. They were arrayed in three rows, and their eyes looked every which way.

"They will ward off the evil for you," said the old man. "They will watch for demons. See, here I have shown that they have broken the lines of the dancing demons. You will take this and wear it around your neck, and you will be safe. Now, you will do as I instruct. You will kneel."

Chala stood, unmoving, his mouth open. Never had he witnessed such a destitute individual, not even among the occasional beggars who appeared in the dooryards of Meraro on their ways across the land.

"Kneel, you fool! I haven't got all day!" thundered the fetid old man.

So close to the monastery walls, Chala could not think of why he should be afraid. The old man lifted his staff and brought it down hard over Chala's shoulder.

"Indet!" yelled Chala. "Hey! What are you doing?"

"Down, I said! Down! Down! Down!"

The blows from the staff rained down on Chala's back.

"All right," said Chala. "All right. Why?" he asked, kneeling. He could have run, but the old man fascinated him, and Chala thought that he could not really hurt him. The blows hurt, but they were not intolerable. They were not that hard. It was sort of like being back in school.

"So I can bless you, you fool!" yelled the wild old man.

"I accept your blessing," said Chala, using the age-old formula.

"Good," said the old man, calming down. "Now listen carefully. I am going to pronounce an incantation over you. It will go into you and into the scroll at the same time. It will bind you together with this scroll. The power of the prayer and the power of the scroll and the powers of the angels will join in you and keep you from harm. Understood?"

"I understand," said Chala, looking at the ground, "and I thank you for this great blessing." He couldn't think of anything better to say, and the old man seemed satisfied with that.

"Good lad," said the vision. "Be quiet, now. Be still. This is very important."

Then the old man was quiet, and the silence of evening fell over the two of them. There was a stillness here, thought Chala. A calmness where something could be worked by itself, without anything else interfering. And then suddenly, sounding like a wheezy old saddle, the old man began to speak.

"Nine angels shall surround you!" he chanted.
"Their wings and swords shall guard you.
The hordes of demons' lines they break.
The howls of hell, the wiles of snakes
Shall never hurt you now. The snares
Of devils cannot win
When cast off by the Cherubim.

Great Lord of Heaven and Earth and
of all things in between;
Great God of the Universe and all
that dwell within;
Send Your angel legions
To Zukquala to protect
This young man, Chala Negassa,
In his life and in his quest.

This I say unto You, while I invoke
The names of your great saints -
The Nine Great Saints of Syria,
And Susuenyos,
And Teklehaymanot.

I have set the seal of the Father,
the Son, and the Holy Spirit
Upon this lad. I have cursed
All you evil demons and unpure spirits.

So say I, Gebre Manfas Qeddus,
Hermit of the heights of sacred Mount Zukquala!

Come Cherubim and Seraphim,
Come Powers and Dominions,
Come Thrones and Archangels,
Virtues and Principalities and Angels all!

Save this servant of the Lord
From any evil that to him may fall!
Ayiee!"

It was just at that moment that Haile Mikael, attracted by the hubbub, poked his head around the wall of a nearby building, took in the situation, and said quietly, with a smile forming on his lips, "Indet?"

What he saw was Chala, kneeling, his mouth still wide open in surprise, watching an apparition of rags and staff and wild hair and gangly arms and flailing legs bounding away over the rocks, with what was left of his clothing flouncing around his buttocks. The old man was racing pell-mell for some unseen destination.

"Wa...was that the saint?" said Chala, struggling to his feet as Haile Mikael came up to him. "Was that Gebre Manfas Qeddus?" he asked with awe in his voice.

"Only if he was six hundred years old," said the bishop. "Did he look that old?"

"Not *that* old," said Chala.

"Well, then," said Haile Mikael, "it was probably not the saint. More likely it was Paulus. Wild Paul, we call him." And he started to laugh.

Now this was another quandary for Chala: a real puzzle. Why was the bishop laughing?

"You should see yourself," said Haile Mikael. "You look like you've seen a ghost." And he started laughing again.

"He called himself Gebre Manfas Qeddus," said Chala. "Was that not the saint of Mount Zukquala?"

"Who lived six hundred years ago?" said Haile Mikael. "Who was an exorcist, and who could cast out demons? And who went naked his whole life to signify his lack of respect for worldly things? He could cure leprosy, too. But no, what you saw was not the saint. What you saw was Wild Paul, who long ago took the name of the saint to emulate him and to draw himself closer to him and to God." Haile Mikael stroked his beard. "He seems to be getting closer to Gebre's lack of clothing, at least," he said, and laughed again.

Chala was looking at the scroll. "This is beautiful," he said. "Reverend Bishop, do you think it has power?"

Haile Mikael's face took on a serious demeanor as he looked at the painting. "Certainly it does," he said. "Look. Nine angels. One from each angel legion. Yes, there is power there. Chala, I may laugh at Paulus, because his antics are really very funny, but he is a hermit, and an artist, and quite possibly a saint, and God speaks through people like that. They can see things that we cannot see, and they report those things to us. So Paulus can see angels, I think, and demons and devils, too, and he can tell us about them. And yes, if you remember what is painted on this scroll, and keep these angels in your heart and mind, they will have power. They will be with you, along with your guardian angel. Paulus has called them to you, and they will help you."

Haile Mikael took the scroll, and rolled it up and tucked it into its leather case. He made the Sign of the Cross over it and said, "There. I have added my blessing to it. May it keep you safe, and in the way of the Lord." And having said that, he put the encased scroll over Chala's head and adjusted its leather strap around the boy's neck.

"Now," said Haile Mikael, "Let's join the fathers and brothers for prayer and dinner."

Dinner was held in the main meeting hall of the monastery. It was a simple affair of injera and vegetable stew washed down with water. After dinner, in honor of the bishop, open discussion was allowed, and news went back and forth and stories were told and retold. There was a question asked of Haile Mikael about the religion of the Ferengis who were invading the land, and the bishop's response that they were Roman Catholics set off a discussion concerning the heresies of the Church of Rome and a general shaking of heads regarding the Jesuits and strange Christian sects in general. Finally an old monk said, "I am reminded of an old story about some so-called Christians who came to Gondar a long time ago."

And once again the story was told of the strange Ferengi Christians who had come to the School of Gondar, the greatest theological school in all Ethiopia, and announced that they had come to show Ethiopia the correct path to God. The Abuna, then present at the school, said to them, "Your church must be very powerful. It seems to have such a direct connection to God. It must be a very old and venerable church. Tell me, how old is your church?"

"Why," said the leader of the Ferengi Christians, "ours is a very old church indeed. It is almost 350 years old."

The Abuna looked at them and said, "Perhaps you should stay here a while and listen to us. Our church is 1500 years old. Perhaps there is something we could teach you!"

The old monk ended his soliloquy. Everyone had a good laugh, and that night, the monks and priests of sacred Zukquala went to sleep refreshed and satisfied, and slept the deep sleep of peace.

In the morning, Chala was again standing outside the monastery, in that place where he had met the fetid apparition of the night before. His angels hung in their scapular around his neck. He was not there to look for the old monk, although he wouldn't have minded seeing him again. What drew him to the spot was the view. For from here, turning in a semi-circle from left to right, he could see 270 degrees of the horizon. In the northwest he could just make out the ridges of Entoto, the high mountain on which was built the capital city of Addis Ababa—the New Flower of the kingdom. Then, directly to the north were the old kingdoms of Shoa and Manz and Amhara. Beyond that, only God knew. The mountains stretched forever, as far as he could see. To the northeast was the Awash River, winding its way east into the Danakil Desert, where it would not reach the sea but instead would flow into a lake which would sometimes disappear in the summer when there was not enough rain. To the east were the Chercher Mountains and beyond them the old walled city of Harar. Beyond Harar were the grasslands of the Ha'ud, where wild Somalis roamed and which no one dared to enter without a large army at his back. To the southeast was Chillalo, the mountain that hung over Assella, the town that was the capital of Arusi. That is where Bedane and Uncle Bedasa and all the rest were camped, getting ready for the fight.

In all that vastness, there was not one sign of a human. So high was Chala, and so huge was the land, that no work of man could be seen. The land flared forth into the nothingness of the surrounding deserts as though the world would never end. Individual mountains were so huge that the eye could not encompass their entire lengths. Above all was the sky, so blue here, reaching up to no one knew where. All was still.

But down there, all over those mountains and hills and valleys, all over those vast highlands and heights themselves dwarfed by the extent of the great continent itself, there was, unseen, movement. All over that great land there were armies moving—the armies of Imperial Ethiopia. The Empire was moving its armies north; north to meet this new threat to the ancient land. From Harar and Arusi and Ba'le and Shoa they came; from Sidamo and Illubabaor and Kaffa; from Gemu-Gofa and Jimma—from all the far-flung kingdoms and principalities where the armies of Menelik encamped, the armies moved.

They could not be seen, but they were there, and soon they would be heard.

PART IV

NORTH

CHAPTER 26

THE ENCAMPMENT AT ASSELLA

"We are the soldiers of the Great Bashaw!
Our fathers were his soldiers in the battles before,
And now we all are ready and it's off to war!
We are the soldiers of the Great Bashaw!

We eat the cattle of the Great Bashaw -
And we eat them raw and we cook them in a stew;
You can call us savage and we know you do.
You'll be lucky if we don't cook you!
We are the soldiers of the Great Bashaw...."

That's what the young troopers sang as they paraded before their officers in Assella Camp. The officers smiled with satisfaction and watched as the soldiers wheeled their horses. Each man held his shield and two spears in his left hand and guided his horse with his knees. Over each man's shoulder was slung a Remington rifle, and around each man's waist was a bandolier full of bullets. The Emperor had not failed them. The supplies had come, and now these men were a crack mounted division, ready to hurl themselves at the enemy with the force of lightning.

After weeks of training, the mounted brigades of Arusi and eastern Shoa and Ba'le could wheel and ride and shoot and advance and kill and retreat and protect themselves as well as any troops on earth. They were in splendid shape, and so were their mounts. From all over the region, supplies had come in. From the hoards of the Emperor and the rases, rifles and ammunition had flowed to the troops in a torrent of greased metal. Here in the clear air of the highlands soldiers had been made out of born fighters, and the sight was as brave as any you could wish to see.

"Ras Michael will be proud of what we have done," said Dejazmach Wube.

"With your leadership, we have made them soldiers," replied Kanyazmach Didda.

"And with your leadership, we will drive the filth we call the Ferengi into the sea and watch them drown or be eaten alive by demons," added Grazmach Roba.

The three leaders sat bunched together on their horses and watched as the hamsa alekas led their cavalrymen past them. Behind the leaders were their officers. There were nearly two hundred of them. Twenty-five were meto alekas: front-line soldiers who would direct the fighting. The rest were the headquarters staffs of the leaders. Each leader had about fifty officers they used to carry messages, to insure that there were adequate supplies, to determine weak points, to generally advise. For the most part they were fierce men, because they had to be. The common soldiers were always ready to sneer at them, to call them cowards and servants, to question their parentage. So they had to be good, if for no other reason than to be able to hold up their heads before the soldiers. It was a built-in rivalry, and it promoted keenness for battle and mayhem in the ranks of the opposing army.

The Dejazmach was the point of the spear. He led the center and directed the movements of the left and right wings. The Grazmach led the left wing, the Kanyazmach the right. Thus there were fifteen hundred fighters in the center, fifteen hundred on the right, and fifteen hundred on the left. In reserve, the Dejazmach held five hundred more men which he could use as he pleased, placing them wherever he needed them.

"There will be twenty thousand of us," said Dejazmach Wube. "That is all of us. We are all from Shoa and Arusi and Ba'le and Wollo, and a few from Lasta and Wokatit. No more are we the great numbers we had of old. No more mounted armies of sixty or eighty thousand men. The famines and the diseases have taken care of that. But no matter. Now we are better armed. Now we can fight both riding and standing. The rifles will make up for our lack of numbers.

"And surely," he went on, "the cannon and the mortars will help us. These also are things we never had before. And Atse Menelik will have 80,000 foot soldiers. Of this we are sure. Ethiopia has not seen such strength since the Old Kingdom, since before the Princes destroyed the power of the throne. What these Ferengi are thinking is beyond me."

I know what they are thinking, thought Kanyazmach Didda. It was something that he could not put into words; something that if he said it aloud would be considered treason. So he thought it to himself: They think

we will turn against each other, like we have done before. They remember
our history. They remember how the British with their elephants and rockets
and bagpipes walked through Tigre and Wollo to capture Fortress Magdala
and cause Theodore to kill himself, and how the rases let them through
and how Theodore's army melted like rancid butter under the hot sun. But
Theodore was cunning and crazy. Menelik is good. He is a good father to his
people. What happened to Atse Tewodros will not happen to Atse Menelik.
We will never desert Menelik. We will never leave him.

*Far to the north, in Asmara, General Baratieri smiled at his maps. It was a beautiful,
sparkling mid-morning, and the sun streamed in through the windows of the house he had
commandeered as his headquarters. Outside, leaves sparkled with drying dew on the garden
trees, and small, brightly-colored birds flitted around chirping.*

*The maps of northeast Africa were huge, and he had spread them out upon the long
formal dining table. There were no troop formations noted on them. Those formations he
kept in his mind. He knew where his troops were—they were striking farther and farther
south, probing and pressing and harrying the defenders of Tigre led by Ras Mengesha.*

*Baratieri stood alone. The war conference for the day was done. After the war
planning had come the reports from his secret service, and that was why he smiled. The
reports continued to confirm his suspicions—that the allegiances of the nobles of Ethiopia
were as pliant as overcooked spaghetti. Today had come replies to his overtures from three
rases. One of them—Ras Hailu of Wollo, he had already in his pocket. That ras would
be with Italy no matter what happened. The other two messages were extremely intriguing.
One was from Ras Mengesha, and it inquired discreetly if some accommodation might
be forthcoming which would allow him to continue as Ras of Tigre in the aftermath of
the coming battle. Mengesha seemed to suggest, although he didn't say it outright, that his
troops might be used most ineffectually in any coming showdown. He also kept referring to
Menelik as the 'Shoan' king and the Imperial Army as the 'Army of the South.' Baratieri
smiled at that. He was keenly aware of the rivalry between the Shoans and the Tigreans.
He knew, like all others who had ears, that Mengesha felt that as the son of Emperor
Yohannes, the throne was as much by rights his as Menelik's. Baratieri knew all that and
smiled. He would keep that pot simmering and do everything he could to make it boil over.*

*But it was the third message that really excited the Italian commander-in-chief. It
was from Makonnen, Ras of Harar. From Makonnen himself! Makonnen, the right hand
of Menelik, as responsible as Menelik himself for the victories of the Shoan armies and
Shoan diplomacy. Makonnen was on his way north, leading his army of 30,000 troops.*

*Couching his message in most diplomatic terms, Makonnen thanked Baratieri for
giving him the opportunity to act as intermediary for the general with Atse Menelik. He felt
that it was unfortunate that Menelik had acted on the advice of some who obviously wanted
war between Italy and Ethiopia. Makonnen himself felt that talks might have ironed
out any differences the two nations might have had with each other, and that Menelik's*

unilateral abrogation of the Treaty of Wuchale was possibly.....well, Baratieri could read between the lines as well as any man, and his eyes gleamed at what he read. What he saw on this paper before him, unsaid, was that Menelik could not even count on his most important general—indeed, on his own cousin!—for support. And Baratieri vowed that as Makonnen came nearer and nearer, and journeyed further and further from his base of supplies and support, that he would find his path strewn with roses—promises and bribes and references to power in the future, once the tyranny of the misguided Menelik was put to rest.

Baratieri shook his head and smiled. By the time Menelik's army came together, it would be ready to melt away. Baratieri's heart swelled in his chest. He would do this. He would continue to throw his battalions at the enemy, driving them farther and farther into their mountains. He would subvert the greedy feudal barons one by one and destroy them. When Menelik was isolated, he would pounce on him and destroy the Shoans. Meanwhile, he would counsel the barons to proceed as though nothing had changed—that their chains of chivalry and fealty had not been broken—that still all the forces of the Ethiopian Empire were marshaled for Menelik's use.

Then at the last moment, when it was too late, all would change. The earth beneath Menelik's feet would shift. Too late this miserable black relic of a dead age would see that he stood alone. And when he did, Baratieri would cut him down.

And honors would be shoveled at Baratieri by the wagon load. He would give Italy a lovely colony in Africa. This land was a prize. It was so beautiful. It was too beautiful to be left in the hands of this mongrelized race of robber barons. Italy would have it, and would make it flower as it had never done before.

Baratieri remembered Garibaldi. He remembered the time of the Redshirts, twenty-five years before, when Garibaldi had swept through Italy, destroying the power of the petty nobles and their farcical little kingdoms and principalities. Garibaldi had taken a collection of ineffective feudal and Papal states and turned the whole rotten mess into an efficient, effective modern nation. As Garibaldi had done for Italy, so now would Baratieri, acting for Italy, do for Ethiopia.

And he would do it quickly. Baratieri knew very well that he had enemies both in Ethiopia and in Rome itself. Some thought him too cautious; others felt his actions to be too precipitous. Crispi, Baldesseri, Piano, Antonelli—all of them were out for themselves, and Baratieri provided them with a lightning rod for their self-centered plottings. But not for long, thought Baratieri. None of them would be able to so much as whisper against a hero of the nation. So he would act quickly, and be in Addis Ababa before any of them could plot against him further. He would do this for the King, and when he was favored by King Umberto, he would be untouchable. And unstoppable.

Baratieri could feel the pulse of the day quickening. He walked out onto the great stone verandah of his headquarters and watched the Italian workmen planning out the streets of Asmara. He saw the buildings going up. He saw natives running to and fro with loads of materials or on errands for their new masters. Look at them. They are happy, he said to himself. They have direction. They have somewhere they are going to. Wait until they spread the news among their brothers in the south that great days are coming when the Italians come to rid them of their oppressors.

All of this Baratieri thought. All of this he acted upon. Machiavelli would have been proud, he thought. And Baratieri smiled.

Dejazmach Wube motioned his Kanyazmach and his Grazmach to come closer. As their warriors sallied down the broad field in a column of fours, their banners flying and their officers bellowing orders, the two men inclined their heads toward their chief.

"Here is what we will do," said the Dejazmach. "We will leave here two mornings from today. We will go directly north. That means we will go through Adama, and go straight north from there, right to Ankober. That will be where we camp next, between Ankober and Debre Berhan"

"The men will be disappointed," said Roba. "They have been talking about Addis Ababa for weeks."

Wube clutched the hilt of his sword in its scabbard and shook it until it clattered. "I told everyone right from the start that we were going straight north," he said through clenched teeth. "How do these rumors get started?" He looked at Roba. "It was you, wasn't it? I know you. You started talking about the girls of Addis, and you've got them worked up into a frenzy about it."

Roba flinched, and Didda could not resist. "He wants to visit Yeshimabet's place on the Jimma road again," he said with a straight face. "Please, sir. Dissuade him. We will never get north of Addis."

"Aha! Yeshimabet again! I have heard this before," said Wube. "I will send you to Addis, Roba, and you send Yeshimabet here. She will lead your troops, and you can play with her girls!"

The three officers started laughing and really whooping loudly. Their junior officers behind them wondered but couldn't hear anything that was said. They were happy that their leaders were happy. That was good enough. When leaders' minds turned dark and stormy, that was when to watch out.

"She is always here anyway." Wube was still talking to Roba. "She is in your mind all the time. What is it about this woman? What is it that she does for you? Or to you?"

"Ah, you have to be there to find out," said Didda.

"What!" said Wube. "You too? What is it.....never mind. I will find out after the battle. That will be my present to myself. The Jimma Road? Yeshimabet's on the Jimma Road. Yes. And you, Roba, and you, Didda, will lead me there. Now, enough of this. We will continue our conference later, in my tent. Tonight. Meanwhile, look at those troops. Is there a finer sight in all the world? Look at those horses prance!"

It was night. The air, so much like wine during the day, turned woody with the singeing of it by white hot charcoal fires in the tent of the Dejazmach. Both Didda and Roba had fine tents, but theirs could not compare with the tent of Dejazmach Wube. Its floor was covered with Persian carpets. The three men sat in comfortable chairs around a small table set in the very middle of the tent, partitioned off from the outer area by canvas drops. On the table was a bottle of Araki and three half-filled glasses. There were no guards, officers, or servants in the tent. The three leaders were alone, and they were warm and safe. That is all a soldier needs when he wants to relax.

"I trust we can leave the question of the Jimma Road behind," said Wube. "I want to keep these boys on the right track north. I want to go straight there. I want to get there before anybody else does. There isn't going to be enough food up there. What there is of it, I want it for us. I don't care what Menelik says. You know we are going to end up living off the land."

"I agree with you about the girls," said Roba, a wry smile on his lips. "There will be plenty of them in the north as well as in Addis, if anyone wants that. But speaking of food, they also talk about the Adarash. They really want to go to the Adarash."

"I cannot blame them for that," said Wube. "I too would like to go to the Adarash. It is an honor to be invited, and it will seem like all of Ethiopia is there. It is a great send-off to a campaign. The feast-hall of the Emperor. Ah! How glorious."

"It has not been used since 1887," said Didda.

"The last of the great campaigns against Gemu-Gofa," said Roba. "Now it is open again. Now Menelik feeds his army again. Now he can do that again, now that the rest of the nation is fed."

Wube clapped his hands for the servants. Knives appeared on the table, and great slabs of beef, and plates of pepper. "Here is our own Adarash feast," said Wube. "We will have another one tomorrow night for our warriors, thanks to Bashaw Indelibu. What is left of his cattle, we will drive with us. Perhaps it will last us long enough, but I doubt it. We'll be down to sacks of teff and water before you know it. Menelik better strike fast; that's all I can say. Then maybe we can come back through Addis and stop at the Adarash on the way home."

"And at the springs," said Roba. "Don't forget the hot springs."

"Not likely to forget the hot springs of Addis," said Wube with a smile. "But this is the strangest war council. We talk of baths and food and women. But we have a war to conduct here. There are three things I want you to know. First, getting to the north. Second, our assignment. Third, our new arms. So, first: We go to Ankober, then camp between there and Debre Berhan. There we will meet the other three thousand of the right wing. I have been appointed Kanyazmach to Ras Mickael, by the way."

Didda and Roba stared at the Dejazmach. "A great honor for you," said Didda. "But what does it do to..."

Wube held up his hand. "You two will be my principal officers. Somehow we will work things out so that our boys get to stay together and fight together. For the most part. At Ankober, we will have to see. Start thinking about how to do this. We have to make our wing as strong as possible. I know the men who are coming. They are good men. You will like them. But we will have only a few days to make it work. We must be strong and know what we are doing, because before you know it, we move on to Wara Illu. And we move just in front of Menelik himself. And the Empress is coming also with her own army of five thousand. We are their shield until it becomes time for battle. Then we have other things to do."

"Get their guns," said Didda.

"Yes, get their great guns. It will not be easy. It will be bloody. Let us hope it is mostly their blood. But we shall see. For now, get your minds back to Wara Illu. There we will be joined by eight thousand other cavalrymen from western Shoa, from Wallo, from Gondar. These will be the left wing and the reserve. The seven thousand of the center will be waiting for us at Boru Meda, north of Dessie. That is where Ras Alula has set up the forward meeting grounds of the armies. Then it's off to the north. It will be one long march, I will tell you that."

"What will the horses eat?" asked Didda.

"The grass is good this year," said Wube.

"And water?" asked Roba.

"We have chosen carefully. There will be plenty of water. You will see."

Didda sat with his chin in his hand, his arm resting on the table. "It will not be easy," he said slowly. "What I am seeing is this: Ras Makonnen coming up from Harar..."

"And going up before us," said Wube, nodding.

"That's thirty thousand. Then us. Twenty thousand. Then Atse Menelik and the Empress. Another thirty-nine thousand. And what of the Gojjames?"

"Ten thousand, from what I understand," said Wube. "They will cross over at Debre Tabor and Lalibela, and come up this way also."

"Not to mention the Tigreans already in the field, and the men of Lasta and Wag, and those of the Simien. And all their servants!"

"This is true," said Wube.

"They shall make the earth quake with their passing," said Didda.

"They will make the earth shake with their droppings!" laughed Roba.

The three of them sat back in their chairs and laughed.

Didda was excited. "There will not be enough room to fight!" he exclaimed. "The Ferengi have only twenty thousand men!"

"There are more coming," said Wube. "This we know. And there are their guns, which unlike ours, fire rapidly, and they have plenty of ammunition. They are deadly. They may be few, compared to us, but they are deadly. There will be plenty of room to fight."

The room was silent, as each of the three men withdrew for a moment into his own mind.

"So," said Wube. "This will be a war of food and will, and sickness and attrition. You will see. That is why we must remain strong and true to ourselves, and keep our boys in good shape. That is your assignment until further notice. Don't worry about the fighting until later. I know you know how to do that. Oh, and there's just one other thing." Wube paused.

Roba and Didda looked at him. The Dejazmach's eyes gleamed.

"There is more news from me tonight that will upset your plans. I will need fifty of your best officers and men. I need to train them for a special assignment. So you will have to replace them. Remember, I want the best, and you must replace them with equally excellent men. I will want them by tomorrow night, before the feast. And I will tell you my reason, but it must never leave this tent. Never!"

Didda and Roba looked intently at their Dejazmach.

"They must be retrained. I need them for the new guns. Machine guns. Machine guns! We have machine guns! We can cut them to pieces!"

At the tenth hour of the following day, the two thousand men of the right wing were drawn up in their squadrons in a semi-circle surrounding a huge bonfire set on the plain to the southeast of Assella. They were standing at attention by squad. They were ten deep to a squad and squads stood doubled, so that their ranks were twenty deep.

Dejazmach Wube, flanked by Kanyazmach Didda and Grazmach Roba, stood before the fire. Behind them were many of their headquarters staff. As they looked out over their troops, they could see beyond the assembled warriors more great fires. Beyond that, servants were slaughtering cattle. Further, beyond the servants and the rows of tents, the horses of the soldiers grazed or rambled across the plain. And beyond that were the high mountains of Ethiopia, hazy in the going down of the sun.

Wube spoke. "My warriors!" he said. "Tonight I tell you that we leave tomorrow at dawn. We go to the north, to the defense of the Motherland, of the Empire, and of the True Cross.

"But before we do that, I have some sad news and some happy news to tell you. They are both one and the same. Here is the news. Tonight, fifty of you will be taken from you. You may never see them again. But believe me when I say to you that those fifty are the best of you, and they shall be at work with you, although you cannot see them. They shall be working against the Ferengi, and when and if you see them again you will be happy about what they are doing.

"I am taking them from you. I am training them with new weapons. So on our march, they will continue their training. And so will you. Here is the other part of my news. Fifty of you will rise in rank tonight, to take the place of the fifty who will depart from you. These I have selected also because they are the best. Now this may cause you some concern, because it is upsetting to lose friends, but let me say this. This will be good training for battle, because in battle you never know when your friend will be taken from you. So do your best. Close up your ranks and protect yourselves. This is a part of your training for battle. Now I will select the men I need."

So saying, the Dejazmach struck through the air with his right arm, slicing downward. At the bottom of his stroke, the first beat of the drum crashed out.

From behind the squads, groups of men split into pairs and sprang silently forward into the ranks. Suddenly, like sounds of lightning, hands slammed onto shoulders from behind. Men were whirled about. Those selected were ripped out of the ranks and made to run up past the officers and into the forest. The drums, the slapping, the silence, the running feet— the rest of the division stood as if in a trance.

This is how it happened. This is how the great warriors were chosen. Few had seen it before. To the new recruits, it seemed like some happening from the gods.

Strange figures raced up through the Meraro ranks. Running up to Bedasa Merga, a figure struck the meto aleka's shoulder from behind. As he spun around, another figure tripped him. The figures grabbed his arms and ran him away past the fire into the trees. Then another pair, as fleet and fast as the first, took Babilla Wami the same way. The Meraro battalion was leaderless in an instant.

Bedane was rooted to the spot. He looked behind him. There stood Mamo, and Mamo looked straight into his eyes and nodded. Then Mamo took his great broad hand and pushed Bedane forward. Stumbling at first, then steadier, Bedane advanced. Five paces he advanced, then planted his feet and drove his spear into the ground. Behind him, the ranks of the Meraro battalion steadied and stood rock firm, and held their position. This is what they had been trained to do. This is what was done.

In the forest beyond the great encampment, Dejazmach Wube divided one hundred men into two groups. To the first group he said, "You will be the salvation of the Empire. In your hands will be the new weapons of the Ferengi, which we have obtained from Janhoi himself. You will learn how to shoot these things, and to carry them fast on your horses. You will learn how to put yourselves in the middle of the enemy and destroy them! We have four of these weapons. They are called Maxim guns, and they make us equal in power to the Ferengi. You will lead us into battle. To you will go the glory of victory. Will you do this for me?"

The answer came in a roar of battle cries from veterans of many wars.

Bedasa was appointed Master of the Guns.

To the second group, Wube said, "You are the best men in the army. You will take the place of your old leaders. You are the leaders now. You will talk to your old leaders and find out their tricks. You will go back to your battalions and lead them. You will appoint new leaders among them. Be sure you choose wisely.

"Before you go back, I want you to do two things. First, each of you go, separately, into the forest. Think of what you are going to do. Take an hour. Do not speak to anyone. Do not speak. Decide what you will do. Then, come out of the forest. Talk to anyone who will listen about what you are going to do. Then go back to your commands, and do what you said you would do. Now go!"

Babilla Wami was appointed Meto Aleka of the Meraro battalion. His first act was to appoint Bedane his Hamsa Akela.

"I cannot do this!" said Bedane to Babilla Wami in a hushed voice. "I am too young. There are others better than me."

"No," said Babilla, smiling. "No, Hamsa, there are not others better than you. Some others may run faster, or throw the spear further, or know horses or medicine better, or do many things better than you. But I will tell you this: you cannot see the men the way I see them. You cannot see how they look at you. They have always looked at you this way." Babilla was still smiling, a quiet, knowing smile. "You are their leader," he said. "They chose you many years ago. That is all there is to it."

Bedane did not fully understand, but he thought he knew what Babilla was talking about. So it was that Bedane thought this: 'If they have chosen me, I must do my best. I must protect them. I must honor them. I must lead. Well, I will. God Above the Skies, help me to lead them well. I promised their parents to bring them home. Now it is not just my ten. Now it is my hundred. Now it is my ketema, my town.'

That night, the fires burned high, and many cattle were eaten. But the feasting ended early. There was much to do to get ready for tomorrow. The men were excited, and found it hard to sleep, and checked their equipment over and over again, and looked to their horses, and counted their bullets. Tomorrow they were truly off to war. That thought caused them to gaze off into the night, and to stare deep into their own hearts.

At the first hour of the morning, Dejazmach Wube nodded his head and the march began. Down from their mountain fastness rode the 2,000 men of Ras Mikael's right wing. Down behind them came their servants, and their women, their mules and donkeys and sheep and goats and tents and supplies. Down came the remnants of Bashaw Indelibu's cattle herd. Behind them there seemed to come a vast migration of nomads, bent on following this army to who-knew-where.

Down through the hill town of Assella they rode, down through the highlands to the flats of the Awash River. They rode through a dry land of struggling trees; through the parched, brittle land of the charcoal makers; through poor land held by poor people. Women sat by the side of the track and sold dried cattle dung for instant campfires, and they sold a lot of it.

In the valley of the Awash they splashed across the fords of the river in long columns. Up the other bank they scrambled and slipped. Into the little valley settlement of Adama they rode, and through it, heading for the high hills beyond. Up the side of the escarpment they went, feeling easier to be in their beloved highlands once again. Now they were on the main high plateau, within the borders of the old and ancient kingdoms, the land of the Amhara and Tigre, the Falasha and Agau and the people of Wag and Lasta and the High Simien. Now history called out to them and drew them on.

Here no steep cliffs awaited them. Here, unlike the valley farther to the south, the sides of the vast lowland led more gently up and up, over trails worn deep into the land by centuries of hooves and feet. Here the columns moved with a gentle pace, higher, ever higher, and with every step they took the warriors breathed easier for their horses, for they were farther from the lowlands and the dreaded horse diseases that could kill horses in a second, it seemed.

They camped nights an hour before dusk, and were off at first light, keeping a steady pace, day after day, moving always higher into the mountains, moving toward the old Shoan capital of Ankober, where Sahle Selassie, the grandfather of Menelik, had built his castle.

On one of those days, Bedane left his duties as hamsa aleka and, taking up his old position, led his old squad out as a company of outriders for the columns. They rode a mile ahead and to the right of the head of their column, and were treated to a great sight.

Cresting a ridge, they looked off into the lowlands, and there, in the mid-distance, along a track parallel to theirs, marched an army. It was unlike anything the boys had ever seen before. It was huge. Its columns stretched into the distance both in front and in back. Only a few officers rode horses. The rest of the soldiers were on foot, and they moved quickly through the dust they kicked up.

Suddenly, far-seeing, quick-talking Shasho said, "Look! What is that?" And they all looked where he pointed, and they saw the cannon. They sat there on the hill and looked at what they had never seen before—huge cannon on wheels trundled along by teams of eight or ten mules.

"They are wheeled cannon," said Bedane. "My uncle described them to me. They are like huge rifles with great exploding bullets that can kill dozens of people with one shot. But Uncle Bedasa always talked about them as if there were only two or three of them in the Empire. I doubt that even Uncle Bedasa has seen so many."

The squad members counted. Except for Shifaraw, they all came up with fourteen. Shifaraw had always had trouble with counting, and they all laughed at him.

"You can laugh," said Shifaraw, "but none of you, I'll bet, can count the numbers of that army."

"It must be the army of Ras Makonnen," said Tula.

"Coming up out of Harar," added Wondimu. "It is said that they number 30,000."

"You will never know that from us," said Bedane. "Shifaraw is right. How can we tell when we can see neither their beginning nor their end? They will be ahead of us on the march," he added.

"It looks like they go straight to Wara Illu," said Taffa.

"How can you tell that? How do you know where Wara Illu is?" said Dabale.

"I don't know," answered Taffa. "I can just feel where it is, and where they are going." Taffa pointed toward the northwest. "They go there," he said. "It is three, four days away for them."

"I will remember that when I go to look for food," laughed Tula. "Before I go to look, I will ask you always where the food lies."

"Better to ask where the army of Ras Makonnen is," said Ibbsa, "and then go the other way."

"Where is Ankober?" asked Mamo. "And where is Debre Berhan?" Since Bedane had been promoted, Mamo had become leader of the squad.

Taffa squinted off to the west. "I would say it is there," he said, nodding toward a high, misty peak on the horizon. "And Debre Berhan would be there." He inclined his head a little toward the south of the mountain where a pass seemed to lead up into high hills south of the old citadel.

They all turned to look in that direction. Then for a few minutes they sat silently, looking all around: at the desert and the army coming up out of it to the east, out of the ancient Muslim emirates of Adal and Fatagar; at the mysterious mountains to the north and west. And some turned and looked back toward the south. Far off, through the haze, they could just make out the outlines of Mount Chillalo and the Arusi highlands.

They were far from home, farther than any of them had ever been before. And once over this hill, they would not be able to see their homeland any more. A chill ran through the body of more than one young cavalryman, and the world seemed large.

After a time of heavy silence, Shifaraw said, "Well, Bashaw Bedane," (they had all been calling him Bashaw ever since his promotion to hamsa aleka) "where do we go now?" And they all laughed.

Bedane looked around. "Let's continue on this ridge," he said, "where we can watch Ras Makonnen on one side and our friends on the other."

Sure enough, when they looked, they saw the head of their column below and to the west of them, just coming up over a lower rise, and heading off to the peak where Taffa thought Ankober was. They looked like ants, but even as far off as they were, through the clear air the boys could see the individual horses prance, and individual soldiers gesture and lean in their saddles. They were a brave sight, all in their white shammas and jodhpurs.

"They all look so clean from here!" said Wondimu, and everybody laughed. After seven days of constant riding, nobody in the squad looked or smelled too clean anymore. "I hope there is a good-sized river at Debre Berhan," he said. "Unless we wash, if the Empress gets a whiff of us, she'll go running back to Addis like a dik-dik."

"Maybe the Ferengi will feel the same as the Empress," said Egersa. "That would save us a lot of trouble."

"Do the Ferengi have cannon like Ras Makonnen's?" asked Tula.

"Yes," said Bedane. "In fact, they have many more. You cannot count them all, there are so many." And Bedane was not joking.

The mood of the squad turned suddenly somber, until Wondimu said, "Well, then, boys, we'd better keep these horses in good shape. Remember, when you see those big exploding bullets heading toward you, ride like hell!"

Everyone laughed but Bedane. Bedane managed to smile, but his smile was grim.

Debre Berhan, the Hill of Light, was an old city. It was situated on the main trade route from Addis Ababa to Dessie and Mekele, and along with Ankober it was deep in the heart of Amhara territory. From it, tracks branched out east and west, north and south, into all the large and small settlements that had thrived on this upland plateau for hundreds of years.

For the most part, wars had not swept this region. Armies certainly marched through on their way here and there, but for the most part they were close to home and well-provisioned, and therefore relatively well-behaved. So the land was fertile and the people strong and happy.

Now here another army came, this one from the south, and it was mounted, and it was friendly, and the people turned out to watch it approach, and to feed it, and to sell it things and play with it and send it on its way.

So in came the right wing of Ras Mikael's cavalry, and it pranced and smiled and preened and commented on the looks of the young women, and then it bivouacked in a field to the north of town, and awaited the arrival of the army of the King of Kings, Elect of God, Conquering Lion of the Tribe of Judah, Emperor of All the Ethiopias Menelik the Second, who would not be long in coming, so it was said.

In four days he would come, and they would be ready for him, and sweep his way clear in his journey to the north. How anyone knew this was never discussed. Just, everybody knew it. That is the way of an army. So it is said.

"So we wait here four days," Babilla Wami was saying. "Then we wait four more." Babilla Wami was not yet used to being a meto aleka. He was still complaining, when now it was his job to thrash complainers. But he was enjoying himself. He was looking around at the mountains and smelling the fresh air through an aromatic leaf he had crushed and shoved up his left nostril. "It could be worse," he said. "This looks like an enjoyable place. I've never been here before. It feels good."

The sun was warm and the breeze was just right. The days were long. The men stretched out on the ground in groups and everyone relaxed. Four days were not too long to do nothing in. So they sprawled on the ground, and waited for Janhoi—and for the battle he brought.

PART V

A NEW WORLD

Eighty miles to the southwest of the Army of Arusi, Chala and Haile Mikael rode in the midst of a raucous stream of life, part of a great band of people and animals all heading toward Addis Ababa, the new capital of the Empire, the New Flower of Ethiopia founded by Atse Menelik and Empress Taitu only a few years before. All around them were merchants and shepherds and farmers leading flocks of sheep and goats and cattle to the Merkato—the great marketplace in the heart of the city. Twining around the herds that numbered in the hundreds and thousands wove caravans of camels up from the desert, bearing goods from Yifat and Adal, from Harar and Djibouti. The roaring of the camels and the bleating of the sheep and the lowing of the cattle kept everything in a continuous uproar.

And there were people by themselves on this highway also, without animals. Some came for war; some came because of war. Some were warriors bearing shields and spears and rifles and little else. Some were family groups leaving the countryside, coming to the city to find their futures, and carrying all their belongings with them.

Here the road was twenty trails wide, and all those trails were filled with animals and people all moving forward to their destinies. Chala felt a soaring of his heart here that he had never felt before. He could feel the quick pace of life around him, and so could Eagle. The horse snorted and pranced and pricked up his ears at the sounds and the sights of this great surging highway of life.

Chala and Bishop Haile Mikael had come down from the heights of Zukquala. They spent a tortuous day picking their way down that mountain's rocky trail. Then they headed north, and spent the night on the shore of a beautiful small lake at Debre Zeit, close by the castle of a noble. There were hundreds of people camped there, and in the morning they all seemed eager to be off at once, all heading for Addis Ababa.

What a sight it was! Thousands of humans and animals stretched in endless lines that moved upward from the valley of the Awash River toward the heights of Entoto, where the great Gibbi Palace of Menelik and the miraculous Cathedral of Saint George welcomed the visitors to the very center of Empire.

And suddenly they were there. Addis Ababa had no gates. It just happened around them. One moment they were in the middle of farm fields. The next, they were in a city. At that time, the capital was like a series of small towns. There were settlements here and there, and roads were laid out, and embassies and hospitals and neighborhoods had come into being, and they could see that at some time in the future a great city would rise here. But it had not yet been built.

But the power of the place was there. They could sense it in the air. They could sense that rases and leul-rases and princesses and kings were about, and Ferengis, and bishops and wealthy merchants—they could sense that they were all here. They could sense the energy behind the high compound walls. There was the energy of a great city, but no great city to match that energy could be seen.

It was scarcely five years since Menelik and Taitu had ridden to the top of Entoto and Menelik stopped and said to his Queen, "Here, my Queen, is my city. Here I will build my city, and it will not move. No longer shall the Emperors of Ethiopia straggle across the land in tents like some kind of nomad band of Bedouin. Once again we shall have our capital, and it shall not be a capital of a province, like Ankober or Makelle or Dessie or Harar. No, it shall be the capital of an Empire, like Axum or Gondar of old. So be it. Let it begin!"

And so the work began.

And together, Menelik and Taitu named the place. The named it Addis Ababa—New Flower. Here the old empire would flower once again, and once again Ethiopia would stretch out its hands to God.

But it was not yet finished. The land reserved for the city was in a great bowl on the southern slopes of gentle Mount Entoto, and it was miles wide, and cut by great rivers that had to be bridged. But the land had to be wide, for it had to accommodate the retinue of the Emperor, and with unification of the country the Emperor needed space and stability. Times were changing. Ambassadors of great powers were in constant attendance on the Court. England, France, Russia, Italy, Japan, America—all had their ambassadors and envoys, their merchants and advisors, their military attaches and spies. All of these needed a place to stay. They could not continue to traipse around the countryside behind an itinerant medieval court that kept pulling up stakes and moving its tents and acting like some vast encampment of locusts. Ah, yes, the camp of the king had become a nest of locusts. It could not be helped. What can you do with over 100,000 people? How do you feed them? How do you find firewood for them? The countryside could no longer take it. The cry of 'The Emperor Approaches!' sent people scurrying, hiding their goods, getting their families out of the way, instead of cheering and feeling good about the government. So things had to change, and Menelik set about changing them.

First he settled his court at Entoto. Then he told the army it could no longer live off the land. Then, after the famines and diseases were over, he told the farmers to farm and the traders to trade, and to be afraid no longer. Then he found out about eucalyptus. He found out how fast it could grow, and he brought eucalyptus trees from Australia and planted them all over where he wanted people to settle. And the eucalyptus trees shot up, and there was plenty of firewood from then on. Then there was the train. The Ferengis wanted to build a railroad to Addis from Djibouti, so they could get their machinery and goods to us easier, and get our coffee and hides to Europe faster, and everybody could get rich. Menelik liked the idea of the train. It intrigued him. All kinds of machinery intrigued the Emperor, even bicycles.

This is the world that Haile Mikael brought Chala to, something that Chala had never even dreamed about in his wildest dreams. And here they were, riding through this new world, and Chala had to take it all in and still stay on his horse, and he had to protect Father Haile as well.

The first place they went to was the Merkato. They just rode by on the edge of it. That was enough. Chala rode in front, making a path for the Bishop. It was all he could do to clear the road. "Make way! Make way!" he shouted over and over again, but almost nobody paid attention to him. The only ones who paid any attention at all were street boys who descended on him and tried to get to the bishop. "Give us money!" they shouted. "We can work for you! We can be your servants! We will clear your path!" The wiry street boys swarmed all over and pulled at him. Then it was that Chala found a strength he did not know he had, and used his shield and pushed them back. The tough hippopotamus hide was effective, and as he used it to push them, and threatened them with his spear, the boys drew back. But still they cried out as Chala and Father Haile passed, and begged alms, and offered to be their servants.

All over the Merkato the same thing was happening. Nobles and clerics and soldiers and people of importance rode through with their servants clearing the way, and street boys chased after them looking for work or begging for money. Chala was astounded. He did not know people could act like this. No one was like this in Meraro, or even in Bekoji. He had never seen people like this before. All across this vast open-air market thousands of people were bartering and begging, haggling and selling. It was a madhouse.

"What do you think?" yelled Father Haile to him. "Should we stop and get you some new clothes?"

Chala whirled to face Haile Mikael, unwilling to believe what he had just heard, and open-mouthed gazed past the laughing priest. The wind was up in the early afternoon, and clothing and carpets on thousands of wooden racks swayed in the dusty breeze. For the dust was up too, and swirled about the bedlam creating dust devils and temporary blindness in unprotected eyes.

"Never mind," said Haile Mikael, still laughing. "Get us out of here. Take that road straight ahead. The one that goes alongside the stream."

Willingly Chala sent Eagle forging ahead.

"Keep going uphill, Chala!" shouted Father Haile. "Pretty soon you'll see where we are going."

Gradually the track became wider, and tree-lined, and there were fewer people. Chala and Father Haile settled down to a steady pace, aiming toward the uppermost part of the city, to where the Abuna's residence was near the cathedral. Chala began to calm down and had a chance to study the city. It was actually pleasant. It would be nice here with fewer people. But the people were fascinating, too. They were from all over and dressed every which way. It was impossible to count the costumes they all wore, and Chala relaxed and began to enjoy the whole scene. And then he saw the Devil.

Or at least he thought it was the Devil. If it was not, it was the strangest kind of being he had ever seen. It was a man, but such a man! He came riding a big royal mule toward them, and Chala forgot his manners and gawked at him as he passed. The man grinned, and he had huge teeth. Then this stranger had the temerity to bow to the Bishop, and lo and behold, Haile Mikael bowed back! Chala was astounded, and when the stranger had passed by a sufficient distance to be out of earshot, he reined in Eagle and waited for the bishop to come up to him.

"Father, what was that?" he whispered. Haile Mikael reined in his horse and said, "That? That was a man, my son."

"What kind of a man could that be?" exclaimed Chala.

"That," said Haile Mikael, "was a Ferengi."

"Indet!"

"A Ferengi. Have you never seen one before?"

"What was wrong with him? Was it leprosy?"

"What do you mean?"

"His skin! It was like, like it had been all peeled off of him, and he showed the red meat beneath."

"That is how Ferengis look, Chala," said the priest. "They all have skins like that."

"All red?"

"Almost all. Some can hardly stand the sun at all, and their skins do peel, and the skin underneath really is red, and they seem to be undergoing torture. I don't understand why they keep coming here. I guess in their own countries the sun is not that hot. For their sakes, I hope not. But still they come. People are crazy."

"What is an enemy doing in the capital of our country?" asked the boy.

"A Ferengi is not necessarily an enemy," said Haile Mikael.

Chala simply stared. All his life he had heard nothing about Ferengis except that they were the enemies of his nation and his people. Now here was Father Haile, who was on his way to pray for the success of his country's arms and Emperor, saying that Ferengis were not enemies. This was puzzling.

"Ferengis are from different nations, Chala," the Bishop was saying, "from different tribes. And they do what is in the interest of their particular tribe. And often, their tribes are at war with each other. When they are not, they are recovering from a war, or likely getting ready for a war."

"They sound like us, Father," said Chala.

"Yes, they do," said Haile Mikael. "They are just like us, except that they are very powerful because of their guns and their machinery. For centuries, we have been trying to get their guns and machinery, so we can become powerful like them and defend the Empire."

"It seems very complicated," said Chala.

"It is very tricky," said Haile Mikael. "It is called 'diplomacy'." The priest drew his breath in sharply and allowed his lips to form a satisfied smile. He nodded at Chala, bobbing his head up and down a half-dozen times. "Let us go on," he said. "We must get to the Abuna's residence. There we will be able to wash and be assigned rooms. It will be very comfortable, for a while at least. And this evening, I must meet with the Abuna and the Itchegie."

CHAPTER 30

BY THE LIGHT OF THE CANDLE

That evening, Chala and Haile Mikael were housed in a small guest cottage in the compound of Abuna Mattewos, the head of the Church of Ethiopia. "Praise be to God," thought a weary Chala.

This was a great honor, but an even greater honor was to follow. After a modest dinner, there was a knock on the door and a servant whispered to Chala and disappeared into the darkness.

"Father Haile, he said that if you would please come to the Abuna's house, Abuna Mattewos would be pleased to receive you now," said Chala. He said this quietly and with reverence, for it had become apparent to him that his bishop was looked upon as a very important person indeed. There was an air of power about this place, as if the air itself knew there were important personages about doing important things.

Haile Mikael smiled, and sighing, he rose and drew his black ecclesiastical robes about him. He adjusted his turban, took a deep breath, and his face changed. In a moment, Haile Mikael took on the aura of a great person, stern of face, mighty in grace and power.

"How do I look?" he asked.

Chala was awestruck by his bishop's change in bearing. "You look like a king!" he whispered, bowing to the bishop.

"Ah. That is good," said Haile Mikael. Then he laughed. "It is best to be able to look important at certain times," he said, "even if you feel like you have been run down by a herd of rampaging elephants!" Then he was out the door, swiftly and quietly.

Minutes later, across the courtyard, the door of the great house of the Abuna opened and Haile Mikael was ushered in by a servant, who bowed low. He was shown to a conference room which held a great table. Around the table were strewn a dozen chairs that looked as though they had been thrown back in the aftermath of a great meeting. Lit candles placed any which way adorned the top of the table and threw mysterious flickering shadows along the walls and across the ceiling.

Haile Mikael's wait was not long. The thick wooden door swung open, and there in the dim light stood Abuna Mattewos himself, in all his eminent dignity. And he was not alone. Behind him was the stooped figure of an old white-bearded man who walked with a limp, his figure hunched over a wooden staff tipped with a silver cross.

Haile Mikael knelt before the Abuna and kissed the cross proffered in the outstretched hand. "Your Excellency," he murmured.

"Your brother in Christ," rumbled the Abuna. "Rise."

Haile Mikael arose, and then fell to his knees again, for the old man had emerged from the shadows, and Haile Mikael recognized him. It was the Itchegie, the leader of all the monks and all the monkish orders in the realms of Ethiopia.

Here then, in this small room, was concentrated in these two men all the power and glory of the Ethiopian Church.

"Rise, my son," said the old man, chuckling. "Have you been out in the woods too long? Are you not used to seeing such great personages as we?"

"We are gratified to see you well," said the Abuna. "How was your journey?"

"My journey went well," said Haile Mikael, struggling to his feet once more. "All was well. The monasteries," he said, bowing to the Itchegie, "were in good order, and the monks were joyous and happy in their zeal for the Lord." He turned to the Abuna. "The priests and the people, too, are faring well. The harvest is good. The weather is fair all over these lands. Except for the conflicts on the borders, all seems right in The Land Of God."

"It is more than a border conflict, as well you know, my good Bishop," said the Abuna, "but your point is well taken. The earth seems fine, and going about its business. But we poor mortals make mistake heaped upon mistake and do the devil's work daily." Mattewos sighed. "If the good Christ knew what would follow, would He have come to us, or gone to somewhere more deserving! Ah, but of course Christ knew what would follow, and He came anyway. Perhaps the more deserving didn't need Him. But the angels themselves fell, and look at that! Were we the best, then? The best hope?" The Abuna shook his head. "But I digress," he said. "If I keep on thinking like this, I may become a monk, of all things!"

The Itchegie grinned and laughed a low laugh. Haile Mikael looked at the two men. He could feel the power coming from them. The Abuna seemed like glowing rays of light, power striking from every finger. The Itchegie was like a brooding old giant, absorbing the sins of the world and transforming them into new hope for the future.

As sacred as these two men were, they were also men of the Earth.

"I understand," said the Abuna, "that you carry with you a letter from our reverend brother in Christ, Tekle Berhan, Bishop of Harar."

"I have it here, Reverend Father," said Haile Mikael. He produced a letter in a modern envelope from within his robes.

The Abuna seemed to sniff. "It looks as if it had come a far distance," he said. "You used it as a napkin?"

"The conditions were unfavorable, but unavoidable," said Haile Mikael. "I am sorry. I kept it close to me. I had to be sure it arrived here. Regardless of how the people feel, there is intrigue afoot. I could count on few friends on long stretches of the road."

"Ah," said the Abuna. "So you felt danger?"

"In some places, Reverend Father. For instance, just last night, when my servant and I stopped for the night at Debre Zeit....."

"That dog of an inconsequential princeling! He still foments rebellion. Did he see you? You are referring to Fitawrari Tekla Maryam, are you not? "

Bowing to indicate his agreement, Haile Mikael said "That is the one. He did not see me, Reverend Father, but it was not from want of trying. His soldiers and spies were all about that fair lake; all around the grounds of his castle. He makes life a purgatory for the thousands who have to stop there on the road to Addis. He extracts money and goods and tribute from all that he can. There is no justice within his domains."

"He is a thorn in our side," said the Abuna, "but he will have to wait. He is one of but a few to oppose the Emperor. We will watch his antics, and when the time is right, he will feel the power of the Empire." The Abuna paused, and breathed deeply. "But how is it with Harar? Let us look at this letter."

Abuna Mattewos ripped open the envelope and beheld a faint parchment, filled with the characters, not of Amharic, but of Ge'ez, the old ecclesiastical language.

"Most Reverend and Exalted Mattewos," it began. "Greetings from your obedient servant, Tekle Berhan, Bishop and Vicar of Harar....."

Mattewos held the letter away from him in the dim candlelight, off to one side for the Itchegie to see. Together, they looked for messages within messages, clues within clues couched within diplomatic niceties and double entendres. The letter was a healthy one and went on about conditions in Harar, and politics there, and the Ferengis there also—all kinds and makes and nationalities of Ferengi, it seemed, and how they were intriguing and plotting, and what Makonnen, Ras of Harar and cousin to the Emperor Himself, was doing to keep control of the situation. According to Bishop Tekle Berhan, Makonnen was doing very well indeed. But the bishop was apprehensive about Makonnen's upcoming march north. He felt a sufficient number of troops should remain behind in Harar to secure it until the crisis was over.

The Abuna smiled broadly and shrugged. "He seems optimistic, overall," he said. Then turning to the young bishop, he said, "Bishop Haile Mikael, We thank you for bringing Us this news of Harar. It is better than We expected, and therefore pleasing to Us. We thank you for bringing Us this news and We are doubly thankful for your presence here. We are glad that you will come to the battle with Us, for We know that your prayers are strong, and your mind is as strong as your prayers, and We will need your help on that fateful day of battle. The Devil himself is within the walls of the Empire of God, and the Land of God must expel him! So help Us, Haile Mikael, and We on Our part will look to you for guidance in the future. It is not for nothing that, while being young, you are already exalted in your worldly position. The Church recognizes greatness and goodness and strength and strong spirit, and you will be of great service to God in the years to come."

Mattewos raised his hands in blessing, and Haile Mikael knelt.

"Bishop Haile," said the Itchegie in a low voice, "I, too, thank you and bless you. But we know that you have had a long and hard journey, and it is fitting for you to sleep a long and deserved sleep. So go back to your room and take your rest. We will talk further in the morning."

Thus dismissed, Haile Mikael was seen to the door by the two old men. A servant, bearing a candle for light, escorted him down the hall and across the courtyard. Soon he was deep asleep in his own cottage in a grand, comfortable Ferengi bed.

Across the hall, in a smaller bed in a smaller room, Chala slept, too, dreaming of strange places, and beings in those places, and dream and reality mixed in his mind. It was good that he slept, for if he had been awake, he would have been very confused. Big white men with huge teeth rode huge pigs through the streets of his dreams. If Chala were not so curious, he would have been very frightened.

As soon as Haile Mikael left the conference room, the Abuna looked at the Itchegie and said, "Now let us see what is in that letter. Come!"

They returned to the table and held the parchment close to heat of the flame of the nearest candle. Between the lines of the Bishop's letter arose other, brighter letters.

"Ah," said Mattewos, "I was afraid that it might be damaged, but this letter, too, has weathered the journey well."

'My Dear Cousin,' the hidden message began, 'I am well. And You? And the court? And the Imperial Guard—is it ready?

'My army is fine,' it continued. 'I head north within the day. Here is the important part: I continue to communicate with Baratieri and his emissaries on a constant basis. He continues to offer me gifts, including your throne!

'Cousin, I will continue to mislead him. By the time I arrive in the north, he will think that I have decided to become an Italian. What a great game! What a fool this man is!

'I will meet You then, next, at Dessie. Send me on to be the vanguard, to relieve Mengesha. I promise you, my troops will not be as good as they can be. My decisions will hold them back. Baratieri will take this as a signal that I am with him. The man is a veritable snake!

'You will receive this from the hands of the Abuna and the Itchegie together. Thus you will be assured of its veracity.

'Yours in Victory!

'Makonnen, Duke of Harar, Ras of Ethiopia'

'PS: I bring my son with me. That is how confident I am of our Victory.'

"This is a good plan," said the Itchegie. "They have taken stock of the mind of this Baratieri. He has taken the bait. They understand him. If he remains in command....."

"We have a chance to destroy the misbegotten son of an ape!" said the Abuna, heatedly. "We must! He has Debre Damo already far behind his lines. We must not lose our knowledge and our ancient Faith."

"Spoken like a true Ethiopian!" said the Itchegie, grinning.

"Ah, my friend," said the Abuna, wagging his finger, "even though I am an Egyptian, Ethiopia is my See, my Vicarage. I know the beauty of this land and the good hearts of its people. It shall not be said that Mattewos did not do everything he could to safeguard The Land Of God."

"Truly," said the Itchegie, "you were chosen well. I am grateful that Alexandria sent you to us. And now, shall we go to the palace?"

"It is always a pleasure to be the bearer of glad tidings!" laughed Mattewos. "Let us go!"

CHAPTER 31

IN THE PALACE OF THE KING

The morning was bright and cheery, with sun streaming in through the windows of Haile Mikael's room. Outside, birds sang in a well-kept garden. Water splashed down Haile Mikael's beard as he lifted his head from the washing basin, and he blew drops of blue water through his moustache before scrubbing his face with a dry towel.

"First we go to the palace," he said to Chala, smiling at him. "Then to the feast, but first to the Gibbi Palace. I will introduce you to a friend of mine there. He went to school with me and Debtera Markos, but life called him in another direction."

"Is he a servant in the palace?" asked Chala, impressed.

"In a manner of speaking," said Haile Mikael. His smile grew wider. "Come, let us go. You are ready? How are your clothes?"

Chala glanced down at his clothes, the same clothes he had worn since leaving home. "They are clean," he replied. "Someone came to my door last night, asked for them, took them, and left them again in the morning. All clean," he said, with some wonder.

"That is good," said Haile Mikael, but with some ambivalence in his voice. "Still, I wish that we had had time to stop at the Merkato yesterday to get you some new city clothes. But..." He paused. "This will do for now. New clothes will come soon enough."

He smiled, but Chala could see that the priest was not satisfied and was somewhat embarrassed.

"Allow me to introduce you to Leul-Ras Daniel," Haile Mikael said to Chala. They had entered the great royal compound of the Gibbi Palace, and after many encounters with guards and courtiers, after much bowing and exchanges of introductions and pleasantries, they had arrived not at the grand front entrance of the palace but at a side entrance. They were in a garden, and two wings of the palace boxed it in, so that it became a very private place in the midst of diplomatic turmoil.

Leul-Ras Daniel. So, a prince! So, Chala dropped to the ground, arms outstretched.

"A friend of my friend Father Haile is my friend. Get up, please, and let me greet you."

Chala, amazed, heard the words of the prince, and looking up with trepidation, he rose. The words had come soft-spoken and kind, and the smiling face above him matched the voice. Chala stood. In front of him was a man of about the same age as Father Haile, but much younger-looking. His face was not lined. He was dressed in royal robes. His fingernails were gigantic. They were at least five or six inches long.

"They show my rank," he said to Chala, turning them around in the mid-morning air. "They show that I do not have to work." Looking at Haile Mikael, he added, "They are coming off tomorrow or the next day. I am going north to the fight. Everyone is going north."

"You seem pleased," said Haile Mikael.

"I sometimes feel like a fool with these things growing out of my fingers, my brother. But to do anything around here, one must adhere to the customary customs. I would not be listened to if I did not follow the rules."

"You could have worn a cross," said Haile Mikael.

"Ah, yes. I could have worn a cross," said Prince Daniel, "but you know it was not for me. In your heart, old friend, you know it was not for me."

"I have always loved the honesty in you," said Haile Mikael.

"And I in you," said Daniel. "Welcome to the palace."

So saying, Prince Daniel extended his arm and bowed toward a door in the corner of the building.

Entering the building was like entering the heart of the kingdom. Long corridors led to even longer corridors. As Chala walked along behind the two old friends, one dressed in the robes of the Church, the other in robes of the State, he marveled at them. Their heads were noble. Their smiles were broad and happy. Their talk seemed more of old fellowship than present duties. They walked holding hands, as was the custom of male friends in the Kingdom, and they chatted much like two brothers would chat on their way to market back in Meraro.

Suddenly, Chala felt very lonely, and wondered about Bedane. Then his loneliness grew to encompass his mother and father, his Uncle Bedasa, and all his friends back in his great golden highland valley. A deep hollowness came into his chest, starting at the shoulders and working inward toward his heart.

But despite how he felt, Chala did not stumble, nor did he appear to be affected in any way. He held onto what he now had to hold onto—in this case a bishop and a prince, and that is a pretty good thing to hold on to if you have to hold onto something. However, he had fallen behind them as they strode along. He could not hear what the two men spoke of, but from the set of their faces, he was sure it was important.

"Don't worry," Daniel was saying. "We will give him to Helena and Mentuab. They will fit him out fine. He will look like a prince in no time, or at least a servant of a prince."

"Who?" asked Haile Mikael, startled. "We will give him to who?"

"My nieces, Helena and Mentuab," said Daniel, smiling.

"My little friends?" said Haile Mikael, delighted. "The little ones I used to twirl about on my arms, to make them fly? The little ones who shrieked with laughter as they flew? Are they here?"

"They are," said Daniel, "but they have changed. They are no longer little girls. How long have you wandered in the desert anyway, my friend? Ten years?"

"Are we to see them?" asked Haile Mikael.

"Presently," said Daniel.

"Ah, how wonderful!" said Haile Mikael. Then he paused, and said, "But listen, my friend, with this subject of clothes for my companion: I will pay for whatever they find for him."

Daniel looked at Haile Mikael and laughed. "Do not say that!" he exclaimed. "It is good that you are a priest. You do not know women at all. Or my nieces, at any rate. They could have him dressed as a Pasha in no time at all, and you would be out of pocket three years' stipend. No, if you want to get him clothes, and I offer my nieces' attentions, allow me to pay for what they find. I will raid the royal treasury. I do not think they will exceed that amount." And Prince Daniel threw open a door on the side of the corridor, and ushered Haile Mikael and Chala into a beautiful room full of light and plants, painted white, and as fresh as the morning light. And standing in that room, waiting for them, were two beautiful young women, the princesses Helena and Mentuab.

Oh, they were beautiful, and they were dressed in beautiful clothes. Their white dresses fell in simple lines, but the wide, embroidered borders of their dresses and shammas were of golden thread that was entwined with red and green design. They wore their shammas draped over their heads and turned around their necks, then fastened over their breasts with golden filigree brooches. Under the shammas, their curled hair glistened. Around their necks were golden necklaces, and from their ears hung golden earrings. On their fingers were golden rings, and on their wrists were golden bracelets. The purity of the white cloth mixed with the flashing gold to set off the dark beauty of their smooth skin. In the finely-chiseled features of their faces, their eyes gleamed.

And suddenly, all this beauty leapt into movement and the squealing shouts of little girls. Now seventeen and eighteen, and sophisticated in the ways of the court and the world, Helena and Mentuab were transported back ten years, became seven and eight, and leaped into Haile Mikael's outstretched arms.

Haile Mikael stood there laughing, holding a princess in each arm while the girls hugged him and kissed his cheeks. He had been their favorite, long years ago, and for them all the intervening years disappeared, and they were happy as they had been in those happy earlier times, when Menelik had solidified the Empire around the power of the Amhara.

"I have some candy for you," said Helena. Not letting go of the bishop, she produced a tiny leather bag and handed it to him. It rattled with the sound of rock candy inside.

"Oh, ho!" said Haile Mikael.

"Do you remember?" asked Helena, beaming at him.

"Oh, yes, I do. I do," laughed Haile Mikael. And he remembered the many times he brought candy to the girls, always hiding it and producing it at odd times, either slipping it to them in the middle of a meal or a ceremony, or equally as stealthily when they were brought to him to be kissed before being carried off to bed by their nurses. It was a game between him and the babies.

"Now it is time for us to return some to you," said Helena. "We are your servants, Father Haile," and she curtseyed.

"Do you remember these, Father?" asked Mentuab. She held out her hand, and in it were two shiny stones. They did not appear to be of much value. They looked like some kind of rock crystals. Haile Mikael held out his hand, and Mentuab placed the crystals in his palm.

"You gave them to us when you left for the south," said Mentuab.

"Ah, I remember!" exclaimed Haile Mikael. They were little rock crystals he had picked up in some desert and brought back for the little girls.

"The candy you can keep," said Helena. "These we will keep, as we kept them before. We will always keep them. These are our most precious jewels."

Haile Mikael placed the rough jewels in the palm of his left hand and made the sign of blessing over them. Then he returned them to the girls and said, "It is a gift from God to be able to give such precious gifts, but to give them twice in a lifetime is more than can be expected by any man."

"It is because they came from you that they are precious, Father Haile. It is because you are so precious to us," said Helena, and she hugged him again.

While Helena was hugging Haile Mikael, Mentuab peeked over his shoulder at the doorway, where Chala had been standing all this time. She frowned and said to him sternly, "Who are you, what do you want, and how did you get into the palace?" Chala stood up straight.

Prince Daniel said, "Girls, this is Chala Negassa, Father Haile's servant, and…"

"Ah," said Haile Mikael, holding up his index finger.

"Oh, of course. I am sorry, Father. Helena and Mentuab, this is Chala Negassa, *companion* of Father Haile, and we have a favor to ask of you in Father Haile's behalf. Chala, come in." Chala walked further into the room. "Chala, these are the princesses Helena and Mentuab. Please introduce yourself."

Chala bowed to the waist, straightened, and said, "I am Chala Negassa of the Shoa Oromo of Arusi, whom you call the Galla. My uncle is Bedasa Merga, and he is Meto Aleka of the Meraro and Bekoji cavalry of the Oromo, as was my father, Negassa Merga, before him. My brother is Bedane Negassa, a troop leader of our cavalry. We are from Arusi, in the shadow of Mount Encuolo. The land was granted to us by Atse Menelik in recognition of our service to the Empire. I go with Bishop Haile Mikael to the north, to the battle."

"He speaks well," said Helena.

"He was taught by our good friend Debtera Markos," said Haile Mikael. "Do you remember Markos?"

"Of course!" said Mentuab, surprised.

"You may have noticed," said Prince Daniel, "that his clothes, while serviceable, do not quite meet the standard required of the companion of a bishop, at least not in the court or in the capital. Father Haile and I were wondering if you might be able to find him some appropriate clothing. His own better clothing was unfortunately lost along the way from the south."

"We would be happy to help," said Mentuab, smiling.

"We would be delighted!" exclaimed Helena.

The beautiful princesses were now young women, but there was still a good amount of girl left in each of them, and they had not had a doll to play with in a long time.

"Come forward, Chala Negassa," commanded Princess Helena, "and let us have a look at you."

Chala did so, and was immediately surrounded by the princesses, who looked at him and touched his clothes and made tsk-tsk sounds and chattered at each other and led him away out of the room and down the long corridor.

"Heading for some secret supply of clothing, I suppose," said Haile Mikael to Daniel as they trailed along at some distance.

"Ha! Heading for the royal tailor," replied Daniel, "wherever he may be at the moment. I think your young companion is in for a tour of most of the palace."

The princesses disappeared around a corner far down the corridor.

"Aha!" said Daniel. "Do you see what I mean? We had better pick up our pace. They will escape us entirely." But their pace remained slow. They had much to talk about.

Helena and Mentuab were guiding Chala along a wide hall which had two rows of columns along its length. These columns divided the hall into three long hallways. As they walked along the central hallway, Chala saw a strange thing he had never seen before. He stopped short to look at it. It was made of metal, and had two wheels, one large and one small, the large one in the front and the smaller one behind. Attached to the metal frame in the middle was something that looked like a small saddle. The thing was leaning against a column.

"It is called a velocipede," said Mentuab.

"Or, a bicycle," said Helena.

"What does it do?" asked Chala.

Helena put her hand on the saddle. "See?" she said. "You sit here. And you put your feet here." she pointed to the pedals attached to the big wheel.

"It is like a horse," said Mentuab. "You ride it."

"Indet?" Chala was in awe of the thing.

"It is a makina," said Helena. "The Emperor has many makinas. All different kinds."

"It is the Emperor's?" whispered Chala.

"Yes," said Mentuab, with a devilish gleam in her eye. "Do you want to ride it?"

"I do not know how," said Chala.

"We will help you. We will help you get on, and then we will push it. And you will put your feet on the pedals, and you push, too. And you will see, it will move forward."

"But it is the Emperor's," said Chala.

"That's all right," said Helena. "He won't mind. He is not using it now."

So Chala, with help from the princesses, got onto the bicycle. They showed him how to stand on the frame and get onto the saddle. Then, standing one to each side, Helena and Mentuab showed him how to hold the handlebars, and how to put his feet on the pedals, and they held the bicycle steady and began to push it forward. That caused the pedals on the big wheel to turn, and the bicycle started going faster and faster. Mentuab and Helena were trotting alongside now, and Helena gave Chala a push in the small of his back, and the bicycle leapt forward.

It was a long hall, and Chala's steed went faster and faster. Balance was no problem for Chala. The princesses were right. This was just like a horse. Faster and faster he went.

"Oh!" said Helena to Mentuab. "Look at him go!"

"He is a true Galla!" laughed Mentuab. "A real cavalryman!"

The bicycle galloped down the hall. Then suddenly, a thought struck Chala and he turned and said "Wait! How do you stop it?"

"Jump!" yelled Helena.

Chala faced front. There was a man standing right in front of him. He must have just stepped out from behind a column. He was a huge man, wearing a broad-brimmed hat and dark robes, and he was staring wide-eyed at Chala.

"Ahhhh!" Chala yelled. The bicycle hit the man square in the stomach. Chala flew over the handlebars. Chala's head cracked into the man's forehead, and Chala and the man and the bicycle went down in a heap on the floor. There was a huge crash, the world spun around, and when Chala looked up, there were dozens of men coming at him. They were drawing swords, lifting spears, pointing rifles every which way, including straight at him. He had never seen such fierce men. And they had all stopped moving. It was like a painting. They had all just stopped moving in all positions of defense. Chala would remember them all his life just like that. He looked at the man he had hit. Neither he nor the man could move. They were both caught in the twisted-up bicycle, their legs tangled up in it. The big man looked at him.

"Who the hell are you?" boomed the big man. He seemed incredulous and furious at the same time.

"I am Chala Negassa of Mareruu..." Chala started to say. But he felt a soft hand over his mouth. Then he heard the voice of Helena behind him.

"He is with us, Your Majesty," whispered Helena.

Chala's eyes opened wide. He tried to dive to the floor, but Helena held him tight. He couldn't move. Haile Mikael and Prince Daniel came running down the corridor. Suddenly, they were attacked by the guards and hurled to the ground. Two of Daniel's long fingernails snapped off. "Ouch!" he said, as a guard ground his face into the hard wood floor. Attempted palace coups were not unknown in this realm, and the guards were taking no chances.

"Who are those men," demanded Menelik.

"This one is Prince Daniel, Your Majesty," said one of the guards.

"The other?"

"Haile Mikael Tesfaye, Your Majesty," said Haile Mikael tentatively, feeling the point of a spear nicking him in the back.

"Who?"

"Bishop Haile Mikael of Ba'le, Your Majesty," said Prince Daniel.

Menelik brightened. "Haile Mikael? Well! Welcome home, lad. Back to the bright lights of the city, eh? Tell me, Bishop. Who is this?" He pointed to Chala. "Is he with you?"

"He is with me, Your Majesty."

Menelik looked at Chala, who was still staring at him. For a few moments the young boy from the provinces and the Emperor of Ethiopia looked straight into each other's eyes. Then Menelik began to laugh. He shook his head. He kept on laughing.

"Somebody pull me up," he said through his laughter, and a dozen men leapt to do his bidding. "Where's my hat?" said Menelik, and the hat appeared as if by magic. Menelik pulled it on. "Attacked by a Galla warrior on a bicycle in my own palace!" he exclaimed. "Wait 'til the Italians hear about this. They will laugh themselves silly. This must not get out, understand?" All heads bowed in obedience.

"I might have known you two would be involved." Menelik scowled at the princesses. He tried to sound fierce, but it didn't work. He couldn't be fierce with these two. "It is you who are guilty of this trick. I can see that," he said. "You must pay the price for this. You must pay a fine. Fix this bicycle. That is your fine. And get this boy some clothes." He looked down at Chala, whose pants were now covered with grease and whose shirt was ripped. "What is your name, son?" he asked quietly.

"I am Chala Negassa, Janhoi," said Chala, kneeling before the Emperor.

"And where are you from, Chala Negassa?"

"From Arusi, Janhoi."

"Ah. I see. From Arusi. It was nice to meet you, Chala Negassa. The next time we meet, please do not attack me with a bicycle."

"I will not, Your Majesty," said Chala, breathing the dust of the floor.

"Good," said Menelik. "Bishop Haile Mikael, it is good to see you again. I will see you later, I trust. I cannot stay. I am off to a feast at the Adarash. Big affair. Ferengi diplomats and observers and spies and all. Dehna Ider, my good Bishop!"

And Menelik twirled his cloak about him and whirled off down the hall, followed by his entourage of rases, dejazmaches, kagnazmaches, balambarases, princes, nobles, earls, and royal guards.

"He has not changed a bit," said Haile Mikael to Daniel. The two men were still lying on the floor.

"Except to grow stronger," replied the prince, examining the remains of his fingernails. "And it is a good thing he does, too. He gathers the nation together just in time. This enemy is not like any other we have ever seen. Will you please help me cut these abominable nails?"

By this time they were up from the floor, looking once again like distinguished and powerful notables. The princesses had dragged the twisted bicycle over to a column and leaned it there. They approached the men. Chala followed behind them, fingering a glob of grease between his index finger and his thumb. It was not like the grease from his father's rifle. It was dirtier and stickier. It fascinated him.

"Find him some clothes," said Prince Daniel to the princesses. "Quickly. Before you-know-who sees him again. You needn't be that finicky about the fittings, just be sure they are good, strong clothes. Father Haile will help me get rid of these useless nails," he said, holding up his hands in front of them, "and when we are finished with that, we will meet you in the little garden. Then we will all go to the feast together."

Helena and Mentuab were finicky, nevertheless, but they were also quick, and shortly they joined the prince and the bishop in the little garden outside the palace. Tagging along behind them was what appeared to be a young prince.

Chala wore new white jodhpurs held up by a wide black belt. He wore a shirt of the whitest white, with fancy white embroidery down the front of it. Wrapped around his head was a more suitable headdress than the one Haile Mikael had given him on the road. A sword belt hung around his waist, and from it hung a scimitar in its scabbard. Setting off all these fine new things was a beautiful tan camelshair cape, which came down to his knees and was fastened around his neck with a substantial brass chain.

"So, you have raided the royal munitions house as well as the tailory, I see," said Prince Daniel.

The princesses laughed with delight. "Is he not beautiful?" said Mentuab. "He looks like a prince."

"Indeed he does," said Prince Daniel, chuckling. "I am honored to be in the presence of such a great personage." He bowed low to Chala and smiled at the princesses. "You have done well," he said.

"Chala," said Bishop Haile Mikael, "you are beginning to look like a true Abyssinian warrior." And to Daniel he said, "He has a spear and a shield back at the Abuna's Residence."

"Ah!" said Daniel. "Then all he needs is a Remington."

"Oh, no, no," replied the bishop. "We must ride fast and far, he and I. He has enough to carry as it is."

"Now including," said the prince, "the weight of princely responsibilities upon his back. Well. Are we all ready? Then it's off to the feast!"

Menelik's palace was not simply a palace; it was a palace in the middle of a great compound surrounded by a multitude of high walls. Within those walls were over fifty buildings. There was Menelik's Palace, and the Empress Taitu's Palace, and the Council Hall, the Treasury, the Court of Law, and a number of churches; summer houses for visiting nobles and dignitaries; a post office; booths for jewelers, embroiderers, tailors and weavers; a saddlery, a smithy, and a joinery; the munitions depot, a pharmacy, stables, vegetable gardens; a forest of eucalyptus trees from Australia; olive and juniper plantations; flower beds, haystacks, meadows for grazing horses and cattle; plowed land planted with vines, cabbages, and celery; a meeting place for lost mules and runaway slaves; fresh water springs; storerooms, lavatories, herds of sheep and cattle fattening for upcoming banquets; guards, beggars, a zoo for lions and ostriches; and eight thousand servants and workers. Two thousand of these worked for Menelik alone. It was a veritable city by itself!

And in the midst of all of this, on the highest hill, there stood The Adarash. Ah! The Adarash! Fabled in memory and song. The Adarash. It was a banquet hall of vast proportions. Menelik caused it to be built at the end of the great famine. Anyone could come there and eat. And they came and they ate and its fame went far and wide all over the Empire.

Inside the Adarash there were thirty-four columns holding up its roof, and on both ends there were, up high, stained-glass windows. On the columns were hung lamps that shone by themselves. I mean that they did not have to be lit with a torch. When light was needed, there was a low rumble and they lit. It was like magic. And there was water in the building, as well as in many of the buildings within the compound. The people made up a song about it:

"Menelik has made the water run uphill!" they sang.

"Soon he will make the Ferengi run uphill as well."

That is what they said. Truly, the feast hall was remarkable.

On both sides of the Adarash, inside, there were raised platforms along the entire length. At the far end there was another raised platform. On these platforms there were placed tables and chairs, and this is where the notables and foreign guests sat. Below them, on both sides, were long tables and benches where the soldiers and the commoners sat, plying away at their food with huge curved knives that were delivered in baskets to the tables by one hundred and ten waiters. The guests drank honey mead and beer and araki, delivered by one hundred and ten bar servers. And there were one hundred and ten ushers to show all these guests to the correct tables.

Prince Daniel and his party had to wait to get into the great hall. Ahead of them was a battalion of five hundred soldiers, all dressed in their finest leopard capes and lion and monkey-fur and feather headdresses, and they were all shouting and waving their spears and singing their war songs. Up the wide center hallway the soldiers marched, right up to the raised dais at the far end of the hall. There, Menelik sat on a golden throne, nodding to them, acknowledging them. To his right sat Empress Taitu on a smaller throne. Stretching out to the left and right sat the nobles of the Ethiopian Empire, seated behind long tables covered with white tablecloths that draped over the front of the tables down to the floor. All of them gazed out over the assembled power of the Ethiopian army.

After the dancing soldiers had been dispersed by the ushers and shown to their seats, the prince and princesses and Haile Mikael and Chala approached the dais, where they all knelt and bowed to the ground in a ceremonial salute to the Emperor. But while he was on the ground, Chala raised his eyes, fearful as he was, and looked up at Menelik. And, glory of glories, the Emperor was looking at him. Again their eyes met, and over the hubbub and roar of the crowd of thousands of guests, Chala swore he heard Menelik say, laughing, "Aha! Addis libs! New clothes. Very good. Betam tiru naew!" He swore he heard that. He lowered his head to the floor again, and he smiled.

Then he felt a tap on his shoulder. He looked up. An usher was beckoning to him, and he followed Prince Daniel and the princesses up a flight of stairs up onto the dais and off to the left, where there were spaces reserved for them. Prince Daniel and Bishop Haile Mikael sat together, and next to them, farther over toward the wall, sat Chala Negassa of Meraro, between the two royal princesses Mentuab and Helena. Here he sat, and gazed out over the vast multitudes, and wondered about how it was that he was here!

Waiters brought all kinds of dishes of meats and vegetables, stews and cheeses, and delicacies Chala had never seen before. Servers brought tej, honey wine, and beer and bubbling water. Raw beef was served, and mutton and chicken, and hot, hot tibs that tasted like candy. Another contingent of soldiers came up the aisle, dancing and roaring out war songs, but none was louder than an old white-haired soldier with very few teeth who jumped up and down right in front of Menelik, jabbing his spear into the air and screaming in a high voice:

"I will kill them for you, Janhoi! I will kill all of them. I will kill them with my spear and scimitar and Remington. And if they cut off my right arm, I will slay them with my left. And if they slice off my left arm, I will kick them to death with my feet. I have done this before, and I will do it again!"

Prince Daniel turned to Haile Mikael and said dryly, "Amazing, my good Bishop. He grows new arms and legs for every battle. How can we lose?"

Haile Mikael began to laugh, and he laughed so hard that it was unseemly for a bishop to laugh that way, and he hid his face behind his robes. But still his body shook with laughter, and tears came to his eyes, and he hid his face in his hands, and laughed and laughed.

"Isn't he a handsome fellow!" said Helena to Mentuab, of the toothless old warrior. "Just the one you have been looking for!"

"I, sister? I? I am not the one looking for a boyfriend," replied Mentuab. "How about this one for you, sitting right next to you?" She nodded towards Chala.

Helena looked at Chala appraisingly, and Chala looked back. "He is handsome," said Helena, "but he is too young for me. Tell me, Chala, about that big brother you have in the Galla cavalry. Is he as handsome as you?"

Chala grinned. He felt like he had just escaped from between two lionesses. "My brother Bedane?" he said. "I don't know. I never thought about it."

"Oh, but he is a warrior, is he not?" exclaimed Helena happily. "That sounds interesting." Talking over Chala's head, she said to Mentuab, "If he is as good looking as this younger one, perhaps I should meet him."

"Chala," said Mentuab, "when we meet the eastern armies, you must introduce your brother to my sister. Is he married? Is he betrothed?"

Chala sat open-mouthed for a moment. Then he said, "No, neither married nor betrothed. You are going with the army?"

"Of course," said Mentuab. "We go to assist the Empress. The whole palace goes, it seems."

"The Empress goes to the battle?" asked Chala, awestruck.

"Definitely," said Helena. "She has her own army of 5000 men. It would be unseemly of her to hold them back. This is a big war, Chala. Everyone who can must go. Otherwise, those people" she nodded her head in the direction of some Ferengis seated halfway down one side of the Adarash, "those people will win the war, and will make us their slaves." She added wistfully, "I do not wish to be a slave."

"I shall never be a slave," added Mentuab strongly.

Chala looked at the group of Ferengis. "Those are our enemies?" he asked, puzzled. "Those are the Italians? But what are they doing here feasting with us if they are our enemies?"

"These are the diplomats," said Mentuab. "The ones who talk and spy. That one in the center is Colonel Piano, the head of their delegation. We let them feast with us. We let them see our power. We let them be afraid."

"They will see that we are united," said Helena. "One nation. One house. They think they will break us into pieces. But they cannot. Atse Menelik has made us into one house; one family. We will crush them."

"It is said they have many guns; many cannon," said Chala.

Mentuab smiled bitterly. "So do we, little brother," she said. "So do we."

"See all those Ferengis, Chala?" said Helena, nodding toward the other Ferengi delegations seated along the walls. "They are our friends."

"For now, at least," said Mentuab.

"Those are the British," said Helena. "Their leader is Sir Bertram Rennell-Rodd. Next to them are the French. The French have the best rifles. Then the Russians. They are good doctors, the Russians. Then the Americans. The Americans have all manner of makinas. And you see those men that look different from us and from the Ferengis? Those are the Japanese. They came from far to the east, far past India, and they brought many gifts with them."

"They brought 10,000 swords," said Mentuab. "You are wearing one of them."

Chala's head began to swim. There was so much to learn; so much to see. The world was so wide, and it seemed very complicated. And the feasting went on around him, with thousands entering and eating and drinking and laughing and shouting and singing and departing, for hours and hours, until Father Haile said, "Oh, my friends. It is time that we should go," and the priest and the prince and princesses and Chala left the dais to make room for others who filled their places almost immediately, and they went out through those surging crowds and into the bright afternoon sunlight.

Thousands of soldiers and civilians were stretched out on the lawns of the palace, basking in the sun, breathing in the sweet air of this mountain capital. Some were waiting to get into the Adarash; others were recovering from the feast. The old soldier who thought he could grow arms and legs sat on a rock by the side of the path, mumbling to himself and staring straight ahead. His jaw hung slack, and he breathed hard.

"That is what too much red meat and araki and ayub will do to you," said Prince Daniel, and they all laughed.

It is said that the Adarash of Menelik the Second was capable of holding eight thousand people. There is no way of knowing if this is true, because there was a constant flow of people in and out of the building. What is true is that on this particular November day in 1895 Menelik fed, or more accurately, caused to be fed, his thirty thousand soldiers, the Empress' five thousand soldiers, innumerable hangers-on, the entire diplomatic corps of Addis Ababa, favorites of the palace, notable citizens of the capital, all the waiters and servers and ushers and guides necessary to direct this mob of people to the correct seats, and Himself and his staff as well. And it was all done in five sittings. So it is said.

When the friends arrived at the little garden outside the palace, Haile Mikael said, "I am afraid that we must go now. We have much to do, and we must leave tomorrow before daybreak."

"We all have our duties," replied Prince Daniel resignedly. "It was glorious to see you again, old friend." He paused and looked down at his hands. "Thank God those nails are gone," he said. "What a terrible custom. Well, perhaps this war will end it."

"We all have our duties," said Haile Mikael, smiling.

Chala looked at the princesses as they hugged the bishop, and he thought, "They may be princesses, but they are beginning an adventure just like mine. I wonder where this will take all of us?" And aloud he thanked the princesses for his new clothes.

"And don't forget your promise," said Princess Helena, smiling. "Bring your brother for a visit."

"Until then," said Chala.

"Until then," said Helena.

Late that night, at the Abuna's residence, there was a knock on his door, and when Chala went to answer it, there was a package in the hallway. He opened it. There were more new clothes, not as fine as the ones he had received earlier, but sturdy clothes, thick and warm, made for traveling through the high mountains of the north. There was a scent of incense about them. It reminded Chala of the palace, and of princesses.

CHAPTER 33
IN THE LAND OF THE AMHARA

In the dim light of the golden dawn, Chala dressed in his sturdy new traveling clothes. He made a bundle of his city clothes and threw them over Eagle's back, along with his other bundles of food and provisions. Then, wearing his new scimitar and carrying his shield and spear, he led Eagle to the main gate of the compound. Father Haile was waiting for him there. Together they mounted their horses and started them out at a walk, letting the horses warm slowly to the day. It would be a long ride.

They rode along the wide avenues between the compounds that made up Addis Ababa, and as they came to the edge of the city, the sun rose from behind the low hills to the east. Just then, they felt a low rumble behind them, and turning in their saddles, they saw a band of mounted warriors coming at a fast canter. They pulled their horses off to the side of the road and watched the horsemen as they passed.

There were sixty horsemen in all, and they rode in a column four abreast. They all wore warriors' headdresses and fine clothes, and they all appeared to be seasoned fighters, lean and fierce and born for killing. At the head of them all, riding alone, was a man whose eyes were made of steel and anger. He seemed to pull the others along through the simple force of his will. Beneath him was a high-muscled night-black horse named Abba Nega—Father of the Dawn—who pawed and snorted and strained to move faster, faster. Fast they all rode down the trail, off into the disappearing shadows of morning.

Chala looked at Haile Mikael, who said, "It is Ras Alula, the great general for Ras Mengesha, ruler of Tigre. He is like a hungry wolf. He lives upon the blood of his enemies. His Majesty has called him back from the fighting in the west, and only now sends him north to Mengesha. Now he will gather his five thousand men and bring them north." He added quietly, "Now the game really begins."

"I have heard of him," said Chala. "He is a great warrior."

"He has killed many and caused many more to be killed," said Haile Mikael. "If that is what makes greatness, then he is great."

"Father," said Chala, "If I may ask, why do you ride to the battle? It seems to sadden you."

The bishop sighed. "It is a choice, Chala," he said, "and it is a choice not easily made. Things must be weighed." He lifted his hands, and seemed to be weighing thoughts and actions with them. "But my choice now, though it seems not to be the choice of a man of God, *is* the choice of a man of God. For this is a war against the people of God. Our enemies say that *they* are the people of God. So why do they come against us? It does not make sense. So I must think that they are not the children of God. Therefore, I must defend the true children of God both with my prayers and with my example. I must go to the battle, whether I like it or not."

The two of them sat silently for a long time. Then Haile Mikael said, "Come! The day awaits us, and it is a long day!"

And so it was, a very long day, and so were the days that followed—days that blurred together in Chala's mind; days of endless riding, of valleys and hills and ambas and plateaus and high towering mountain ranges. Out over the road to Debre Berhan they rode, and north from there, stopping only at night, or for hurried handfuls of food during the day, or to let the horses rest. And all along that journey, they rode past others going the same way. Units of cavalry and infantry; hordes of servants leading herds of donkeys loaded with tents and food and blankets for the soldiers; great men seated high upon royal mules that never tired; women following their husbands and lovers to the battle; merchants following the armies to sell them wares at higher than ever prices; women looking to sell their services at every night's camp; children eager to help as servants—all flowed along in a great white-clothed stream to the north. It was as if the whole nation were heading north, as if it had uprooted itself from its land and was heading north to defend that land against anything the foreigners could bring against it. It was a happy multitude that sang war songs and boasting songs and love songs and beat its chest and swore that it would make the enemy rue the day it had ever heard of the land called Ethiopia. And even though that vast throng contained within it the seeds of its own destruction, no one in that crowd could or would choose to see those seeds. All minds bent upon the same service: north to the battle; north to the oldest home of the Empire, where the ancient capital stood; north across the heartland of the Amhara, and through the ancient kingdoms of Simien and Lasta and Wag; north to Tigre, and the holiest of churches and monasteries; north to the place of Ethiopian birth. North, to drive the Ferengis from the land of Ethiopia.

After five days of hard travel, with Addis Ababa and Debre Berhan far behind them, Haile Mikael and Chala arrived at Wara Illu, and there they rested, but not for long. For one day only they rested. Wara Illu was a gigantic plateau in the middle of three high mountain ranges. It was a traditional marketplace for the central highlands. Thousands upon thousands of people could fit there easily. Right now, with the main armies yet to arrive, there was plenty of room. It reminded Chala of his own highland home. Haile Mikael and Chala turned their horses out to graze on the lush green grass of this highland plateau, and to drink deep of the waters of the streams that flowed in deep ravines that cut through that fertile place. That night, they wrapped themselves in their robes, used their saddles for pillows, and slept under the starlit sky. The next day they checked their gear and repaired it. They checked their food for mold and dampness and their waterskins for leaks, and breathed the wild, cold mountain air that swept across the land.

That second night at Wara Illu, Alula's five thousand fighters arrived. The lights from their fires covered the plateau.

The next morning, Haile Mikael and Chala saddled up early and left, long before Alula's soldiers had roused themselves. Where the main road went straight north, Haile Mikael chose a road that went northwesterly. For four days they rode in that direction. They passed through a haunted valley under the towering fortress of Magdala, where, over twenty-five years before, Emperor Theodore had dared the British army to attack him. And when it had, and was victorious, this was the place where Theodore had placed a revolver to his head and shot himself to death rather than face defeat. Now Magdala was deserted and eerie, and the cries of hunting hawks hung weirdly in the misty air.

Once past Magdala, the travelers splashed through a small rocky stream that was the headwaters of the great Takkezze River. A thousand miles from here this water would join the Blue Nile in the Sudan and travel down through Egypt to the Mediterranean Sea.

Crossing the Takkezze, they rode up into the mountains again. Coming upon the great road to Debre Tabor, and making excellent time along that route, in one more day they rode into Lalibela.

Sacred Lalibela held them for two days: sacred Lalibela, with its eleven beautiful churches carved out of the living rock. They were said to have been carved by angels. It was said that Emperor Lalibela could speak with those angels and direct their work. They were ancient and mysterious, these works of angels. They were over eight hundred years old when Chala saw them. These were not simply stones carved out of the hillside and piled one on top of another. No, these churches grew out of the rock itself, were chiseled out of it, were part of it, and they were magnificent churches. Their interiors were painted with beautiful pictures of the saints. They were holy, holy, holy places. Haile Mikael said mass in the one called Kidit Mariam, blessed the monks and priests and pilgrims with the sacred blessing of a bishop, and on toward the north they rode.

A day-and-a-half north of Lalibela, as Chala and Haile Mikael rode through a narrow valley covered with great trees, Haile Mikael reined in his horse and motioned for Chala to stop. Then he pointed up into the trees and said, "Well, Chala. What do you suppose that to be?"

Chala followed the bishop's pointing finger and, looking up, he saw high in the trees a rope, or what appeared to be a rope. It was thin and black in color.

Hailemikael's hand moved, and Chala followed it. "Indet!" he exclaimed quietly. "What is that? Why is a rope in the trees?" For the rope stretched through the trees from south to north, as far as Chala could see.

Haile Mikael smiled and said, "It is not a rope, Chala. It is called a wire."

Chala frowned.

"It carries words," said the Bishop. "It carries messages."

Chala was stunned. "How?" he asked.

"I do not know," laughed Haile Mikael quietly. "It is a miracle, I guess. It is one of the Emperor's makinas. All I know is, someone can put a message into it in Tigre, and at once the Emperor can hear it in Addis Ababa. And people can hear it in several places along the way. It...."

"Man naew?" yelled a harsh voice from the trees. The horses jumped. "Who are you? What are you doing in this place?" Three soldiers stepped out of the bushes.

Now Haile Mikael did not pretend to be a simple country priest. He held aloft his bishop's cross, studded with jewels, its silver shining in the noonday sun. He threw back his cloak, showing off his fine clothes.

"I am Haile Mikael Tesfaye, Bishop of Ba'le!" he said in a commanding voice. "I have been sent by the Emperor Himself to judge how well you guard the Emperor's secret."

Four more soldiers stepped out of the forest. Haile Mikael bent down from his horse and held out the cross. Each man in turn advanced, kissed it, and then knelt before the bishop, looking down at the ground. One of them said without looking up, "Your Excellency! We were told of your coming. We had word of your coming from the post just to the south, although we were not told when you would arrive. We greet you, Excellency!"

"My good soldiers!" said Haile Mikael. "It is good to see you. Your duty is most important. Through your work, we will win. Be sure, above all, that you keep this wire safe." The Bishop lifted his cross once again and blessed the soldiers.

"How may we help you, Excellency?" asked the leader of the soldiers.

"Show me and my companion the best path along the way of the wire," said Haile Mikael, "and introduce me to the soldiers to the north of you."

It was a sentence that the bishop would pronounce many times before this journey was finished. The wire was four hundred miles long, and stretched from near Addis Ababa to within thirty miles of Makelle, the capital of Tigre, and every mile of it was patrolled by twenty-five soldiers. Ten thousand men guarded that wire.

Makelle was occupied by the invaders now, and they were pressing south. Their goal was to reach Amba Alagie, a natural fortress. Then they would go on to Magdala. That was their plan. So farther toward the north, the wire that told Menelik of their movements was guarded by many more men, who could give battle to the invaders in case they turned to the west and seemed likely to discover the secret.

Haile Mikael and Chala rode north, always north, passed along from one group of soldiers to the next. Always they followed the wire. Soon they entered the borders of Lasta, an ancient kingdom surrounded by the highest mountains in Ethiopia. On the morning they arrived in Sokota, Lasta's capital, Haile Mikael brought Chala to a small building on the outskirts of the town. Here, the wire dipped down out of the trees and into the building, and out again the other side.

"See, Chala," said the priest. "Here is a place you can hear the messages."

They went inside.

There was a man seated at a desk that had a strange contraption on it. There were strange sounds coming from the contraption.

"The message is from the north end," he said to the cluster of officers in the room. "From Samire. Scouts say that the Ferengis are marching south from Makelle. There seem to be about two thousand of them. Whites and askaris together. The scouts say they appear to be headed for Amba Alagie.

They think it is an advance guard. The rest of the Italians stay in Makelle, and continue to turn it into a fort."

The officers went outside, and Haile Mikael and Chala went with them. All stood and looked at the huge Amba Alagie, some forty miles distant. The great mountain, looking like a misty mirage, soared up into the sky in the northeast.

"I hope we have somebody there to greet them," said a grazmach. "If we don't, and they take the amba, we might as well retreat to Magdala."

It was dawn on the morning of December 7th, 1895. Amba Alagie stood like a giant fortress astride the main trading route from north to south. The mountain rose five thousand feet from the plains both to the north and the south. There was no way to get around it. If you went to the west, you ended up in the tangled mountains of Lasta. If you went east, you were in the Danakil Desert. It had always been true that the army that held the heights of Amba Alagie held the key to victory.

Major Tomasi Toselli and his staff officers stood on the southern edge of Alagie's escarpment and looked down into the plains to the south. The heartland of Ethiopia stretched out before them. The Italian column had arrived in the saddle of the amba at dusk the night before. They had deployed their pickets and patrols and settled in for a long night's vigil. All through the night, they had watched the campfires of the armies of Ethiopia thousands of feet below. They felt good about their position. They held the saddle. Even though they had only two thousand men, those men were well-equipped. They had new rifles and two machine guns. They had two heavy mountain artillery pieces. Their front faced to the south, where their fire could enfilade any army approaching up the main track. Their left flank was heavily defended against any marauders who might be climbing up the broken ground from the east. On their right, the huge mountain rose steeply another thousand feet, and on its flank they had placed a strong detachment with orders to be wary of any snipers that might try to move around that side and make life miserable with their plinking.

Late the previous evening, a message had arrived from General Baratieri. Their mission was to hold this ground at all costs. No Ethiopians should be allowed to gain the heights. This would enable the Italian engineers to complete the fortifications at Makelle. Also, Baratieri wrote, reinforcements were on the way, and other movements were afoot, movements that Baratieri would not mention in his dispatch for reasons of security. But the implication was that the Italian army was on the move forward, on several fronts.

All this was good news to Toselli and his men, because try as they might, they could not shake the feeling that they were very far out in front of their support.

That dawn, down in the valley, the smoke from thousands of Ethiopian campfires created a haze. Then, out of the low lying haze, riders appeared. The figures were tiny, almost like ants, but there were thousands of them. They were heading up the main track, directly toward Tosellli and his staff.

The Italian officers peered through their spyglasses and binoculars.

"Galla cavalry," said Toselli.

"It is said that Ras Mikael has 20,000 of them," murmured a captain, who then swallowed loudly.

"No matter," said Toselli. "This place is as good as any fort. If they come straight ahead, we will slaughter them. If they try to go around to our left, we will slaughter them. It will be a day for the Ethiopians to die." He paused. "It will be hours before they arrive. We will see to our defenses, and prepare for reinforcements to arrive."

A horse neighed in the still dawn, from somewhere up on the mountainside where no horse should be. Toselli and his officers turned and looked. Far up on the mountain, a single horse and rider appeared silhouetted against the morning sky. The rider raised a pistol and shot into the sky. Suddenly the mountainside erupted with Ethiopian soldiers who rose up, fired a tremendous volley, and charged down upon the weak Italian right flank. The Italian soldiers and askaris, startled out of their wits, broke immediately, and began to run at a dead heat back onto the center.

"My God!" exclaimed Toselli. "Get back to your posts and reinforce the right wing! Draw them into a line along the road. Wheel the center around. Bring over the left. Form a line! Form a line!"

No longer was there any talk of slaughter. Now only a few guards were left to watch the pass from the south, and all the other men of the detachment wheeled to defend themselves against the new enemy, and they were terrified.

For it was Ras Alula. It was Ras Alula and his five thousand veterans of the battles of the north. They had been there all through the night, had arrived early the previous day, had hidden in the rocks on the heights of the mountain, and now they were leaping like lions down the mountain, firing and yelling war cries and shooting to kill.

Toselli stopped giving orders and looked up once more. Now the horse was pawing the air with its forefeet, rearing high and screaming. Not neighing. Toselli swore it was screaming. It was the horse Ras Alula had named Abba Nega—Father of the Dawn—and it was screaming out in anger at the Italian troops. And in its saddle was Ras Alula, waving his pistol. Toselli swore that the Ras was laughing. The old man had his head thrown back, and he was looking at the sky, his mouth open. Toselli could just make out the outline of the old warrior's open mouth.

Then the horse came down to earth, planting his feet firmly on the rock, and Ras Alula seemed to look directly at Toselli. Down came the pistol in an arc, and it pointed directly at him. The next thing Toselli heard was the screech of the bullet as it passed close to his ear. The second bullet ripped through his uniform at his right shoulder, and the Italian commander leaped into the rocks, scrambling for cover.

All along the right flank, his men were falling back. The machine-gunners kept trying to re-set their guns into position to rake the mountainside, but every time one of them tried to fire, he was shot down. Every time the artillery gunners tried to get to their pieces, they were shot down. Along the whole line, his men were being cut to pieces. The detachment watching the Galla horsemen ride up the road became more nervous by the minute, as those small, ant-like figures grew in size and came closer and closer to them. And always, the men of Ras Alula rained down fire and lead on the Italian and askari troops alike.

Major Toselli, hidden behind a rock, looked to his right and saw Captain Isthia. "Captain!" he yelled, and Isthia spun around and looked at him.

"Yes, sir!" he yelled back.

"Tell Lieutenant Barrada to get those machine guns into a better position. We can rake them from that knob as they try to come down."

"Lieutenant Barrada is dead, sir!" yelled Isthia.

"Do it yourself, then. If you do nothing else today, do that!"

"Yes, sir!" Isthia saluted and ran toward the right, taking cover behind every rock he could find. Suddenly, he fell and remained motionless.

"Oh, God!" thought Toselli, "It's Dogali all over again!" Ten years before, during the last war, Alula had caught an Italian detachment in a ravine at Dogali and had slaughtered them all—550 men. No survivors.

"Not this time," thought Toselli. He was enraged at the thought of Dogali and this wiry, evil old man. He jumped from behind his rock, his sword in his right hand and his pistol in his left. "Rally, my men! Rally!" he yelled. "Rally to me!" He ran to that little knob in the middle of the mountain pass, that little fortina, gathering men around him as he ran. When he got there he gave frantic orders, pushing men left and right, encouraging others to leave their cover and come to him, and they came. They came fast, running like the wind, and threw themselves down in the rocks, and turned and fired at Alula's pursuing fighters.

"No Dogali here," muttered Major Toselli to himself. "I will not allow it." He steadied his men and looked around. Behind him, he saw what he was looking for. It was a ravine heading northward down the mountain and commanded by this little fortress at its head. It was too far away for Alula's men to reach. A rear guard could hold this fortress until he had extracted the rest of his men, and then he in turn could cover the retreat of the rear guard. In this manner, he could arrive at Beit Mariam, the small town at the base of the mountain, and hold out there while reinforcements came up to aid him.

Reinforcements! Where were the reinforcements? Baratieri had promised reinforcements. Another reason to fall back. If he met the reinforcements while he was struggling down the mountain, there would be chaos. Better to retreat right now. He would lose his artillery, but there was plenty more of that back at Adigrat depot.

Just then, there was a tremendous amount of firing from the detachment guarding the escarpment to the south. Toselli could see them in the distance, breaking and running. Then, coming up behind them were the horsemen—hundreds of white-clad horsemen. On they came.

"Retreat!" yelled Toselli. "Follow me! Retreat!" He turned to go down into the ravine, and when he did, he saw a sight that chilled him to the bone. Over against the eastern horizon, lines of Galla horse had appeared, heading north, passing by him. They were outflanking him, enveloping him. Soon they would engulf him.

"Follow me, men!" yelled Toselli. He began to run down the ravine. His men needed no encouragement. Soon many of them were ahead of him, officers and men alike.

Then Toselli realized his mistake, for from the heights above the ravine came rifle shots, a few to begin with, then growing in number until there was a steady fusillade. Like rolling thunder, the rifle shots followed the Italians down the ravine. Somehow, Alula had taken his men and thrown them along the ridge. Toselli's safe ravine had become a place of carnage. Men dropped to left and right. Men stopped and fired up at the ridge, then ran again for cover. The bottom of the ravine filled up with dead and dying bodies, some still, some crawling, some screaming in pain, some crying. All of these wounded knew what their fate would be if Alula's soldiers had time to find them.

But Toselli had no time to gather them up and save them, and Alula's men, under orders from their Ras, did not come for them. They were too busy running along the ridge and firing down on what was left of the Italians. For Alula's orders rang in their ears, and these men of the north, the remnants of the once proud army of northern Ethiopia, had vengeance in their hearts, and Alula's war cry raging in their minds. "Kill them!" Alula had cried. "Kill them all!"

Toselli's wounded were left in the ravine, and neither came Italian to rescue them nor Ethiopian to maim them and disfigure them and at last to kill them. That night, the hyenas came to finish them, and the hyenas did not care who was alive or who was dead. That night, the hyenas had a feast for themselves.

CHAPTER 3 5

BEIT MARIAM

As Toselli's troops retreated from the heights of Amba Alagie, Colonel Rudolfo Galliano led a column of reinforcements into the town of Beit Mariam at the northern base of the amba. His fifteen hundred men were not in a hurry. Earlier in the day, a few of them had noticed some puffs of smoke up on the amba, but they didn't think much of that. No one had heard any sounds of firing; the wind was from the wrong direction and carried the sounds away into the south and west. So the troops of Colonel Galliano took over the little town and leisurely prepared a solid defensive perimeter. They would go up to the amba the following morning.

At two in the afternoon, Galliano's pickets saw three black men racing towards them, dressed in the tattered uniforms of the Massawa Brigade. These askaris from the Red Sea coast tribes were wild-eyed and frightened and excitedly grabbed the arms of their protectors and repeated over and over, in a frenzy, the words "Abba Nega! Abba Nega!"

Everyone on the picket line knew what those words meant. Everybody in the north knew who owned that horse.

Now more stragglers came running toward the town. Officers and interpreters were called up. "Ras Alula!" the stragglers babbled.

"Where?"

"Up there." They pointed. "Coming down. Many men. Many men. Tigre. And Galla horse. All over."

"Where are your commanders?" asked Colonel Galliano, frantic to make some sense out of this. "Where is Major Toselli? The officers? The artillery and machine guns?"

"Lost. All lost. Gone. Major Toselli is dead."

"The guns. Were they spiked before you retreated?"

"No, sir."

"Damn!" said Galliano. "How could this happen?"

"He was there," said the soldier. "Waiting for us. Ras Alula was waiting for us."

There must have been two hundred stragglers. Then, about four o'clock, a body of two hundred troops in good order came in. Then more stragglers; and finally, a small, courageous rear guard detachment, maybe fifty more in all. Then there was silence.

Some four hundred fifty men came into the line that day. "This can't be," thought Galliano. He almost went into shock. "Steady," he said to himself. "Steady." This meant that 1700 men had been lost. Twenty of them were Italian officers. The rest were askaris. Oh, there would be hell to pay for this.

"Sir," said an askari, "The Galla horse are on the amba. Thousands and thousands of them. They were going around us." He pointed to the east. "They will go around you too if you stay here."

Galliano looked at the soldier, then at the land surrounding him. He looked with the practiced eye of a veteran officer. Beit Mariam was easy to defend. It was a little fort itself. The land around it was not easy to defend. It was a land where detachments could get lost easily, where an army could come apart and be hacked to pieces like a segmented worm.

Colonel Galliano made his decisions quickly. He gathered his officers around him and said, "We will use this night to figure out the best plan of retreat. Tomorrow morning, at the crack of dawn, we will be out of here. We will fall back on Makelle."

"But Baratieri's orders, sir!" protested a young captain. "We are to go forward."

Galliano looked at him sternly. "That is enough, Captain," he said. "The General is not here. Conditions have changed. We retreat in the morning, and believe me, there will be no consequences from our having done so. But we must not lose a man. Not one man. Understood?"

During the night, Colonel Galliano lost three hundred men. They were the three hundred men of Ras Sebhat, a minor chieftain of the northern reaches who had allied himself with Italy. Sometime during the night, Ras Sebhat's men, after sizing up the situation, left the camp as silently as cats. All of a sudden, they were just gone.

When Colonel Galliano learned of their absence, he shrugged and smirked. "Fortunes of war," he said to himself. "Fortunes of war." He had half expected it. In truth, Ras Sebhat's men had been lost hours before, as soon as they had heard that Alula had smashed Toselli's column.

"So much for Baratieri's plan of eating Ethiopia ras by ras," thought Colonel Galliano. Baratieri's plan had depended on the minor chiefs knowing that they would be protected by the might of Italy. Now that had changed. When word of Amba Alagie got out, every human between here and the Red Sea would know that their safety would depend on whatever force was climbing over that dark amba tonight.

Galliano looked up at the dark, towering massif. What was over there? What was coming at him? Toselli's survivors had wild stories of campfires in the plains to the south, campfires that stretched to the horizon. What power had Menelik massed against him? Could the rumors of an army of 60,000 riflemen be true? No. Impossible. "There is just one thing I am certain of," he thought. "I am glad I am not Baratieri. I am glad I will not have to explain this to the government. All I have to worry about are these crazed Ethiopians coming toward me."

And having thought this, he returned to making his defenses.

The Oromo cavalry attacked at dawn, on foot, running through the trees and firing and looking for weak spots in the defenses. But Colonel Galliano had prepared well, and the Oromo could not find any weak spots. They retreated almost at once, with only a few men lightly injured on each side. They mounted their horses and rode off toward the north. Galliano knew what that meant. If they found a place to close him in a trap, they would. Immediately, he ordered the retreat to begin. The ranks remained tight and disciplined, and moved off in good defensive order. They even managed to take most of the artillery shells they had been carrying forward to resupply Toselli's column. They moved in a dense mass, like an army phalanx of old. They presented a formidable front to any enemy. And coming across the plain to the south of Makelle, they held their order to the last.

Ras Mikael had divided his horsemen into three brigades. One, the left, he sent to Beit Mariam to probe the Italian defenses there. The center he aimed in a wide semi-circle toward Makelle. The right wing he ordered into an even wider arc, far out to the east, and swinging around to the north of Makelle. It's job would be to cut Makelle off from the main Italian force stationed at Adigrat. It would also report on movements of Italian troops trying to relieve Makelle, and to keep up a harassing fire at Makelle's fort.

As Colonel Galliano's force moved nervously toward Makelle, they were always aware of Ras Mikael's left wing nipping at their heels. The cavalrymen would approach in squads, fire a volley, retreat. This went on all day long. Galliano was satisfied with this. There were just a few minor wounds among his troops, since the Ethiopian cavalry took pains not to approach too closely.

Galliano, though, wondered at this strategy, then put it down to Ethiopian reluctance to stir up a hornet's nest among troops who were already in retreat and going in the direction the Ethiopians wanted them to go. So his column plodded on, heading into the north, ever watchful, ever hopeful. Their hearts lightened as they approached Makelle. They could see the outlines of the larger buildings of the town. They knew it was well-fortified. Their steps quickened. They knew they were almost there.

It was then that the Oromo center came down at them from the hills to the east, galloping their mounts furiously toward the Italians in a spear charge. It was a terrifying sight to troops who had thought themselves, until seconds ago, safe in the fort. They quickly formed into ranks, leveled their rifles, and fired. Horses and riders went down, but the charge continued. Just then, loud reports rang out from Makelle Fort. The mountain guns were in action. Shells cascaded into the Oromo charge. Then there was turmoil, as horses and riders crashed to the earth, ripped apart by the splintering shells. Great gaps appeared in the Oromo lines. A formation of Italian troops came out of the fort and began advancing toward the battle. Suddenly, from being attackers, the Oromo were in danger of being flanked.

"Back!" yelled the Oromo leaders to their men. "Back! Back!" The long-range guns fired again and again from the fort. Shrapnel everywhere. More horses going down, crashing together, rearing in terror. The white clothing of the troops splattered with the red blood of men and horses. Back the Oromo went, back into the hills, back out of the range of the fort's artillery. Soon they were gone, out of sight, except for the dead and wounded men and horses they left to mark the site of the battle.

The Italian column reformed, and marched jauntily into Makelle, victors for the day, victors for their King Umberto, victors for their lives.

The next day, the right wing of the Oromo cavalry came up out of the eastern lowlands and took up positions to the north of Makelle, cutting off the Makelle garrison from the main Italian army at Adigrat. These were the troopers of Kanyazmach Didda, the men of Arusi and eastern Shoa. They had not yet had a taste of battle, and they were eager for it, but for the time being their orders were to sit on the road to Adigrat and defend that road against any relief attacks that Baratieri might prepare. And gradually, they extended their lines to the west, up onto a ridge that overlooked Makelle and the Italian fort.

From here they watched as day after day Ethiopian armies arrived at the siege and attempted attacks, all of which were beaten back. The Italians had 300,000 cartridges and 3,000 artillery shells and used them with abandon. Seemingly, the Ethiopians could do nothing against that fort. During one attack, the Oromo troopers saw a man reach the wall of the fort and try to bring it down using nothing more than a hoe, which he swung wildly over his head. Truly, the Ethiopians were courageous, but the Italian defenses were strong.

Still the Ethiopians attacked.

To understand the fury of these attacks, it must be understood what the Italians had done. They had made their fort out of the old church called Enda Iyasus. They had camped in its graveyard. They had broken the tombstones and fitted them together to form the outer walls of their fort. Their artillery fired from the graveyard.

There grew a desperation in the armies of Ethiopia to rid their sacred land of those Ferengis who would do this sacrilegious thing to their churches, their saints, their ancestors. It was not a question of being able to do it; it was simply that it must be done. So it was done. Day after day, charge after charge, death after death—it was done. Hundreds of Ethiopians died, but they never stopped attacking.

One day, Bedane Merga, Hamsaleka to Meto Aleka Babilla Wami, sat on a rock on the ridge north of Makelle, and shading his eyes with the edge of his gabi, looked down on yet another attack on the town. He could see the Italian soldiers scurrying about in their fort, which seemed to grow stronger and stronger by the day. He could see Ethiopian soldiers approach through the ruins of the town, fire, reach close to the gravestone wall, charge forward, fall, die. "Aieee!" he said under his breath, and he thought, "This is impossible. This is the wrong way to do this. It may be right in their hearts, but it is not right to kill yourself for nothing. What can I do?"

And after that morning's attack was over, when all the other troopers had gone back to camp, Bedane continued to watch the fort. He could see right into the fort. He could see the Italian soldiers relaxing after the attack. He could see them checking their weapons, stockpiling shells and ammunition, rebuilding and extending the fort's walls, taking breaks from their work, going to the well and drinking deep. Going to the well and drinking deep.

Bedane's eyes brightened and he became alert. His eyes focused on the well and the men around it. They not only drank there, but filled buckets and skins full of water there, and carried these containers all over the fort. Suddenly Bedane's breath came out of him in a gasp of understanding. This was their only water.

"Whey!" said Bedane, as he continued to look. "Whey!" He watched the ant-like figures of the enemy soldiers. "I wonder if my Remington could reach them from here," he thought, and immediately he knew he was far out of range. "There must be some way of reaching them from here," he thought. He sat and he gazed, and at night he went down to his encampment, and with a furrowed brow, he thought long and hard.

The next morning early, he was up on the ridge again. Once again he watched the morning attack, the dead Ethiopian soldiers, the Italians drinking from the well. All morning he pondered.

In the afternoon, there was a new sight that caught his eye. Far to the south of the fort, miles away, out in the plain, a huge red tent was being erected. It was the Imperial tent, and it could only mean that the Emperor Himself was nearby. The tent was a deep scarlet color. It was over sixty feet high. It was the Emperor's home when he traveled. Its framework was fashioned from huge logs. Its sides could be lifted twenty feet into the air. Hundreds of people could be in the tent all at once, and when they were there, they walked upon Persian carpets which stretched from end to end and from side to side over the whole floor space of the tent.

Down at one end of the tent stood the imperial dais. Upon it was placed the imperial throne. At night, the sides of the tent came down, and the tent became a building of many rooms. It became the palace of the Emperor. Always, the emperors had traveled through their realm; and always, this tent or one like it had been their moving capitol. This had been happening for over a thousand years.

And now Bedane could see not only the royal tent going up, but also many other tents—large enough, but nowhere near the size of the Emperor's—going up as well. These were the tents of the kings and princes of Ethiopia. There was one for the Empress. There was Ras Mengesha's from Tigre, where now the armies fought. There was Ras Makonnen's from Harar. King Teklehaymanot's from Gojjam. Wagshum Guangul's from Lasta. Ras Mikael's, from Wollo. There were the tents of Dejazmatch Balcha, who led the army's right wing; and Dejazmatch Abate, who led the left. Then there were those of other rases: Ras Wole, Ras Mengesha Attakim, Ras Darghie, and Ras Hagos, all of whom led armies loyal to the throne. Surrounding all these great tents were all the tents of the followers of the rases. They stretched to the horizon. Bedane was awed. Surely, how could this little fort stand before a force such as this? But stand it did.

At the end of the day, Bedane once more went down the ridge to his camp, but this night he did not sit alone and think. This night he went to the tent of his aleka, Babilla Wami. "I have seen something I think may be important," said Bedane after the usual greetings. "I think I know how that fort can be taken, but I don't know how to do it."

The next morning, Babilla Wami walked with Bedane to the top of the ridge. They watched as troops from Wagshum Guangul's army, just arrived the night before, tried to storm the fort. They were turned away as were the others before them, leaving the usual complement of dead and dying soldiers.

"Now, watch," said Bedane. "Look at the right end of the fort, in that grove of olive trees. Watch what happens."

Once more the Italian troops converged on the well, drank, filled their pots and skins and buckets, and went back to their duties.

"They all go there," said Babilla. "What of it? I can't see what they do."

"I have watched for three days now," said Bedane. "I know what they do. That is their well. They go for water. They carry it off. It must be their only water. They all go there."

"Ah," said Babilla. "You have the eyes of an eagle."

"We can take the fort if we take their water," said Bedane, "but I don't know how we can do it."

"Ah," said Babilla, and he laughed a low laugh. "I do not know either, my good lieutenant." His white teeth flashed in the strong sunlight. "But if I were a Ferengi, I would know."

"Sir?"

"If I were a Ferengi, I would get a couple of my long-range mountain guns up here and blast that well into hell. I would put them far enough away so they could just reach, and so the guns in the fort couldn't reach back at them. Then I would hold target practice with them until that well was blasted into King Solomon's mines. That is what I would do." Babilla hawked and spat. "All we need is a few Ferengi mountain guns and a lot of muscle to get them up here."

Bedane stood silently for a minute. The two men looked down at the fort.

"So my idea is useless," said Bedane.

"No," replied Babilla. "It is not useless, Hamsa. It is a good idea. We will bring it to Kanyazmach Didda directly. You should get credit for it."

"You honor me," said Bedane, and he bowed, "but my idea is useless. We cannot do anything. Your idea is good: to bring the mountain guns up."

"But I cannot do that," said Babilla Wami, shrugging his shoulders. "No, your idea is the most useful. It shows us what their weak point is. So that is the best idea. Then other ideas will flow from that." Babilla paused. "You say I honor you, Hamsa. But you deserve that honor. You have a good idea; now all we need is the way." Babilla looked down at the dead and dying Ethiopian soldiers outside the fort. "See, Bedane!" he said. "God has made us Ethiopians so courageous! We don't need guns. We just go out and run at them and scare them to death!" Babilla laughed a great laugh. "But come. We must tell the Kanyazmach your idea immediately, to make your idea safe. Otherwise, the word will spread and one of those Amhara princelings out there in those tents will take credit for it." Babilla looked down the slope toward their camp. "See?" he said. "Here comes one now. Soon, they'll be all over the place. Have a thought of them and they turn up. Nobles! Faugh!" He jerked his head and spat.

Bedane looked in the direction of the camp. Sure enough, a horseman was riding up the ridge. He was small, scarcely larger than a boy, but he wore all the finery of an Amhara noble. "Well," thought Bedane, "some of these Amhara lords are pretty small..." But there was something about this one that seemed.....

The small nobleman reined in his horse and looked up at them. His hand rose in greeting, and his shout came up to them through the still morning air: "Bedane! Bedane, my brother! It is I, Chala. How are you? By the grace of God, I am well!"

Bedane stood transfixed. All he could think was, "How could this be?"

"It is a spirit," said Babilla Wami. He sounded frightened.

Bedane stood still.

"Did you not hear me?" demanded Babilla. "It is a spirit".

Bedane smiled. "If it is a spirit," he said, "it is riding Eagle, my brother's horse."

Babilla didn't know what to do. This apparition was definitely a spirit— good, evil, indifferent, it didn't matter. If a spirit wanted this ground, he thought, well, let the spirit have it. And the spirit definitely did want this ground. It was coming closer. Babilla wanted to run, but he could not run in front of Bedane.

Bedane smiled broadly. He could see the horseman's eyes. "It is my brother."

"The spirit has taken his body, and takes your soul. It is a dream. It is not your brother."

The horseman was within ten feet of them now. He slid out of the saddle and walked quickly toward them, grinning.

"My brother!" he said, holding out his hands.

"My brother!" answered Bedane. "How....."

Chala started to giggle.

"See?" said Bedane, turning toward Babilla. "It is Chala." He turned back toward Chala. "Meto Aleka Babilla Wami thinks you are an Adbar spirit."

Chala began to howl with laughter. "No," he laughed, "No, I am not a spirit, but I do have a wonderful tale to tell!"

And so Chala told Bedane and Babilla how he had come north with Father Haile, and of all the adventures they had had, and of being in the palace at Addis Ababa, and of Lalibela and Lake Zwai, and he did all of this in thirty seconds. Then he stood and looked at Babilla, puzzled, then he looked afraid. The blood drained from his head and he swayed. "Meto Aleka Babilla Wami," he almost whispered. "Meto Aleka Babilla, were you not Hamsaleka to my uncle, Bedasa Merga? Where is my uncle?"

"We do not know, Chala," said Babilla. "But do not be afraid. He is well. He was taken by Kanyazmach Didda and the other officers to be the head of a special group of soldiers. There are fifty of them."

"We haven't seen them since before we crossed the Awash," said Bedane, "but we know they are safe. They are doing something secret. So, Hamsa Aleka Babilla Wami was promoted to Meto Aleka."

"And your brother Bedane was appointed to be my Hamsa, Chala. I would not have it any other way."

"Who leads the boys?" asked Chala.

"I gave the appointment to Mamo," said Bedane. "He does a good job. Strong and solid. And all the boys are safe and well."

"I saw some of them on the way up," said Chala. "They told me where you were, but I did not ask them about anything else. They all seemed well and happy."

"And as surprised as we were to see you, I'd say," said Babilla. "But come. We must find Kanyazmach Didda. Bedane has found out something important to tell him."

They turned to go down the ridge. Just then, there was the sound of a cannon shot from a long way off to the south. They stopped to gaze off in that direction. Two minutes later, there was another shot. This one sounded sharper, clearer, more powerful.

There were no more shots. Bedane, Babilla, and Chala were puzzled, and waited a couple of minutes. Then Babilla said, "That is strange. Perhaps some kind of a signal. But come, we had better go. Who is this Bishop Haile Mikael, Chala? And how did you come to meet him?"

If there was one thing that Menelik liked better than ruling his empire, it was tinkering with machinery. Menelik was a born mechanic. Every time a new machine entered the borders of his realm, he had to get his hands on it and take it apart and put it back together again. The Emperor was very proud of his ability to put things back together again. Many men couldn't do that. Most men were good at taking things apart and looking at the parts and wondering how they went back together. Menelik *knew* how they went together. He just *knew*.

That's why he liked traders, who could move all the parts of a caravan from one place to another and get there with the caravan intact. That's why he liked farmers, who knew how to sow and weed and reap and feed their families and keep those families intact and strong. That's why he liked mechanics and engineers. He knew that it was by putting things together and keeping them together that progress was made, and people benefitted from that progress.

So when he heard that Ras Alula had captured two Italian long-range mountain guns at Amba Alagie, he had to take a look at them. He ordered Ras Alula and Ras Mengesha to bring them to Makelle, and the morning after they arrived he set about testing them. First, he had a troop of cavalry clear a wide area in front of the encampment. Then he had Ras Makonnen bring one of his cannons to that place, and he had Ras Mengesha bring one of the Italian guns. After looking at the Italian gun from all sides, and crawling around it, and running his hand along the barrel, and testing the breach and the loading mechanism, and feeling its wheels, and cradling its shells in his arms like they were very heavy babies, Menelik said to Ras Makonnen, "Cousin, have your gunners fire your cannon."

Ras Makonnen did so. The cannon boomed out, the ball flew, and all the rases and gunners and officers marked where it fell and exploded. Then Menelik said, "Now, cousin, have your gunners fire the Italian gun."

The gunners went to their task with care, never having fired one of these new guns before. But they did it right, the cannon fired with a loud, sharp report, and its shell landed so far in front of the first one that it was almost out of sight.

"It flies a third as far again as our cannon," said Makonnen, looking troubled.

"That is good to know," said Menelik. He was silent for a moment, then he said, "Our meeting will be at the third hour after noon. Everyone must be there. I want every ras, every noble, every grazmach and dejazmach and kanyazmach there. Everyone. No excuses. This changes everything. If we do not find out how to counter this new weapon, they will cut my army to ribbons with it. They will take our country and everything that is in it and they will turn it to their own use. And we, Cousin, will become their slaves. Royal slaves, perhaps, but slaves nonetheless. I do not wish that to happen."

"Nor do I, Your Majesty," said Makonnen, and his smile was forced.

When Babilla, Bedane, and Chala arrived at the tent of the Kanyazmach, they found him in front of it, waiting for his horse to be saddled. Babilla approached him and bowed, as did Bedane. Chala stayed back, and held Eagle's reins.

Didda looked at them. "Well, Aleka? Did you come over to pay homage to my person, or what?"

"Permission to speak, sir," answered Babilla, still bowing.

"So stand up and speak, unless you are here to tell me that you have hurt your back and you want to go to the hot baths in Addis instead of to the battle."

Babilla straightened and said, "Sir. We think Hamsa Bedane has discovered an important thing that you should know, sir."

"Make it quick. I am on my way to a conference."

"Tell him," said Babilla, and he pushed Bedane forward.

Bedane told the Kanyazmach what he had seen from the ridge, and Babilla added that while Bedane didn't know exactly how this could be done, he himself had thought about how to place a cannon to shoot into the fort, but that they would need powerful cannon like the Italians had.

Kanyazmach Didda snorted, and watched his servants tightening the cinch on his horse's belly. "So what do you propose? That I send a trader to Adigrat to buy a gun from Baratieri? Or would you rather lead a troop into the Italian encampment yourself and bring one or two back for us?"

Babilla was abashed. "Sir," he said, quietly for him, "we just thought you should know that somehow it could be done."

The big barrel-chested officer looked at him. "Forgive me, my good aleka," he said. "Just, I am frustrated with the situation. I too have watched the attacks on this skimpy little fort. I too have watched day after day as our soldiers die and as the ones left alive eat everything in the countryside that can't run fast enough to get away. But yes, what you say is important, and what your lieutenant has discovered is important. Say, why don't you come to this conference with me? If everyone is as frustrated as I am, maybe they will listen to you, and maybe one of them will have an idea of how to do this thing."

The Kanyazmach tested his saddle, and turned back to Babilla and Bedane. "Well, get your horses," he said in a loud voice. "We are in a hurry!"

Bedane murmured something to Babilla, who said "Sir?"

"What now?" said Didda, irritably.

"My hamsa wonders if his brother can come along with us." Babilla jerked his head in the general direction of Chala.

"His what?" the Kanyazmach said.

"His brother, sir."

"You mean that scrawny little Amhara princeling over there is your lieutenant's brother? I thought you had made a mistake and captured him instead of taking orders from him. What the hell is he doing in those clothes? Where did he get that scimitar?"

"Sir, he..." began Bedane.

Kanyazmach Didda put up his hand. "Stop. I do not want to know. I want you to get your horses. We have to go. Yes, bring him if you wish, as long as he does no harm."

"He may prove useful, sir," said Babilla.

"Oh?" said Didda. He arched his eyebrows.

"Sir, he was not born in those clothes, sir. He....."

"Get your damned horses!" shouted the Kanyazmach. "Let's get out of here! You can tell me on the way!"

The Council of War began at the third hour of the afternoon in the royal tent. Menelik stood in front of the royal dais, but below it, on the floor. Behind him, stretched across the dais, was his staff. At the right end of the dais stood Abuna Mattewos, and on the left was the Itchegie. Both church leaders held on high their crosses of silver and gold.

In a semi-circle facing Menelik stood the nobles of Ethiopia. To Menelik's right was Dejazmach Baltcha, leader of the right wing of Menelik's army, who led 10,000 men for Menelik. Next to him stood proud Empress Taitu, leader of her own army of 5,000. Then came Wagshum Guangul, King of Wag and Lasta, leading 10,000 fighters. After him was Ras Mengesha Attakim of the Simien, 5,000 men.

Directly opposite Menelik was his cousin, Ras Makonnen of Harar, who brought 30,000 soldiers and thirty cannon across the desert. To his right stood Ras Mengesha Yohannes, Duke of Tigre, and his wily old general, Ras Alula, who led what was left of the Army of the North, some 5,000 fighters. Next was King Tekle Haimanot of Gojjam, who brought 5,000 men. Next to him stood Ras Mikael of Wollo, leader of the 20,000 Oromo cavalry. Lastly, standing on Menelik's left, was Dejazmach Abate, leader of Menelik's left wing of 10,000 soldiers.

In the center was Menelik, who led the center of his own army—15,000 men. So the half-circle was complete: two dejazmachs, five rases, two kings, the empress, and Emperor Menelik. Behind each of the leaders stood their staffs, so that there were some two hundred army leaders included in the circle. Altogether, they represented a force of 115,000 soldiers.

Menelik spoke:

"Abuna Mattewos, Reverend Itchege, Empress Taitu, my cousins, my brothers, my warriors. Here we are, all together. Finally, after two hundred and fifty years, we are an empire again, and we are strong. No longer do we fight each other. Once more, we are One House. One House! And now our enemies will see our strength. Now we are armed, and strong, and willing, and we shall throw our enemies into the sea."

Menelik paused, and sighed. "But we have problems, my brothers," he said. "Here they are. First, we know we can beat our enemy in a fight. Our good servant Ras Alula has proven that over and over again. Just a week ago he drove them from the heights of Amba Alagie, and We deeply thank him for that. But we have never been able to throw the enemy out of one of his forts. Now here he is again, blocking our way. But we must go north. We must go around Baratieri's army and cut him off from the sea. We can do that, but we must not leave this fort behind us. For if we do, Baratieri will join with this garrison and we will be trapped. He will cut us off from our supply lines. We will then have to rely on the supplies of northern Tigre and the Hamazien, and God knows that these areas have been so savaged by warfare that they can no longer support their own people, let alone us. So we must take that fort and keep our supply lines open. But how do we do it? They have excellent arms in there. Many machine-guns and artillery pieces. I myself have tested one of their guns only this morning. We cannot bring up our cannon against them. Their guns can shoot a third further distance than ours. We would lose all our artillery, and our infantry and cavalry would be slaughtered. What can we do? I await your answers."

King Tekle Haimanot spoke up immediately. "My cousin!" he exclaimed in a loud voice. "My army arrived yesterday. Already they are rested. Give my army the honor of taking this fort. Surely that little place cannot withstand the charge of five thousand Gojjamis. Remember, my lord, that we are used to forts and castles, both how to defend them and how to destroy them. Give us the honor, I beg of you!"

At this speech a wild laugh of derision came from Ras Alula. King Tekle Haimanot's hand went to his sword hilt, and his lips curled in anger.

Ras Alula said, "You wild men of the west! Do you not think that we of the north know castles and forts as well as you? And look at us! The remains of Emperor Yohannes' proud army, once 100,000 strong. Now we can scarcely find five thousand men. Over and over we have gone against the Ferengi forts, and I tell you, this is nothing like what you are used to. They will cut you to pieces. That is not the way." He turned away from Tekle Haimanot, turned his back to him, and the King of Gojjam would have drawn his sword, but Menelik said,

"My good cousin, do not be angered at the words of Ras Alula. He has fought long and hard against the Italians, and I fear he is right. I myself have watched as day after day our armies have swept gallantly up to the walls of the fort, left their hundreds of dead and wounded, and retreated, feeling disgraced. First, the Galla cavalry, then the Hararis, then my own army, then the men of the Simien, lastly the men of Wag and Lasta, as late as yesterday. No, there is no disgrace here. Alula is right. It is not lack of courage. Remember, it is said that God gave the Ethiopians ninety percent of the world's courage. This is something else. We are up against new things, and we must use our minds and come up with new means of attack, or we are defeated. We cannot let that happen. Think! Think! Give me a new way of attack! Give me a new weapon!"

There was a minute full of silence. No one had an answer. No one had a new weapon, or a new way of attack.

Then Ras Mikael of Wollo, leader of the Oromo, spoke in a low but penetrating voice. "My Lord," he said, "I bring you a weapon, but it is not a new weapon. It is an old one."

Menelik looked at him. "Speak, Ras Mikael."

Ras Mikael took Kanyazmach Didda by the arm and drew him forward. "This is the leader of my right wing, by name Didda Bokku. He is a good, tried and true and valiant soldier. One of his men has discovered something about the fort which may be of use to you."

Kanyazmach Didda bowed low, knelt, and touched his forehead to the ground.

"Rise and speak, Kanyazmach Didda," said Menelik. "What have your men found?"

"Janhoi, Excellency, Your Majesty," said Didda, rising to his feet, "one of my men spied on the fort, and noticed that there was but one source of water in the whole place. The entire garrison depends on it. He reported this to his aleka. Together they came to me and told me their idea. I brought them with me, in case it might be useful."

"They are here?"

"They await without, Your Majesty."

Knowing it was the custom of the Oromo for news to be brought directly from the one who had seen the thing, Menelik said, "Bring them in."

Babilla Wami and Bedane were ushered in to the gathering by men of the Imperial Guard. And Chala trailed behind them! Bedane heard him and turned, but a guard spun him around and motioned him forward. The three came through the ranks of Ras Mikael's staff until they arrived where Ras Mikael and Kanyazmach Didda were standing. There was nothing between them and Menelik but a few yards of Persian carpets. They prostrated themselves before the Emperor. But, as now seemed to be his custom, Chala looked up to see what was going on, and stared again right into the eyes of Menelik.

And what was going on in the mind of the Emperor at that moment? Suddenly, for no apparent reason, he was thinking of bicycles. "What the hell?..." thought Menelik to himself. He shook his head slightly, as if to clear it. Then, recovering himself, he said, "Will the soldier who spied on the fort rise and identify himself?"

Bedane stood, trembling, and said in a low voice, "My name is Bedane Negassa, son of Negassa Merga, former Aleka of the Shoa Oromo of Arusi. My home is in Meraro."

"Speak louder," commanded the Emperor. "What did you see?"

"Your Majesty," said Bedane. "I saw that all the soldiers in the fort, after every battle, came to one place to draw water. It is a well in the westernmost part of the fort. After seeing this over and over, I came to the conclusion that it was the only water in the fort. I saw this from the ridge to the north of the fort. I thought of shooting at them with my Remington, but I realized that it was too far. I thought my information might be of value, so I reported it to my meto aleka.

"And he is here?" asked Menelik.

"He is, Janhoi."

"Rise, Aleka ," said Menelik, "and tell us who you are."

Babilla rose. Bedane glanced at him. For all his vile vocabulary, his roughness caused by years of soldiering, his real toughness brought on by seeing death and suffering all around him—at this moment, Babilla Wami looked noble. He stood straight and stiff, his jaw jutting out and his moustache gleaming, and he said, "Your Majesty, I am Babilla Wami, Meto Aleka of the cavalry forces of Meraro, Bekoji, Siltana, and Lemu, all of

Your province of Arusi. My hamsaleka, Bedane Desta, came to me and showed me what he had seen in the fort. He told me he had no idea of how to do anything about this, but I am a veteran, and I have seen many things, and I told him that if I were a Ferengi I would know what to do." Babilla was becoming more confident. "I told him that if I were a Ferengi, I would take one of my mountain guns up to that ridge and blast that well into hell, pardon my language, sir, I mean, Janhoi, sir!"

"Aha!" said Menelik. A broad smile grew across his face.

"I said that if it were placed right, we could destroy the well, and the Italian guns, being placed further away in the fort, could not return our fire," said Babilla loudly.

"Aha!" cried Menelik.

Babilla continued his train of thought, more to himself than to anyone else. "But I did not know what to do, because we do not have any of those guns. But I thought Kanyazmach Didda should know....."

"Ahhhh!" cried out the Emperor. "But we do have those guns, Aleka Babilla! We do have those guns, Hamsa Bedane Negassa! I have two of them, and by God, by tomorrow morning—Makonnen, Baltcha, are you listening? Do you hear me?—by dawn tomorrow, I want those guns up on that ridge. Have them sighted. I don't care how you do it. Carry them up on the backs of hyenas if you have to. Get them there. Then, Cousin Tekle Haimanot, I will give you your glory. Lead your men in a charge against the fort. Give them a hot fight, but keep your men just out of range. You know how to do it. Give those Ferengis a hot time. A long time. Then retreat."

Menelik turned to Makonnen and Balcha. "Then when the dogs go for their water, blast the hell out of that well, as Aleka Babilla says. Get as many of them as you can, but concentrate on that well. Crush it. Cave it in. Destroy it. Then we will see how long they last. And Ras Mikael, post Kanyazmach Didda's troopers in position on that ridge, in case the Ferengis try to attack our guns. And I will personally reward these men!"

Thus spoke Menelik of Ethiopia.

Thus it was done.

CHAPTER 3 9

THE CAMP OF THE EMPRESS

"Aleka Babilla, I ask your permission to delay our return to your camp for just a little while. I want to bring my brother to meet some friends I made in Addis Ababa."

Chala, Bedane, and Babilla Wami were standing outside the royal tent, beyond the rows of Imperial Guard troops. They had been ushered out at the close of the war council, along with most of the staffs of the nobles.

Babilla Wami turned to Bedane. "Who is this?" he asked. "He shows up dressed like an Amhara lord, he babbles strange tales about bishops and battles, now he follows us into the Council of War, and if I remember, the last time I saw him he was learning to read and herding goats."

Bedane began to laugh. "Maybe you were right the first time, Aleka Babilla. Maybe it is a spirit."

"No, it's not a spirit," said Babilla. "It's Chala, all right. I can tell by that stupid look in his eyes." He turned to Chala and said, "You have my permission to take your brother to meet your friends, Your Royal Majesty of Whatever, but I warn you: do not involve him in any adventures." And to Bedane he said, "I give you two hours' leave. You must be back in camp early tonight. I will want you. It will be up to us to show the gunners where to place the captured guns. Two hours. If you are not two hours behind me, I will...I will...I will string you up, if I can find a tree in this godforsaken country strong enough to hold you."

"It will not be even that long," said Chala.

As Bedane and Chala walked away, Kanyazmach Didda came out of the tent and saw Babilla. "An excellent speech, Aleka!" he said. "An excellent speech. I am glad I brought you. Now you will be rich, eh? A gift from the Emperor himself. Very good. Where are they going?"

Babilla smiled quizzically and replied, "Sir, His Royal Princeling of Somewhere wants his brother to meet some friends he made in Addis, sir."

Didda Bedane laughed. "Good!" he said. "Maybe it's the Minister of the Pen, or Dejazmach Baltcha, or the Empress. All I know is this, Aleka Babilla: I think that boy is good luck for us. I do not know where he has been, but let me tell you—you do not know this, but I saw it. While you and your lieutenant were burrowing your faces into the carpet in there, your lieutenant's brother looked up, straight at the Emperor, and the Emperor looked straight at him, and I swear the Emperor recognized him. It was strange. Why would the Emperor recognize him?"

"I have no idea," said Babilla Wami. "He is full of surprises."

"Surely, that is the truth," said Didda Bokku.

Chala and Bedane rode over to the camp of the army of Empress Taitu, and passing by the royal tent of the Empress, Chala pulled Eagle up in front of a large white tent that stood next to the royal one. He dismounted, and Bedane followed suit. Leaving the horses with some servants, they approached the door of the tent. Chala spoke to the guard at the door, who was a large eunuch.

"I am Chala Negassa of Arusi," he said to the guard, "and this is my brother, Bedane Negassa. I am here to meet with the Princess Helena."

The eunuch bowed and disappeared inside the tent.

Bedane looked at his brother with alarm. "Are you crazy?" he whispered. "What do you mean, you are here to meet with a princess? Do you understand what you have said?"

The guard reappeared in the doorway. "Princess Helena is not able to meet with you at the moment," he said, "but Princess Mentuab bids me usher you in." He bowed low, and with a wave of his hand, bade them enter.

They walked into a large antechamber. The floor, like that of the imperial tent, was covered with Persian carpets. There were several chairs surrounding a low table in the center of the room. Standing next to the table was Mentuab, resplendent in a purple gown. She was smiling.

"Chala Negassa!" she exclaimed. "It is good to see you again. How are you?"

"I am well, Princess," replied Chala.

"And how is Father Haile?"

"Very well also. He is at a meeting of the clergy. But you should see him soon."

"That is good. It was very hard to have only the memory of him for so many years. But tell me, Chala, who is this warrior you have brought with you?"

Bedane looked very much the warrior. He was fully armed, with his rifle slung across his shoulder and his shield and spear in hand. He seemed to have grown taller and leaner on the way to the north, and the features of his face had a sharp angularity to them.

Chala bowed to the princess. "Forgive me, Princess Mentuab, for being presumptuous, but if you remember, at the feast in the Adarash, Princess Helena said to me that I should bring my brother and introduce him. So I have brought him. Princess Mentuab, this is my brother, Bedane Negassa, Hamsaleka of Aleka Babilla Wami, serving under Kanyazmach Didda and at the pleasure of the great Ras Mikael."

"It is my pleasure to meet your brother," said Mentuab. She curtsied rather than bowed, something which Bedane had never seen before. He didn't know what to do—speak or be silent, bow or fall to the floor. Consequently, he simply stood there, ramrod straight, slightly in shock.

"I am sure that Princess Helena will be happy to meet you, Bedane Negassa," said Mentuab, smiling. She turned to Chala, "Yes, Chala, I do remember her saying that. Presently, she is preparing herself in formal attire. We must be in attendance upon the Empress within the hour, you see. But it is just a short walk to the Empress' tent. We will have time for a nice visit. I will go and tell her you are here. Oh, but I forget my manners! Do sit down, please. The servants will bring you some coffee while you wait."

With that, Mentuab slipped behind one of the hanging carpets that partitioned the tent, and disappeared. Chala and Bedane sat. Servants brought fresh coffee beans and hot water, and ground the beans, and Chala sat and smiled. Bedane stared at his brother wordlessly, in wonder at where he was and what he was doing there. But he could not speak in front of the servants. He would look like a fool if he did. That is what he thought, and he would have been right.

Mentuab walked down the center hall that divided the rooms in the interior of the tent. All the way at the back, on the right hand side, she came to the carpet that was the front wall of Helena's room. "Helena!" she called quietly.

"Yes?" asked Helena.

"It is I, Mentuab. May I come in?"

"Of course," came the muffled reply through the wall.

Mentuab pushed aside the carpet and entered. The afternoon sunlight, coming through the white cloth of the tent made the room bright. Helena was standing before a small mirror that hung on the canvas wall. She was holding a set of earrings to her ears. "Ooh, Mentuab," she said petulantly, "I cannot decide between this pair and that one. Help me." She put the earrings down on a small folding table and picked up another pair.

"Those," said Mentuab to her younger sister. "The golden starbursts. They are spectacular with your white dress."

Helena held the delicate filigreed earrings to her ears, looked in the mirror, and sighed.

"They are just right," said Mentuab.

"You are right," said Helena. She was already pushing the pin of an earring through her earlobe. "What brings you to my room, my sister?"

Mentuab waited just a moment and then said, "Your Galla warrior awaits you in the guest room."

"What?" said Helena. Startled, she looked back at Mentuab through the mirror.

"You ordered a Galla warrior, remember? He is back up there having coffee, waiting for you."

Helena spun around. "What are you talking about?" she said with alarm.

"At the Adarash, in Addis Ababa, you told Father Haile's little friend Chala to bring his brother to you if he got the chance. Well, he got the chance. He is without." Mentuab covered her mouth with her hands. She was shaking with laughter.

"Be clear," said Helena sternly. "What are you saying?"

Mentuab could hardly contain herself. Her eyes began to fill with tears of laughter, and she said, "I said, Chala Negassa has brought his brother to meet you."

Helena's hands flew to her face. She could feel them turning cold against her cheeks, the blood draining out of them. "Oh, my God!" she said breathlessly. "I didn't mean it. I was just playing with him!"

"Beware of playing with unsophisticated people," said Mentuab. "They may take you at your word." And she doubled over with laughter.

Helena's eyes flashed. "And you let them in?"

Mentuab straightened. "And what was I to do? Send them away like beggars?"

"You could have told them that we were needed at the Empress' tent. That is the truth."

"I did tell them that. I told them we would be needed there within the hour. So it will be a short visit. You will be able to get through it."

"What! You have set this up, you conniver, you schemer, you idiot! You have done this just for a good laugh!"

"What?" said Mentuab, continuing to laugh. "You accuse me?"

"You are an idiot! What am I to do? I can't go out there."

"Yes, you can."

"I will feel like a fool."

Mentuab became serious. "You will look like a princess," she said. "You will remember your training, and you will act like a princess. He will be in awe of you."

"Oh, my God, you are an idiot. Chala has told him all about me and....."

"I don't think so."

"Why do you say that?"

"The poor young man seems to be in shock. I don't think he actually believes where he is at the present moment."

Helena's eyes narrowed. "You deceiver. You and Chala set this up."

"I and Chala? Don't be silly. Where? When? No, little sister, this is a plot between Chala and you yourself. Ha! Ha! 'Bring me your brother', you said."

Helena took a deep breath. "Does he have a bone through his nose?" she asked quietly.

"Not that I noticed," said Mentuab.

"Is he ugly?"

"Well, no, I wouldn't call him ugly," returned Mentuab.

"Does he smell?"

"No more than any man who has been riding around on a horse for three months. Shall I instruct the servants to waft incense over him?"

"Oh, dear," said Helena. "Oh, dear. Oh, of course not!"

"Are you ready?"

Helena looked at her sister. She felt like a lamb being prepared for slaughter. "I must compose myself," she said.

"Take a deep breath," said Mentuab. "You look lovely, by the way. You do not need to worry."

"You are right, sister. I did this to myself. I must live with it." Helena drew herself up. "I can and I shall," she said.

Bedane was sitting in a chair that faced the outer wall of the tent. Across the table from him sat Chala. Bedane saw Chala rise and bow. He stood up, automatically grasped his spear, and turned toward the interior of the tent. And then he stopped and stood absolutely still. He did not breathe. He did not blink.

For before him, Bedane saw a vision.

Helena stood alone in the center of the room. She was dressed all in white, with the golden jewelry she had selected for the day setting off the white against her beautiful dark skin. She held her head high. Her eyes were distant. Her full lips were pressed together in an attitude of command. She was truly a princess. All else in the room flew from Bedane's sight.

So they stood for an age, looking into each other's eyes.

For Helena, too, had seen a vision. When she entered the room, she saw Chala rise and bow. Then she saw a tall warrior rise and turn toward her, and as he turned, his gabi flowing about him, he seemed to her as a shadow warrior from the past come to life. And while her countenance remained unchanged, and her royal attitude remained outwardly intact, inwardly she sighed and said to herself, "Oh! He is beautiful!"

And so the two of them remained, and neither of them knew what time had passed. And for them, time ceased to be.

The soft sound of Mentuab pushing back the curtain and emerging from the interior of the tent brought Helena back to her senses. She looked at Chala and, with arms outstretched and a beautiful smile, she approached him. She took his hands and said, "Why Chala, my friend! You kept your promise! Introduce me, please."

"Princess Helena, my brother, Bedane Negassa..." was all that he could say before Helena had returned her gaze to Bedane. She stood facing him as quietly and as regally as a statue. Taken totally by her beauty, Bedane stared in amazement. Then, acting upon some unrealized knowledge stored deep within him, he bowed and said, "My Lady. I am honored."

The two princesses of the royal court and the two sons of the warrior Negassa Merga sat around the table and drank coffee. They spoke of their journeys to this spot and their beliefs and fears of what would come tomorrow and the days that would follow before they were once again all safe in their homes. It was a pleasant meeting.

Everyone said the proper things and did the proper things. But for Bedane it was a time of magic. There was something about this meeting that changed him forever. It seemed as if he were suddenly filled with the thoughts and dreams of another person. It was like another life was being poured into him. All kinds of possibilities that had never occurred to him before seemed to well up in him. And as he sat there, he automatically sat up straighter, and listened more carefully, and said things more clearly than he had ever said them before. And he did all this not in a bad, or snobbish, or officious, or supercilious, or oafish way, but in a very natural way.

As time had stopped before for Helena and Bedane, when they all sat down to coffee time started up again, and as if to make up for lost time, time raced on, so that in a very short time there was no time left at all. Chala and

Bedane stood and bowed, and the princesses stood and walked with them to the doorway of the tent, and bade them farewell.

After the men had left, Mentuab said, "See, sister? You did fine. Just like a real princess."

Helena said nothing. She stood looking at her sister. Then she swayed slightly, and put her face in her hands.

"Come. We will be late," said Mentuab.

"I cannot leave just yet," Helena whispered.

It was Mentuab's turn to be startled. "Why? Is something wrong?"

Helena stood, holding her face in her hands. Then she said, "Oh, dear. Oh, dear," in the smallest voice in the world. She looked at Mentuab with pleading eyes.

"Oh, no," said Mentuab. Then she said it louder. "Oh, no. No, you cannot. You can not have feelings for him. You are a princess. He is a commoner. And a Galla! Nothing can be worse. It would come to no good. Listen to me. Take a deep breath. Get over him. You will never see him again. Do you hear me? Remember your duties, you silly girl. You are a princess!"

Helena stared at her sister for a long time. Then she said, "I am more than a princess, sister. I am a woman." And having said that, she put her face into her hands again, and sat in a chair, collapsed into it. All was quiet in the tent, and Helena sat quietly for many long minutes. But her heart was beating fast.

Chala and Bedane rode Eagle and Star side by side into the dying day, heading back to their camp north of the besieged town.

"Well, my brother," said Chala, "how do you like my friends?"

"I don't know who you are anymore, little brother," said Bedane grimly. "I don't know what to say to you. What will you conjure up next?"

"I do not conjure, elder brother. I just meet people. How did you like Princess Helena?"

Bedane was silent.

"She liked you. It was easy to see."

"I have never seen such a beautiful woman in all my life," said Bedane. It was as if the words had tumbled out of him all by themselves. Bedane looked shocked that he had said them.

"Good," said Chala, grinning.

"She asked you to bring me to her?"

"At the Adarash feast. She said, 'Bring your brother to see me.'"

"She was playing with you," said Bedane. He laughed. "I guess you are not a conjurer after all. You are a simpleton."

"Not such a simpleton as you are right now," said Chala, laughing. "I can see inside your head. There is a princess in there, and she is beautiful, and you cannot get rid of her. She will be with you forever, and make *you* a simpleton." Chala laughed again, and slapped Eagle's rump. The horse plunged forward. "Race you to camp!" yelled Chala. "Che, Eagle! Che!"

Bedane dug his heels into Star's ribs. "Hid, Star! Innehid! Che!"

The two brothers galloped their horses across the land, feeling the wind rushing across their faces, feeling the ground turning to dust beneath their horses' hooves, feeling the smooth rhythm of the horses' gallop. They felt like they were riding the back of the roaring wind across a thundering sky.

They arrived in camp as the sun was setting. The campfires were already blazing, and the warriors were sitting around waiting for the chickens to finish broiling. The chickens were in huge iron pots placed over the fires. They were there through the efforts of the two food finders, Tula and Dabale, who had scoured the land for miles out, looking for dinner.

"It was not easy," Tula was saying. "Every day it is harder to find anything. Today we went all the way into the hills to the east. We cannot go further that way. The people told us that if we went further, we would meet the Italian army. And we had to pay a lot for these scrawny birds."

"I wonder what the infantry is doing," said Ibbsa. "They cannot go as far as we. They have no horses. What are they eating?"

"They are eating stones," said Egersa, laughing. "They are turning stones into soup."

"Oh, tell us!" said Shiferaw. "Tell us, medicine man, the story about the stone soup!"

"I cannot do that," said Egersa. "I cannot tell a story the way it should be told. That is what the teller of tales is for. Taffa, teller of tales, tell us the tale of the soup."

All their eyes turned toward Taffa. His eyes twinkled with pleasure at being the center of attention. Slowly he sat down near the fire. His friends sat too, around him in a circle. On the edge of the circle, many others stood. Taffa was a great teller of tales.

"Once upon a time," he began, "Once upon a time, there was a man going from Geddeb to Bekoji. His name was Babilla—not our very own Aleka Babilla Wami—heaven forbid that I speak of that great warrior with disrespect...!"

"You better not if you value your skin," laughed Shiferaw.

"No, this was another Babilla, and this one was a cheat." Taffa paused for effect. His friends strained to listen. "Now on the way," continued Taffa, "it rained very much. Babilla was wet and cold. He ran very fast to a house that he saw beside the road. As he arrived at the house, he shouted, saying 'Please open the door! I am a poor man!'

"Only the maidservant was in the house. She was cooking injera. She felt afraid, but she opened the door for him.

"After he got warm by the fire, Babilla became hungry. He wanted some injera. He said to the woman, 'I have a stone here that makes good stew.' He patted the pocket of his trousers. 'If you will allow me, I'll show you how it is done.'

"The maid thought that this must be a wonderful stone, and she said, 'Fine! I will give you butter and many kinds of spices for the stew.' She brought him a pan. She brought the butter and spices, and Babilla began to cook the stew.

"He put a pot on the fire. The maidservant brought water and poured it into the pot. 'Careful,' said Babilla. 'Just a little. That's good.' Then Babilla removed that magic stone from his pocket. He blew on it, and muttered incantations over it. Then, very slowly and with great reverence, he dropped the magic stone into the pot.

"Soon the water began to boil. Into the pot went the butter. Into the pot went the spices. Around and around Babilla stirred the butter and the spices and the magic stone. Many minutes he took to stir that stew, and all the time the maidservant sat and watched him work. She sniffed the wonderful scent of spices and butter in the air, and she became hungrier and hungrier.

"Finally, Babilla stopped stirring. He put down the stirring spoon and stuck his finger into the pot. Then he stuck his finger into his mouth. 'Ummmmm!' exclaimed Babilla. 'That's good! Come. Bring some injera and let's try it out.'

"The maidservant was starving by this time, and she ran to get the injera. She brought two huge injeras. She gave one to Babilla and kept one for herself. They began to eat. Oh, that stew was good! Of course it was good! There was all that butter and spice in it.

"Babilla and the maidservant ate all the bread and stew. After they had eaten, Babilla took the stone out of the pot and said, 'I bought this stone from a merchant. It was very expensive. It cost me ten thalers. But it was worth it, was it not? Look at the fine stew it made.'

"The maid said, 'That stew was wonderful. I have to have that stone. Please sell it to me. I will give you some cloth that cost me nine thalers in the market.'

"'Done,' said Babilla. He took the cloth and went on his way. After a while, the maid's master, Ato Bekele, with his wife, Waizero Alemitu, came home. When they were seated, the maid brought them coffee and told them about her wonderful stone and how she bought it from Babilla. Ato Bekele and Waizero Alemitu became very angry. Shaking his fist in the air, Ato Bekele raged and said, 'Oh, how men can cheat their fellow men!'

"But there was nothing Ato Bekele could do, for Babilla was long gone, far to the north. It is said that he joined Ras Mikael's cavalry, and every night he goes from campfire to campfire, always with his magic stone, and every night he eats well, and....."

"For God's sake, let's eat this chicken before he gets here!" yelled Shiferaw.

"Wait, boys!" ordered Taffa. "Listen carefully. This Babilla, now. Every night he eats well, and every night he sells another stone to an unsuspecting cavalryman. Last night it was Shiferaw. Tomorrow it may be you!"

"It was not I!! It was not I!" yelled Shiferaw. But his words were drowned in the laughter of his friends.

As their laughter slowly died and their eyes turned toward the greasy chicken steaming in the iron cooking pots, a voice of authority came booming down the mountain out of the dusk: "So my valiant cavalrymen have turned back into ten-year-old shepherds!" cried Babilla Wami. "Is this what I have to work with? Well, get your boyhoods out of your systems! Eat up those chickens and get your gear together. I need coolies....I mean soldiers! I need gun haulers. Eat quickly and enjoy that chicken. You may never see a chicken again, by the great god Waaqa! Come on, my great warriors. Eat up and join me on the ridge in fifteen minutes. Bring ropes and rifles and enough cartridges and water to last you two days. Leave your horses here. You are now real coolies....I mean soldiers!" He let out a roar of a laugh and disappeared into the night's gloom, off to the next campfire to bring his message.

Up and down the line went Babilla Wami, campfire to campfire, until all of his men were up in arms, and then he went to the next battalion, and he did not rest until they were all up, and he led them up the shank of the ridge to a place where they could look down the other side, and there were the two Italian mountain guns. Around them sat Ras Makonnen's gunners, grinning up at the soldiers through the dusk.

"Now," said Babilla Wami, "we take them from here. The gunners will follow. Rope these beasts. Drag them up. Carry the shells. You who do not carry or pull, take the rifles of your comrades."

All through that night, the cavalrymen turned coolies dragged those great guns up the ridge. On each gun there were a hundred and fifty men in front, dragging the guns with strong sisal rope. Behind, a hundred more held the guns in place when they came to spots where the ridge dipped down, so the guns would not bound into the men in front. Another mass of men silently carried the guns and spears and water and dry kolo cereal for their friends, and all together ascended that twisted ridge. Up and up they went, for hours and hours, until they arrived at the spot where Bedane had looked down into the fort.

Then, in the light of a three-quarter moon, the gunners conferred, and decided on a spot: a flat surface behind some rocks where the guns could shoot into the fort unseen, and there they had the soldiers drag the guns, and place them well, and by 4 AM in the morning, with the moon setting in the west and the stars becoming brilliant in the chill hour before false dawn, they were ready. The gunners bowed to the soldiers, and Babilla Wami led his sweating men forward, into the rocks down the hill from the guns, so that if the Italians came out of their fort to take those guns back, they would get a surprise they would never forget.

At dawn, with a great shout, King Tekle Haimanot's men charged the Italians out of the west. Screaming and shouting, they streamed toward the church that was now a fort. Down they went into the dust whenever the Italian machine-guns raked the earth where they had stood. Behind the blasted walls of burnt-out buildings they dove when the Italian artillery in the graveyard opened up on them. Down in the dust they screamed and howled and cursed the enemy.

Up on the ridge the Harari gunners grinned and sighted their guns to where Bedane pointed, down into the fort, to the well, where the hot Ferengi soldiers would go when they had beaten back another attack.

At the second hour after sunrise, King Tekle Haimanot called back his men, and for once, unlike the earlier attacks, there were no bodies left behind. The King had spoken truthfully when he told Menelik that his men knew castles and sieges. Tekle Haimanot brought them all back to safety, all but a few, and these few, wily and sinewy and as strong as wild jackals, hid in the dust in the heat of the day and waited. All was silent.

In the fort, sensing the departure of the enemy, the Italian soldiers came out from behind pillar and post. They brushed themselves off and checked their weapons. They posted just a few sentries, and took their waterskins and canvas water bags and began to converge on the well. They went slowly, relaxed, as though the work of the day had been done. From the ridge, they looked like a colony of ants converging on a piece of honeycomb.

Then came the bark of a mountain gun, and a shell exploded in the midst of the ants. The other gun fired. That shell too blew up a group of ants. The ants started to run around in all directions. The gunners on the hill didn't care. They hadn't come to kill ants. They had come to close up the well. The gunners stood on the ridge and looked at the fort with their binoculars. They talked among themselves with satisfied smiles. The first two shells had come very close to the well.

The gunners went back to their guns and recalibrated them. The shells flew again. This time, they hit even closer to the well.

On the third try, they hit the well.

The ants in the fort turned their mountain guns toward the ridge and fired them. But they didn't know where to fire, and there was no damage.

Ras Makonnen's gunners fired again and again. Stones and dust fell into the well. The sides caved in. They kept firing until the well was a pile of rubble. Even if the Ferengis cleaned it out, it would be useless. Their water would be mud.

A column of Ferengi soldiers came out of the fort, formed a line, and started up the ridge.

"They are black," said Bedane.

"Eh?" said Babilla Wami, peering down at them.

"They are black," repeated Bedane. "I thought the Ferengi were white."

"I wish I had your eyes," said Babilla Wami. "Those are not Ferengi. Those are askaris—men from the coast, paid by the Ferengis to kill us." The aleka laughed. "They will get a lesson today. Listen, sharp-eyed soldier, look even more carefully and you will see white men. Those are the officers. Aim for them when they get up here. It is more fun. If you hit enough officers, you can watch their soldiers run around like idiots, yelling and diving."

"Oh, like they will be shooting at us to watch our men acting like monkeys," said Bedane, sighting his rifle.

Babilla Wami gave a twist to the leaf in his nostril, pinching it for more aroma. "Except," he said, "since we are the same color as our men, it is harder for them to tell who we are." He smiled. "It is somewhat of an advantage," he said.

Down in the fort the Italian guns blazed away at the ridge. The Ferengi line came steadily up the hill. There were hundreds of them. Babilla Wami looked to his left and right. Six hundred of his men lay out of sight, down in the rocks.

The Ferengi were closer now, and Babilla Wami stood, put two fingers to his mouth, and blew a piercing whistle. Six hundred men came up out of the rocks, rifles at the ready. "Fire!" yelled Babilla Wami, and six hundred rifles went off with a roar. There was the smoke, and the smell of it, and in the aftermath of the fusillade what was left of the Ferengi line stood for a second as if dazed, then dove for cover.

"Fire! Fire!" yelled Babilla Wami over and over.

Some of the askaris were bolting for the fort. The bullets caught a few of them and dropped them, and made the others run even faster. Soon other bunches of askaris and even some Italian officers were running down the hill.

"Cease fire! Cease fire!" screamed Babilla Wami. Some of his soldiers began to run after the askaris.

"Do not follow! Do not follow!" roared the Aleka. Some of the men ran down anyway, to take the guns and belongings of the fallen enemy. They went no farther than that before their officers caught them.

"Why chase them?" asked Babilla Wami, shrugging his shoulders. "They are dead men anyway. They will dry up and blow away without their well. Why risk death for no reason? We will save ourselves for the big battle. That is the time for a worthy death."

He looked at the muzzle of his rifle, blew at it, and winked at Bedane. Bedane looked at the older warrior grimly, and nodded.

The white flag came out of the fort one hour after daybreak the next morning. Three Italian officers on horseback carried it, walking their horses slowly and steadily, directly toward the imperial tent.

Menelik did not wait for them to arrive. He summoned his Minister of the Pen and said to him, "We have the fort. There is no question of that. We have the garrison, and the relief force for Amba Alagie, and what is left of the Amba detachment. I'll bet we have three thousand men, or close to it."

"A good reckoning, my Lord," said the minister.

"Here is the letter I want you to take to Baratieri...."

"I, my Lord?" exclaimed the minister, with some alarm.

"No, of course not. Look over this letter, put it in graceful language, and have it delivered to Baratieri at Adigrat. Send...who should go?"

"Send a ras and a dejazmach. That is protocol," said the minister.

"And a guard to protect them. Let's see. Who should I send? I'd like to send Alula, but they'd murder him on the spot. Let's send Wagshum Guangul. They've been trying to turn him. They will think that he will want to talk on his own behalf. They will think he will be of value to them, so they will honor his flag. Little do they know! With him I'll send.....I'll send..... no, no dejazmach. I'll send that kanyazmach that brought the news about the fort. What's his name? Didda? Didda. That's it. I'll send him, and for a guard he can take that bunch of troopers who hauled those guns up the ridge. Ha! They'll scare the hell out of Baratieri. And he will see how far south my support comes from. I know him, my brother. He is a driven man. He will want to destroy Us as soon as he can, and the whole Empire with Us.

"Now, the letter...." The Emperor paused. "Here is what I want you to say: say to Baratieri that I give him back his soldiers with no conditions attached. Say that they have fought bravely and that...."

"My Lord!" gasped the Minister of the Pen. "You would just give them away? Let us keep them. Send them to Addis. Who knows what will happen tomorrow? Keep them for bargaining if we need them. Don't just throw them away!"

The Emperor's eyes narrowed and his speech became formal. "Do not question this," he said. "I have thought this out. Tell Baratieri that We do this as a token of Our interest in peace. Say that We wish this war to end; that We wish the frontier to be at the Mareb River, as was stated in the treaty; that We wish talks to begin between our nations. Tell him that the only demand We make is that Italy recognize the complete independence and sovereignty of Ethiopia. Then, Minister, take that letter to Wagshum Guangul and send him on his way. And then," Menelik's eyes gleamed, "then you will give copies of that letter to the French, the English, the Russians, the Americans, the Japanese, and to every newspaperman you can find!" Menelik paused, then said, "You know as well as I do, my Minister, that the world grows larger and larger for us every day. Our fate will be determined not simply by what we do on the field of battle, but by how our victory appears to the world at large. I am determined that our ancient empire be seen as such— an ancient civilization. I am determined that the world see this invasion for what it is—a land grab by a bunch of fools. This nation will not bow down before a horde of pirates! We will slaughter them first. But we must be seen to extend the olive branch. That will be reported all over the world."

"But to simply let this cache of three thousand enemies just go!" said the Minister of the Pen. "I cannot see it."

"Do not worry yourself about it," said Menelik. "I intend to use these men to our great advantage, not just in world opinion, but in this war. I know Baratieri. He will snap up this offer. His only thought will be to put his army back together again, and use it to strike us as hard as possible. And when he does, he will have a surprise worthy of his motives. He will find himself as thirsty as his soldiers in this little fort are now. That will be very satisfying to Me."

So it was that Bedane and Babilla Wami found themselves in the front rank of a guard of three hundred mounted riflemen, accompanying Wagshum Guangul and General Albertone, commander of the Italian Makelle division, to Adigrat, the headquarters of the Italian army. Down they rode toward the east along an ever-narrowing valley between jagged mountain ranges.

At last they encountered a mounted Italian patrol, which, seeing their white flag of truce, stood its ground. Wagshum Guangul halted, and behind him his cavalrymen came to a quiet stop. Emboldened by this turn of events, the patrol's lieutenant demanded to know their business. Guangul rode forward, holding the reins of Albertone's horse, and the king spoke to the lieutenant in Italian.

"We have come," he said, "as an emissary of His Majesty Menelik, Emperor of All the Ethiopias. We announce the capture of your fort at Makelle, along with its garrison. We wish to speak with your general, Baratieri. We bring a peace offering." With that, the Wagshum jerked at the reins of Albertone's horse and brought him forward. "Bring us to Baratieri," he commanded, "and no tricks, or this man dies instantly."

The Italian lieutenant's face hardened, and he was about to speak harshly, but then, astonished, he recognized General Albertone, and thought better of it. Fifteen percent of the army was under the command of Albertone, and this Ethiopian warlord was saying that they had captured it. The lieutenant swallowed his words, composed himself, and said, "We will lead you. When I tell you to stop, you must leave your men. You and the officers of your choice will then come forward under the flag of truce."

"Agreed," said the Wagshum. "General Albertone will stay with my troops as surety for my safety. Should anything befall me or my officers, he will die immediately. And," the Wagshum paused for emphasis, "as soon as Menelik hears of my difficulties, your three thousand men at Makelle will die."

"Agreed," said the lieutenant. "Be pleased to follow us, sir, you and your men." He wheeled his horse and led on.

As they rode, the valley opened wider, and on the plain before them the Ethiopian troopers could see the camp of the Italians far in the distance. Above them in the hills to the left were machine-gun emplacements. To their right, in a row, were fifty of the powerful mountain artillery guns. Only God knew how many others there were, and where they were. Directly in front of them, in the distance, were the tents of the army, and beyond the tents, the town of Adigrat itself, sheltered below the cliffs of a towering escarpment.

"Halt!" said the lieutenant, and his arm went up. "Emissary and selected officers forward!" he yelled, and his arm pointed out straight. He and his patrol moved forward. Following him at a distance, Wagshum Guangul, three of his officers, and the truce flag bearer rode proudly toward the distant tents. Kanyasmach Didda was left in charge of his troops and of the Italian general. For show, he kept his pistol squarely at Albertone's chest.

A vast stillness came over the warriors and their mounts. All were quiet. None spoke. Here and there a horse snorted and then was still again. Whatever thoughts the men had, they kept to themselves. The minutes went slowly and the hot sun beat down on their heads. The men pulled the folds of their gabis up over their heads. There would be no sunstroke in these ranks.

Suddenly, from the cliffs above them, there came a shout in Italian, followed by laughter. The men gazed up, only to see an Italian machine-gunner pointing his gun directly at them and grinning. He shouted at them again and laughed. "Dah dah dah dah dah dah!" he said, swiveling his gun back and forth like he was mowing them down. "Dah dah dah dah dah dah!"

Another Italian jumped up on top of some sandbags and shouted, then jammed a bullet clip into his rifle, aimed at them, and shouted at them again.

Kanyasmach Didda wheeled his horse and faced his men. His stentorian voice barreled out over the sands: "Do not respond, men! Do not respond to them in any way. Do not shoot, or shout, or raise a fist to them. Stay in your ranks and be still."

"Yet abatih?" came a shout from the hills in Amharic. "Min abatih?" "Where is your father?" "Who is your father?" Then more laughter. And in Italian, unintelligible to the troopers, but understood clearly by them nevertheless, "We will cut you to ribbons! We will massacre you, you goddamn savages. Go back to your jungle!"

The troopers sat and stared sullenly ahead. Didda alone glared at the Italians on the cliffs. "Monkeys!" he thought to himself. "Hide in the rocks like baboons. You are going to get one hell of a surprise soon."

The minutes drifted into hours. The Italians tired of their game, and soon, once again, there was nothing but silence.

In the mid-afternoon, riders were seen approaching from the Italian camp. At first they appeared simply as moving specks, but soon the troopers could make out Wagshum Guangul and his officers and other men: white men. There were three of them. They came quickly, and Guangul motioned Didda to bring Albertone forward. Guangul took the reins of Albertone's horse and handed them back to the general, who nodded to him. "You are free," said Guangul.

"My thanks," answered Albertone in Amharic. "What of my men?"

"Soon," said Guangul. He turned his horse toward the west and signaled Didda.

"Wheel to the right, in place!" thundered Didda. Three hundred horses turned as one. Didda, Wagshum Guangul, and Guangul's officers galloped to the head of their command. The Italian soldiers on the cliffs started yelling again. "We will get you! We will get you, you savages! You fools!" they yelled.

But Albertone was having none of it. Once again a general in command, he glared up at them and shook his fist. "If I find out who you are," he yelled, "I will have your eyes cut out of your heads! What kind of idiots are you? You are soldiers? You sound like a bunch of street vendors! Silence! You have disgraced our army! Silence!" And there was silence. Immediate silence.

Wagshum Guangul led the Oromo troopers back down the valley to the west.

When they had ridden nearly to Makelle, King Guangul halted. "Kanyazmach Didda, come here," he said.

Didda dismounted and approached the King of Wag and Lasta.

"Your troopers behaved well, my friend," said Guangul. "Extremely well. I am happy you are with us. I hope we are near each other in the fight."

Didda bowed low, then reached up to grasp the King's hand, which he kissed. "We are happy to be of service, my lord," he said. "We will be there when you need us." He bowed again and remounted.

Guangul and his officers rode off. When they were some distance away, Kanyazmach Didda turned to Babilla and said, "A fine nobleman, that one."

"Yes, sir," said Babilla.

"He was pleased with our men," said Didda, "and I was too. Double rations for them tonight, if you can find any, and tella, too, if there is any left in this godforsaken place. Dismiss your men, sir."

"Yes, sir," said Babilla.

After Didda had ridden off, Babilla Wami turned to Bedane and said, "We did well."

"I thought someone would start shooting when those men on the cliffs were hooting at us," said Bedane.

"It is well that no one did," said Babilla Wami. "There is an old saying: 'He who raises his voice, loses.'" The aleka paused. "Except in battle, of course," he added. "In battle, you scream like a banshee. It feels good."

"I am puzzled," said Bedane. "Why do we give back three thousand men who will turn around and fight us again?"

"I don't know," said Babilla, scratching his head. "Perhaps Atse Menelik wants to even the sides, to make it a better fight. I don't know." He grinned. "Come," he said, "let's get these boys back to camp, and find us some tella."

That evening, in the Italian headquarters, Baratieri welcomed Albertone and, as was usual, told his generals what was happening. It seemed he always had to tell them, he thought to himself. Why were good soldiers like them such dullards when it came to the big picture? Well, that was why he was in command and they were not.

"So," said Baratieri, "You question Menelik's motives? They are transparent. One, he has no food. Two, he has no water. Three, he has foreign observers with him. He wants to impress them with his civility. So," he continued, ticking off his points on his fingers, "he gives us back our soldiers that he can neither feed nor water, and he looks good in the eyes of the foreign press. As if that makes any difference." He paused. "So," he began again, his bushy eyebrows lifting and his moustache wiggling, "here is what we do. The exchange is scheduled for two hours after sunrise three days from now? Get the army ready to move. Once we have our men, we conduct a full-scale assault. We re-take that town. We move south from there. We aim straight for Menelik's tent. We back them up against the escarpment, open up with every mountain gun we can find, and destroy them. Wreck their formations. Wreck their will. Give them hunger and thirst like they have never seen it before! By God, I am going to destroy this jungle chieftain and deliver this place to King Umberto if it is the last thing I ever do! Leave me alone. Let me think."

At dawn on the appointed day, three Italian generals stood on the crest of a ridge overlooking the valley of Makelle from the east. There they awaited the return of the captured Italian troops. Behind them, out of sight, were the massed brigades of the Italian army. Before them was the brooding plain of Makelle. They stood looking through their binoculars.

"See," said Albertone, "you can just make out the top of the church down there."

"Where now there is no water, and six of our mountain guns, I presume," commented Dabormida. "Any chance of getting our cannon back?"

"Not negotiable," said Arimondi. "Lucky to get Albertone's men back."

"Well, I guess we'll get them soon enough," said Dabormida, "when we smash through their camps."

The day grew brighter by the minute, but still the mist hung low in the valley. Dabormida scanned the terrain. "Now after we take the town, then we continue straight south, straight toward Menelik's tent," he said to no one in particular. His glasses rested on the southern reaches of the plain. "I cannot see Menelik's tent. I cannot see any tents, as a matter of fact."

"It is too far away," said Albertone. "Four miles at least from the town."

Dabormida sighed, then grunted. "No, Albertone, I mean I can see no tents at all. I should be able to see some tents down there."

"The mist is thick," said Arimondi, "thick with cloud and thick with cooking fires."

Behind the generals, a blood-red sun rose in a cloudless sky.

"As if they have anything left to cook," said Dabormida. "Well, enough of this. Everything is set. Let's have breakfast, then come back for another look. They are not due for what, another hour-and-a-half? Plenty of time. This will be fun."

An hour-and-a-half later, their bellies full of breakfast, the three generals and their staffs walked up the ridge again. "I will take the center," said Arimondi as they walked. "I will take the town and head for Menelik's headquarters. Dabormida, you will be on my right. Seize the ridge they shelled Albertone from, then swing west and south, and cut off their retreat to the west. Albertone, take your brigade to my left, sweep down the eastern reaches of the valley, then cut in and press them towards me. It will be a slaughter."

"I still cannot see any tents," said Dabormida, cresting the hill.

"Still the mist?" asked Arimondi. He looked up and his jaw dropped. The morning mist had lifted, and Dabormida was right. There were no tents.

But there were dust columns everywhere. Dust was being kicked up into the air everywhere along the valley. Instantly the generals brought their binoculars up to behold a striking sight.

Everywhere in the valley there were columns of Ethiopians, mounted and on foot, and they were heading north.

"They are trying to flank us!" shouted Dabormida.

"Steady, General," said Arimondi. "They have flanked themselves. They are wide open."

"They don't know we are here!" exclaimed Albertone. "They think we are just a party to pick up our troops. They don't know our army is all here. What an opportunity. We will sweep them away. Lieutenant. Carry a message to General Baratieri. Get him up here. A miracle has happened. We have just conquered Ethiopia!" The lieutenant ran down the hill towards the main army.

But a second later, a colonel cried, "Generals!" with such force and alarm that all three of them jumped and looked around at him. The colonel was pointing downhill.

There, coming out of the trees, was a single line of three thousand men. The line was over a mile long. There were both Italians and askaris. All of them had their hands in the air, and were shouting at the generals not to shoot, that they were friends, comrades. They came up the hill through the fields, until they were about twenty-five feet from the tree line.

Then, behind them, out of the trees walked a double row of Ethiopian infantry. There must have been five or six thousand of them. The sight of them took the Italian generals absolutely by surprise.

A single Ethiopian rider, carrying a white flag of truce, galloped his mount furiously up the hill until he was within a few feet of the Italian soldiers. He was finely dressed, and had a regal bearing. It was the Ras of Tigre himself.

"A tu servicio!" said Mengesha. "Here are your men, as we promised. And no funny business, gentlemen. We know your army is near. We know exactly where it is. And I will tell you this: I have given full command of my troops over to my general for the day." Mengesha pointed downhill with his white-flagged spear. "I have no control over him now. I think you know him?"

Down at the bottom of the hill, a rider walked his black horse slowly out of the trees. The rider was of slight build, and carried a rifle crosswise in his arms. It was Alula.

The Italian generals looked glumly at the Ras.

"Ah, I see by your expressions that you do know him," said Mengesha. "Well, what can I say? You know as well as I just what he is capable of if he gets nervous. Wouldn't that be a fine sight—a mass execution?"

"You wouldn't!" exclaimed Arimondi.

"Of course I wouldn't, General," said Mengesha. "Neither would you. But neither of us is Alula, eh?" The Ras paused. "Now, gentlemen, we will give you your men, but it may take some time. First, we need to inspect each of them, to make sure they aren't taking away anything that doesn't belong to them."

"What could they take away, goddammit!" exploded Dabormida. "All they have are their pants and shirts. You've even taken their shoes!"

"Ah, yes," said Mengesha coldly. "Well, you see, that is the problem. You know the old story about how Ethiopians view their earth as sacred. Well, all of your men down there—their feet are covered with Ethiopian dust. We will have to remove it before they come any further. They cannot take it out of our country. This may take some time. Should we brush it off or wait for water? You see our quandary? At any rate, we shall see. Perhaps it will depend on how the day goes, eh?"

Mengesha glanced back at the distant Ethiopian columns. "Our forward units are probably in Adua by now," he said. "Soon we shall cross the Mareb. Then we shall have a struggle with that gentleman down there." He pointed at Alula. "He will want to go further north. He wants his old capital of Asmara back. The rest of us will want to circle around to the northeast, to cut you off from the sea and watch you starve."

Another group of Italian soldiers was walking quickly up the hill, surrounding General Baratieri. Mengesha glanced at them. "My complements to your commander," said the Ras. "Tell him I am sorry I cannot stay to speak with him directly. Etcetera. Tally ho, what?" he ended in English. He wheeled his horse and sped back down the hill.

"You are the ones who will starve!" shouted Dabormida angrily at the departing Ras.

"What is this shouting about?" asked Baratieri, coming up the hill. "What....what is this?" he asked, his voice trailing off to a whisper. "Who are those men down there?"

"My men," said Albertone quietly. "As hostages."

"The Ethiopians are moving to flank us, sir," said Arimondi.

"This is your good news? Should I have the messenger shot, or you?"

"Sir, it was what we saw before they pushed the hostages out of the trees."

The cold steel of understanding riveted Baratieri to the ground. Instantly he assessed his position. Forward. Exposed. Possibly cut off from reinforcements. A race to the Mareb. A race to the edge of the escarpment. A battle to maintain the passes down to the sea. Abandonment of Adigrat, of Asmara and Keren and Kassala and Bogos, of the garrisons of those places and at the string of small forts along the roads of Eritrea. A defense of Massawa, while they waited for the 10,000 reinforcements said to be coming any day. What? What did 'any day' mean now? The loss of Eritrea instead of the conquering of Ethiopia. My God, thought Baratieri. And just two days before, the telegram from Prime Minister Crispi insisting on a victory at any price. At any sacrifice, he had said. Italy would prefer a loss of two or three thousand men to a retreat which would seem dishonorable, he had written. Indeed, I cannot retreat, thought Baratieri. It would turn into a rout.

"Sir? Sir?" Arimondi's voice broke through his reverie, his calculations. He turned toward the voice.

"Should I prepare the army for a retreat on Adigrat, General Baratieri?" asked Arimondi.

Baratieri swallowed hard and said, "General Arimondi, my fine brave generals, prepare the army to move. But not to Adigrat. Simply ready them for a march, and then meet me in my tent in one hour."

PART VI

ADUA

One week later, on a frosty highland morning, Menelik and his rases and commanders sat on horseback on a mountain ridge northeast of Adua and looked off toward the south. They looked at mountains as jagged and blasted as any on earth. Those peaks looked like a jumble of smashed teeth in the mouth of a deranged hyena.

To the west, the land softened into a plain. On the edge of that plain stood the town of Adua. A year before, Baratieri's troops had occupied that town, and it was only through the tireless efforts of Mengesha and Alula that he had been forced to withdraw. He left behind an Ethiopian population that with one heart hated the Italian general.

Now Baratieri was back. His army lay in these hellish mountains south of where Menelik and his men now sat on their horses. There were 20,000 Italians and askaris down there, and they were giving Menelik fits.

Menelik had expected Baratieri to fall back on Adigrat, and then fall back further, into Eritrea. He had expected the general to be frightened of encirclement. But Baratieri had not done what the Emperor had expected. He had not retreated. Instead, he had confronted the Ethiopians once again, and now he was down in those hills, constantly repositioning his forces, moving about, making Menelik wonder when and where he would strike next.

"I say we leave him here and go further north," said Alula. "Take Asmara and Keren. Invest the passes to Massawa. Starve this son of a dog."

"We already have half the cavalry out doing just that," said Ras Mikael. "Except for taking the towns, we control that country right now. Of what use is an army of 100,000 if it runs around looking for thirst and famine?"

"The power of the enemy is right here," said Ras Makonnen. "This is what we must destroy. We cannot run from that fact."

Menelik had already tried to run from that fact twice now. First he had tried to outflank Baratieri by his march to Adua. Just this past week, he had sent Makonnen and the Wagshum north and east, to the banks of the Mareb, in an attempt to lure Baratieri away from the heartland. It hadn't worked, and Makonnen's weary veterans had staggered back exhausted, thirsty, and famished. Menelik had had to open up some of the last reserve food supplies to get them back into shape.

Alula's idea had a lot of merit, thought Menelik, but he just couldn't do it. First, by staying here, he could count on a trickle of supplies coming in from the west, from beyond Adua and Axum, from the people of Tigre and the Simien. If he moved north, perhaps his army could scour the land for food, but the border people up there had allegiances that swayed back and forth with whoever controlled the area at the time. It would be like pulling teeth to get any supplies out of there.

Second, Menelik wished to abide by his word. He had signed a treaty stating that the Mareb River was the northern border of Ethiopia, and although the Italians had tried to trick him by that treaty into handing over his imperial powers to them, in effect making Ethiopia a province of Italy, still he wished the Europeans to see that he kept up his part of the bargain. Menelik was playing on a larger stage than most of his countrymen. His warriors were defending their motherland; as for Menelik, he was making sure that the world would see the struggle of a great and ancient civilization against foreign invaders.

Third, Menelik was truly confounded by the actions of Italy. For fifteen hundred years Ethiopia had been beset and besieged by hostile Muslim imams and mullahs and crazed mahdis of one kind or another. Even though Mohammed himself had declared that Ethiopia was never to be the victim of a jihad, that proclamation had never held sway. The fanatics that grew in the surrounding deserts had always tried to destroy this highland fortress of Christ. For hundreds of years, Ethiopia had struggled to maintain ties with the rest of Christendom. For centuries, the rumor of King John of Ethiopia had swirled through the Christian kingdoms and principalities of Europe. Now, at last, fellow Christians had come to the borders of Ethiopia; strange, pale-white Christians, to be sure, but in numbers sufficient to turn back the Muslim tide. From Britain they came, and from France and Germany and Switzerland and Russia, and from Italy.

And when they got to the borders of Ethiopia, what did they want to do? They didn't want to join Ethiopia in throwing back the Muslim enemy.

No, they wanted to overthrow Him, Menelik, and reduce his empire to slavery! This truly perplexed Menelik. He simply could not understand it.

But these Italians now: although they had made themselves his enemy, still, they were Christians, and Menelik found it very difficult to kill Christians. There was something dreadfully wrong in that. What Menelik really wanted to do was to make them go away—by diplomacy, by an overwhelming show of force, by intrigue—by whatever means it took to make them leave. The last thing he wanted to do was to kill them. But they were making it very hard; very hard. And his army was full of Muslims and animists—pagans, for Christ's sake! He was killing Christians with pagans! He could scarcely believe it.

"So now he has moved his lines again," said Menelik.

"Yes, my Lord," said Makonnen. "Now he faces west, toward Adua. Now he threatens Adua again, and Axum."

"So he stretches us out. He holds the interior. Good planning on his part. With a smaller force, he can control a large adversary."

"Yes, my Lord," said Makonnen. "He wants to stretch us until we snap—from hunger."

"Well, we can stretch, and a lot further than he thinks we can. King Tekle Haimanot."

"Janhoi?"

"Bring your army around to the south of Makonnen's. You will anchor the right wing. King Guangul, you will support Tekle Haymanot. Makonnen, you will become the new center, right in front of Adua, along with Ras Mikael's cavalry. Then Ras Mengesha, your Tigreans will be on the left. Behind you, in reserve, will be the troops of Ras Sebhat and Ras Hagos. And right here, this will be the left wing. Ras Alula, you will anchor our lines here, please. Be prepared to move down on the enemy at a moment's notice. And Alula, be vigilant. Keep your spies out and your patrols strong. I want to know what that man does before he does it. Understood?"

"Delighted, Your Majesty."

"My army will be behind yours, Makonnen, in reserve. We will be ready to move right or left, or forward with you if the situation demands it. Dejazmach Baltcha, you will be my liaison with King Tekle Haimanot and you will command the right wing. Makonnen, you will be my Fitawrary and command the center, and Grazmach Abate, you will command the left. Ras Alula, you will take your orders from Ras Mengesha. Is that clear? Further, you will not go off by yourself on your own. You will stay with your troops except when you are in conference with the rest of us. You are a valuable soldier, Alula, but I must be able to find you when I need you. Agreed?"

"I am your servant, Janhoi," hissed Alula.

Menelik, satisfied with his deployment, sat silently and looked out over that ragged wasteland below them. Then he said, "Brothers, cousins, here is the problem I see, and here is where Baratieri is strong: shortly, if there is no battle, our armies will starve. If that happens, we must disperse our armies. If that happens, Baratieri will take Tigre. Next will be Lasta. Then Wollo. One by one your kingdoms will fall. If we do as Alula suggests and go north, we will just let our armies starve in a different place, and the final result will be the same. No, somehow we must bring him to battle. But if we attack him, he will slaughter our armies with his long-range guns. So, we must make him attack us. There is one way we can make him do that," said Menelik. "We can make him think we are weak. Makonnen, what has he offered you lately?"

"I, my Lord? Nothing much, really. He keeps offering me your Empire. I keep asking for Somalia as well, but he won't give it. We are at an impasse."

"Guangul?"

"Nothing like that. Only the empire. No talk of other nations. I do not think he is serious."

"He offers me only Tigre!" said Mengesha. "I am insulted. No talk of empire at all. And he refuses to grant me trading rights at Massawa and control over the trade routes."

"All he has offered me is a few guns to defend Gondar and cooperation in taking Kassala from the Dervishes," said Tekle Haimanot. "I too am insulted."

"That is what you get for living so far away," said Mikael. "Go back to your mountains and sulk."

"I too am insulted," said Alula. "All he offers is 10,000 thalers for my head. I am worth much more!"

Amid the general laughter, no man was more amused than Menelik himself. "Gentlemen," he said when the laughter had run its course, "I am shocked, shocked, at how easily you are insulted! And you, Makonnen, my cousin! Not even my entire empire is enough for you? What an appetite!" The Emperor paused, and said, "Now, my brothers, my cousins, here is what I ask of you: when the Italian's spies come again to you, appear to be more interested than before. Soften your demands. Makonnen, give up on Somalia. Mengesha, drop your request for trade rights. And whenever you meet with them, be sure to indicate that there is hardly any food left. That is what I want him to hear. Make him think that we are weak. Make him think that if there is a battle, your armies will suddenly disappear. Make him think that he can destroy us with one well-placed thrust. Make him attack us. We must get him out of his fort and away from his guns. Then we can win."

"How is our supply of food, Janhoi?" asked Guangul.

"We have three days' supply," said Menelik. "We must pretend that once again we are all poor shepherds in the hills, and stretch that food to last ten days. Then perhaps more will come in from the south."

"It will not be the first time Ethiopian bellies have shrunk," said Tekle Haimanot.

"In that respect," said Mengesha, "perhaps the famine was good for us. It gave us practice."

"So," said Menelik. "There is our plan. Make him think we are weak and starving and we will break at the first attack. Good luck, and may you all find vast empires! Now, let us go and swing our armies around to contain that jackal down there! Innehid!"

February 29, 1896—10:45 am

The Italian army had stationed itself on the Hill of Sauria. It was a strong position. To the southeast was Adigrat; to the southwest, Makelle. To the north was the small town of Entichio; to the west, Adua. Baratieri could strike at Adua at any time. He could retreat to Entichio at a moment's notice, or to Adigrat. Either town brought him closer to his base at Asmara and his seaport at Massawa. It was a good place to be: compact, easily defended, a spearhead aimed at Menelik and the African rabble.

But the place was becoming indefensible. It had nothing to do with the hill. It had to do with food. The Ethiopians, starving as they were, were constantly sending out columns to cut the Italian supplies and capture the goods for themselves. Transportation from the coast was beginning to break down. The army was down to seven days' rations. It was time to do something.

Around the table in the Headquarters tent sat Generals Arimondi, Albertone, Dabormida, Elleni, and Colonel Galliano. Baratieri stood, fidgeted, and paced back and forth, occasionally pointing at the large map of the area spread out over the table.

"It is time to do something,' he said. "We must decide. Here are two courses of action. One is to fall back for the time being, wait for reinforcements, replenish our supplies, and then move forward again, striking hard. By doing that, we force Menelik to continue in the field. We know his army has only about two days' rations left. We force him to disperse his troops in search of food. His army sees his weakness, begins to lose faith. It begins to fall apart. Our overtures to certain rases begin to take effect. Major desertions. Major problems for Signore Menelik. His coalition falls. His Empire falls. To us. That is one course, and here is the bad side of it. It takes months, and Rome wants a quick victory."

"It seems to be what we have already been doing for two months now," said Arimondi. He ran his hand through his hair. "It has not worked before. Why should it work now?"

"It works now because of the timing," said Baratieri. "The stretching of the resources of the enemy to the breaking point. But it takes time."

"The enemy," said Elleni wryly, "seems to be able to stretch a long distance, and for a long time." Elleni was older than the rest, with dry, taut skin under a wispy white moustache. A good soldier. A good technician. Baratieri looked at him.

"Here is the second course of action," said Baratieri. "It is to strike. Now. Advance on the whole front. Achieve forward positions. Bring up our guns to where they can play the devil with the Ethiopian formations. Pound them. At the same time, under cover of the barrage, charge the center, break them in two, drive their flanks up against the mountains, bring up the guns again, and smash them to bits. Scatter them. Break them into hordes of hungry scavengers. Finish them now!"

"By God, yes!" Dabormida shouted, slamming his meaty fist down on the table. "That is what we should do. That is what we must do, for the glory of Italy!"

"But if they do not break," said Albertone, remembering Amba Alagie, "we find ourselves surrounded by sixty thousand shrieking hellions, and in the middle of an artillery duel. They have cannon too, you know."

"Popguns!" exploded Dabormida. "Ancient garbage!"

"And six of our guns, too, General Dabormida," said Elleni quietly. "And ammunition. Do you remember Makelle?"

Arimondi waited for silence, and then asked of Baratieri, "My General, what is the latest we know of their willingness to fight? Have you assurances from any of the rases that they will desert Menelik and come over to us?"

"I have assurances from all of them, even that back-biter Makonnen, who tells me he wants to be King of Ethiopia under a regency of Rome. I tell you, I don't trust him as far as I can throw him. All the others—Mengesha, Tekle Haimenot, Guangul, Mikael—every one of them wants the kingdom for himself. Every one of them has told me he will come over."

"Like Ras Sebhat?" asked Galliano. Galliano had been given charge of the brigade of askaris. "Ras Sebhat was with us. He swore it. Now he sits next to Menelik. Heard the name Alula and left. You cannot trust any of them, General. They will go with the one they think will win."

Baratieri brought himself up to full height. His medals shook on his chest. He pounded his fist into his hand. "Then we will give them a winner!" he exclaimed. "I have made up my mind. It doesn't matter if any of them come over, Galliano. Even if none of them do, their armies are starving. A third of their men are away at Axum. A third of them are out foraging, stealing our supplies, ravaging the countryside, useless. More of them are sick. It will be a battle of equal strengths, and we will smash them! We must attack!"

"Bravo!" cried Dabormida. "I salute you, my General! We are with you all the way. We will tear them to pieces."

"If we do this right," said Baratieri, "we will win the day and keep our casualties to a minimum."

"Why even speak of casualties?" boomed Dabormida. "Let us get after them. Two or three thousand casualties will be worth it if it brings us Empire!"

Baratieri looked at him with steely eyes. "Exactly, General Dabormida," he said. "Exactly. We must be prepared to pay the price. For the prize is Empire! Now, all of you. It is decided. We attack. Go back to your commands and make ready your men. Then return here in an hour. I will have maps ready for you, and I will show you the plan."

Here is what Baratieri knew: as for his political game, the rases could still be won over. All he needed was to show them a great victory.

As of the previous night, he had sent a letter to Menelik suggesting that two sides consider a truce. No reply had yet been received. It was inconceivable that the Emperor would attack him until after he had replied; nor would he expect an attack until after he had replied. This was an old rule of warfare, one which Baratieri was willing to bend to gain a victory.

His spies had told him of the sickness and hunger in Menelik's army. Whole divisions and units were already on their way back to the south, or not coming forward.

Menelik did not have the strength nor the will to strike northward. Consequently, what was left of his diminishing army lay hungry and sick in this spot, ripe for the picking, afraid of his guns, afraid of his crack mountain battalions.

All of these things he considered, and he saw an opening. He would feint to the left and to the right, establish a strong central position, barrage the demoralized Ethiopians, and then sweep forward, ripping apart the African center, taking the town of Adua, threatening Axum, and splitting and mangling the two wings of the Ethiopian army, leaving them hanging onto their eerie, evil crags, starving and dying of thirst.

Two other things Baratieri knew. First, five days ago, he had received a wire from Crispi, the Secretary of State. In that wire, Crispi had said that his 10,000 reinforcements were already on the sea, on their way to him. But Baratieri remembered also that earlier message from the Secretary, in which Crispi had said that time was of the essence; that a victory needed to be won or grave international consequences would follow; that two or three thousand casualties would not be looked upon as too many; and that he was not to wait for the reinforcements but to begin an offensive immediately.

He had not discussed that earlier message with anybody. "Two or three thousand casualties would be acceptable." That is what Crispi had written to him. He, Baratieri, was the only one who knew that. But Dabormida, that buffoon, that great, insufferable braggart, that bully, that blunderer! Dabormida had just repeated Crispi's statement word for word. That could mean only one thing: Dabormida was in on it. Dabormida was Crispi's man in the colony. Or one of them. Could there be more? Could there be a cabal, a nest of them, plotting to get rid of him, plotting to get rid of Baratieri? Was this fleet of troop transports also bringing his successor? Fools! He could not let this happen. It would be the ruin of the colony if he were to be replaced. What did Crispi know about running a colony? What did any of them know, sitting around in their posh villas in Rome and Venice, in Milan and Palermo? What did Dabormida know, for God's sake, about anything other than bluster and braggadocio?

That is what had put the icing on the cake for Baratieri. So they wanted casualties? So they wanted a great victory? Well, he would give them casualties! As for the victory, there was a fine chance of it.

At noon, the generals gathered once again in the headquarters tent. On the table, on top of the large map, were scattered smaller field copies of that map, a copy for each of them. They were all used to this. Baratieri was fond of maps. Sometimes they joked that maps were more important to the commander than the ground they represented. But they also knew that his maps were detailed and accurate. They listened carefully as Baratieri outlined his plan.

"The map is aligned with magnetic north," he said. "See how the battle sweeps toward the west. Tonight, at 9:30 PM, your brigades will begin to move. The keystone of the plan is here, the Hill of Belah. That is where we will build our center for tomorrow's barrage. Almost all of our artillery will be stationed there. Arimondi, your brigade will hold that line."

Baratieri turned to Albertone. "General," he said, "your unit will be the left flank. You will proceed on this track south of Belah. It enters a small valley, and then comes up against this hill called Kidane Meheret. You will take up a defense position there. If there is a charge by the enemy against the center, you will provide support. You will have six guns with you, and machine-guns. I also give you a battalion of Alpini."

"There will be no charge at the center,' snorted Dabormida. "The savages will be holed up behind any rock they can find, covering their eyes."

Baratieri turned toward Dabormida. Ignoring his outburst, the Commander said, "General, you will advance to the Spur of Belah, and fortify it heavily. You will extend your lines across the valley to the north, to where the cliffs of Mount Atgebat come down. This is most important. You will be facing Ras Mengesha and Ras Alula. Even if Mengesha at the last moment is unwilling to fight us, you know Alula will. Mengesha will not be able to control him."

"Alula and a few tired ragamuffins. That is nothing," snarled Dabormida.

Baratieri took a deep breath. 'This man is a fool,' he thought to himself. 'I will replace him somehow right after this battle. Alula burns to return to his home. His men are tested veterans. They give no quarter. They are like animals. Let us see how this buffoon likes tangling with them.' Aloud, he said, "General Dabormida, you may wish to confer with General Albertone regarding the capabilities of Ras Alula and his men. But regardless of what you may think of him, you must be in a position to stop him. Also, you will provide support for the center. You, like Albertone, will have six guns and a battalion of Alpini. The balance of the Alpini, Arimondi, will go to you. Use them wisely. You will have thirty-five hundred of them. Protect the guns at all cost."

Baratieri moved his index finger across the map as he continued. "General Elleni, your force will be held in reserve on Mount Rebbi Arienni, and yours, Galliano, on Mount Rajo. Elleni, you will support Arimondi and Dabormida. Galliano, you will support Albertone. You will all have trusted local guides. Now, that is it for the first phase."

"A good, simple plan," said Arimondi, pleased that he would have the bulk of the Alpini. "What happens next?"

"Next, at 7 AM, we begin our barrage. The forty-six guns in the center will concentrate their fire on the enemy center. Especially on Makonnen's and Menelik's troops. On their headquarters. They will not know what hit them. One of two things will happen. If they charge..."

"Bah!" snorted Dabormida.

Baratieri continued. "If they charge, we will shoot them. That is simple enough. They must come over this central plateau, if they come in any force. We will be in our positions. They will be sitting ducks. If they do not charge, the left and right brigades will leave their positions, move along the sides of the plateau, slice Mengesha and Tekle Haimanot away from the center, turn inward, and meet at Menelik's tent. From there, they will move back upon the left and right flanks and push them against the mountains, while the center moves up and through to Adua. We will fortify Adua and the hills around it, and make it safe. Elleni will move up with the guns and place them in Adua. That should do it for the day. Now, Dabormida, see on the map: there are two roads that lead toward the west in front of you. The one hugs the lip of the plateau; the other goes down into the Valley of Mariam Shavita. When you advance—if you advance—be sure to take the plateau road. Then if Alula comes against you from the north or west, you will have the advantage of high ground. Albertone, on the south you will not have that advantage. Once past Kidane Meheret, you will be going uphill. Take care. It is an easy enough slope if no one is shooting at you, but not so easy if they are waiting for you. If there is resistance, then Arimondi, you will give Albertone all the support he needs with the guns. Make the way clear for him."

Baratieri paused and looked at his generals, then summed up. "Now," he said, "go back, confer with your officers, and study the maps. Report back here to me at five o'clock with any questions you might have. And get some sleep. Tonight will be a long night. You must be alert."

February 29, 1896—1 pm

"Chala."

"Yes, Father Haile?"

"Chala, one never knows what life may bring. So, if there is time, and if there is something to see that you have never seen before, it is best to see that thing before you move on to another place."

They were sitting in the outer room of a very comfortable large tent that had somehow miraculously appeared and been given to Haile Mikael for his use. It was the middle of a dry day, and the sharp cold of the early morning had been replaced by a warm wind out of the west. It was pleasant here, even in the midst of an army. It was strangely quiet inside the tent, and Chala's mind was conjuring up splendid carpets and wall hangings, and in the corner a palm tree had sprung up, and beneath the tree, a spring bubbled up and created a stream that would flow in any direction Chala desired—in his mind.

"Chala," said Father Haile with a smile, "Are you listening?"

Chala shook his head and smiled, and said, "I am sorry, Father. I was directing this stream that comes up from beneath our palm tree."

"Ah! Is that where you were!" exclaimed Father Haile. "Well, that is a very good place to be. But did you hear what I said about seeing things?"

"Yes," said Chala. "Some of it."

"Listen, Chala," said the priest. "This battle that is coming. It may come within the hour—although that is not likely—or it may not come for days. It may never come at all. We and the Italians may all starve to death waiting for it to happen!" Haile Mikael chuckled and shook his head. "But while we are waiting, you have a chance to see what everyone in the empire wants to see. We are ten miles from Axum. Half of the army has already been there, seeing the sights and receiving blessings. Tomorrow is Saint Mikael's Day. It is a good day to see the holy places. You should go. Yes, you should get on Eagle and go."

"Will you not go also, Father?" asked Chala.

"I have been there many times, lad," replied the bishop, "and I have a strong feeling that, for some reason, I should be here. I don't know why. But, I feel just as strongly that you should be there. What do you make of that, my boy?"

A small smile played upon Chala's lips. "I cannot make anything of it, Father. You seem to talk in riddles. But I guess I would like to go. I would like to see what is there. But why do you not come and show me? Surely it would be a good thing for me if you could show me the place."

"No," said the bishop. "For some reason, I should be here. You can take care of yourself, and you will not have to take orders from me or anybody else. It will be a holiday for you. Go now, and have a good time."

Chala rose and bowed. He went outside and saddled Eagle, all the time wondering about what Father Haile could have on his mind. Well, possibly he just wanted to be alone, to meditate, perhaps. Who knew?

Chala had little curiosity about Axum itself. He had no need to see this ancient capital. He already knew the story of Sheba, and the story of Ezana, the king who fifteen hundred years ago had become the first Christian king of Ethiopia. He knew about the crowns of the Emperors and the tombs of the kings and the Bath of Sheba and the ancient stelae and the stones enscripted in ancient Ge-ez and Greek and Serbian. But on the other hand, he was really curious about the Ark of the Covenant, and if it really were in Axum. If it were there, he wanted to see it.

And then again, it was one thing to know about the imperial crowns, but another thing entirely to see them. So when Chala went to Axum, he searched out the old relics, and when he found them he gazed at the crowns in awe, wondering at their antiquity. He visited the tomb of King Caleb, who in the Fifth Century had a fleet of ships that controlled the Kai-Bahr—the Red Sea. He looked up in wonder at the magnificently carved granite stelae, some of them sixty or eighty feet high, and tried to figure out how they were erected. He tried to get into the part of the old cathedral where the legend said the Ark was kept. But the entrance to that secret place in the cathedral was well-guarded by a multitude of priests who were wary of the number of soldiers in town, and who were being careful to keep everybody away from the rumored hiding-place. So he was not successful in that attempt. But he was amazed at how many other things there were to learn, and amazed too at how interested he was in learning all about that ancient history. It filled him up, filled his soul somehow.

Axum was filled with visitors that day. There must have been 20,000 soldiers in town to see the sights. That afternoon, Chala fell in with a squad of Oromo horsemen from Wollo. They spoke a different kind of Orominya than he, but he could still understand it. They had a good time going around the town. They watched each others' horses and helped each other out, and at the end of the day they found a good pasture just outside of town and settled in for the night.

The soldiers ate a simple dinner of kolo and injera, and talked and dozed and waited for midnight. At midnight there was to be a special mass in honor of St. Michael. There would be hundreds of debteras and priests drumming and chanting, with the cathedral and the holy grounds surrounding it lit by torches, and nobody wanted to miss that.

February 29, 1896—9:30 pm

Four tracks led out of Sauria to the west. The northernmost one led between Mount Atgebat and the Spur of Belah. Beyond those two hills, it split. One fork went west through the valley of Mariam Shavita and the other went west along the edge of the high plateau. Onto this road Dabormida led his brigade this starry night.

Another more central road led between Mount Rebbi Arienna and Mount Rajo. Here General Elleni and Colonel Galliano led their reserve troops to their stations on those mountains.

South of Mount Rajo, a track led toward the Hill of Belah, toward the main position. Along this track Arimondi led his Alpini and askari units, and behind them came the guns. They would skirt Mt. Rajo and climb a gentle saddle between that hill and Belah; then, at the top of Belah, they would deploy and march half-way down the western side of the hill. There they would fortify the place, and then the artillery would come down behind them and dig in. It would be like a fortress. Dabormida would be to their right; Albertone to their left. Before them, miles away, they would be able to see the campfires of the Ethiopians.

From the south side of the Hill of Sauria led still another track that circled in a wide arc around to the west. From that point, it skirted the side of Mount Kidane Meheret. Albertone led his men along this road, moving fast. Where the slope of Kidane Meheret turned south, there he would deploy his division facing west and northwest, his left at the mountain crags, his right guarding his road and Arimondi's flank.

It was a good, simple plan.

Axum: March 1—Midnight

At midnight in Axum, the sacred drums beat for the chanting priests. The Tabot—the Ark of the Covenant—was placed in procession, and the Midnight Mass of St. Mikael began. The ceremony was lit by the flickering torches and candles held by thousands of worshipers. The drums boomed out over the ancient hills, and the chants echoed across the stelae fields and murky tombs even to the monastery on the top of the cliff. Before the doors to the cathedral, twenty thousand warriors prayed under the stars, all enraptured with the night, all awed by the chanting and the drumming and the presence of the Lord. They stood there, hour after hour, all through the night, praying and watching. The mass lasted until four in the morning, and even then, thousands were waiting for communion.

South of Mount Rajo: March 1—1:30 am

Baratieri's plan was a good, simple plan except for one thing—Baratieri's map was wrong. It did not show where Arimondi's road and Albertone's road met. For they did meet. To Albertone, at the head of his column, the faint track coming out of the night to the north of his own did not appear significant. He noted it in his mind and hurried his men on. He wanted to be in position before Arimondi came down the Hill of Belah so that he and Arimondi could coordinate and adjust their lines, and make them as effective as possible.

What he did not know was that coming down that insignificant little track that entered behind him from the north was Arimondi's whole brigade, followed by the artillery train. Albertone passed by, oblivious of what was happening behind him. His four thousand men followed him, crossing the path of that track, and when half of them had passed, here came the head of Arimondi's column down the other track, and it came to a sudden halt in the darkness. There it waited and waited until the last of Albertone's men and cannon had passed in front of them. After that, there was a time of puzzlement, while Arimondi checked with his officers and scouts and compass. Arimondi finally decided that he knew where he was, and that he was in the right place. When his scouts reported that indeed the roads did meet, he puzzled a bit about how Baratieri hadn't known about that. Then he pushed on. But by then, he had lost almost an hour. In a few minutes, his little track veered north, climbing the saddle to Mount Belah, so Arimondi could see that he was on the right path. But he was late.

It has been said many times that both Saint Michael and Saint George were seen on the battlefield of Adua, fighting for the Ethiopians; but it has never been explained by anyone how Baratieri, the master of maps, did not know what happened with these two roads that came together and went apart again and held up the advance of the Italian center. Perhaps it was those two saints, working with Baratieri to create a mistaken map. It is something that is incomprehensible. We do not know the answer. Perhaps we shall never know.

False Kidane Meheret: March 1—2:30 am

Albertone had arrived at his objective. All around him the night was dark and full of stars. He deployed his left wing, stretching it to the cliffs. He ordered his center to take up its position. He ordered his advanced guard—the alpine battalion—forward to watch for Ethiopian marauders.

Then he waited with his officers and scouts for news of Arimondi's brigade. This march had gone well for Albertone. He had reached his objective well ahead of time. It had almost been too easy. "Well," thought Albertone, chuckling to himself, "Sometimes things go right."

But forty-five minutes later, he was still waiting, and he began to worry. He had achieved this position so quickly. Could it be that he was not in the right place? He called his officers together. "Arimondi should have been here by now," he said. "We should have made contact with his left flank a long time ago, but we have neither seen them nor heard them. And we arrived here so quickly. At first, I thought that was good news, but now I wonder. Are we where we are supposed to be? Are we at Kidane Meheret?"

One of Albertone's captains turned to a junior officer. "Lieutenant. What do your guides say?"

The lieutenant motioned his local guides forward, and pointed to the black bulk of the hill that loomed behind them. "Kidane Meheret?" he asked.

There were the low, explosive sounds of Tigrai, the language of southern Eritrea. There were alarmed eyes, and arms that gestured toward the west, and the lieutenant said, "Sir, they say *that* is Kidane Meheret, not *this*!"

Far to the west, the mass of another dark hill stood out against the sky.

"I knew it!" said Albertone, letting out a deep sigh. "I knew we had reached it too soon. But gentlemen, look. Look at the map. Here. Bring the torch. Look at the map and the way this hill lies. Does it not look as though this is the place? This hill fits perfectly. Look. Across our little valley, there is Belah. I would swear it. We seem to be in the right place...."

"Unless," said a captain, "that across our little valley what we see is a spur of Rajo, and that in fact Belah is further west."

"But the map says *this* is Kidane Meheret. And *that* hill corresponds to Belah, not Rajo."

"But sir," said the captain, "the guides say that *that* is Kidane Meheret up there, not this one here, and if *that* is Kidane Meheret, then Belah must be somewhere up there too, and this must be Rajo."

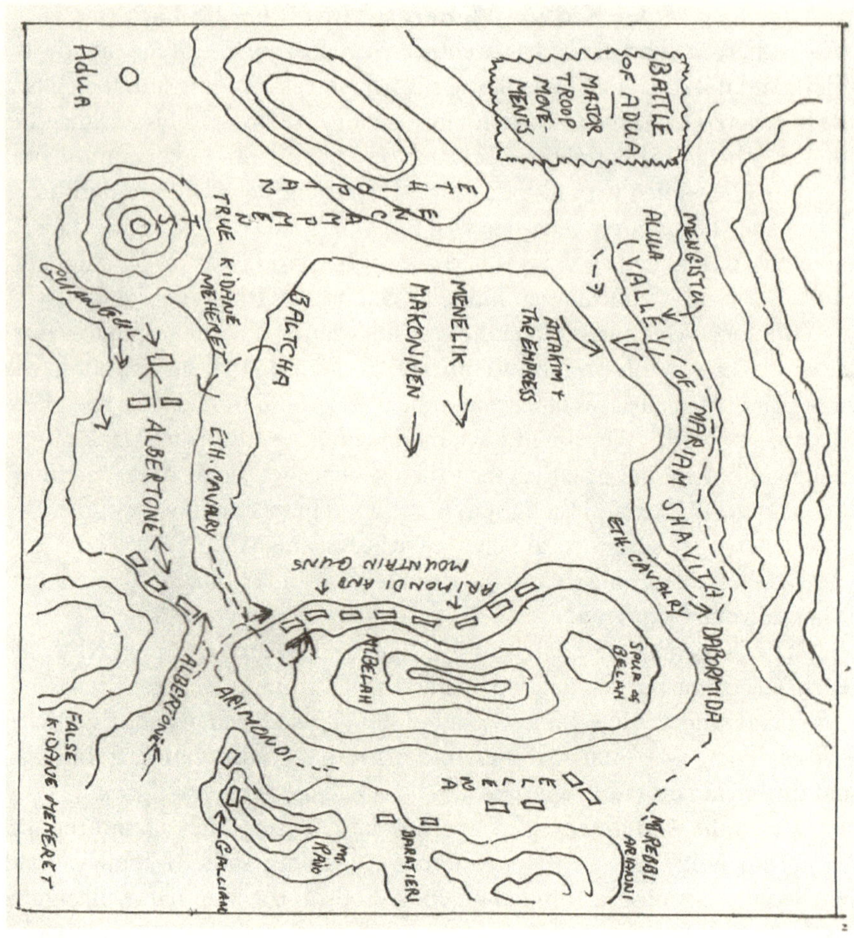

BATTLE OF ADUA
MAJOR TROOP MOVE- MENTS
Adua
ADUA VALLEY (OF MARIAM SHAVITU)
MENGASTU
ETH. CAVALRY
ETHIOPIAN CAMP
BALTCHA
MENELIK
MAKONNEN
ATTATIM & THE EMPRESS
TRUE KIDANE MEHERET
ETH. CAVALRY
GULANGUL
ALBERTONE
ALBERTONE
ARIMONDI
FALSE KIDANE MEHERET
ARIMONDI AND MOUNTAIN GUNS
M. BELAH
SPUR OF BELAH
DABORMIDA
M. REBBI ARIANNI
MT. RAIO
GALLIANO
BARATIERI

"But Belah is not up there. Look. Do you see anything?"

They all peered through the black night. They could see nothing.

"The dark can play tricks," said a colonel. "If this is not Belah, maybe Belah blends into those western mountains."

"Perhaps," said the captain, striving to see. All the officers peered again through the dark night, looking for Belah. And as they did, a strange feeling came over all of them that they were in the wrong place, that Albertone was right, that they were far behind the place they should be. It was strange. They all felt it at once. They all fell silent. Then Albertone said, "Contact the advance guard. Tell them to be careful, but to go forward to that hill out there—to Kidane Meheret. That is where we belong. Form the flanks and center into three columns. We go forward."

"But, sir," said a major, "what if we are in the right place? Then, if we go out there, we are too far forward. We are exposed, and we expose Arimondi. Then what do we do?"

Albertone looked at his map again, and up at the nearby silent hill. It certainly seemed to be the right one. But it couldn't be. No, the right one was out there, his eyes were playing tricks on him, and he had to be in position to support Arimondi. "Then, Major," he said, "we can always come back. Colonel, give the order to advance. We go forward to Kidane Meheret."

But where Albertone stood was exactly where Baratieri wanted him to be. Arimondi wasn't on the other hill simply because Albertone's column had held him up. But only the ranks knew that, and the ranks weren't talking. They were spread out all over the plain, in the dark, doing what they were told to do, and that was keeping them busy.

The guides did not lie. That hill out there in the dark *was* Kidane Meheret. This one was not.

But Baratieri had thought that this one was Kidane Meheret and had marked it as such on the map. He had mislabeled the map. No one knows why. But for some reason, God willed Albertone to leave his good position and march forward into the night, leaving his men exhausted and Arimondi's flank open to fate.

Between Two Hills—4 am

"There is no Hill of Belah out there," said Colonel Fanta. "It is obvious to me, General. Belah is behind us. Look back. It is easy to see."

Albertone and his staff were halfway between the two Kidane Meherets. The shadows of both hills were easy to see from here. The sky, while still black, seemed to be just a tone less dark than before. Albertone and his officers stood in an open circle and looked forward and back. They were in the middle of nowhere, in a truly precarious position. To their north, there was a deep valley, and the main plateau started beyond it. To the south, great mountains bordered their position. Albertone and his men stood in the middle of a vast rolling meadow, with no strong place to make a defense or a rally. Albertone began to sweat.

"Stop the advance," he ordered. Couriers ran out to all the units. The General and his officers stood silently.

"We are going back," said Albertone. "Something is dreadfully wrong here. That may be Kidane Meheret up there, but that is not where we are supposed to be. Here is what we will do. Before we are trapped out here in the daylight, we will go back to where we were. We will from there send a strong detachment over to what we think is the Hill of Belah to look for Arimondi. If no one is there, still there will be signs of their passing. If we are too far behind, and it *is* Mount Rajo, fine. We can always advance again. But always, we will be closer to Arimondi than the Ethiopians can ever be. If he is in front of us, we can come up to his assistance. But one thing I know: something is very wrong here, and we must think defensively."

A runner came up to the officers. "Sirs," he said, out of breath, "we cannot find the advance guard!"

The officers stood silently, looking at him.

"Those damned Alpini, they must be charging right along, to get to the new position as fast as possible!" exclaimed Albertone. "Scout, go out again. Find them. We cannot leave them out there."

Suddenly, far to the front, there was a roar of guns. Then it subsided, then rose again in a second fusillade. Then there was the constant sound of individual shots, rising and falling in waves of intensity.

"My God!" said Albertone. "We've got to get them back here! Colonel Fanta, take the left column up. Make contact with those Alpini officers. Lead them back. Cover them. The center stays here. The right takes position along the rim of that valley. The guns go back right away. We cover them at all costs."

"That is no small patrol out there" said Lieutenant Tourilla.

Albertone turned on him with a snarl. "Do you take me for an imbecile?" he yelled. "Get out of here. Do something useful. Here is something for you to do. Get out to the end of the left line. Tell the officer there to....."

There was another roar of rifles, closer this time, near where the left flank column should have been, somewhere out there in the dark.

"Wait," said Albertone, and he spoke quietly as he addressed his officers. "We are in a perilous situation here. This is what we must do. We will have the center create a defense line. The right will act as a reserve. The Alpini and the askaris will have to fight their way back. They are good men. They will do it. When they arrive, then we will move everyone back."

Just as before, but now from two locations far out in the darkness, there was the peppering of shots. Out there in the dark, the askaris had come up against King Tekle Haimanot's pickets, and the Gojjamis had responded like a nest of hornets. There were five thousand of them out there, streaming down from the heights of True Kidane Meheret, searching for the enemy. The sky was just beginning to get light.

The huge red Imperial tent soared into the air, its peak so far above the ground that it began to catch the early morning light while all around it was still caught in darkness. Before the tent stood the massed war drums of the Empire of Ethiopia. Inside, in the great audience hall, Abuna Mattewos was saying the morning mass for St. Michael's Day. He was assisted by three bishops, one of whom was Haile Mikael Tesfaye, Bishop of Ba'le. A chorus of a hundred debteras chanted, and fifty holy drums boomed out accompaniment.

At the mass were Their Royal Majesties Menelik and Taitu, along with most of their personal staffs. Two kings, Wagshum Guangul and Tekle Haimanot of Gojjam, were there, as were many members of the diplomatic corps. Dejazmach Baltcha and Grazmach Abate were there, and many rases and lesser nobles. Half the Emperor's court seemed to be in attendance.

The sounds of chant and drum hid the sound of the galloping horse that arrived at the entrance to the tent. The guards recognized the interloper and bowed to him as he strode over the carpets. Past the ranks of nobles and clergy he almost ran toward the altar. Bowing perfunctorily to the Abuna, he turned and knelt before Menelik. It was Tafesse, the Kanyazmach of King Tekle Haimanot's army.

The Abuna looked at Menelik and Menelik nodded. The Abuna signaled the drummers and debteras to cease. Silence reigned in the tent.

"Tafesse, what is it?" whispered Menelik.

"Janhoi, we are attacked in force on the right."

"You are sure? They are not just sniping with patrols again?"

"Thousands of them, Your Majesty. They come straight ahead."

There was the sound of more horses approaching. From far off, the dull sounds of battle made their way into the tent. The Emperor looked at the Abuna again. The Abuna raised his staff and intoned, "May the glory of Saint Mikael and Saint George be with you today. May all the angels of the Most High Lord be at your side. Go. The mass is ended."

Led by Menelik and Taitu, the entire congregation, along with the clergy, left the tent. Menelik's staff clustered around him.

Outside the tent, Ras Alula and half a dozen of his men were dismounting and pulling two other men out of their saddles. The men were white, and they wore the uniform of Italy.

"A gift for Your Majesty, Janhoi," said the old warrior. He licked his lips. "They were coming up the Miriam Shavita Valley. They are scouts. Behind them is a brigade at least. They march directly toward us. I think they have taken leave of their senses, but there they are, and onward they come."

"They advance on our left?" asked Menelik, startled.

"Directly toward Mengesha," answered Alula.

Menelik was bewildered. This was incomprehensible. He had half expected an attack, but this! It made no sense. He turned to Dejazmach Baltcha and looked into the Oromo general's eyes. There was no answer there. Baltcha was as surprised as the Emperor himself.

Two more riders galloped up. This time it was Ras Mengesha and a rider who rode well but was dressed like a peasant. Mengesha, himself dressed in his war trappings, jumped from his horse and said, "Your Majesty, this man is named Alawon. He is a spy for us. He is a cook for the Italian generals. The Italians are coming. All of them. They are bringing their guns up to the Hill of Belah!"

"Sir! I wish to be a soldier for you!" yelled Alawon.

"Conference of War!" bellowed Menelik. He turned on his heel and strode back into the tent. The rases followed. Makonnen, Baltcha, Wube, Alula, Mengesha, and Mikael were there. Senior officers under them, as many as were at the service, were there also.

"My sword!" yelled Menelik. "Bring my sword!" Then he addressed the rases. "Now, my brothers," he said. "Now it seems they come. What do you think they are doing?"

"They are extended," said Dejazmach Baltcha. "They come both on the left and right, and bring their guns into the center, to a position where they can barrage us even as we stand here."

"We must get the dependent people to the rear," said Makonnen, "then dig in and wait for the enemy. That way, the army will not be exposed."

"That is good," said Mikael, "but what about my horses? If everyone is scurrying around in the rocks, the horses will scatter or die, and then what is the use of the cavalry?"

"Better some dead horses than thousands of men," said Wube. "I am with Makonnen. Let's wait for them and shoot them as they come."

"Yieee!" screamed Alula. The old man jumped into the middle of the circle. "Have you all gone crazy? Hide in the rocks? That is just what they want you to do! While you are hiding, their guns will murder your men, and more men will flee. Their brigades come left and right just now, but they will stop, and after a few hours of artillery, they will come again, push in what's left of your center, and roll you up into these hills. They will scatter you like dry leaves. That is what they will do!"

The old warrior, breathing heavily, leaned on his spear. The rases looked at him.

"What would you do?" asked Menelik.

"What I have always done," said Alula. "I would attack while they are out in the open. That is the only way to get at them."

"You would attack both wings?" asked Baltcha.

"I would attack them all!" cried Alula. "All! I would attack them at once. I would sever both wings from the center. I would attack the center, before they could set their gunsights correctly."

"You would lose thousands," said Menelik.

"Janhoi, my great Emperor, my father, my friend," said Alula, "you will lose thousands anyway, and your armies and your Empire as well. By attacking, we rid ourselves of this beast. He will spend all his ammunition. He will lose thousands. He will lose all his supplies. We will be rid of him! May Menelik die if I do not speak the truth!"

Alula collapsed in front of Menelik. They all looked down at him. He looked like a bundle of old rags.

"Give me some time to myself," said Menelik, "and pick him up." He walked alone into the recesses of the tent and disappeared behind a partition.

This is what Menelik knew: twenty thousand of his army were at Axum or Adua. Ten thousand more were scattered throughout the countryside, either scouting or raiding supply lines or requisitioning supplies from the peasants, and these thousands were far out, since food was scarce.

Another ten thousand or so were too sick to fight well, if at all. Some could hardly move, lying and shivering with the wasting diseases and fevers that followed all armies.

Another ten thousand he had sent back toward the south just two days ago because there was no food for them.

Taking away Taitu's small army and his own personal guard, Menelik had some 65,000 effective troops.

He also had rases that, if he showed weakness, would lose faith in him. Their doubts would spill over into their troops. But more important, if he were defeated here, some of them would go over to Baratieri. He knew they would. That was the way of the world.

And he had food for just two days.

Menelik stood and thought through these things. For two minutes. Then he sighed, shook his head to clear it, and returned to the front of the tent.

"Alula is right!" said Menelik in a loud voice. "We attack. We attack right now, on all fronts. Baltcha, you command the right wing. Take care of that column there. Abate, you and Mengesha take the left. Let that old maniac loose on them, if he can stand up. Take Wube as well, and Attakim. Mikael, take half your cavalry and go up that little valley that leads to the right of Belah, then turn and rake them across that hill. Do what you can. Take those machine-gunners of yours with you there." Menelik pointed out into the gloomy pre-dawn plain. "The other half goes down the plateau on the left, to the left of Belah. Do you see? Do not let their center aid that extended left wing that is coming up the valley. Keep them apart at all costs.

"Makonnen, my cousin, you and I will go straight ahead, right at Belah. Gentlemen! My rases, my kings, my cousins! Today we conquer or die. Today we rid our land of this scourge. Today Ethiopia is strong. Let us go! Follow me!"

"And I, my Lord? What am I to do? Sit in my tent and knit you a sweater?" It was Empress Taitu.

Menelik looked at her and laughed. "You, my Empress," he said, "you will take your army and go to the left. Go and be a reserve to Attakim. Follow him everywhere, and go forward!" Menelik strode out of the tent. Outside, thousands of warriors were assembling. Alawon, the spy, howled at him, "Janhoi, let me be your soldier!"

Menelik turned to Mengesha. "Ras Mengesha, take this lunatic and give him to Alula and let him fight. I am convinced. He is on our side. Let him fight!" Mengesha and Alula galloped off, with Alawon hot on their heels.

Dejazmach Baltcha approached the Emperor. "My Lord, I will need more help on the right. I will have only Tekle Haimanot's and Guangul's armies. That is only eight thousand. How will I push them back? How will I make them run?"

Menelik looked at Makonnen. Instantly, Makonnen said, "How many?"

"Seven thousand," said Baltcha.

"Will that leave you enough?" Menelik asked Makonnen.

Makonnen smiled. "It will have to, won't it?" And he laughed.

"Very well, Baltcha," said Menelik. "Take them, but don't throw them away. Makonnen may need them later."

"I will treat them as though they were prized princes," said Baltcha with a grin, and in a split second he was up on his horse and galloping away.

"Leave me my artillery!" yelled Makonnen. Without looking back, Baltcha waved an arm.

"Well, Cousin," said Menelik, "shall we go then?" The Emperor grinned broadly, and unsheathed his sword.

"Are you all right?" asked Makonnen, "You look like you are going to a party."

Menelik laughed. "I have nothing to worry about," he said. "I have done all I could. I believe I have done right. Now, whatever happens, happens. I feel as fresh as a baby. For the first time in twenty-five years, I have nothing to worry about! Come on, cousin, let's go have a battle!"

The two men mounted their horses. They rode past the massed war drums and ranks of trumpeteers, out to where the troops were massed in the fields in front of them.

"Beat the drums!" shouted Menelik. "Sound the trumpets! We attack! We attack now!"

The drummers and the trumpeteers stood as if in a trance. It was as though they were cast in stone. There was not a sound from them, not a movement.

Menelik whirled around and looked at them, unbelieving. On all sides, the troops milled about, uncertain of what to do. The priests, who had been blessing the troops and distributing communion to them, stopped. There was a great silence.

Ras Makonnen, on his horse next to Menelik, lowered his sword and stared at the Emperor.

"What is wrong with you?" yelled Menelik. "Who are you? What are your fathers? Beat the drums!"

The drummers did not move. They stared at Menelik with wide eyes.

In the crowd of priests and soldiers, Haile Mikael Tesfaye looked up and saw this strange, silent, unmoving scene. It was as though the entire Ethiopian army had become frozen in time and space.

Haile Mikael looked at a debtera near him. The singer held a sacred drum. Quickly, the bishop strode over to the man and took the drum away. Holding the huge drum under his arm, he looked up at the Emperor, took a deep breath, and pounded the drum.

Once, twice, three times he pounded it. It set up a rhythm. Other priests joined in. Suddenly, Haile Mikael turned away from Menelik and began to walk toward the enemy. Then, still striking the drum, he began to sing in a high, quavering voice at the top of his lungs:

"This is the day that the Lord has made;" he sang. "Let us rejoice and be glad in it!..."

The familiar sound of the psalm resounded through the air. Priests and debteras and monks took up the song and began to follow Haile Mikael as he walked through the army, heading east, aiming for the dark Hill of Belah far in the distance.

"Look at this!" Menelik yelled to the soldiers, "The priests lead us! The priests are not afraid!"

Makonnen spurred his horse up to the nearest petrified drummer. Placing his sword at the man's neck, he said firmly, "Beat that drum or I will kill you."

The man jumped, yelped, raised his arm, and down came the drumstick with such force that the boom of that single great war drum drowned out the sounds of all the priests' drumming and singing. And on the second stroke, he was joined by all the other drummers. The sound of those drums was like that made by a great streak of lightning that lands right next to you, unexpected, and knocks you to the ground.

The drums beat and Menelik raised his sword in the air and bellowed, "Forward! Forward! For the Motherland! For Ethiopia! We strike!" He spurred his horse and galloped to the front of his army, with Makonnen riding beside him. His horse rearing, Menelik pointed east with his sword and began to ride toward the enemy. The army cheered and followed, running to keep up with the Emperor, running to be near him, running to die with him on Saint Michael's Day.

MENELIK

Back on the crest of Rebbi Arienni, protected by the Elleni brigade, Baratieri sat on his horse and looked out toward the west. His staff surrounded him. The sky behind him brightened by the minute, and the panorama of his chosen battlefield began to be filled with the light of day.

Directly west of him lay Belah and the Spur of Belah. On the far side of those hills, he knew, the troops of Arimondi and Dabormida were digging in. The artillery was preparing to blast the Ethiopian encampment, three miles distant. All was set there.

To his south, he could see Galliano's fifteen hundred askaris on Mount Rajo. From there, they could cover the roads leading back to Sauria, but more important, they were in excellent position to join Arimondi or Albertone. They were light infantry troops, capable of moving to wherever they were needed at great speed.

To the southwest was the hill Baratieri still thought to be Kidane Meheret. That was the only fly in the ointment. There was that constant rattle of rifle fire far out on the plains beyond it, where none of Albertone's troops ought to be. Baratieri waited for a messenger to explain this situation to him. He had sent out a courier at about 4:30 AM, but the lieutenant had not yet returned. All the Italian commander could think was that Albertone's advance guard had somehow gotten too far ahead and had run into a detachment of Ethiopians. In that, without knowing it, he was correct.

And then Baratieri heard the war drums, and knew that the Ethiopians were coming. His first thought was to disrupt the Ethiopian army, and to that end he sent off a courier to Arimondi to see how far he had come along with the artillery. Second, off galloped another messenger to Dabormida, to see how that brigade's preparations were advancing. Then Baratieri waited.

At last, at 7:30, a courier came from Albertone. Baratieri opened the note. "Seriously engaged with the enemy," it read. "Moving the brigade to better defense position. 6:00 AM. Albertone."

Baratieri looked across at Kidane Meheret. He could see no sign of any kind of a battle there. Baratieri looked at the courier, puzzled.

"Sir," said Major Bassi, "I noticed the other day that you can get a good view of Kidane Meheret from that side of Mount Eschaho, across the valley. It is only, perhaps, a fifteen minute ride. It might be advisable..."

"Right you are, Colonel," said Baratieri. "We leave at once." And the commander and his staff left for Eschaho.

They arrived there twenty minutes later. Baratieri scanned the valley beyond the Spur of Belah with his spyglass. Far, far in the distance he could see dim signs of activity in the Ethiopian lines. Troops were lining up and moving forward. Formations were on the march, not yet covered in dust in the early morning air. Cavalry units were setting out.

The general swept his glass around to Kidane Meheret. He could see no sign of troops there, either Italian or Ethiopian. Then he moved it slowly to the west. There! There in that meadow between Kidane Meheret and that other hill. Puffs of smoke. Distant sounds of guns. Big guns. What the hell? What was anybody doing way out there?

Another courier, delayed by chasing Baratieri from Rebbi Arienni to Eschaho, galloped up and saluted, and thrust a message directly into Baratieri's gloved hands. The messenger looked tense, and Baratieri quickly scanned the terse message: "We are surrounded. The fighting is hot. Reinforcements would be useful and appreciated. 6:25 AM. Albertone. Send Reinforcements!"

The last two words were scrawled in a hurried hand.

Baratieri, alarmed, looked at the messenger again, then back at the note, then back at the field of battle. The note had been sent at 6:25. Baratieri checked his watch. Now it was 7:50 a.m. Almost an hour-and-a-half! And no help sent to Albertone in all that time!

"Where the hell have you been?" exploded Baratieri at the unfortunate lieutenant.

"Sir," said the lieutenant, "there are Ethiopians all over the place out there. I had to be careful, always on the lookout, riding here and there, back and forth, hiding, dashing. I am sorry I took so long, but I am happy that I am here at all." The lieutenant diplomatically refrained from saying anything about Baratieri's not being where the courier expected him to be.

Baratieri grunted and looked back over at the field again. "Go back and tell General Albertone this: tell him I send him reinforcements from both General Dabormida's and General Elleni's forces. Tell him to hold on. We will get him out of there. Tell him to keep trying to move back to Kidane Meheret. He will find his reinforcements coming up to meet him. Go now, and tell him that."

"Yes, sir," said the lieutenant, "but General, sir, which hill is Kidane Meheret? This one or the far one?" The lieutenant pointed toward the True Kidane Meheret.

"This one, you fool!" yelled Baratieri. "What do you mean, which one?"

"General, sir. The guides told us the far hill was Kidane Meheret!"

"What!" screamed Baratieri. "What?" Then the full enormity of what had happened to Albertone hit him. "*This* is Kidane Meheret. Get General Albertone and his brigade back to it. Hurry! He must secure that position."

"Yes, sir!" said the lieutenant, and wheeled his horse and galloped off, chanting to himself "OhmyGod OhmyGod OhmyGod" in time with the galloping horse.

Almost immediately, a courier from Dabormida—not the one Baratieri had sent, but another sent by Dabormida himself—arrived at Baratieri's traveling headquarters. Baratieri hastily tore open the envelope. "We are reaching out our hands to Albertone. 7:15 AM. Dabormida," was all it said.

The feeling of panic that was beginning to well up in Baratieri subsided just a bit. "Your general has anticipated my wishes," he said to the young officer. "Go back to him and say this: whatever size relief column you have sent, send another of the same size. Albertone is surrounded, and is in real trouble. Tell him to make haste! And you do, likewise."

"Yes, sir!" The lieutenant saluted and sent his horse thundering off.

Baratieri went back to scanning the battlefield, but within a few minutes another courier appeared before him. This was the man he had sent to check on Dabormida's position on the Spur of Belah.

"Sir, General, sir!" said the courier, saluting. "I could not find General Dabormida, sir."

"Well, he's out there, lieutenant," said Baratieri sarcastically. "You mean no one in his brigade could find him?"

"General, sir, I scoured the place looking for him. I could not find him. I was all over the Spur, sir, and to the valley between it and Mount Atgebat. He is not there, sir. I mean his whole brigade, sir. The brigade is not there!"

Baratieri turned pale. "I...I have just received a note from him," he said. "He says he is reaching out his hands to Albertone. You say he is not there?"

"General, sir," said the courier, "there are traces of a large detachment of troops moving west. I followed to the point where that road divides, where the left-hand road moves along the edge of the plateau and the right-hand one goes down into the Mariam Shavita? That large detachment took the right-hand road, General. There was a wide band of footprints. Wheel marks from cannon. Hoofprints. They went down into the valley, General. I thought it wise to return and report to you, sir."

"You say there are none of our men on the Spur of Belah? None?" Baratieri's face drooped, almost as if he had become an old man in the space of seconds.

"Not a one, General."

"My God," said Baratieri.

General Vittorio Emanuele Dabormida was in a foul mood when he led his brigade out of Sauria fortress on the evening of February 29th. At the same time, he was strangely elated. He had finally managed to coerce Signore Baratieri—that supercilious, blundering fop with his chestful of silly medals and his moustache brushed and waxed just so—he had finally gotten him off his ass and into a battle that was worthy of the name, and it had taken a lot of energy and wheedling and outright bullying to do it. He was happy about that, but he was mad about this damned waffling back and forth and losing ground and time. Dabormida felt that they should be halfway to Addis Ababa by now. Instead, they had been beaten back and outfoxed by a couple of aborigines with spears and shields and chicken-feather headdresses. He wanted to get to Addis Ababa. Now. Fast. And straightaway, instead of taking this damnable territory ras by slovenly, cowardly, whining ras. Now he, Dabormida, was going to have to kick their butts out of the way once and for all, slice up their piddling little semi-states, and apportion everything out to the settlers, and do all of this while at the same time having this simpleton figure of a posturing idiot of a commander looking over his shoulder and whimpering about what Rome thought.

Dabormida knew what Rome thought. Rome thought Baratieri was an idiot. He was causing a lot of trouble for the government, which was besieged by the radicals of the left because Baratieri was preventing Dabormida and the other generals from slicing through this baboon-infested kingdom and taking it over once and for all.

Dabormida was in a furious rage, and woe to the junior officer or private or guide who crossed him, for that man would pay.

At the same time, he was exhilarated. Finally, he was in a position to do something, and woe to the Ethiop stupid enough to stand in his way. Now he had his men—good, trained, tough fighting men. He had his command. He had his assignment, and at the end of the assignment there was no closing. That ridiculous Baratieri had never said, "When you get that done, come back and stand here." So Dabormida could do just what he judged to be correct.

What Dabormida judged to be correct was to make sure the glory for this fight belonged to him, and that everybody knew about it. So while Signore Baratieri was conducting this battle for the glory of Rome, he, Dabormida, would see that the battle was fought for his own glory. He would see to it that everyone knew that he was the hero of this massacre. He would emerge from this combat bathed in blood and guts and glory; and when word of the battle went back to Rome, and when he himself went back to Rome a conquering hero, his accomplishments would outshine Baratieri's as the sun outshines the moon.

All of this was swirling about Dabormida's envious mind all through that long night's march.

But Dabormida had it easy. He had a relatively straight and level road. No other brigade fumbled around in the dark and ran into his; and when he had arrived at the spot in the valley between the Spur of Belah and Mount Atgebat, he had plenty of time to throw out pickets, assign bivouacs, and collect his battalions. He ordered a rest there in the valley, just where he could see across the dark plateau past the heights of Belah rising on his left.

That is where he was at 4:00 AM, resting comfortably, preparing orders for his men to turn the Spur and the valley floor into a fortress. That is when he heard the sounds of King Tekle Haimanot's attack on Albertone echoing across the plateau. Dabormida sensed opportunity. He stood and listened. When one of his officers approached him with a light and a map, he simply said, "Quiet. Put out that light," and continued to stand. When he heard anyone approach, he simply waved them off with his hand, refusing to even turn to acknowledge them.

Finally, Dabormida left his vigil on the edge of the plateau and called a conference of his colonels and majors, and said to them, "Gentlemen, I hope you will forgive me for this delay, but I did not wish our men to be caught spread out and occupied in fortifying positions if we had to move fast, which is what I believe we will now have to do." He paused for effect. His great shaved bullet head bobbed up and down in a cajoling, friendly manner as he continued. "You can hear as well as I that Albertone is in trouble over there. We must go to his assistance. That is the way our plan is set up, so that either wing can assist the other if need be.

"But you see, I am confident that the battle is setting up this way: the Ethiopians are obviously attacking our left wing, and will try to fold it in upon the center. Then they will try to roll down the center. At that time, our artillery will be useless, and only Elleni and ourselves will be able to help turn the tide." Dabormida began to stride back and forth in front of his officers. "At that time, gentlemen, we don't want half our force strung out along this hill, taking potshots at leaping Ethiops, and the other half out there somewhere in that dark grassland, leaping around with the black beggars. Something extraordinary must be done if our entire army is to be salvaged, and so here is what I propose to do."

Dabormida breathed deeply. His chest expanded and he seemed to grow in height and bulk. "I propose," he said, "to go up this Mariam Shavita Valley, and at dawn, or as soon as possible thereafter, to attack the center of the Ethiopian line. To explode out of that valley and destroy their center, send them into confusion, and go west and destroy Adua. What do you think of that, my men?" Dabormida laughed, and some of the men laughed nervously along with him.

Only one officer, Colonel Ferreria of the Torino Alpini battalion, dared to say anything. "Sir, does not that valley lead directly to the armies of Ras Mengesha and Ras Alula?"

"Alula! Alula!" Dabormida sneered. "All I ever hear is Alula. Bah! Alula is a wizened-up old lunatic windbag with a few thousand ragamuffins. Mengesha is little better. Both of them have taken the blows of our assaults for the past five years. Alula got lucky at Amba Alagie, but that's all. His men are old and sick. There are no strong warriors in all the Tigre anymore. Anyway, Ferreria, we will not go straight at them. Just before we get within shooting distance of them, we veer off to the left, climb the side of the valley, emerge on the plateau, and head for Menelik's tent. Our artillery and machine-guns cover our rear and blast hell out of Alula and that sniveling Ras of Tigre if they dare to come at us. That will fix them. Meanwhile, we destroy their stores and wreak havoc with their goods and camp-followers. Then we torch their tents. That's the best thing we can do for Albertone and the rest of our boys. Once we get the fires going well, we circle around to the south and Albertone and I have their right wing in a vise. We squeeze. We squeeze the life out of them. Then we sit and watch Arimondi and the artillery slaughter whatever is left of their center. Then we mop up. Then we clean up. Then we go home." Dabormida's laugh boomed out through the dawn light.

"Now, boys, I have already sent out pickets and scouts. We must move quickly. All extra baggage stays here. Light it is. Double-time march through that valley. Then up and a run for their tents."

The officers scattered to their posts and began to hustle their men into quick-march order.

Dabormida motioned to a lieutenant on his staff. "Lieutenant Preda, son of my good cousin Antonio, I have a special task for you. Take this letter to General Baratieri. But listen—do not set out until I have left with all the troops. Then, go carefully. Slowly, if you must. Ask directions if you have to. Be wary of lurking Ethiops. I will be truthful with you. You see, Lieutenant, General Baratieri may be a bit perplexed by this maneuver, and may wish to change it somewhat. So I must have some time to make it work. It would be good if he did not see this letter until, oh, say, seven o'clock. Around there. Then he will just have to trust me, eh? You understand? Eh?"

The lieutenant swallowed. "Yes, Uncle," he said. "Our family will be proud of you."

"Ah, it is good then. You understand. Now, stay with the Commander as short a time as possible. Then come back as quickly as possible. Ride up this valley quickly, so you can join the fun and share in the glory, eh?"

At 6:30 a.m., when Baratieri's courier arrived at the Spur of Belah to look for Dabormida, the last of the brigadier's men were an hour away. Dabormida was marching down the Mariam Shavita . He had his rifles at the ready, his artillery protected, and his patrols out. He felt great. The sun was striking the tops of the mountains, the air was still, the morning was coming in clear and clean. In fifteen or twenty minutes he would wheel his brigade left, emerge onto the plateau, come in behind the Ethiopian center, and wreck their base. The valley was still dark, and his army was hidden. There had been no sign of discovery.

One thing that Dabormida did not know: two of his scouts were already at Menelik's tent. They had been there for over an hour. They had been among the original set of scouts and pickets sent out at 4:00 a.m., and one of Alula's patrols had pounced on them, trussed them up, gagged them, gave them a wild ride, and gleefully presented them to Menelik. Dabormida did not know that.

The first thing Baltcha did on the Ethiopian right was to tighten King Tekle Haimanot's line. The next was to swing Wagshum Guangul's men around to the right of the Gojjamis. Then he divided Makonnen's seven thousand men. Four thousand he sent around Guangul's army, extending the Ethiopian lines around Albertone even further. The other three thousand he sent down into that little valley that separated Albertone's grassland from the main plateau. Whenever some of Albertone's men popped their heads over the rim of the valley they were met with a volley from the nearest of Makonnen's men. Meanwhile, on top of the grassland, Baltcha kept lengthening and tightening the net around Albertone.

The Italians and askaris fought well and hard, but the odds were too high for success. Baltcha had left Makonnen most of his artillery, but he had taken six Hotchkiss guns with him. These he had set up by six-thirty, and suddenly artillery shells were bursting over the heads of Albertone's troops. The Italian mountain guns replied, and an artillery duel began, the guns booming away and the echoes of their firing reverberating through the hills and across the plains beyond.

All through the morning, Baltcha kept tightening that noose. A charge here, a salient there, and always the movement past Albertone toward the east; always the threat of flanking the Italian brigade; always, the fear of being encircled building in the Italian ranks. By eight o'clock, except for a small outlet to the east, Baltcha had them surrounded. He left that small opening for panicked stragglers to run through, and when they did, Baltcha's sharpshooters picked off as many of them as they wanted. The rest were let go, to spread fear through the rest of the Italian army.

Axum—6:30 am

The Midnight Mass at the cathedral ended at 4:00 a.m.

At 5:00 a.m., there were still people receiving communion.

At 5:30 a.m., the communicants were sitting in groups in the town or in the fields around the town, wondering whether they should go back to sleep or try to get through the day without any. They sat around campfires eating dry kolo and yesterday's scraps of injera and talking quietly.

At 6:00 a.m., some thought they heard thunder coming out of the east. Their friends scoffed at their hearing, and laughed at them for thinking of thunder. 'Look at the sky,' they said. 'Look at the stars. Look at the clear sky.'

At 6:30 AM, Baltcha let loose his artillery barrage against Albertone's brigade, and Albertone's artillery replied. In Axum, men and women leaped to their feet and huddled together and for a few seconds, simply listened. Then there was bedlam. People went running to and fro, saddling horses, grabbing spears and shields and swords and rifles. Warriors began running down the road to Adua, as fast as their fatigue and weapons would allow.

Chala saddled Eagle in a flash, picked up his sword and shield and spear, and jumped into the saddle. Down the road toward Adua he sped, but soon a running warrior turned toward him and yelled, "Give me a ride! Give me a ride!" Chala stopped. The warrior jumped up onto Eagle's back behind the saddle, grabbed Chala around the waist, and onward they sped. All around them, horsemen were stopping and picking up fighters.

"My name is Gebre Medhin Wolde Amanuel," shouted the warrior in a dialect of Amharic Chala could scarcely understand. "I am from Lasta. Who are you?"

"My name is Chala Negassa. I am from Arusi. I came through Lasta on the way north."

"What is your unit?"

"I am a servant to the bishop Haile Mikael Tesfaye of Ba'le," shouted Chala into the wind. "My brother is with the Oromo horse of Ras Mikael."

"Oh-ho!" said the Lastani. "That is some cavalry! I myself am a balambaras for Wagshum Guangul. Can your horse go faster?"

Chala dug his heels into Eagle, and the horse stretched his legs.

All around them, horses and men pounded down the road to Adua. As they flew along, they could see other men and horses also, running across the fields from all directions, all running toward Adua.

No one can ride like an Ethiopian horseman.

No one can run like an Ethiopian warrior.

It is ten miles from Axum to Adua, and it was five miles further to Menelik's tent. The first of the horses streamed through Adua in under half an hour. The first of the runners were not too far behind.

Up into the hills galloped Eagle, up and over the passes that led to Menelik's tent. Coming over the last rise, Chala could see the red tent far below. He reined in Eagle, and Chala and the general from Lasta gazed at the scene below.

There was firing everywhere. Everywhere they looked, the armies of Ethiopia were advancing.

"Hurry up! Hurry up!" yelled Gebre Medhin. "We don't want to miss this battle!"

Chala gave Eagle his head, and the highland pony sped down the hill toward the tent.

There was no one at the royal tent. The drums stood alone before it, abandoned. Only one old priest hobbled along on a stick, and Chala halted Eagle beside him.

"Where is everyone?" cried Chala. "Where is the Emperor? Where are the drummers and trumpeteers?"

The old priest leaned on his stick. He looked up and winced. Then he smiled and pointed to the east. "All gone," he said. "Gone to the battle."

A roar of guns came from the Mariam Shavita Valley.

"Where is the Emperor?" asked Gebre Medhin, incredulous.

The old priest cackled. "He leads the army," he said, pointing east again. "At the very head of the army, with his sword and spear."

"Indet!" exclaimed Gebre Medhin. "And the army of the Wagshum is where?"

"I do not know," said the priest. "Out there somewhere."

"Hell," said Gebre Medhin, and slid off Eagle. He turned to Chala and shouted, "Chala! Many thanks. May God be with you today." He held up his hand, palm outward.

"Gebre Medhin! God and Saint Michael be with you!" yelled Chala, saluting the balambaras. "Where are you going?"

Gebre Medhin was running east. "To the battle!" he yelled, without turning.

"Old Father," said Chala. "Where are all the priests, the Abuna, the bishops?"

"Out there too, somewhere," said the priest matter-of-factly. "Heading for the battle, or in it by now, I would guess." He pointed to his leg. "I would be there as well," he said, "but I can't walk. I fell over something. I think it is broken."

Chala pointed behind him. "Thousands come," he said. "Stay here and tell them where to go. Where are the bishops?"

"Straight out, as far as I know," said the priest.

"Thank you, Reverend Father," said Chala. "May God do something good for you on my behalf!"

"Likewise," said the old priest, weakly. Beads of sweat dotted the old priest's forehead. He began to sway, and looked for a place to sit.

Chala dug his heels into Eagle, and hurled him east at a gallop.

CHAPTER 51

THE VALLEY OF

THE MARIAM SHAVITA

It had taken Dabormida more time than he would have liked to get to the head of the valley. The road had deteriorated into a jumble of rock-strewn paths on the way. The land itself had become rockier and steeper. Still, he was happy with the results. Now he was at the head of the valley, and began to form his troops for the assault against the Ethiopian camp. They would go up the side of the valley on a wide front. When they got to the top, they would form into a phalanx and storm the camp. But they had to be quick about it. It was already almost 7:30.

Looking down on Dabormida from the heights of Mount Adi Abuna, Mengesha and Alula sat on their horses. They couldn't believe what they saw.

"He is crazy," said Alula, over and over. "He is crazy. The man must be mad."

"When they are driven back down into the valley," said Mengesha, "then we will come down on them from this side."

"It will be simply slaughter," said Alula. "There is no glory in this."

"It will be necessary," said Mengesha.

"My heart is sick," said Alula. "I hate them, and I want them dead or out of my country, but this....."

"It is no fight," said Mengesha, shaking his head.

"It is a slaughter," said Alula.

The two rases, high up on the mountain, could see what Dabormida could not. Just back from the rim of the valley, on the edge of the plateau, Ras Wole waited with 4000 men. Just behind him was Ras Attakim with 3000 of his men of the Simien. In reserve, behind them all, was the Empress Taitu, with 3000 of her men. Ten thousand waited for four thousand Italian soldiers who were tired from an all-night march; who were being driven to attack uphill by a lunatic with maniacal eyes.

Far beyond the rim of the valley, the Tigrean rases could also see the armies of Menelik and Makonnen as they, in their thousands, swept toward the Hill of Belah. And far off to the east, they could make out a long, winding column of white-clad Galla cavalry. Those horsemen were almost to the Spur of Belah, and they were beginning to turn down into the valley where Dabormida should have been. There would be no hope for Dabormida's refugees, running back down the valley from the battle. The Galla would spear them like pigs.

Down in the valley of the Mariam Shavita, Dabormida shouted "Charge!" He lifted his pistol straight up and fired once into the air. The Italian troopers cheered and began to climb the side of the valley.

Just as they cleared the lip of the valley and emerged onto the plateau, even before they could really see anything, Ras Wole screamed "Fire!" and his men released a volley into the massed Italians. Then there were the screams of the wounded, and the disbelief of the unwounded, and officers yelling to go forward, and the lines wavering, and Wole's men went down into the grass to reload, and behind them, Attakim's men fired.

Then, behind them all, something happened that the Ethiopians never forgot. Empress Taitu shouted "Forward, my men!" and she herself, Mauser pistol in hand, began to walk toward the battle. Her ladies of the court went forward with her. Her soldiers cheered and ran forward, and soon Wole's and Attikim's and Taitu's troops were among the Italians, and men fought hand to hand, and knife to gun, and men went down in death by the hundreds, and the Italians tumbled back down from the rim of the plateau, back down into the bottom of the valley, the Ethiopians right in back of them and among them, and there was pandemonium until Dabormida rallied his troops around the mountain guns.

Then, high up, Mengesha shouted "Now!" and Alula, his moment of compassion ended, screamed "Kill them!" Down from that mountain, running, came the Tigreans, the remnants of the great Northern Army, the hardened veterans of the northern front; and they came with vengeance in their eyes.

Mt. Eschano: Baratieri—8:15 am

"You say there are none of our men on the Spur of Belah? None?"

"Not a one, General," said the courier.

"My God," said Baratieri.

Every officer and guard with the general turned their eyes toward the Spur. It sat there looking like a little fort with sparse grass and trees on it. In the early morning sun, a mile-and-a-half away, it looked like the perfect defensive position. And Dabormida was not there. He was gone. He had taken his entire force, leaving not a single patrol behind.

As Baratieri and his men watched, there was movement on the crest of the Spur. There were horsemen there, dressed in white robes. Tiny in the distance, they rode across the crest and looked around. There were not many of them—perhaps a hundred—and they did not stay long. Almost immediately, shells from Arimondi's guns fell among them. Some men and horses went down and the others pulled back out of sight. But they were Ethiopians, no doubt of that, and they were on Arimondi's flank. They were almost flanking Arimondi!

"General, sir," said Colonel Branca, "I believe, sir, that we may be in danger of being outside our lines....."

"Whatever lines are left," said Baratieri. "Come. We go back to Rebbi Arienni, to Elleni's brigade. From there, over to Mount Rajo, to see what is happening with Albertone. Let's go!"

Baratieri returned quickly to Elleni's headquarters. As soon as he spotted Elleni, he called out, "General, send three of your battalions to the Spur of Belah. It is the key, and it is not held. Get them up there quickly."

"But Commander, isn't Dabormida...."

"Dabormida is gone, General. Gone! Just gone! I don't know where. I don't know why. He has simply disappeared. Hurry. Get your units up there. We must hold that spur. Your three other units, hold them here. One to move at a moment's notice, another to cover that road over there. In case we have to leave in a hurry. Don't want to have to fight over who gets the road, do we? Now, I am going over to Mount Rajo to see Albertone's situation for myself. I have already told Albertone that I am sending him some of your men. So, I would like to see that last detachment of yours following me. When they arrive at Rajo, I will direct them where I think it best."

As he climbed the side of Mount Rajo, Baratieri looked behind him and was relieved to see Elleni's battalions heading quickly for their new positions on Belah. Behind him, at the double, came another of Elleni's crack battalions. This was stretching things too thin, but he had to get some help to Albertone. He had to have those troops right with him, to hurl them forward with tremendous force, to save Albertone.

Baratieri crested the ridge of Rajo and looked down into the valley between Mount Belah and False Kidane Meheret. Halfway down the hill,

Galliano's line of askaris were in position. All of them were intently watching the valley. Baratieri saw what they saw, and sucked in his breath.

Below, for the length of the valley, broken soldiers were running back toward Sauria. They ran in clumps and singly, and every once in a while one of them would drop and stay still. Hardly any of them had their rifles or any equipment. There were hundreds of them. They ran with a single purpose—to escape the battle; to flee from the fight. And across the valley, in positions on Kidane Meheret that these men should have occupied, there were Ethiopians. All along that hill, there were Ethiopian sharpshooters, homing in on the running figures.

From far off, in the plain beyond the corner of the hill, came the sounds of a tremendous battle.

"Colonel," called Baratieri, motioning the battalion commander to him, "take a position to the right of the askaris. Somewhere where you can take some shots at those Ethiopians on that hill. More important, where you can assist Arimondi at a moment's notice."

"But General Albertone?"

Baratieri's jaw tightened. "I'm afraid it is too late for Albertone," he said. "The best thing we can do for him now is to have a good position here for him to retreat to. If he is too mangled, you can direct him up here, then back to General Elleni's headquarters. If he still has some troops in decent condition, keep them here with you. Perhaps try to re-occupy that hill over there; keep those sharpshooters off of it. You have a grave responsibility, Colonel. Do as you think best. You are the core around which we will build a new line. Above all, support Albertone as he retreats. But don't try to go out for him. That would only lose you your own men."

The colonel led his troops down onto the saddle between Mount Rajo and Mount Belah. Here he could command the road and give cover to the retreating troops. Here, also, he was covered by Galliano's askaris, stationed higher up the hill. And here, he could quickly, if necessary, form a reserve for Arimondi, dug in on the far side of Belah.

Dejazmach Baltcha

At 8:30 a.m., Baltcha launched a total assault against Albertone's position. He began with a renewed artillery barrage against the Italian guns. Then, twelve thousand men attacked what was left of Albertone's brigade.

By 9:00 a.m., it was over. Two thousand of Albertone's men were dead. A thousand were injured. A thousand were streaming over the lip of that little valley, guns thrown away, hands in the air. As they ran down into the valley, they were met by the three thousand fighters of Ras Makonnen that Baltcha had stationed there. These lucky captives were marched off towards

Avanti, i mei alpini!

Adua. Five hundred more unlucky Italian troops were running for their lives back toward the main Italian lines, and being shot to pieces as they ran. These were the men Baratieri could see from Mount Rajo.

Albertone was dead. No more would he be a victim of fate or of another man's bad judgment. He came to his end fighting against overwhelming odds, in a situation not of his own making, in a place not of his own choosing. If he had a fault, it was believing in a resurgent Roman Empire, in a dream of a nation's glory. He never knew that the Prime Minister of that nation considered him and two or three thousand others "expendable" for the glory of a new nation and the pride of men who sat behind desks and lolled in manicured parks far away in a beautiful homeland. Far from the grandeur of Italy, in a nightmare of horror and fear and stupidity and ignorance, Albertone died.

At 9:15, Baltcha signaled Ras Mikael to bring his troopers forward, to bring them up that little valley. Five thousand Oromo warriors rode up that protected valley toward Mount Belah. To one side of them they saw the prisoners being marched away, and that gave them hope and lightened their hearts. Before them lay the unknown future, filled with guns and fear and the smell of death. Onward they rode, and their horses stamped the ground and made it quiver. They rode like a wave in the sea, and they looked fierce and lean and wrathful. This was the time for the spilling of blood. This was the time of killing, and they were ready and eager for it to begin.

Menelik—9:45 am

In the center of the great plateau, Menelik and Makonnen waited on horseback in a small hollow while their armies surged about them and picked their way forward toward the Italian lines. For the plateau was not a mesa, nor a table top, but it rolled and flowed and formed little valleys and small hills, and the soldiers moved sometimes protected by the terrain and sometimes not. Whenever a formation of Ethiopians crested a hill, the Italians would open fire with their artillery and send them scampering for the next small bit of cover. So it went, the Ethiopian armies moving steadily forward, taking losses, looking for cover, keeping together, getting into position for the final charge.

"Jesus Christ!" exclaimed Menelik, as an Italian shell howled overhead and plowed into the hill behind them, and the exclamation was not a prayer. He turned to Makonnen. "Where the hell is your artillery?"

Makonnen coolly withdrew his pocket watch from his robe and looked at it. "Some time yet," he said. "Ten-fifteen minutes, maybe, they'll be up, be in range. Another few minutes to sight them....."

"We may have to go without them," said Menelik. "We can't just sit here and get shot at."

As he spoke, riders converged on his position. From the south came Kanyazmach Tafessa, and he was grinning. He slipped from his horse and prostrated himself before Menelik, then jumped quickly to his feet.

"Great Emperor," he said. "I bring you glad tidings. Under King Tekle Haimanot, Wagshum Guangul, and Dejazmach Baltcha, we have dismantled that enemy brigade on the right. They are finished. They are prisoners, dead, or running for their lives. We have captured six guns, thousands of rifles and pistols, two machine-guns, and some officers."

"Officers!" said Menelik from the saddle. "Who led that army?"

"General Albertone, Janhoi. He is dead."

"Dead?" said Menelik. "Dead?"

"Yes, Your Majesty."

Menelik looked at Makonnen as if to say, 'I don't know if that's good or not,' but there was no time to ponder the question. A rider came in from the north. This one did not bother to dismount. It was Ras Attakim of the Simien. "We have them! We have them!" he yelled "They are trapped in the Mariam Shavita! They are running down the valley with Mengesha and Wole and Alula nipping at their heels, and thousands of Galla horse waiting for them down there at the end. And your wife, Janhoi! Your wife!"

"My wife? What about my wife?"

"She was right there, Your Majesty! She was right there with us. Marched right into the middle of the battle with a Mauser pistol in her hand. I've never seen anything like it." Attakim threw back his head and laughed. "And the fool who led them is dead."

"Baratieri is dead?" said a startled Menelik.

"No no no," said Attakim. "I am sorry. His underling. Dabormida. The Tigreans got to him before we could, and there's not much left of the body, but it's Dabormida, all right. Oh, and we have eight guns and six machine-guns and all of their supplies. Found them just lying around over there. We'll eat well tonight."

"Where is my wife?" asked Menelik, fearing the worst.

"She is leading her troops, and some of mine, up along the left side of the plateau. She is concerned about you."

"Concerned about me? The idiot. She should be concerned about herself!"

"She does not know where you are, Majesty. She fears for your safety."

"I can't understand that," said Menelik, as two more shells plowed up the hill behind them. "As you can see, we are perfectly safe."

"I shall report that to her, Janhoi?" asked Attakim.

"Tell her we are at tea with the British observers," said Menelik wryly.

Attakim laughed again. "May I go then, Your Majesty?" he asked.

The Battle of Adowa:
The Last Rally of
General Dabormida

"Go by the grace of God" said Menelik, and as the young ras rode off, the emperor turned toward his cousin and said, "Well, Makonnen, what do you think of that? Both their right and their left demolished. Done for. Finished. It is incomprehensible!"

"They still have steel left in their hands," said Makonnen. "This is the hard part. Ask anyone of the north when was the last time we took an Italian fort. And that hill up there—they have made it into a fort. They probably have fifty guns up there, and their troops are dug in. It will be hard. We will do it, but it will be hard."

"Your Majesty, Your Excellency," broke in Tafessa. He was standing next to his horse, preparing to mount. "The rest of my message: Dejazmach Baltcha earnestly requests that you hold your armies at the ready. Ras Mikael rides through a valley on the right, and will come out on the right of the Hill of Belah. He will attempt to turn the flank. If he does so, then it will be the time to attack." Tafessa hurtled into the saddle. "Dejazmach Baltcha humbly requests that you wait for the next messengers, who will let you know when the time is good."

"Kanyazmach," said Makonnen, "did Dejazmach Baltcha say when this would happen?"

There was a tremendous roar of rifles from the front, where the Hill of Belah dipped down to meet that little hidden valley. Tafessa grinned. "Right about now, Baltcha said. Permission to go, Your Majesty? I want to be in on this!"

"Go with Saint George at your side, Kanyazmach!" yelled Menelik to him. "You have done your duty today!"

Behind them, over the hill that the Italian gunners had ripped up, more men were coming. They were not in formation. They were running and riding. They came singly and in groups. As they ran, they shouted, "Your Majesty! Wait for us! Ethiopia, be happy!" and on they ran, leaving the Emperor behind as they tried to reach the frontmost units of the army.

The troops of the Italian center were crack troops. Here were stationed most of the Alpini—3500 of them—plus other seasoned units, machine-gunners, and the bulk of the artillery. There were over forty artillery pieces placed on the Hill of Belah, and as the morning wore on and the infantrymen began to be satisfied with their digging and fortifications, they amused themselves by watching the artillery play havoc with the Ethiopian troops and tents.

From here, the Italian heavy guns could reach the Ethiopian encampments, so the artillerymen divided their time between trying to take down Menelik's red tent and homing in on the Ethiopian formations trying to advance across the plateau. It was fun to watch them. They appeared and disappeared among the small hills and valleys like pieces of flotsam and jetsam cresting the waves of the sea.

The soldiers decided that the Imperial Tent was like the Leaning Tower of Pisa, and they waited to see just when a shell would blow it over. They took turns watching it through their officers' binoculars. The soldiers took bets on what the artillery would do next. They sat back, checked their weapons, and smoked their cigars.

The disturbance began calmly enough. First there was the distant shooting on their left flank, and the warning shots fired by their compatriots on that end of the line. The soldiers stood and craned their necks to see what was happening. Then there was a sound like the low rumbling of distant thunder. Suddenly, coming up over the gently rising slope to the south there was a horde of horsemen, all yelling like banshees and urging their horses on up the hill. The Italian troops started firing, but the horsemen came on. There were thousands of them, and they were having a hard time of it. Riding uphill, their horses were nowhere near a gallop. Soon they began to fall—men and horses together, and those in the front ranks were being badly mauled. But on they came. The Italians stood and scrambled to places where they could fire at will, and fire they did, and suddenly, the horsemen turned aside and started to run their mounts uphill, away from the Italian line. The Italians poured fire into them, but soon the Ethiopians were too far up the hill, out of range, and then, they kept going, up and over the ridge.

Only then, in the sudden quiet, did the infantry realize what had happened. They were outflanked! The enemy was behind them. Quickly orders were given to go up and attack. Units formed and started up the hill, but the men were unsure of the situation. They would be attacking uphill. It would be hard. Suddenly, their advantage was gone. Those horsemen could divide the army, splitting it into two or three parts... This could not be happening.

Then again from the south came the sound of more shooting, as the units on the far left began to fire on what appeared to be Ethiopian stragglers left behind by the charge. The soldiers looked, and fired, and looked again. The stragglers were unhorsed, on foot, and were running back and forth. There appeared to be about fifty of them. Strange. There were horses running around, too, and other animals. Mules, it looked like. Well, they would be dead horses and mules and Ethiops before long. The Alpini aimed their rifles.

"Hurry, boys, hurry!" Bedasa Merga yelled. "Set up quick! Remember the drill! Sharpshooters! Protect us! Protect your gunners!" He looked to the north along the slope of the hill. Already, Alpini were running toward his position, firing as they ran. Two of Bedasa's guards went down, shot down as quietly as trees. They never had a chance to even raise their rifles.

"Ready, men?" Bedasa looked around. Gunners nodded at him. Bedasa raised his sword and brought it down. "Fire!" he screamed. "Kill them! Kill them! Kill the bastards!"

The four machine-guns burst into fire. Bullets flew down the Italian line hissing lead death. Bedasa could see men jerk and fall and go down in pieces. He could see more of them come on, running straight into his guns.

"Kill them! Reap! Reap!" yelled Bedasa. "Kill them all!"

Artillery shells burst among his men. Bodies went flying everywhere. One of his guns was left without a crew. Bedasa rushed to it and grabbed a sharpshooter on the way. The two of them righted the gun, and Bedasa fired.

"A great day to die!" Bedasa screamed. "A great day! Look at them. Look at them come. How brave they are! How brave these soldiers are! It is an honor to die with them!"

The Italians were still firing and running toward them. Another of Bedasa's machineguns exploded in a shell burst.

"Let us show them what Ethiopians are!" Bedasa screamed. "Keep firing! Keep firing!"

Then there was a sound that came through the earth. It came as if it were the father of all other sounds. It came over the sound of machine-guns, over the sound of artillery, over the screams and shouts and howls of men dying and being cut to pieces. Bedasa and the other one of his gunners who was left stopped firing for a second. Even the Italians stopped their attack. They all looked up, up the hill, to see what shook the earth.

And there—coming down the hill in a wild charge—there were the cavalrymen of Arusi and Ba'le, of Shoa and Wollo, the five thousand men of Ras Mikael who had turned on the ridge, turned back down the slope, and now they were charging downhill in a wild charge that could not be stopped, and it was rifle against spear, pistol against sword, bodies against the muscle of horses and wild cries of attack against the terrifying screams of death, and the horsemen of the south roared down upon the left of the Italian line, and Bedasa kept his Maxim guns firing their deadly cross-fire, and the Alpini went down in heaps, but fighting to the end. Their officers took out their pistols and aimed at cavalrymen and were speared as they aimed, but they never gave ground. Their soldiers followed them into their graves. Never was a battlefield more ribboned with death than this. Never were bodies piled on bodies like this. It was carnage. It was murder. On both sides. No one did right or wrong. All did what they could to live and kill. And always, the chatter of Bedasa's Maxim guns kept on, and always men died.

It all happened in fifteen minutes, and then it was over, and the left wing of the Italian line was gone. Dead. Along with an equal number of Ethiopians. All that was left was the scream of the dying.

Then, far over to the north, a wild howling mob of Ethiopians rushed over the Spur of Belah and started for the right flank of the Italian line. They were not led by anyone. They had come up from the Ethiopian rear and just went for the hill. Arimondi's troopers slammed into them with everything they had, but it never stopped them. On they came, driving a wedge between Arimondi and Elleni. Far beyond them, riding down the north road to Sauria, having done with Dabormida, went the left flank cavalry of Ras Mikael.

Reap! Reap!

"Come! Come, you fool! We have work to do!" yelled Kanyazmach Didda at Badilla Wami. Badilla only laughed. He sat there on his horse, halfway up the Hill of Belah, and faced out toward the plateau, and he laughed. He did not heed his bloody sword in his right hand. He did not heed the words of the Kanyazmach. He just sat and watched. He could not believe it.

"Look, sir! Look!" he shouted to Didda. "Look at this. I have never seen anything like it. Look at them come!" Didda looked where Badilla pointed, and saw what Badilla saw. All the way across the plain, out of every crevice and nook and cranny, the Ethiopians were up; the men of the Imperial Army and the Army of Harar were up and running. Huge formations were hurling themselves forward. The Italian guns roared, and great holes appeared in the Ethiopian formations, but the holes filled up and the armies advanced. "Listen to them cheer!" yelled Badilla. "You can hear them even up here!"

"It is a beautiful sight, Aleka," said Didda, "but if you do not follow me I will have to take off the top of your head with my sword."

"Not just the army, sir!" yelled Badilla. "Not just the army! Look beyond!"

Behind the army formations, thousands of horsemen and infantrymen ran toward the front. All over the plateau they were running forward.

"They look like ants! Like bees!" yelled Badilla.

"Locusts! Rats! Whatever! Come, Aleka! I need you! We have work to do!" The Kanyazmach took his whip and sliced it against the side of Badilla's horse. The animal lurched forward. Badilla's mouth opened wide in surprise, then he understood his position and moved with a will. Never before had he seen this. Always before, armies fell apart. Men went back, holding their wounds. This did not happen here. All day, everyone moved forward. All day, people came out of nowhere and attacked the invaders. All day!

As Badilla gained the ridge, he turned in his saddle to once again view the field of battle. From here the view was superb. All across the plateau, lines and formations of soldiers were rushing forward. In the center of Belah itself, where the Italian lines still held, the mountain guns continued to thunder. Badilla grinned and shook his head in wonder, then kicked his heels into his horse and took off after Didda.

The Kanyasmach was far ahead, trying to catch up with Ras Mikael. The Ras and his staff were riding through the mass of horsemen on the ridge, dividing them as they went. Some they headed down the back side of the hill on foot—maybe a thousand of them forming a skirmish line—and the others were drawing up in a new charge formation. This time the charge would be to the east, downhill into the battalion placed down there in the saddle between Belah and Rajo by Baratieri. Badilla could see them waiting down there, getting ready.

Bedane came galloping up to Badilla. "Aleka Badilla!" he shouted. "I thought you were dead!"

"Me, dead?" Badilla jeered "From what? I see no lions here. I see your sword is red. Good work. Where are our men? Are there any left?"

"I have seen many of them," said Bedane, "but they are all scattered. I think we did all right. The boys from Shoa were hit hard, though."

"Well, we'll think about that later," said Badilla. "It looks like a lot of us are left. Enough to scatter those foot soldiers down there." Suddenly he exclaimed, "Look over there!"

Bedane looked down into the valley between Belah and the False Kidane Meheret. Where before the disheveled bands of Albertone's soldiers had run, now Ethiopian soldiers ran toward the east, toward Sauria.

"It looks like they are running a footrace!" said Bedane.

"True," laughed Badilla. "Tekle Haimanot and Guangul must be hungry! They are each trying to get to the Italian food first!"

"There's Mamo and the boys."

"Go see to them. Rally our men as best you can," ordered Badilla. "I follow the Kanyazmach." He galloped off.

"Mamo!" yelled Bedane, riding up to him, "How are you? Is everyone all right?"

Mamo's eyes gleamed like steel. He was enjoying this fight. "Only Ibbsa, Egersa, and Wondimu are here with me," said Mamo. "The others are all right, I think. Here, there, everywhere. There are no units anymore. Just thousands of us riding together." Mamo smiled. "Still, it's quite a force, isn't it?"

"That it is," Bedane agreed. "Come, let's get these boys lined up. I think we'll be going down this hill before you know it."

The line of skirmishers was moving slowly down the hill. Kneeling, firing, up again and moving forward in a tenuous white-clad line a half-mile long, they gradually began to close on the enemy.

Behind them, the horsemen formed up, and at a signal from Ras Mikael they moved their mounts forward at a walk, gradually coming up to and through the skirmish line. Then, as they waited for the signal to charge, they could see that the Italian troops below were starting to move. Beginning with a quick-march that soon turned into a run, the enemy battalion abandoned its position and headed back toward the hill of Rebbi Arienni.

Ras Mikael had raised his hand for the signal to charge, but quickly lowered it. Now he issued new orders. On the left, fifteen hundred men would chase the Italian unit back to its old lines. Another fifteen hundred would gallop down to the former battalion position, get off their horses, and start up Mount Rajo to attack the askaris. The skirmish line would follow them and become the second wave of the attack. Dejazmach Wube would lead the left up toward Rebbi Arianni. Didda would lead the attack on the askaris. Grazmach Roba would back up Didda with the skirmishers. Ras Mikael raised his hand again.

"Forward!" he yelled, and the troops, mounted and on foot, surged down the hill.

Up on Mount Rajo, the askaris were stunned. They saw the Italians retreating below them, leaving them alone to face the oncoming Gallas. To their right, they could see that other Galla warriors would cut them off from Baratieri's force. To their left, they could see Guangul's and Tekle Haimanot's soldiers chasing the remnants of Albertone's men down the valley. Far to the north, they could see the battles around the Spur of Belah and the Ethiopian column heading toward Sauria over the northern road.

Soon they would be surrounded, at the mercy of the fierce Galla. In a flash, a panic came over all of them. This could not be. They could not stand against the horror of the Galla. To a man, they rose from their positions. Some turned around. Shots were fired, and their Italian officers went down. Their colonel, Galliano, died instantly from a multitude of bullets. Then the askaris turned toward the onrushing Gallas and throwing away their rifles, thrusting their arms into the air and sending up a cheer, they began to run downhill.

Didda, down in the col, stopped his advance and ordered his men to aim their rifles at the oncoming askaris. The askaris slowed to a walk, but still came on. "We surrender!" they yelled in Tigrean. "We want to join you!"

None of the Gallas knew Tigrean.

"Keep those rifles up, boys," yelled the Kanyazmach. "They look like they want to surrender, but it's better to be sure." Didda's words did not carry to all his men. The askaris kept on coming, and suddenly some shots rang out. A few askaris went down. The rest of them fell down on their knees, on their faces, wailing out their surrender.

" Aleka Badilla," said Didda, "They appear to be surrendering. Take five hundred men and circle them. Then march them back to Adua and beyond. Disperse them into bands of a hundred. Give them to Atse Menelik's army."

Badilla was distraught. "Sir!" he exclaimed. "Leave the battle?"

"Your sword is red," said Didda. "You have done your part, and done it well."

"Sir, it is not over!" said Badilla. "I am a soldier, not a jailor. Please, sir! Please!"

The Kanyazmach sat in his saddle and sighed and frowned. He mulled over the possibilities. He could use five hundred men as jailors and lose them for the rest of the fight, or he could just have them shoot these askaris. But the askaris might prove useful later on. He might even use them as a first wave of attack against the Ferengis. Or he could -

"Aleka," he said, "take those five hundred men I gave you and find ropes, straps, cloth, anything. Tie these traitors up and leave them here. When you are finished, we will move on. Meanwhile, I'll tell Grazmach Roha and Dejazmach Wube what we are doing."

"Yes, sir!" yelled Badilla, grinning.

"Aleka!" exclaimed the Kanyazmach. "There are plenty of horses down on the far side of the hill. Use their harnesses to tie up these fellows if you have to. Then assign whatever wounded or worn-out men you have to guard them."

"Yes, sir, Balambaras Didda!" yelled Badilla.

Kanyazmach Didda laughed, tickled at his instant, if unofficial, promotion.

Baratieri—10:45 am

From their vantage point on Rebbi Arianni, Baratieri and Elleni surveyed the wreckage of their army. They knew Albertone was gone, and they suspected the worst for Dabormida. They knew that Arimondi still held; they could listen to the fight he was waging. But on both sides of Arimondi, the Ethiopians were raging around them like a storm tide at sea.

To their right, Elleni's troops were just holding on to their positions. Ethiopians were swarming over the Spur of Belah and up the lower slopes of Belah and Rebbi Arianni itself. Alarmingly, there were Ethiopian cavalry heading down the north road toward the base at Sauria. As much as Elleni's few guns punched at them, they kept riding east, from where they could either attack the base or encircle Rebbi Arianni.

To their left, they watched more Galla cavalry come down from Belah onto Colonel Bellini's position. They saw Colonel Bellini abandon that position at a run; then, horror of horrors, they watched as the askaris turned on their officers and shot them.

"We have to give Arimondi a chance to get back here," muttered Baratieri. "As soon as he gets here, we call retreat, and get back to Sauria."

"What about Dabormida?" asked Elleni.

"I think he's done for, Emilio. I don't know where he is, he sends no messages, the Ethiopians pour down the Mariam Shavita.....Look at them! Just hold on here, please. Be sure your men know to cover Arimondi's. Get your troops back here in a tight defense, and we'll extricate as many as possible."

The two generals stood looking out to the west. From their position, the ground sloped down into a shallow valley, then up again to form the ridgeline of Belah. Beyond that ridge the artillery still boomed and small-arms and machine-gun fire kept up a huge racket.

Then, one by one, the mountain guns began to fall silent. Soon there seemed to be only a few of them still firing. With each gun that went silent, the rifle fire intensified. With each gun that went silent, Baratieri and Elleni grew more nervous. Baratieri shuffled his feet; Elleni compressed his lips and tugged at his moustache.

Finally, only two or three artillery pieces continued to fire. On the skyline of Belah appeared a vast mob of men. Some were Italian; most were Ethiopian. Some Italians were still in units, fighting as they retreated. But the Ethiopians were in among them, attacking. Always attacking. As Baratieri and Elleni watched, the Italian units wavered and broke and gave way, and the fight began to tumble down the side of Belah, a great melee of shouting and hacking and spearing and hand-to-hand combat. What was left of Arimondi's command made a run for Ellini's lines, but Elleni's soldiers could not cover them. There were no targets for Elleni's guns. The Ethiopians were right in among Arimondi's men, reaching for them, pulling them down. And there were thousands upon thousands of Ethiopians, for in truth all of Menelik's and Makonnen's troops were on that hill and coming over the top, and they were mad. They had taken the fire of Arimondi's brigade and the artillery it had protected. Thousands of their friends and comrades had been killed and butchered by that fire, and now they sought revenge.

The Italians fought back as best they could, but the odds were incredibly great. As Baratieri looked at the wave of Italian troops rushing down that hill, it looked like a wave of the sea that crests on a beach, only the live water still rushing onward, leaving the fallen behind to die in back of it on the sand. So terrible was that fight that bodies fell on top of one another. There was no room to move without stepping on the dead and wounded. On the fight came, now down into the little valley, with Elleni's troops still helpless to aid their countrymen.

"It is over!" exclaimed Elleni. "Sir, save my men at least!"

"Sound retreat," ordered Baratieri. "Get them back in as good an order as you can. We aim for Sauria, and we'll dig in there. Forget the guns. Get the men out, and try to keep them in good order."

General Elleni did a remarkable job that day. Not only did he get his men off of those hills, he picked up the stragglers from Arimondi's and Albertone's brigades and brought them along too. He had his soldiers keep in formation and double-timed them out of there, with the Ethiopian armies all around. He almost got them back to Sauria, but as he neared that fortified hill, the Italian and askari troops that had been stationed there came running from that base, for it was already under attack by the armies under Dejazmach Baltcha. Elleni could see the Ethiopians swarming over the wreckage of that hill. That Galla cavalry was there, too, and forming up for another attack. To the north, more cavalry could be seen, and more Ethiopian foot soldiers. These were the troops of Mengesha and Alula and Wole and Attakim and Empress Taitu, who, having finished with Dabormida, were ready now for another fight.

The Italian army was not ready for another fight. The eyes of its soldiers were dazed and dull. They were in shock. All they wanted was to get out of there.

Baratieri and Elleni shepherded their beaten troops away from that valley of death; away from the hill fort of Sauria. They brought them through the small town of Entichhio, then across the Mareb River. Always the Ethiopians were at their heels, snapping away like jackals at a wounded antelope. All that afternoon the Italians retreated. Finally, in the night, the Ethiopians left them alone.

But if Baratieri and his army were finished, back on the battlefield the Ethiopians were exultant. They had carried the day. They had changed history. Now Europe and the world would forever look on Ethiopia as a sovereign nation.

From that battlefield, the Ethiopians took all the Italian mountain guns—sixty-six of them. From that field also, they took 11,000 rifles and huge supplies of ammunition. They took and ate right away all the food that Baratieri had abandoned. From that field they took fourteen hundred prisoners, and marched them far into Ethiopia—to Addis Ababa, to Harar, to Gondar and beyond, to wait for peace negotiations to be concluded.

They had destroyed the Italian army. No one knew how badly the Italians had lost until two days later when Baratieri, cowering behind the walls of Asmara, took stock.

Of an army of twenty thousand, only eight thousand one hundred men straggled into Asmara. Seven thousand Italian and askari soldiers were dead. Two thousand five hundred were wounded. A thousand askaris had defected. Fourteen hundred Italian prisoners were marching into Ethiopia. Generals Albertone, Arimondi, and Dabormida, and Colonel Galliano, were dead.

On that field the Ethiopians had left sixty-five hundred dead men and women. From that field they dragged eight thousand Ethiopian wounded. Among their dead were Fitaurari Gebre Iyesus, Commander of the Imperial Army; Fitaurari Damtew Ketema, the Emperor's former envoy to Russia; Kanyazmach Taffesse Abayneh, first to bring word of the battle to Menelik; and Balambaras Gebre Medhin Wolde Amanuel, who had ridden from Axum with Chala Negassa on the back of Eagle. And along with them died a strong, happy young man of Arusi named Dabale Ariti.

There was exultation and grief in the Ethiopian camp that night. As the armies straggled back in, exhausted, friends looked for friends and finding them, embraced them and laughed and danced. Soldiers shared food taken from Sauria. More food began to trickle in from the countryside, both from the army scouting parties and from country people seeking to join in the victory celebrations.

There were many missing. Soldiers and followers alike stood by the edge of the plateau and, looking across it, recounted what they had seen there—the bodies, the beaten enemy, the thousands of wounded—and they mourned and wept. But they consoled each other, saying that their comrades had died for them, for their freedom, for the Motherland. They swore they would never forget them, that they would hide their faces in their shammas and weep for the fallen.

Out on the plateau, priests gave the last rites to the dying and consoled the injured. Doctors from the Russian Red Cross gathered the wounded and brought them to the field hospitals.

Badilla Wami bounded down the hillside to the camp of the Meraro band. "Hey, boys!" he shouted. "How are you? How did you fare?"

"We are well, Aleka!" said an animated Mamo. "We all came back except Dabale. He's probably visiting somewhere. Tula and Ibbsa saddled up to look for him. Not a scratch on anyone."

"That is even better than I thought," said Badilla, smiling. "You haven't, by any chance, seen Bedane, have you?"

"No," said Mamo, "but others have. He, too, searches for Dabale. He is well, I hear."

"He is an excellent soldier," said Badilla. "An excellent fighter. As are you, Mamo. As are you all. You really proved yourselves today."

From the next camp a couple of the Bekoji boys shouted. "Hey, Wondimu!" they called. "Come over here and lead us in a song!"

Wondimu grinned, grabbed his shield and spear, and loped off toward the Bekoji camp. Shiferaw jumped up and followed him over, and so did

Shasho. The Bekoji soldiers were up and brandishing their spears and yelling. They gathered around Wondimu as though he were the hub of a wheel and they the spokes. They jammed in close to him, and others, seeing the dance forming, came running to join in. Soon there were nearly fifty warriors clustered in that circle, jumping up and down, yelping and hollering, and Wondimu started to sing: "The Ferengi came to Adua to fight against the savages!" he sang.

The men, howling and laughing with glee, replied in chorus:

"This we know! This we know! This we know! This we know!"

"They came to fight but stayed to die!"

"This we know! This we know! This we know! This we know!"

"They fought against an army that had marched a thousand miles to them! They died by spear and bullet, by the knife and by the Maxim gun!"

"This we know! This we know! This we know! This we know!"

"We killed their generals, killed their captains, killed their famous mountain men. We drove them from our land so fast we'll never see them back again!"

"This we know! This we know! This we know! This we know!"

"Now they cower in their forts; our nation now is free again. Tomorrow we will drive them to the sea and into hell, my men!"

"This we know! This we know! This we know! This we know!"

At the end of the chorus Wondimu leaped for the sky, and the others followed. They came down hard, their feet stomping into the earth.

"YaHey! YaHey! YaHey! YaHey!" they chanted. "YaHey! YaHey! YaHey! YaHEY!"

In the Imperial tent there was likewise royal jubilation, with old Ras Alula laughing and cackling with glee, calling out to Menelik to lead them through Asmara and to the sea. Menelik smiled broadly as his rases and generals came in. Servants moved through the crowd bearing platters of meats and trays of tej. Then Menelik clapped his hands and called for order and began to speak:

"My brave soldiers!" he said. "My brave kings and barons! My warriors of the Ethiopian motherland! Now is the time for joy and sorrow. Sorrow for our dead comrades who have given their lives for us; but great and glorious joy for the preservation of the motherland. What can I give to you to make this day worthy of you? Here is what I will do: I will rain down blessings upon you from the Most High, and I will give you presents to take home with you. First I will give you this: for all of you who have stood by me in battle, I swear to you that I will stand by you even unto my death. If there is ever any trouble again in this land, and you call on me for help, my armies and the power of the Empire will be at your side. This I swear.

"Now, King Tekle Haimanot of Gojjam and Wagshum Guangul, King of Lasta, I pronounce that you are kings of your kingdoms forever, free to rule forever as such, and to each of you I give five mountain guns and as many rifles as your men can carry.

"To Ras Mikael, Protector of Wollo, I give you likewise five artillery pieces and the hand of my daughter in marriage, if that pleases you, as I think it might.

"To Ras Wole of Simien, here are your five guns, and machine-guns too, to guard the passes against the dervishes of the Sudan, and I give you men to show your men how to use these weapons to best advantage.

"Ras Attakim of Begemder. Guard Gondar well, my faithful cousin. It is for you to rule in that ancient city full of history, and here are the guns to help you do it."

Menelik turned and smiled at Ras Alula. "Alula, Old Man of the North, Defender of the Realm, I know you want me to drive the Ferengis into the sea. That may be possible, or it may not. But whatever happens tomorrow, here is what I say today, and I tell you that your Lord Ras Mengesha concurs in this. To you, Alula, I give my greatest thanks for your wonderful advice. For it was you it was who told Us what to do when We needed to know that. To you, Ras Alula, we give you the district of Axum, the most holy city of our Empire. Also, I give to you a gift of 100,000 thalers of silver. You have earned your rest."

Alula bowed low. What Menelik gave was great, but not what he wanted. Alula wanted Asmara. But thinking about Menelik's gift, he smiled to himself. One hundred thousand thalers would make him strong, and important. Perhaps in the future, Asmara....

Menelik looked at Dejazmach Baltcha. "Baltcha, faithful friend, know that I hold you in the greatest esteem. Though you are not of royal blood, I give you command of my army for as long as you wish it. I also command you, when we are done with this, to lead that army into Kaffa. We will finish that problem once and for all. And I make you Ras of Gemu, Gofa, and the other Oromo kingdoms in the southwest, with full powers to govern as you see fit. Thank you, my loyal general. Ras Mengesha, son of Yohannes, Keeper of Tigre, Defender of the North, to you, who have fought tirelessly for the integrity of the Kingdom, I confirm you as Ras of Tigre. Stay here in your home, defend the Empire, make the land sweet with peace. I pledge whatever you ask in help. All of us will always be ready to defend Tigre against any aggressors. Now to help you defend this land, beset on the north by the Ferengi, on the west by the Dervishes, and on the east by the ancient enemy realms of Ifat and Adal, I give you twenty new mountain guns. I give you 20,000 rifles, and 5,000,000 rounds of ammunition to go with them. I give you 300,000 thalers. Use this money well, and help your people. And I further confirm that your son and his sons forever will rule the land of Tigre. We shall be as brothers."

Menelik sighed and smiled and turned to Makonnen. "Cousin," he said, "what can I give to you? You already have everything you need. I would give you Europe, but you have already been there!" All the rases laughed low, and looked at Menelik and Makonnen. "You already have Harar. Keep it! Be my strength against any aggressor from the south. Here is what I will do. Where is your son?"

From behind Makonnen, a boy, small for six years of age, came forward. Menelik looked down at him and placed his large hands on the boy's head and showed him to the gathered nobles.

"Makonnen," said Menelik, "I cannot make you ras, for you are already ras. I cannot make you rich, for you are already rich. I cannot give you provinces, for you already have provinces. But here is what I can do. Here and now, I can make your son ras, and I give him the Province of Sidamo to rule. You, Makonnen, must train him to rule. Train him well. You will be his regent."

Makonnen smiled and bowed. Menelik had just given his family rule over two great southern provinces.

Menelik looked down at the thin, tiny boy, and moving his hands to the boy's shoulders, he said in a loud voice, "Tafari! Tafari Makonnen! Today I make you Ras of Sidamo! Govern well. Learn quickly. Be strong."

Then Menelik looked up at the assembled rases. "Nobles of Ethiopia!" he said. "Cousins! By the Grace of God and by My authority as Emperor of All the Ethiopias, I give you Our new governor of Sidamo, the son of Makonnen of Harar: I give you—Ras Tafari!"

On the western slope of the Hill of Belah, where the Oromo charge had come down on the Alpini, Bedane sat and looked out toward the red sun setting in the west. It was going down through an orange haze that painted mountains and sand and rocks and trees alike in a red and purple hue. Rising from that glorious red mist made out of the evening dust and haze came the moans of the wounded and dying. Voices begged for water and home and friendships lost forever. All through that haze, priests bent low and murmured over corpses and wounded alike, over friend and foe, and chanted them to heaven. Doctors and medics moved about the field, looking for the ones they could save. Friends brought water to their fallen comrades, and sometimes hope, and sometimes not. For as far as Bedane could see, bodies of men and horses stretched across the plains and hillsides. A great reek of death would come soon from this field.

Bedane looked down now at the lifeless form of Dabale Ariti. He looked to see where the bullets had ripped away Dabale's throat. He let his hand linger along the edges of the wounds. He felt the sticky, congealed blood of a boy who had turned quickly into a man and followed him north into battle.

Bedane closed Dabale's startled eyes. He sat and held Dabale's head in his hands. "Aiyee, Dabale!" he said to himself. "The battle is done. We have won. You did your duty. Now you are dead." Bedane gasped. He had forgotten to breathe. Now he took in the dusty, death-ridden air in great gulps. His body shuddered and quivered uncontrollably. "Dabale," he went on, "Dabale, Dabale. Who now will laugh so deeply at Wondimu's jokes, and sit with such attention listening to Taffa's stories? Who now will discuss the bible for hours never-ending with Ibbsa? Who now will race his horse like the wind against Tula's fine gray? Who will be so willing for work and play? Who will be our strength in battle and on the long march home?"

Bedane stopped his whispered mourning chant and sat gasping slowly. He held his hands open, like claws, and gazed at the blood on them. "Enemy blood. My blood. Dabale's blood," he thought. Bedane's mind plunged down into a red sea of blood, where rocks turned liquid with it, and sands flowed sluggish with it, and the air was full of the stink of death. "What is this? What is this?" he asked himself in his mind. "Of what use is this? What have we done? We have killed Dabale. Of what use is Empire against the death of this good man?"

Bedane had killed three men this day that he remembered, and the feel of those killings were with him, and they did not bother him. The killings were done to bodies that were trying to kill him, and they had the feel of steel plunging and cutting into flesh, and these killings were no different than the feel of hacking at a cow or a sheep. But he did not know them. Now, here was a friend, and he was dead, and this was different somehow. But suddenly he thought, "How? How is this different? How is it that I mourn for Dabale and not for the others? Is it that I do not know the others? Ah, but I do. I know all the others. All of us today fought Death together. Some won. Some lost. Here they all are, waiting for Death to eat their bodies. I know them all. Why did we all come so far, and march so hard, and make such sacrifices to get here? Just, was it simply to meet Death and give him dinner? Of what use is this? What is the purpose?"

Bedane arose and gazed out into the gathering dusk. Two riders were coming slowly toward him. He would know them anywhere, at any distance.

He would wait for them here, by the side of Dabale. Together, Bedane and Tula and Ibbsa would take Dabale back to camp. Together, they would find some good place away from this hellish field and lay him to rest; somewhere where beautiful flowers grew and water ran free.

PART VII

HOMEWARD BOUND

The cadence of a victorious army, even a hungry and uncertain army, is a wonderful thing to see. The battle is over, the army is heading home, the smiles of the warriors are carefree under a glorious blue sky. All is joined and joyous under heaven.

Thus it was with the Ethiopian armies of the south as they made their way home, going down along the old trade route from Makele. Leaving Tigre behind, the soldiers marched and rode over Amba Alagie. Some of them took time to look at the site of Ras Alula's battle with the Italians. More stopped at the small towns along the route, and sat around the village fountains where beautiful clear water bubbled out of the old stone pipes. There they sat and bantered and joked with the Tigreans and enjoyed themselves simply by sitting for a while in the sun.

Once over the heights of Amba Alagie, the road looped gradually down across meadows and forests and ambas never-ending, through a fairytale land of beauty and peace. Here the grasses had turned a deep yellow, mature in anticipation of the Little Rains. All across the land, farmers were hard at work preparing the soil for the second planting of the year, for notwithstanding the fighting, the year had been good for growing. There was peace across the land, and across that land rode Haile Mikael Tesfaye, bishop of Ba'le, and his companion, Chala Negassa of Arusi.

"Ah, Chala," said Father Haile, "See this land! Is it not beautiful? Are we not lucky to be here? Is God not good to us? Look at this!"

Before them the world fell away in ribbons of field and forest, and across that land walked or rode thousands upon thousands of soldiers, wives, girlfriends, servants, sutlers, slaves, hangers-on, the whole claptrap of a traveling army, laden down with booty and stories and laughter and glory. Oh, how many thousands of tales would come out of this march, out of the great battle, out of the minds of a people made one by one great man and one great battle. Ah, this march would never be forgotten!

"Now see, Chala," said the bishop, "See far off in the distance, the way the land goes on and on? Just about as far as you can see, maybe three days' distant, we will come to a beautiful lake: Lake Haik, it is called. On the shore of that lake is a great monastery. That is where I was trained. I can't wait to show it to you. It is beautiful!"

On they traveled across the meadows, until presently a priest came riding up to ask a question of the bishop. Chala, wishing to give Father Haile some privacy in his conversation, urged Eagle forward until he was some twenty paces in front of the bishop's horse. Then he turned and looked behind him. Far away, beyond the winding lines of people in the valley, he could see the cavalrymen of Arusi just beginning to pick their way down a distant escarpment. He smiled happily. That night, they would camp together, and he would see his friends once again.

Chala turned to face front again and his smile disappeared in an instant. His eyes froze in disbelief. Out of a small forest to the west of the trail, uphill from it, rode a band of a couple of hundred men. On they came, swinging their scimitars and spearing the marching people.

Pandemonium broke loose. People ran this way and that. Those with weapons turned to defend themselves. They could not. The horsemen came on too quickly and cut them down. Men and women ran this way and that. Some fell in the path of the riders and were trampled. Others screamed and fled.

Chala swung Eagle around. "Save yourself, Father!" he yelled. "Ride for the troopers. I will cover you!" But Hailemikael, instead of turning back, stopped his mount, reached into his tunic, brought out his cross, and held it high.

"Run, Father! Run!" yelled Chala. He swung Eagle around again. Coming toward him were a half-dozen riders, up in their saddles, yelling and brandishing their curved swords.

"Che, Eagle! Hid!" Chala yelled. The horse bolted forward into an instant gallop. Chala raised his shield and lowered his spear straight out, aiming for the heart of the foremost rider. By the time the two men met, they were both going at full gallop. Chala's adversary was a big man, and that gave Chala a big target. Holding the spear like a lance, he thrust straight into the man's chest. There was a burning in his hand as the spear shaft seared back through it. Chala heard the wild war cries of his rival, looked up, and saw the man's startled face as the spearhead raced through him. He saw his enemy start to scream in horror, felt or heard the swoosh of the spear going through the body, and that was all he knew.

The Azebo's sword, in the motion of coming down on Chala, suddenly shot up again, then down. The warrior's grip gave. The blade, freed from the dying arm's strength, came down on Chala's face. It hit him across the forehead and cheek and knocked him out of the saddle. Chala went down like a sack into the brown grass and rocks. He lifted his head just for an instant, just long enough to see two other riders gallop up to Haile Mikael. One grabbed the cross out of his hand; the other grabbed the bishop's horse by the bridle. Then the blood came down into Chala's eyes. There was a blaze of pain and he collapsed into the ground. He was like a bundle of rags thrown down into the grass, and the last thing he heard, or felt, was Eagle's thundering hoofbeats sounding fainter and fainter as the horse galloped away across the plain.

Up on the ridge to the north of the valley the Arusi cavalry began to form. All along the ridge it formed, fifteen hundred strong. The troopers gazed down at an amazing sight. All through the valley, Azebo riders galloped back and forth spearing and knifing terrified people, looting their bodies, stealing their horses and goods. It was mayhem.

"Let us go! Let us go!" cried the men to their officers. Badilla Wami and Bedane ranged up and down the line. Badilla lifted his sword to announce the charge. Just then, Bedasa Merga galloped up to him, shouting, "No! No! Not yet! Not yet! Listen to me!"

Badilla Wami looked at him. Bedasa ripped off his headdress and threw it on the ground. "All of you! All of you!" he yelled. "Look down there. The bandits all wear Oromo headdresses! You will not know enemy from friend. You will kill each other. Take off your scarves! Take off your headdresses!"

Badilla and Bedane took off their headdresses and threw them to the ground. Badilla turned to the troopers. "All of you do the same!" bellowed Badilla. "No headdresses! No headdresses!" All along the line men ripped their monkeyhair and lionmane headdresses off and threw them to the ground and sat bareheaded on their horses.

"Stay with your squads!" yelled Bedasa. "Don't separate!"

Then Badilla Wami gave the signal, and he and Bedane and Bedasa led the Arusi Oromo at a gallop down onto the field of carnage. Squads went after the marauding Azebo with a will, spearing them, shooting them, hacking them out of their saddles with their swords. That day the

Azebo found themselves in a great battle against great soldiers. They found themselves cut to bits. This was not what they had bargained for. They cut and ran back across the plain and into the forest, the Arusi Oromo in hot pursuit.

In the forest there was confusion. The Azebo dismounted, let their horses go, lay in wait for their pursuers.

Up to the edge of the forest the troopers came, dismounted, stood confused for a second. Then some began to plunge into the forest. One of the first was Wondimu. He ran at full speed into the trees, with the cries of his comrades in his ears calling him back. But he didn't stop. He was hot with the spirit of battle, and charged on.

Suddenly there was a man before him. Wondimu cocked his arm to throw his spear, and the man yelled, "Brother! Brother! Why do we fight each other? Are we not relatives?"

Just for an instant Wondimu paused, but that instant was enough. A shot rang out, and another, and Wondimu felt his arm go numb, and then his shoulder, and the man in front of him jumped forward and cut Wondimu's throat with his sword. In another second, the rifles of Shasho and Taffa rang out, and Tula and Ibbsa raced forward and finished off the wily Azebo. The rest of the squad came up and soon the area was cleared of any living Azebo. The Azebo had lost big again. Four dead to one Arusi trooper down. But that trooper was Wondimu, the singer of songs, the quickest of warriors, and Wondimu, too, was dead.

The fire flamed high. Firelight gleamed off clothes once white and eyes that once shone with the glory of adventure. The remnant of the squad that had left Meraro with the highest of hopes and the élan of youth sat in a circle around that living fire and grew older and grayer with every minute that passed.

Dabale was dead from Italian guns. Now Wondimu was dead from an Azebo spear. Now people were captured, held for ransom, gone into the night. Now sentries were out, and there was fear, and strangers wandered from campfire to campfire looking for friends, looking for help.

"It is not like Wondimu," said Shiferaw. "He was quick. He was deadly in battle. How could these brigands take him?"

"It was a trick," said Mamo. "It must have been a trick, boys. He was too tough and quick to get that spear any other way."

"They were waiting for him," said Shasho, and he spat into the fire. "They were waiting for all of us. We are lucky we are not all dead."

"Thanks to you, Shasho," said Egersa. "Thanks to you."

All the men nodded in agreement. Egersa, Taffa, and Ibbsa had seen the power of Shasho's rifle that day, as he cut down the three Azebo Oromo bandits. The rest of the squad had found out quickly from them. They had all been there; had been ready to rush through the woods, killing anything in their path in exchange for the death of their singer Wondimu. But Bedane and Babilla had stopped them. "Not for nothing have the Azebo lived here these two hundred years, boys!" Babilla had shouted.

"Come! Bring Wondimu, and come out of this forest. Re-form up on top of the meadow."

So reluctantly, but now with the skill and understanding of blooded fighters, they paid attention to Babilla who, along with Bedane, covered their retreat.

Now the boys from Meraro sat in silence around the fire. Theirs was a long, long silence. Then there was a snarl from Shasho, who said, "Well, Taffa, it is time for a story. Tell us one of your tales. Tell us one of your stories tonight if you dare. Tell us about our lost brothers. Tell us the fun in that, and make us believe in a happy ending. Tell us that. I dare you."

Taffa looked up at Shasho across the fire. Taffa's eyes were glazed over. Wondimu was dead. Wondimu, his brother in tales, who could sing a song, make a song, live a song better than any man alive. In his mind, Taffa saw Wondimu dancing, his strong muscles rippling along his ribcage as he hurled himself into the air, bringing fifty more warriors into the air with him.

And now Shasho dared Taffa to tell a story. Taffa looked around the campfire. Across the flames, the eyes of his comrades stared at him, and Taffa sighed. He ran his hands through his hair, and looked across the fire into the black night, and he said,

"I will tell you a story, boys. It will not be a happy story, but maybe it will give you strength. May it give all of us strength. Here is the story I will tell, just as I heard it from a storyteller back in the hills of Meraro."

And here is the story Taffa told:

God, Death, and Winter one day walked a far distance. They were tired and wanted to rest. They came to a house, and God said to the owner,

"How are you?"

The owner replied, "Thank God, we are all well."

Then God said, "The night is coming. Please let us stay in your home."

Then the man asked, "Who are you? Where do you come from?"

God answered him, "I am the God who made heaven and earth and all things."

The man stood up and said, "Please go from here. You did not make people equal. You made one rich and then one poor and sick. For this reason I do not want you to stay in my house."

And God and Death and Winter walked again a far distance.

Soon they came to another house. God and Death sent Winter.

Winter went to the man's home and said, "Please let us stay in your house. The day has been converted into night."

The man asked, "What is your name? Where do you come from?"

"My name is Winter. I have come a far distance to meet all the people."

The villager said, "You are a bad person. You made one country desert and another country rainy and you dropped much snow and ice on the people. We don't want you to stay here. Go somewhere else."

Winter went away and told God and Death about his journey.

Then God and Winter sent Death to the villagers.

Death went to them and said, "The night is coming. Please let me and my friends stay in your homes this night."

The villagers asked, "Who are you? What is your name? Where do you come from?"

"My name is Death."

The owners of the homes said, "Come in, please, and bring your friends. You do not choose poor and rich. You make all men equal. You do not make one country desert and one country cold. You make all countries equal."

That night men held Death in high honor. Death does not lie. Death is true.

That is the story Taffa told over the fire that night, on the trail back home, with his best friend dead. That is the tale he told with the sparks of the fire circling high and his friends gathered around him in the night. That is the tale he told when the blackness of life descended on his soul and held him in the embrace of despair.

He looked up. Some of the men were staring at him. Some were covering their faces with their gabis. Tula was looking straight at him and crying.

"That is my story for the night," said Taffa, his voice breaking. He hid his face in his gabi, and his body shook with grief.

And a despairing voice out of the night said, "Help! Help me! I am looking for my brother! Does anyone know of the town of Meraro? I search for Bedane Negassa of Meraro! Can you help me? Who can help me?"

Everyone looked up. Out of the shadows of the night a strange apparition staggered toward their fire. A dream-like figure, a wraithe dressed in blood-stained clothes, lurched toward them, almost falling into the flames.

"My God!" said Ibbsa, and leapt up to help. He grabbed the sack of clothes and, guiding the blood-covered being around the fire, sat him down.

"Ahhh!" said the apparition. "Where is my brother? Where is my brother?"

"We are all here, brother. Who are you?" said Shiferaw.

"Who am I?" asked the ghost. It laughed, and asked again, "Who am I?"

Egersa answered. "Chala!" he said, leaping toward him. "Chala! It is I, Egersa. We are all here. We will help you. Let me see your wound."

"Ahhhh!" sighed Chala, and his head drooped on his chest. Egersa could see nothing in the bad light.

"It is Chala?" asked Tula, incredulous. "Egersa, how can you tell?"

"Ibbsa, bring a brand from the fire," said Egersa. "Tula, look. When I bring his face back up, to where it should be fixed to his skull..."

"Ayiee!" said Tula softly. "His face hangs in air."

"Tula, go to my pack. Bring it here."

Tula went and found the medicine pack. Egersa kept his hands on Chala's head, feeling, exploring, considering.

"Mamo," said Egersa. "Mamo, sir, please send someone to find Bedane. It is Chala."

"Are you sure?"

"I am sure," said Egersa. "Please, sir. Bedane will be the best news for him."

"We must find the Bishop," gurgled Chala.

"Hush. Quiet, Chala," said Egersa. "Later."

"Now," said Chala. "Now." Chala's voice was becoming drowsy.

Mamo sent Shiferaw and Shasho to search for Bedane, and turned to build up the fire.

"This is bad," whispered Egersa to Ibbsa and Tula. "He grows sleepy. We must keep him warm."

"I will get straw," said Taffa. He disappeared into the night.

Tula and Ibbsa looked over Egersa's shoulder into the nightmare that was Chala's face. They watched as Egersa, using his thumbs, pushed the face back up onto the skull.

"God, he is lucky!" exclaimed Egersa. "Look. Look at his eye." The eye was in place, and undamaged. The sword-cut had come down across the forehead into the cheek, glancing off the eye ridge on the way, so that there were two wounds, one over and one under the eye.

"Ibbsa, Tula, I will need three things right away. First, Tula, I need a poultice made of the wide leaves in my pack. Mix them with water. Pound them with a pestle. Make them into a dripping mess. Then, Ibbsa. You will find in that smaller sack some narrow black leaves. Crush them in your hand and give them to me. I need them right now. Mamo, sir, hold the light steady."

Egersa, all this time, kept pushing and pushing on the loose skin of the face, moving it into better and better position. Suddenly he smiled. "See." he said, "It is Chala."

"Bishop Haile! Father Haile!" said Chala, his voice rasping. "Where is my horse? Where is Eagle?"

Ibbsa held out his hand to Egersa. "I must hold his face," said Egersa. "Drop those leaves onto the wounds, Ibbsa. Rub them in. Get them in everywhere. They stop the poison."

Ibbsa let the crushed leaves rain down on Chala's face, then took his fingers and began to push the medicine into the wounds. As he did so, the leaf particles seemed to melt and flow into the wounds. It seemed almost a miracle.

But Chala did not think so. "Ahhhhh!" he screamed. "It burns! It burns!"

"It burns the poison," said Egersa. "Stay with it, Chala! Stay with it." He nodded to Ibbsa to continue to rub in the leaves.

"Now, Mamo, sir," said Egersa, very quietly. "Give the torch to Ibbsa. Ibbsa, I will need all the light I can get; but Mamo, even more I will need your strong hands. Hold, please, the back of Chala's head."

Beneath the light of the torch Egersa, still holding Chala's face in place with his left hand, fished in the medicine pouch for what he needed. Finally, he brought up a huge curved needle with string already through it.

"Ready for anything, hakim," said Tula, grinning.

"Thank the great winds of Waaqa for that," murmured Egersa. "Chala, hold steady, now. This will hurt, but it must be done."

"What are you doing? What are you doing to me?" asked Chala, almost delirious with the pain of the leaf medicine.

"I am sewing you up," said Egersa quietly, "just as the sewers in the marketplace stitch up our garments."

"Oh," said Chala.

Egersa started at the top of the forehead, where the cut began. He pushed the flesh together and in one motion pushed the curved needle through. Then he took the end of the string and tied it off, leaving a crude stitch in the wound.

"How did that feel?" he asked.

"I felt nothing," said Chala.

Egersa looked puzzled, but without pausing he moved his fingers down the wound. About a half-inch down, he pinched the skin together again, and sent the needle quickly through it.

"Ahhhhh!" screamed Chala. "What are you doing to me?"

"That is better," said Egersa to Tula. "I was afraid with that first one that the flesh was dead. That would have been bad. But see, Tula, it is alive here. That is good. Let us hope it is alive from here on. Be ready with the poultice when I need it."

"See, Chala," said Tula cheerfully, "you have a lot of life left in you. At least in your voice."

"If I could see you, I would kill you with my eyes. Ahhhhh!" he screamed again, as Egersa drove the needle home.

"Keep him steady, Mamo," muttered Egersa, fishing once again for a good piece of flesh.

Soon Egersa had the forehead sewed up. "Now," he said. "Ibbsa, come forward toward the front with that light. This will be tricky. See, how the face drops away? It has been simply sliced in two. It will be hard to hold. Is everybody ready?"

For the first time the curved needle dipped like a red-hot poker into the flesh of the cheek underneath the eye. Once more Chala screamed, this time louder and longer than ever. It was like fire was eating his face. He screamed and screamed as the needle cut through him. Then suddenly he gasped, and his body went limp, and he felt nothing.

"It will be easier now," said Egersa. "Lay him down flat. It will be easier working on his face if he is flat. I'll be able to tug it into the right shape."

And that is what he did. Ten stitches later, Chala's cheek was sewn together. Egersa pushed and pulled at it a bit, trying to match it up with the cut on the forehead. "I'm trying to make it look, you know, even," said Egersa.

"He'll have a story for every girl he ever meets," said Mamo, grinning.

"Bring him over to the straw," said Taffa. He had returned unnoticed. "I found an extra blanket, too," he said.

"Good," said Egersa, and they lifted him quickly onto the straw. Taffa put the blanket over him.

"Now, Tula, put that poultice on him," said Egersa. "Pat it on gently. Now I need some cloth. A bit torn from a gabi? Do we have an extra gabi?"

Mamo was first off with his gabi, and speared it, and ripped a wide piece off of it.

"Just right," said Egersa. "Now we'll wrap him up for the night. In the morning, we can take the bandage off and check for poison and put new medicine and new poultice on it, and we'll need more gabi cloth, too."

"On this march, there are always extra gabis," said Ibbsa. "More and more each day, it seems."

It was very quiet, late in the night. Chala lay sleeping, breathing heavily.

"I will take the first watch," said Taffa.

Down in the valley, hyenas howled and called, licking their chops over the dead. It was a bonanza for them.

At dawn, Shasho and Shiferaw came riding over the gentle hill. With them was Bedane, riding Star and leading Eagle. He had found the horse wandering over the battlefield late the day before, when he was scouring the area looking for Chala and Haile Mikael. He had found no sign of either of them, but he had found Eagle grazing quietly.

All night Bedane had stalked through the valley. He had roamed into the hills, stopping at campfires, talking to fighters and refugees alike. Everywhere there seemed to be hurt people. Their hurts were good news to Bedane. These people would have been dragged off or slaughtered if it had not been for the great charge of his unit. So if they were hurt, that was good. At least they were alive. At least they were not in the evil hands of the Azebo, acting as slaves while they waited for a ransom that never came. Many of these would live to reach home again, even with pain and difficulty. That was good. But no one had seen his brother.

Bedane entered the circle by the fire and looked down at the sleeping figure of Chala. In the lightening day, the camelshair cape, blood-smeared and matted with dirt and straw, showed this form to be his brother. As Bedane watched the sleeping Chala, Taffa pressed a hot glass of coffee into his hands.

"He will look bad," said Egersa quietly, "but I think it will look worse than it really is. Be prepared, Bedane, when I take off the bandages."

Saying this, he knelt by Chala and began to unravel the bandages. Then he pulled off the leaf poultice. Chala muttered in his sleep, and his teeth chattered.

Bedane knelt by Chala's side and peered at his brother's face. It was raw; discolored. The jagged wounds seemed to flare out with deep red and purple edges. The strings of the stitches, dirty with blood, looked like they had been trailed in horse manure. But the cut was straight and good.

Egersa fingered the stitching string and said, "It was clean when I started. Don't worry, Bedane. There is nothing on it but his blood and flesh, and some bits of leaves."

Egersa washed Chala's face, and the boy groaned. Then Egersa applied more black leaves and patted them into the cuts. Tula brought another poultice, and Mamo shredded more material off his gabi, and they rebound the wounded head. Then Egersa said to Bedane, "While I was unwrapping the old bandage, I found something else," and he guided Bedane's hand to the top of Chala's head. There was a huge knob there, swollen and hot. "It must have been where he hit a rock when he fell. Thank God he was wearing that fancy Amhara lionmane headdress they gave him. He would have split his skull if he hadn't been wearing that."

Bedane let out his breath and shook his head as if to clear it. "But you say he will be all right?"

"He will sleep a long time, I think," said Egersa, "but yes, I think he will be all right. The trick will be to keep the wound clean, and keep him so that the blood will come back into his face and heal the wounds. Some good food will help. Some beef, or even a chicken."

"Beef!" exclaimed Bedane. "A chicken!" He looked around. All over the hills and valleys thousands of people were up and making preparations to go on the march, and none of them had more than a handful of kolo to eat for breakfast. "We are all starving. Where do you expect to find a cow?"

Egersa just stared at him, helpless. "That is what will help him," he said, but he said it with no hope in his voice.

Suddenly, Chala sat bolt upright in the straw. "Arrrggh!" he screamed. "I am blind! I am blind! I cannot see!"

Hurriedly, Egersa removed the bandages from around Chala's eyes. "Ah!" said the boy, blinking. Then he groaned and said, "I can see, but my head. My head. What happened? Where is my horse Eagle?"

"He is right here, little brother," said Bedane softly. "So are we all, everyone from Meraro."

Chala looked up at Bedane. "What happened to me, brother? I can see, but it is all blurry." He lifted his hand to his head, but brought it away fast. "Ah!" he said.

"Stitches," said Bedane. "Your face is sewed up like the mouth of a bag of grain. You will look very pretty later, after you have healed. You will look like a great warrior."

"I am a great warrior," said Chala. "I remember now. I got him. He was riding right toward me, screaming and waving his sword—a huge Azebo— and I spurred Eagle and lowered my spear and I got him. Right between the ribs. I could feel it squoosh deep into him. Then there was a great light, and I don't remember anything else. But I got him." Chala stopped for a moment. Then his breathing stopped, and he tried to focus on Bedane's face. "Wait. They were going for Bishop Haile. I saw that. Where is the Bishop?" he asked. "Where is Bishop Haile Mikael?"

"We don't know," said Bedane. "We tried to find him. He is gone."

"It is my duty!" said Chala fiercely. "To protect him. My duty! Where is he? Is he dead?"

"We found no body, Chala," said Shasho.

"And no horse, either," said Shiferaw.

"No one has seen him," said Bedane. "We asked all over. No one has seen him."

"We must go after him!" said Chala excitedly. He tried to struggle to his feet, but he couldn't rise. Bedane pushed him back gently onto his bed of straw.

"Not you, little brother," he said. "You must rest."

"We must get the bishop back," said Chala weakly. "We must. It is my duty. A bishop of the realm. A bishop of the Empire. What can those thieves want of him? What?"

"Ransom," said Mamo to Bedane.

Bedane stood and looked at Mamo. "Perhaps," said Bedane quietly. "Or worse. If they find out who he is...."

"They will," said Ibbsa. "He is a man of God. He will hold up the cross to them. What are these people?"

"The Azebo?" asked Bedane. "No Christians there. Muslims, if anything. And friends of the Italians into the bargain."

"They will torture him," said Shasho.

"But not enough to kill him," said Bedane. "They will recognize him for what he is. Remember his cross that he carries with him? The one with the precious stones in it? When he blesses them with it, they will know instantly what he is. They will not take him for a poor country priest."

"They will hold him for ransom," said Mamo. "He is a prize."

"But what will they do to him before they ransom him?" asked Shasho. "That is the question. What will they do to him? He is an infidel to them, and a great one. They will make sport of him."

Bedane walked away from the camp, a few paces down the gently-sloping hill. He stood squinting off to the east, down into the plain between the mountains and the desert that was the home of the Azebo. The plain stretched far away. Bishop Haile, if he still lived, was down there somewhere. But where? And what were their chances if they went down there? He returned to camp. "Mamo," he said, "go find Babilla Wami. We need his advice, and we need his blessing, and his orders, for whatever we do."

Mamo found Babilla in conference with Kanyazmach Didda and his officers. They were trying to figure out how to re-group their far-spread battalions, and how best to make the way safe for the hordes of civilians streaming south. The Azebo were not likely to be satisfied with the small returns from yesterday's raid. They would come again.

Mamo reined up, dismounted, and stood at a respectful distance from the group of officers. The Kanyazmach looked up as he arrived, and said to Babilla Wami, "It is one of your boys from Meraro. I recognize him. I wonder what he wants. They are like bees, these fellows. Always buzzing around."

"Unlike bees, they do not come bearing honey," said Babilla Wami. "Always they need something."

"Find out what he wants," said the Kanyazmach.

When Babilla returned to the group of officers, he said, "The message is from my hamsa, Bedane Negassa. I was wondering where he was. His brother Chala came staggering into camp last night, ripped up and bloody. Your nephew, Aleka Bedasa. The one who rides with the bishop. The bishop has been taken by the Azebo. Chala says we must get him back. He babbles away. He has lost a lot of blood, but he got an Azebo before the bastard got him. Anyway, Bedane wants to know what to do."

Kanyazmach Didda's eyes narrowed, and he nodded. "Tell this one to wait. What is his name?"

"Mamo Wolde Mariam, sir."

"Ah, yes. Frightening-looking fellow. Why don't we send just *him* against the Azebo? He'll scare them to death." Didda chuckled. "Tell him to wait until we are finished."

Mamo waited, and presently the knot of officers broke up. The Kanyazmach, followed by Bedasa and Babilla, strode toward him. "Take us to Bedane and Chala and your men," ordered the Kanyazmach.

It was noon when the little group of officers rode up to the Meraro camp. Chala was asleep again, his head sheltered from the sun by a priest's parasol. Egersa and Taffa fanned him slowly with their hands, keeping the flies at a distance. Didda strode into the camp. All the men jumped to their feet and stood at attention.

"How is he?" asked Didda, his usual booming voice for now gentle. Before anyone could answer, he said, "Get back to fanning him, you two. Keep him alive."

Bedane bowed and said, "Sir, the Azebo have taken the bishop. We are afraid that once they find out who he is they will torture him."

"This I know," said Didda. "This they will do. They are like that."

"We must get him back, sir," said Bedane.

"Hamsa, here is my problem," said Didda. "My men are spread from here two days to the south and two days to the north. Look around you. All over the place, thousands and thousands of civilians with nothing to eat, trying to get to the granaries of Addis Ababa. A month away, if not longer! If I leave them, the Azebos will fall on them. It is my responsibility to keep them safe, or at least try to. I cannot spare an army to beat the bushes for a bishop. But I understand what you say. We must get the bishop."

Kanyazmach Didda was no fool. If he let a bishop slip from between his fingers into the hands of the Azebo, the Abuna and the Itchegie and the Emperor Himself would have his head, or at least his career.

Chala, hearing him speak, raised his head, and in a weak voice said, "Sir, we have an army that can get Bishop Haile."

Didda looked at him and frowned.

"He babbles, sir," said Babilla.

"I know where there is an army," said Chala, wincing.

The Kanyazmach squatted down next to Chala. "Hakim," he said to Egersa, "let me see his wounds."

Egersa unwrapped Chala's head and removed the poultice. "God above," said Didda, with some awe in his voice, "You are one lucky young man, Chala Negassa." The Kanyazmach looked up at Bedasa Negassa and grinned. "You have quite a family, Aleka Bedasa. This one conjures up armies where there are none. He is always full of surprises." Didda looked down at Chala again. "Where is this army of yours, Chala?" he asked.

"To the west, sir. All the men we need."

"Oh? In Lasta?" Didda frowned. "The Lastani were cut to ribbons at Adua, Chala. Lasta is a power no longer."

"No, sir. Not that army. The Emperor's army. Makonnen's army."

"They are all still far north of Makelle, still near Adua," protested Didda. "They cannot help."

Chala raised himself onto his elbows. "Sir, they are thirty miles away. A day's ride. Less than the ride from Lemu to Assella. I can get them."

Didda shook his head. "They are not there, son."

"Yes, they are," said Chala, fixing his good eye on Didda. "They are there in the wire."

Didda looked at Bedasa, startled. "He knows the location of the wire! Does he know *all* the state secrets?" Bedasa could only look bewildered.

"In the wire," Chala whispered. "I can call Atse Menelik. In the wire."

"Where is the wire, Chala?" whispered the Kanyazmach.

"Near Sokota. There is a station near Sokota, up in the hills beyond the town."

"What will you say to Atse Menelik?"

"I will tell him, 'Janhoi! Bishop Haile Mikael is taken by the Azebo.'" Chala paused and looked straight at Didda. "He will do the rest."

The Kanyazmach looked into Chala's eyes, and thought, and considered. He remembered the council of war before Makelle, and how Chala and the Emperor had looked at each other. He remembered how puzzling he thought it was then that they seemed to know each other. The Kanyazmach remembered that, and made a decision. He looked up at Egersa. "Hakim," he said, "Can he ride?"

"No, sir, he cannot," said Egersa. "He will fall."

"Tie me onto the saddle!" yelled Chala. "I will ride!"

Didda rose and spoke to Egersa. "Son," he said, "I know you have the good of your patient at heart, but I must also have the good of the nation at heart." The Kanyazmach motioned with both hands in the air. "Boys, here is what I will do. Gather round. Now, this squad will bring Chala Negassa to the talking wire at Sokota. You will protect him every inch of the way. If you let him fall or die, I will have you slaughtered. Understood? I am not playing with you here.

"You will leave tomorrow morning at dawn. Today you will rest and..... and mourn, and bury the dead. I understand you have lost your friend. Today, rest. Mourn. All of you. I will find you food and bring it here. Now, Mamo, you strike me as a good soldier, but you will not lead this squad. Bedane, you are a true warrior, but you will not lead the squad. Aleka Babilla, you are demoted for the time being. *You* will lead this squad, and you will be proud to do so, for this is the best squad in the army.

"Now, here is your assignment: after Chala talks to Atse Menelik, rest for a day. Then head south. Stay to the west of this march. Take extra mules with you. Fill the backs of those mules with grain. Ride like the wind. Go through the valleys to the west. Circle around behind Lalibela and Magdala, and meet us at Wara Ilu with all the grain you can carry. And be sure, all of you, that when Chala talks to the Emperor, he also talks to Addis. Tell them in Addis to send grain north. All the grain they have." The Kanyazmach paused. "You must be in Wara Ilu in ten days, because that is when I will be there, and I will be hungry. I will want to see the grain from Addis. I will want to see the grain you bring, also. Without it, we will starve. Do you hear me?"

Then the Kanyazmach went on. "Bedasa Negassa, you will attach your gunners to the Arusi battalions once again, and you, sir, will lead the battalions of Meraro, Bekoji, Lemu, Siltana, and Geddeb home. In effect, you will be my Grazmach. You will guard this left flank with your life, and if you as much as *see* one of those Azebos, you will machine-gun the son-of-a-bitch on the spot. Do you understand me?"

"Yes, Sir," said Bedasa, grinning. "When do I start?"

"Right now!" ordered the Kanyazmach.

"This," thought Bedasa, "will be my last command. It is a fitting way to end."

The next morning, at the first hour, they tied Chala into the saddle and started off to the west. Above them, the last of the stars still twinkled. They went west over the hill, past the new grave of Wondimu. Each man held his thoughts within as he passed the grave, but all were grief-stricken by this new death, and over that small band there hovered a great sadness. It followed them even as the day brightened.

Presently, they were away from the big trade route with its thousands of soldiers and civilians heading south, and the air turned cooler and cleaner as they wound their way up into the hills. It would be more than thirty miles; more even than from Bekoji to Assella, for Chala was right about the miles, but wrong about the conditions. Here the land went up and up, in ravines and terraces, and here the horses and mules had to pick their way carefully and slowly. Far off, but still seeming to tower over them, rose the ramparts of the High Simien, the heartland of the Old Kingdom.

So it was slow, which in a way was good for Chala. He had to stop and rest many times. It took a day-and-a-half instead of a day, but still it was faster than going all the way back to Makelle or beyond, trying to find the Emperor. That night they spent on the outskirts of a small hamlet of fearful people who were wary of these fierce young warriors. "We are like God, Death, and Winter combined to them," laughed Mamo, and in truth they were.

As soon as they stopped, Chala lay down and slept. They covered him with blankets, and Egersa checked him for infection. The wounds were clean. Tula once again made up a poultice, and once again they covered his wounds, and on through the night he slept.

In the morning they went on again, forever marching their horses up steepening hills, until at last they came to the town of Sokota. Through the town they rode, and beyond it, until at Chala's direction they stopped at what appeared to be a small hut. There were two soldiers outside of it, and more inside. The mounted men could hear them talking. The two soldiers on the outside looked at them warily, their rifles at the ready.

"I am Aleka Babilla Wami of the Arusi Brigade of Ras Michael's cavalry," said Babilla. "These are my men. We wish to speak to the Emperor."

"Indet!" said one guard. "Are you an idiot? Do you think this is the Emperor's palace?" The other guard began to laugh.

"I am not a fool," snarled Babilla Wami. "I know what is inside. Get your commanding officer."

"And who was it who wanted him? Ras...umm...Ras...Babilla, was it?"

"Don't fool with me!" yelled Babilla. "Get your officer."

"Don't be so cocky," yelled back the guard. "Before you make trouble, look around. You will see, through the trees, a good number of rifles leveled at you. A very good number. You are not a fool? Neither are we. You will not move until I find out who you are and what you want."

Another man appeared in the doorway to the hut. He was tall, thin, and looked like an aristocrat. He held a Mauser pistol at the ready.

"Wait!" said Bedane, raising his hand. "The one who needs to speak to the Emperor is this one. He has been here before. He was here before the battle, with Bishop Haile Mikael of Ba'le." He swept his arm around, indicating Chala.

The aristocrat, evidently the officer, said in a high thin voice, "You show us a bandaged head and ask us to identify it?" He smiled a thin smile.

Without losing a moment, Egersa unwrapped Chala's bandages. When he was finished, Chala sat there on his horse, blinking with his good eye. "I am Chala Negassa of Meraro," he said through clenched teeth. "I was guard and servant for Bishop Haile Mikael. I came here with him before the battle, inspecting the wire. You may not recognize me but I know you, and I know the inside of your house. I can tell you what is in there. What I say is true. How else would I know about this place and what you do?"

The ride had been hard on Chala. As he sat there on Eagle, he looked like a rag doll whose head had been sewed together. The mouths of the guards dropped open.

"What happened to you?" asked the officer.

"Sabre cut," said Babilla Wami. "Azebo raiding party."

Chala's voice grew stronger. "The Azebo have taken Bishop Haile Mikael. Somehow, we must get an army together to get him back. I must speak to the Emperor!"

"And if you speak with the Emperor, how will the Emperor know you?"

"He will know me from what I tell him. I will tell him something only he and I can know."

The officer considered these strange words and came to a decision. "Get down. Come in. You two, also. Just the three of you," he said, pointing to Babilla and Bedane. "The rest of you, stay on your horses and don't move."

Babilla and Bedane dismounted and helped Chala off Eagle.

"If the Emperor does not know you," the officer said to Chala, "you will never leave this building. Understood? All three of you." He turned to the men on horseback. "Give your rifles to my men here. You will get them back when your friends come out again. Pray that they come out again. If this is a trick, you are all dead men."

Chala, Bedane, and Babilla followed the officer into the house. In the back, seated at a table, was a young man who looked like a student. On the table before him was a writing tablet and a pencil and a machine that Babilla and Bedane had never seen before. It was a simple machine. There was a platform about the size of a man's foot, and a thing that hovered over it and that clicked down on the foot part. From it a wire ran across the table, up the wall, and out the window. The young man who operated this device, thought Bedane, looked like a student waiting to take a test.

"Lieutenant Tefferra," said the officer, "This person wishes to speak to the Emperor. Please be so kind as to put a message through."

The lieutenant's eyes widened. He looked at Chala and said simply, "Speak. Speak slowly and distinctly. Tell me to whom you wish to speak, your name and title, and then give me the message."

Chala swallowed. There was a lump in his throat and his mouth was dry. He wanted water like at no other time in his life. He spoke: "To His Imperial Majesty Menelik the Second, King of the Kings of Ethiopia. Greetings. I hope you are in good health. This is Chala Negassa of Meraro, servant and companion to His Excellency Bishop Haile Mikael Tesfaye of Ba'le Province. Your Majesty. Bishop Haile has been taken prisoner by the Azebo. We need an army to get him back."

The young lieutenant of the Imperial Guard listened, and his hand moved, and the machine clicked. The message went winging over the wire, north to the palace of Ras Mengesha that overlooked Makelle. Since Adua, Menelik had been staying at the Makelle palace as a guest of the Ras, and the line had been extended to reach him there.

The lieutenant who received the message at Makelle wrote it down and handed it to his kanyazmach, who looked at it and thought. "Send this back," he said to the lieutenant: "How do we know you are who you say you are? Identify yourself. Give us proof."

Lieutenant Tefferra listened to the clicks on the wire and looked at Chala. "They want proof that you are who you say you are. What can I tell them?"

Chala replied, "Tell them this: I am a friend of Prince Daniel and of the Princesses Helena and Mentuab. I am wearing the camelshair cape that the princesses gave to me." Babilla Wami looked at the aristocratic officer as if to say, 'And what do you think of that!'

Back came the message, "Anyone can say that. You could be a thief who has killed the cloak's owner. What else can you say to prove yourself?" Lieutenant Tefferra looked at Chala and waited.

"Tell them this," said Chala. "Say, 'Janhoi, I am the boy who ran into you with your bicycle at the palace in Addis Ababa and knocked you down.'"

Everything in the room stopped. Everyone in the room looked at Chala. Bedane spoke in a gasp. "That is how you met the Emperor? You knocked him down?"

"Are you sure you want to send that?" asked the officer. "Because if it is not true, it could mean that, since I let you in here, I could die. But before I did, I would make sure that you and all your friends died. That would give me great satisfaction."

"I wish to send that," said Chala.

The officer looked at him.

"How could I make that up?" asked Chala.

"It had better be the truth, and be recognized as such by His Majesty," said the officer. "Otherwise....." He made the motion of a knife across the throat. "I think you are crazy," he added.

"He is not!" said Bedane. "I know enough of this to know something. I thought he was crazy, too. He's my brother. We are simple soldier-farmers from Arusi. Yet before the Makelle battle, he introduced me to these princesses. Walked right into their tent and said who he was and they came right out and met with us."

"And our Kanyazmach, Didda Bokku," said Babilla Wami, "said to me that Atse Menelik seemed to know this one somehow. Why else would we bring him here? Are we all crazy?"

"Whatever you think of me," said Chala, "the fact is that the Bishop is gone." He pulled himself up to his full height, and the skin of his face stretched tight against its stitches. He looked like a deaths-head. "The Bishop is a favorite in the palace," he continued. "All in the Royal Family know him and love him. The Emperor now knows that somebody has reported him taken. If I were an officer near that place where the Bishop was taken, and I had the power to send a message, and I killed the messenger instead, I would be a very sorry Imperial Guard officer very shortly down the line. I wish that message to be sent. Send it!"

Bedane and Babilla looked at Chala with awe. They had never heard anyone speak so strongly, much less this squirt. They could hardly believe it was Chala speaking.

And the speech was enough for the officer, too. "All right! All right!" he yelled. "Send the damned message! By God, you had better be who you say you are!"

There was a moment of great silence. Then Lieutenant Tefferra said, "Would you repeat that message, please, sir?"

The lieutenant in Makelle spelled out the message syllable by syllable as it came across the wire. He asked that it be repeated, and checked the original words. Then he handed the message to Kanyazmach Abayneh.

"Jan hoi. I am the boy who ran in to you with your bi cy kel at the pa lace in Ad dis A ba ba and knoct you down."

"It must be some kind of a code, sir," said the lieutenant. "It sounds crazy."

The kanyazmach read the message slowly and then began to chuckle. The chuckle turned into a laugh, the laugh turned into a belly laugh, and the belly laugh into a howl. "No, lieutenant," laughed the kanyazmach. "No, it is not a code. This happened. I was there. I saw it happen. This is the kid on the bicycle who ran into the Emperor and knocked him flat. It was very funny—the kid and Menelik and the bicycle all in a heap on the floor. We were all sworn to secrecy. Which, by the way, you now are also."

"Yes, sir," said the lieutenant, grinning. "I will not say a word. I have already forgotten what you have said. But sir, what shall I reply?"

Kanyazmach Abayneh regained a serious mien. "I will have to pass this along," he said. "I believe it will be answered quickly. Tell them to wait."

"Just 'Wait,' sir?"

"Just 'Wait,'" said the kanyazmach.

Kanyazmach Abayneh searched the palace for Balambaras Sabagadis, who brought him to Ras Hailu, who brought him to Ras Attakim of Simien, who knocked on the door of the dining room where the Emperor was meeting with Mengesha, Makonnen, Alula, and Dejazmach Baltcha. Baltcha opened the door and the kanyazmach whispered the news to him. "Come in," said Baltcha, and Ras Attakim and Kanyazmach Abayneh entered the room.

The kanyazmach bowed low, and Menelik said, "I trust this is of importance, Kanyazmach Abayneh?"

"Yes, Your Majesty."

"Speak."

"Yes, Your Majesty. A report by wire from Sokota. A boy named Chala Negassa reports that Bishop Haile Mikael has been abducted by the Azebo, who are raiding our people heading south."

"Bishop Haile Mikael? The Azebo have taken Bishop Haile Mikael? Who did you say reported this?"

"The bishop's servant, Janhoi."

"And we know this to be true because....."

"He identified himself sufficiently, Your Majesty."

"How so?"

"He said you knew him, Sire."

"How?"

"He said he was the one who rode into you on your bicycle and knocked you down."

Menelik laughed. Menelik laughed a long, long laugh, in a most unaristocratic manner. "Of course!" he said. "Who else?" He laughed deeply again. "Someday, Mengesha, I will tell you that story. But this is serious, kanyazmach. Bishop Haile Mikael is a good man. His loss would be a tremendous blow not only to the Church but also to the State. Makonnen, do you remember, just before the battle, when the drummers would not drum and the army would not move? This is the very priest who took the drum and sang and led us into battle. He is very important to us all. And the Azebo, it seems, have allied themselves with the Italians, or are just out for themselves again. It wouldn't be the first time. At any rate, Mengesha, they are on your flank, and on mine, and active. I must do something."

"Let me do this for you, Your Majesty," said Ras Mengesha. "Let me get him for you."

"What can you do, Mengesha? Your army, what is left of it, is needed here on the northern front, in case the Italians come again. They have just disembarked 10,000 new troops at Asmara. All of them are frightened out of their wits right now by the tales of the others who survived Adua, but who knows how long that will last? No, I need you and Alula and Makonnen right here for now."

"I do not need my army for this, Janhoi," said Mengesha. "There is another way; another force. A different kind of force. I will go and get them, Sire. Let Alula represent me on the northern front. I swear to you that I shall be back in ten days, and I will have the Bishop with me."

"Are you sure you can do this, Mengesha? I must stress that this is of extreme importance to me. How will you get him? What is this other force?"

Mengesha smiled. "It is a question of alliances, Janhoi. It is the importance of old alliances. You never know when you will need old friends." He paused. "I will go to the Danikil," he said. "I will ask the help of the Danakil."

"Oh, yes," said Menelik, with a wisp of a smile. "Your old friends, the

Danakil. You believe they will help?"

"I know they will, Janhoi. They are an honorable people. They will do this for me. I have always treated them fairly."

"Which is why I suppose you still have all your parts," said Menelik.

"Ah!" said Mengesha, "I see their reputation precedes them."

"Hundreds of years of people going into the Danakil Desert and never being seen again is what precedes them, Mengesha. And your reputation, my good Ras, is of being the only man who visits them and lives to tell about it."

"My father, my grandfather, my great-grandfather, all the way back to the great Ras Mikael of Gondar, have enjoyed a good relationship with them. They are fine people, if you don't get them upset. They are usually upset with the Azebo. They don't like them too much. They will see this as an opportunity to throw terror into them once again, and keep them away from their desert."

"Go get them, then, and get Bishop Haile Mikael from those bandits," said Menelik. "But before you go, would you mind if I place Alula here under the command of Baltcha, before he gets us into another war?"

Alula, with the petulance of a great old warrior, contrived to look disgusted.

"Your Majesty," broke in Baltcha, "with Your permission, may I go to the wire room? I wish to find out the situation in Sokota."

"Go," said Menelik. "Thank the boy for me. Tell him I will take care of the Bishop, and tell him to wait for me in Addis Ababa before he goes home. I want to see him and his friends."

Dejazmach Baltcha bowed. Signaling to Ras Attakim and Kanyazmach Abayneh to follow, he hastily left the room.

"Now, Makonnen, Alula," said Menelik, turning back to the maps on the table, "here is what seems to be the situation in Asmara...."

It had been a long wait. The aristocratic officer had brought a chair for Chala, who sat with his head hanging down, exhausted. Then the wire clicked. Lieutenant Tefferra wrote the message down and read it. "From His Imperial Majesty Menelik II to Chala Negassa of Meraro," it said. "Greetings. I will take care of Bishop Haile. As for you, await me in Addis Ababa along with your friends. I wish to see you."

All their heads were swimming. Chala smiled. "See, I told you he would take care of it," he said.

The officer looked at Bedane. "It seems your brother has made some very interesting friends," he said.

But the wire was not finished. It began to click again, and Lieutenant Tefferra read the message.

"This is Dejazmach Baltcha," it said. "Major Bekele, I need to know what troops are near you, and what the Azebo are doing."

Major Bekele answered, "I have someone here who has new information. I will let him answer." The major motioned Babilla Wami forward. "Tell him," he said.

Babilla stood at attention and said, "This is Aleka Babilla Wami of Kanyazmach Didda's Arusi Brigade. Kanyazmach Didda has fifteen hundred cavalry directly east of us, but the rest of the troops are scattered up and down the road, separated by days. Kanyazmach Didda is trying to round them up. We did not expect this. It was only by luck that we did not lose thousands of civilians the other day. We do not have sufficient forces to attack the Azebo and protect the people all at the same time."

The message came back: "Major Bekele, send two of your fastest riders to Kanyazmach Didda. They will tell Kanyazmach Didda this: that five thousand troops will leave Makelle for his position tomorrow morning. Tell the Kanyazmach that he should guard the road until they arrive. Then he can retire southward. Then, Major, do this for me, please. Let Aleka Babilla and his men rest. Take care of the boy Chala and anyone who is with him. Give them some food. Third, try to intercept any units heading south through your district and swing them to the east, by my authority. Promise them money if they will do this. I will take care of it. Meanwhile, I will try to find Ras Mikael in Waldiya, or wherever he is, and try to move some of his cavalry north fast, so watch for movement from the south. Have you received all of this?"

"Yes, I have," replied Major Bekele.

The wire clicked again. "Is this not interesting, Major, this new way of warfare? Thank you for your help. I am finished. Baltcha."

Without realizing it, Major Bekele, too, had been standing at attention. Now he relaxed and said, "Come. Let us go outside."

When they emerged from the telegraph hut, Major Bekele looked up at the cavalrymen, still up on their horses. Men and horses were wilting in the midday sun. The mules were fine.

"Guards!" he shouted to his men. "Bring water for these men and their horses and mules. Give them their rifles back. And bring food out of the storeroom. We will feast together, for this is a great day!"

Out came servants with water pitchers and towels for the men to wash. Out came more servants with ewers of tej and glasses to be filled. The Imperial Guards and the Oromo cavalrymen raised their glasses together, and together they sat for a feast in the forest. First came the lamb tibs, tasting like candy in thick brown sauce. Then the vegetable stew. There were potatoes and onions and leeks and cabbage and carrots, and other such delicacies as that, hardly ever found in the highlands of Arusi. Then came the raw beef slabs, carried around to the circle of warriors by even more servants. The soldiers took out their knives and cut off thick slices of red meat for themselves. They shoved the meat into their mouths and cut off what they couldn't fit just beyond their lips.

Babilla Wami wolfed down his meat, belched, and chuckled at Lieutenant Tefferra, seated next to him, who wrinkled his nose and shrank back from Babilla's crudeness. "You think I am an animal?" laughed Babilla. "You guys have had it too easy. I haven't seen food like this for three months. I don't suppose you have any ayib, do you?"

Politely Tefferra replied, "The ayib comes next. Delectable herbed ayib, from Ankober. Seasoned with just a hint of berbere."

"I knew it!" exploded Babilla. He threw back his head and guffawed. "Where do you get this stuff? Look at this meat." He held up his piece of beef, dripping with blood. "Look at it. You can see the fat in it. I haven't seen a cow with this much fat for four years."

"We are the Imperial Guard," said Tefferra. "We get the best."

"Best seats at the battle, too," said Babilla. "Back here guarding wires."

"Somebody has to do it," laughed Tefferra. "*Every*body can't get all the glory. That we leave to warriors like yourself. Where did you earn that lotti, that earring, by the way? Don't see many of those around."

Babilla snorted. "Down south," he said. "With Ras Gobena. Kaffa campaign."

"I'm impressed," said Tefferra, and he was.

Babilla sat staring at Tefferra, not willing to say more. His stomach was full. It was a strange sensation, and he wanted to concentrate on it.

"Anyway," said Tefferra, breaking the silence "most of us went up to the battle. As soon as Makelle was secured, we left a skeleton crew here and went up to Adua. We were with Menelik in the center."

Babilla grunted. "You did well," he said. "We were the guys who came pounding down that hill in front of you. Between us, we cracked the hell out of those Ferengis, didn't we? We did good work, brother."

"That we did," said Tefferra. "We saw you coming down that hill. That didn't look like fun."

"It wasn't fun for the Ferengis, at any rate," said Babilla. "I liked it fine. Say, do you have any other stations along the way from here to Addis? We've been ordered to show up at Wara Ilu with tons of food. We could just follow the wire along and raid your offices on the way and leave the peasants alone. We could feed the whole damn southern army with your supplies."

Tefferra snickered. "Tell me, wild warrior," he asked, "How did you like your reception here today? I'll bet you still don't know where the machine-guns are."

"We'll sneak up on them," said Babilla. "We'll steal the stuff in the middle of the night. Injera, vegetables, cows, tej, the whole thing."

"No, you won't," said Tefferra, filling his and Babilla's tej glasses from the bottle in front of them. "I'll just send a message to them and tell them to look out for a bunch of savages on horseback looking for tej."

"Damn," said Babilla. "This new warfare is ceasing to be fun. Machine guns, Ferengi observation balloons, masses of artillery.....now you can't even sneak up on anybody anymore. I'm telling you, Tefferra, as soon as I get back to Addis I'm signing up for Baltcha's new Kaffa army. No wires out there. Good forest to hide in. Beautiful girls, too, and happy to be captured by anyone who isn't marching them toward Cairo. Think of themselves as lucky to get to Addis Ababa. That's the kind of fighting I like. You look like a good guy. Want to go?"

"I'll go if my unit goes," said Tefferra. "And while I'm waiting, I'll go look for some of those Kaffa girls who are in Addis already."

"Hah!" said Babilla. His eyes held a faraway look. He yelled at Mamo across the circle. "Hey, Mamo! I'm going with Baltcha to Kaffa. Want to come?"

"Sure," grunted Mamo. "I'll do that. I like this army life. Where's Kaffa?"

"Somewhere out west, in the forests, before you get to the Nile. The Emperor needs its coffee. Baltcha wants its king in chains, too."

"Coffee," sneered Mamo, forgetting his glass and drinking straight out of the bottle. "I don't like coffee. They have this?"

"Sure," said Babilla. "This, and lots of good-looking girls."

"Baltcha know where they are?"

"Sure."

"Sign me up," said Mamo. He finished his bottle, lay back on the ground, and gazed at the sky.

The feast went on into the evening. When the sun went down, the Arusi soldiers thanked their hosts and staggered off to their appointed sleeping places. That night, the wire did not sing.

In the morning, the Arusi squad took leave of their new friends, got on their horses, and led their train of mules south, down through the small valleys of the central highlands. They would feed themselves and requisition supplies along the way from the villages they passed. They were looking forward to Wara Ilu, some ten days south, and they rode with a will. Even Chala rode straight in the saddle, for the morning, at least. Then his stitches began to hurt. The squad stopped at a small stream so Chala could bathe his face. They ate a sparse lunch. Then they were up and moving south again. Always south. Always fast.

CHAPTER 57

HAILE MIKAEL

Ras Malakot of the Azebo seethed with anger. For two centuries or more his people had controlled the trade route between north and south, extracting tolls from peasant and lord alike. Thirty years past, they had stood aside and let the British Ferengi go through to finish off Theodore, that usurping dog who pretended to be king. That proved to be a mistake. When they left, the British gave arms to the Tigreans, but only a pittance to the Azebo. They were treated like dirt, and at that instant the Azebo made a vow that no one, no matter who, would come down that road again without paying a price.

Now up from the south had come this huge scavenging army demanding food and animals and equipment from them. Menelik, like Theodore before him, obviously did not understand the power of the Azebo. Malakot had the Azebo hide and lay low, so that it appeared that they had dwindled to a few scattered settlements. It was easy to do. Plagues ravaged the land continually, wiping out entire communities, so it was not surprising to find abandoned villages and whole districts where no one could be found. With a solitary people like the Azebo, everyone would understand that no word had come out about any disaster in that land. The Imperial Army, heading north, had other things on its mind besides counting Azebos.

There the matter had rested, until that rag-tag army had come streaming south again, fresh from its victory over the Italians, but hungry and thirsty and sore from walking or riding for days on end. Then the Azebo saw their chance. Then the Azebo struck.

Those were good days, those days of the lightning raids. They lost few men, except for one day, and gained much loot and many horses and many slaves. Horses were always good. Slaves were even better, easily sold to the Arabs across the Kai Bahr, easy to sneak through Tigre between the highlands and the desert, and there were always Arab traders prowling about, eager to pick up valuable merchandise.

This haul seemed to be especially nice. Along with the horses and slaves and loot there was a man who seemed to be a big churchman of the infidels. A bishop, he said he was, and his belongings seemed to bear him out. The silver crucifix he carried was not the usual kind. It was studded with precious stones. His prayer book was of the finest parchment, and its pages, besides the usual infidel writing, were covered with fine pictures. His clothing was of the best. Truly, if this infidel leader proved to be the person he seemed to be, he was even more valuable than a slave. He could be ransomed for a princely sum. The infidels would want him back.

Ras Malakot gathered up his soldiers and loot and horses and newly-made slaves and the big churchman and headed east. For two days they traveled, heading down into that vast plain between the highlands and the desert that was the domain of the Azebo. Deep in the heart of that domain, Malakot dispersed his forces, and the tribesmen went their separate ways, taking their share of the booty with them to their settlements. Then Malakot took the path to his own village, followed by his guards and his own personal soldiers, all with their loot and captives. That night they arrived home, and the excitement of their people was great. The women and children exclaimed over the goods and horses, and taunted and spit on the captives, and the Azebo feasted long into the night.

Sitting on his raised chair in his great tukul, Malakot glowed in the obeisance of his retainers, who came in constantly to throw themselves face down in the straw before him and scream out their loyalty. For each of these displays, Malakot would nod slightly and grin.

Beside the ras stood the gaunt figure of the tall highland bishop, his hands bound, his eyes blindfolded, a worthy prize for the Ras of the Azebo. Malakot thought long and hard about how to make this priest worthy of a large ransom. Slowly through the night he developed a plan. He would let the Tigre and Amhara rases know where the captive was, and he would set a price on him. But he would not just wait for them to come to him. No, he would make them *want* to come to him.

He would exhibit this churchman at the market. He would tie him to a post and have him whipped. That news would get back to the highlands quickly, and the offer would come. And for every day it did not, the price would go up. Surely, certainly, an offer would come quickly. Malakot mulled over in his mind an appropriate price. It would be steep. He would be ready with it when the emissaries came...

On that next market day, Malakot's soldiers led Haile Mikael Tesfaye to the whipping post in the middle of the market square. There they stripped him and one of them began to lay the rawhide horsewhip across his back. A crowd of people looked on, laughing at the cries of the captive. It was good sport, but it was not going well enough for Malakot , who strode up to the post, yanked the whip out of the guard's hand, and cried out, "Fool! Who taught you to whip? Your mother? A leper? A blind man? Here! I'll show you how it's done!" And with that, he lay a lash across the bishop's back that opened the skin and caused the blood to fly out all over. Haile Mikael, tethered to the tall post, screamed and jumped. His body twitched and he gasped for air. "Let that god of yours help you now!" raged Malakot.

Haile Mikael was transfixed. He could not believe what was happening to him. He was naked, laughed at by hundreds of people in a circle all around him while he dangled from a tall post and twitched uncontrollably with pain. He could feel the blood running down his back. He could feel the muscles in his arms convulse as the ropes held him high, stretched out, his toes barely touching the earth.

Malakot slashed at him again. Haile Mikael howled in pain. The crowd laughed and applauded. Again Malakot whipped him, this time across the back of his thighs. Haile Mikael threw back his head and a piercing scream came from his throat. His body began to twitch in spasms.

Suddenly, not knowing how, Haile Mikael went deep into himself. He could still hear the whip as it cracked across his skin. He could still hear the delighted shrieks of the crowd. He could still feel his body jerk and dance like a live sheep being roasted over a fire. "Thank God that's not happening," he thought. He could feel his throat sear in screams, feel his lungs dry up under the sun. But somehow it all seemed distant. His mind went down into a place where the hurt didn't matter, somewhere deep inside of himself, somewhere where it was all dark and red and bright all at the same time, and there he stayed, with a bright golden glow shining all about him, and even as he could hear his body yelling in pain somewhere out there, inside in that safe spot full of light and peace he cried out in disbelief, "Lord! Why are they doing this to me?"

The answer came, soft but strong. "I don't know, Haile. Why did they do it to Me?"

Haile Mikael was silent for a moment, and then he said, "They are ripping my body apart. They are taking the skin off of me. I do not think I will be able to live."

"You will live," said the Voice. "You will always live in Me, whether you are in Heaven or on Earth. But your work on Earth is not yet done, so be prepared."

"Lord!" cried Haile Mikael. "Why are they doing this? What did I do wrong? I have always tried to follow You!"

"I told you to follow the reed."

"Yes."

"You did not. Still, you must follow the reed."

"How must I do that?" exclaimed Haile Mikael. "I do not know how. I tried."

"Time will tell," said Christ. "Time will tell you everything. Just, follow the reed, and it will lead you to Me." Christ's voice was growing faint.

"Wait!" cried Haile Mikael. "Wait! Don't leave me!"

It was growing dark. The circle of light was growing smaller all around him. The darkness, the red and black darkness, was encompassing the light, killing it, destroying it.

"Don't leave me!" the priest screamed.

"We shall meet again," said the faint voice of the Christ.

And the darkness came in total, and there was nothing but the darkness. Haile Mikael was afraid as he had never been afraid before, and he screamed in anguish. Then there was nothing except the echo of his scream. And then, after that, truly nothing.

The circle of onlookers was jostled, then shoved aside. A half-dozen men appeared through the empty space and walked into the circle. Each held a spear in his right and a spear in his left hand. The men were naked. Each wore a crude belt around the waist, and from the belt hung a huge curved knife in a scabbard. The skins of the men gleamed red. It was as though they had brought the color of their desert with them. They had bodies like great hunting cats, all sinew and lean hard muscle and bone under their shining skins, and there was nothing shameful about their nakedness. These were men designed for the hunt; for the kill. These were the Danakil.

"Give us the man," said their leader.

Ras Malakot spun around, whip in hand, and in rage and arrogance he said, "What! Who are you! Don't you know who I am?" His hand reached for his sword. He took two steps toward them even before he realized what he faced.

Malakot had not obeyed. He had broken the rule.

The Danakil never negotiated. They spoke and acted.

They struck.

"No!" shrieked Malakot. "No! Wait!"

It was too late. The spears did not listen, and now they were flying toward him. Three spears. They struck him in the chest, severing an artery, collapsing a lung. One went through him and snapped apart two vertabrae in his backbone. Malakot crashed to the ground, blood gushing from his mouth, a look of terror on his face.

And suddenly there were spears flying everywhere, like living steel snakes in the sky. Danakil appeared from everywhere—from behind houses, from behind groups of people. They seemed to spring from the very earth.

People went down screaming under the flying spears. Men, women, children—it seemed to make no difference. A second volley of spears was in the air. More Azebo went down. All at once, the knot of people, howling in terror, went running like ants from the desert devils who had appeared out of nowhere. Even before the spears had found their marks, the Danakil were among the Azebo, knives out. They caught them from behind and slit their throats. They circled in front of them and drove them back. Like a pride of lions working a herd of antelope, they came among them and slashed them down, cutting the sinews of their legs.

Now there was a terrible screaming in the town of the Azebo, and wailing, and terror was loose in the broad daylight. Now the nightmares were realized, and Death stalked the Azebo on legs faster than the fastest horse, closer than the fired bullet. Now the Four Horsemen of the Apocalypse appeared and the red devils of the desert took their knives and spears and killed and killed.

"Enough!" said their leader. He ran up to Haile Mikael and cut the ropes from his hands. Gently his men lowered the priest of the highlands onto the shoulder of the strongest man among them, and at a signal the Danakil retrieved their spears. Three of them picked up discarded Azebo gabis. Then they loped out of the screaming village and ran toward the desert.

A sufficient way out of the village, their leader halted his men in a spot where they could see for a long way all around. It was a spot of huge dry boulders and dryer sand, a place of foreboding; a sign of the desert yet to come.

Here the man who carried him gently lowered Haile Mikael's body onto a shaded rock where the coolness could penetrate his shattered skin. Another warrior opened a small leather pouch and began to cover his wounds with salve. Haile Mikael looked up at the warrior who had carried him and shuddered. The warrior was covered with blood. It ran down his body in rivulets. Haile Mikael knew it was his own blood. His body began to quiver and shake spasmodically. His mouth said weakly, "Ah! Ah! Ah!" as the salve went over him. He drew deep breaths, but those gasps were not enough to keep away the pain. At one point he simply howled, and the warrior with the salve covered the priest's mouth with his hand and said nothing, but only waited for the howling to stop.

The one who was the Danakil leader took a small gourd from a cool spot in the rocks where it had been hidden and held the spout to Haile Mikael's lips. He raised the priest's head so that he could drink. Haile Mikael felt the cool milk trickle down his parched throat, and heard the quiet words of the Danakil chief. He did not understand any of the words. "By this milk, this man now becomes our brother," said the chieftain in Dankali. "Any who would injure him, beware the anger of the Danakil."

The Danakil took two spears and removed the metal spear tips from the wooden shafts. Then they took the shafts and lay them side by side. They took two gabis and crossed them back and forth over and under the shafts. They took strong leather strips and formed a resting place for the head, and another for the legs.

They lay Haile Mikael on the stretcher, and placed the third gabi over him. They did this because they knew how the mountain people valued clothing and did not like nakedness, and also because the man was sick and also because it was the right thing to do. They did this with the gentle mercy that only the strong can show to those they choose to honor. They placed a light cloth over his head to shield his eyes from the sun. Then six of them picked up this warriors' stretcher and began to run. All thirty of the Danakil took turns running with the stretcher. They ran for two-and-a-half days, always deeper into their beloved desert.

At noon on the third day, they reached their camp. At the edge of their camp the great tent of a highland chieftain stood, and they took Haile Mikael there.

Outside the tent, the Emir of the Danakil stood next to Ras Mengesha Yohannes. The Ras uncovered Haile Mikael's head. Haile Mikael was raving. Spittle drooled from the corners of his mouth. Hardened as he was to death and battle, Ras Mengesha's stomach turned. His heart swelled with anger against those who would do this to any man, and he vowed vengeance upon that rebel tribe who could not understand the power of the Kingdom.

Mengesha let Haile Mikael rest for two more days, then, realizing that the priest would never heal without the greatest care he could offer, he carried him gently into the mountains, to his capital of Makelle. There, he took him to his castle, and brought in the Russian doctors who were still caring for the wounded of Adua. Then Mengesha wired Menelik: "The bishop is safe. His wounds will heal. He is here in my home, where he will remain until he is whole again. Then I will send him to you." He signed the telegram, "Mengesha Yohannes, Ras of Tigre, Guardian of the Northern Gate."

When Menelik received the wire, he nodded. He was satisfied. Deep in his heart he pledged that the Azebo would pay for this. Not simply for what they had done to Haile Mikael, but also for all the other good people they had slaughtered and robbed and harassed; not just in this campaign but in all the years past as well. And Menelik and Mengesha kept their pledges, even down through many generations.

Teglat Meda was a small village of farmers. There were ten houses. There were fifty people. They paid tithe to Balambaras Asrat Meta, who was away to the war. Teglat Meda was on the border of Shoa and Wollo, and with the dominance of Shoa over the latter kingdom for the past thirty years, the times were peaceful and the crops were good. Situated as it was in a small hidden valley away from the main trade route, the village was quiet and serene.

But lately times had changed. Two months before, the armies had swept north past the entrance to the little valley—men and women and horses and mules and donkeys and oxen and cattle—all of them in a hurry, and that, from the viewpoint of the villagers of Teglat Meda, was good. Now the pieces of the army were sweeping back south again, this time hungry and tired and sick, and that was bad; for sick, famished men needed food; and tired, starving men went far to get it, and they did not care how they got it.

The people of Teglat Meda were not at home. They were hidden in the cliffs above the valley, watching their houses from afar. They would wait in the cliffs until the armies had passed.

The cavalrymen crested a small hill and reined in their horses. There were ten of them, and they were hungry, but still strong. They surveyed the valley, the position of the tukuls, the location of the fields. At home, these men too were farmers, and they liked what they saw. They could appreciate well-tended fields and well-kept farmsteads.

Babilla and Bedane nodded to each other. Their horses moved forward slowly. Shasho and Taffa took positions on the flanks. The horsemen moved across the fields toward the nearest house. Bedane and Mamo slipped off their horses and cautiously approached the house. They yelled for the people to come out. When they heard no reply, they went inside, their rifles ready. The rest of the men dismounted and formed a relaxed circle of defense. Babilla Wami scanned the hills and forests for signs of life. There were not even any donkeys about, much less edible animals. Nothing moved.

The houses were empty. There was nothing in any of them of any value at all. The people of Teglat Meda had planned well.

"Well, Tula," said Babilla Wami, "you are the food gatherer. Where is the food?"

Tula looked grim and thought. Then he said, "There may be some stray cattle around in the woods."

"I have seen nothing move," said Babilla, "but it might be well to see to that. But right now, let me show you an old trick." He smiled. "Come on, boys," he said. "Gather round and listen to me. I learned this trick in the Gojjam campaigns. For a while, it seemed like all the armies in the world were going through there. Every time they got a crop, here came an army along to eat it. So the peasants out there thought of a trick, and I'll bet they know it here, too.

"Now," he continued, "let's have some fun. Tula, Mamo, Shiferaw, and Taffa, get on your horses. Look at this beautiful field in front of you, all plowed and waiting for the Little Rains. We'll start here. ('This is where they would put it,' he thought to himself, 'Right here in the middle, where they could all get to it easily, and easy to watch, too.')"

"Good," he said when they were mounted. "Now get your horses into a line. Bunch them together tight. Okay. Here's what you'll do. Go down to that end of the field. Keep your horses as tight together as possible. Then, just like you were dragging a giant plow, trot them all the way across the field to the other end. When you get there, turn them around and start back, just like you were at home and you were plowing one furrow after another. Keep them going back and forth across the field. Keep at it until I tell you to stop. Okay, go."

"But what are we doing?" asked Shiferaw.

"You are following my orders," said Babilla Wami. "Ha! Ha! No questions needed. Just keep those horses all together, at a trot, back and forth, until I tell you to stop."

The young soldiers rode off together, shrugging their shoulders. Tula was grinning at Taffa and shaking his head. Nobody could hear what he was saying, but they didn't need to.

"Ha!" said Babilla Wami, smiling. "Tula thinks I have gone crazy. Ha Ha! Now, the rest of you, come with me."

Babilla Wami walked quickly out into the middle of the field, and the rest followed him. When they got to the middle, Babilla waved at the riders to start their journey. On they came, straight into the middle of the field. They passed in front of their comrades and kept riding to the far side of the field.

"Sir, what are we supposed to do?" asked Shasho.

"You are supposed to keep absolutely still and listen," said Babilla Wami. "If you hear anything funny, tell me."

"You mean from the forest?" asked Ibbsa.

"I mean from the ground," smiled Babilla. "But keep your eyes on the forest. I don't think any of these villagers are near here, but we don't want to be caught unawares. While you are looking, though, continue to listen. Listen!"

The horsemen reached the far side of the field and turned. Babilla whistled them back, waving his arm, pointing the path they should take. They came back right beside the path they had made the first time, making a wide new path just as Babilla had ordered.

Back and forth they went across the field, time after time, Babilla Wami guiding them with his hands closer and closer to where he stood. Finally, on their eleventh pass, Babilla said, "Hah!"

Bedane and Chala looked at him. So did the others. Babilla stood there nodding his head up and down, his jaw set grimly. He yelled after the horsemen, "Turn your horses! Come back the same way; the same path." They did so.

"Listen carefully," said Babilla Wami to the group around him. "Tell me what you hear."

They strained their ears to hear. As the riders crossed in front of them, Egersa said, "I just heard what sounded like distant thunder. But there are no clouds," he added, puzzled.

Keen-eyed Shasho stood transfixed, looking at the ground where the horses had passed. "The ground moved," he said to no one in particular. "I swear, the ground moved."

"Hey, boys!" shouted Babilla Wami, "Bring them around again. Pass just where you passed before. But this time, at a gallop."

Then came the riders down the field as before, but faster, their horses thundering down in a charge. When they passed this time, the sound of their hooves on the ground changed, so that the ground sounded like a hollow drum.

"I was right!" yelled Shasho. "The ground moved! I was right!"

But Babilla was already running to the place where the sound had changed. As the others came running up to him, he shouted, "Dig here! Dig here! Use your spears; your hands. Dig!" and he fell to his knees and began to throw the dirt to one side.

"What is it?" said Ibbsa, digging for all he was worth. "What are we looking for?"

"Our supper!" laughed Babilla.

"Potatoes?" asked Ibbsa, incredulous.

"Hell, no," said Babilla. "Teff, tej, tella, cabbages, onions, sides of beef, who the hell knows what they have in here?"

"How do you know it's here?" said Egersa.

"It's here all right!" said Shasho, who had already figured it out. "Just keep digging!"

The men on horseback got back just in time to hear Babilla Wami exclaim, "Aha!" The aleka stopped digging and took his knife from his belt. He held it up in the air and said, "Now, boys, I hope you learned something from the Wild Warrior today! How to eat on a campaign, for instance!"

Babilla took his knife and plunged it into the soil. It went in a few inches and stopped. Then Babilla began to hammer whatever had stopped it with the knife. It made a low, hollow sound.

"Indet!" exclaimed Shiferaw.

"It's wood!" said Ibbsa.

"Aha! Wood. Yes," said Babilla Wami. "Lots of wood. Come on, boys, get the dirt off of it."

Soon, all working together, they uncovered plank after wooden plank, until they had an area of planks about twelve feet long by eight feet wide.

"Take the three middle planks and put them to the side," said Babilla.

There, under the soil of the field, was a great storeroom dug into the earth. It was deep, and dark, but they could just see, glimmering in the darkness, the outlines of many white sacks filled with teff, and probably other grains, too. The smell of the aging grain came up out of the hole. All the men were lying on the boards, trying to look down into the dark.

Taffa had the idea first. "I'll jump down and see what we've got," he said, grinning. He grabbed the side of the plank and lowered himself over the edge.

"Careful," said Babilla, "It looks like a long way down. Wait for a rope."

"It can't be that far" said Taffa. He looked up at them as he swayed in the air. "I'll send you up some good stuff." Then he let go of the plank and dropped into the dark.

Immediately, he screamed. His scream pierced their guts. He kept screaming. They scrambled about, trying to see what was happening. Babilla ran up with a rope, tying it around him as he ran. "Mamo!" he yelled, "Tula! Shiferaw! You big guys. Hold this rope!"

Babilla dropped over the edge, and they lowered him slowly into the hole. Taffa was still screaming, but softer, and they could hear the gurgling in his throat.

Babilla swung down on the rope, slowly, his feet kicking in the air around him. Once or twice he hit thin shafts of wood. They fell away as he flailed at them with his legs. Then he was down. He peered through the gloom. "Jesus Christ," he said.

Taffa was impaled on two spears. One had gone in low in his belly, and had not come out. The other had gone into his back and stuck out of his chest.

"Send Egersa down," shouted Babilla, untying the rope around his waist. "Wait! Wait a minute! They have spears down here. Must be a dozen spears. Wait!"

Up on top, they could hear the clatter as Babilla cleared the upright spears, ripping them out of the ground and throwing them into the dark corners of the storeroom.

"Now!" he shouted. "Egersa. Get down here!"

Babilla looked into Taffa's eyes. They were startled and wild, and the light was going out of them even as he looked. "Why didn't you wait for the rope!" Babilla whispered. He began to lower Taffa to the ground. "Why didn't you wait...."

Taffa's eyes dimmed even more. Blood streamed out of his mouth. He was silent. Now there were only gasps as he reached for air with hapless lungs.

Egersa came quickly down on the rope and hurried over to them. "My God!" he said softly.

Babilla and Egersa watched Taffa die. There was no sound from above, and neither did they speak. Babilla cradled Taffa in his arms. Egersa dabbed with a cloth at the streams of blood coming from Taffa's lips. Babilla hugged the storyteller and patted his back and said, whispering, "This was not deserved." He felt the choking in his throat, and tears came, and once again he said to Taffa, "This was not deserved."

Up on the ledges of the hills, beyond the forests, where the trees became sparse and the grasses grew on the rocks, the people of Teglat Meda peered down upon their homes and their fields and watched the horsemen who surrounded their hidden cache. They looked like ants at this distance. They watched the interlopers as they rode back and forth and as they dug in the earth. They watched as one, then another and another disappeared into the hole in the earth. And they watched, too, as one of the men who had gone down into the hole was lifted up from it and placed in the field. They watched as the other men picked him up and carried him off the field and placed him on the green space in front of one of their houses. From that distance, they could not see the blood. But they could see that he had been destroyed.

Sartsa Dengel, the head of defense for Teglat Meda, was elated. His eyes glimmered with satisfaction as he spoke to Zara Yaqob, the mayor of the small settlement. "See," he said. "We got one of them. May he suffer for this! Thieves! We got one."

The white-haired mayor did not look at the younger man. "You are a fool," he said in a voice loud enough to be heard by many others who stood nearby. "There was no need to do this. If they found our hole and took some of our grain, so what? They could not carry it all away. We still would have something to eat until the next harvest. Now, you have driven them mad with your spear idea, and they will take revenge."

Sartsa Dengel turned on the mayor in fury. "Who was to say so few would come? How do you know that there are not many more just beyond the trees? They would have taken all our food and goods and spit on us and laughed at us and called us peasants. I swore that no one would do this to us. Now, they have paid for the goods they would steal. Now at least they have paid a price!"

"Now they will take everything," said the mayor. "You must look beyond your spite. Now we will have nothing, and we will starve."

"We will get seed from others," said Sartsa Dengel, just then beginning to think of the future. The mayor's words had chilled him, although he didn't show it. "We will barter for food with other towns."

"With what?" asked the mayor.

Sartsa Dengel was silent. He and the mayor and all the other people of Teglat Meda stood silently and watched. They saw the thieves as they took sacks of grain and loaded them onto their horses and mules. They watched as the horsemen placed their dead comrade across the saddle of his horse.

"See," said Sartsa Dengel, "they cannot carry it all. They will have to leave most of it for us."

Then they saw the first faint wisps of smoke coming out of the hole.

It was Mamo's idea to destroy the crops they could not carry. Mamo burned deep within like an angry volcano. Now his anger came forth. "I cannot carry the food of these bastards," he said to Babilla Wami. "It is probably poisoned anyway. I want to find them and kill them."

"Yes," said Shasho. "Let us go after them and kill them."

"Shasho, be reasonable," said Bedane. "Look around. What point of that circle of hills will you attack first? And even if you ride straight at them, they will see us coming and move somewhere else. And who knows what guns they have? Do you want more of us dead?"

Mamo leaped onto his horse. "Who will ride with me?" he yelled.

"I will!" said Shasho. He too leapt into the saddle, rifle at the ready.

"And I!" said Shiferaw.

"And I!" said Ibbsa, moving toward his horse.

"Like hell you will," said Bedane. He pulled Shasho off his horse like he was a scrawny chicken, and shook him. "Come to your senses. Taffa is dead. You cannot bring him back. You must not do this!"

At the same time, Tula restrained Ibbsa from jumping onto his horse, and Shiferaw simply stood, confused.

Bedane felt Shasho relax. "He was my friend!" said Shasho. "He was my partner. We were the eyes of the camp. We were the guardians, the ones out in front, the warriors."

"We will need you now even more," said Bedane gently. "Calm down. Calm down."

Mamo whirled his horse around and galloped off into the field. He rode up to the hole and jumped off. The others watched as he upended plank after plank, sending them down into the hole. They could hear him shouting his war cries as he went on like a maniac. Then he came riding back to them.

"They will pay for this!" he shouted, brandishing his spear. "They will pay! Who will help me? Come on, boys. Help me find all the hay we can. We will burn their damned food!"

Bedane was about to order Mamo off his horse when he felt the pressure on his arm. He turned to see the blood-covered Babilla Wami beside him. "Let him do this," said Babilla quietly. Then in a loud voice he said, "Go and do that, Mamo! Boys, go help him. Finish off whatever food we can't carry. Get that straw!"

The aleka turned again to Bedane. "We have to let him do this. If he doesn't, he will explode and do something really stupid. Let him take out his vengeance on the food, or he will rebel and we will have to kill him. We don't need more dead."

The men of the squad went running for straw. They found straw and kindling wood, and firewood, and they hauled it over to the pit and dropped it all in until it was almost full. Then Mamo lit the pile, and they all laughed and cheered. They stood around as the fire gained strength and began to roar. Flames shot up out of the ground, and the heat was intense. Soon some of the planks began to burn and the fire, like a caged lion, roared in its pit, consuming itself and anything around it that would burn. The spear shafts burned, and their metal tips melted into the earth. The sacks of food blistered and fell open, and the fire caught each grain and exploded it. The fire whirled the freed grain around in the pit air in a huge exploding fireball, and the men stepped back. It was a magnificent show.

Then Mamo grabbed a fiery brand and, leaping onto his horse, rode for a nearby house. Before anyone knew what he was doing, Mamo had torched the roof of the house. The grasses of that house, dry since the last big rains of eight months past, went up in a flash.

Before Bedane could stop him, Mamo had fired three houses, and while Bedane was wrestling Mamo out of the saddle, Shasho started on the other end of the town. Soon all the houses were on fire, roaring away to ashes in a great conflagration.

Up on the mountainside, Zara Yaqob turned to Sartsa Dengel and said, "Behold the results of your stupidity. Now we have no food, no shelter, just the clothes on our backs."

"At least we are men!" said the hotheaded defense chief defiantly.

"We will starve like men," said the old mayor. "And our women will starve like women, and our children like children."

"We will rebuild," said Sartsa Dengel. He laughed. "We can sell the potash from what is left of the houses. There is always something that can be done."

"You are a man who has set fire to his own house and lost everything, who then pretends he has lost nothing. You are an idiot."

"Shut up, you old fool," said the defense chief. "We will have everything back in no time."

"True," said the mayor. "In no time. In no time that any of us will ever see."

Babilla Wami stood next to the body of Taffa, which was draped over his saddle. With both hands he touched Taffa's back. It was like he could not stop touching Taffa, like if he kept touching him it would bring him somehow, suddenly, back to life. But finally he sighed and patted Taffa's back one last time and said, "Mount up!"

The squadron mounted. All carried sacks of teff behind them on their horses' backs, and each led a mule loaded down with great amounts of grain. They started off for Wara Ilu, five days away, to bring the food to Menelik's hungry troops. But none of them could even think of eating any of it.

The next day they came upon a country church up on a hillside. They summoned the priests and the gravediggers and the local professional mourners, and they found a nice spot in the church's graveyard. There, Taffa could enjoy a good view of a beautiful valley, looking south toward

Arusi. They buried him there, and paid the priests.

Then sadness came down on them all for Taffa and Wondimu and Dabale. Boys they had grown up with were dead men now, dead all over the hills and plains and valleys of the Empire. Into all of the men Grief came and would not leave. All of them felt Grief in different ways. All of them now knew that there was far more to war than drums and courage and exciting rides. There was more even than Death and Disease and Famine and Pestilence. Here was another thing of war—deep, abiding Grief, that in some of them would never let go, ever. So that was another gift of war—that shroud of melancholy over the earth, over the lives of all people, as horror was added to horror, and death to death; and cold and hunger lived in the bodies and minds of all of them, and they longed for home.

THE EMPEROR'S GARDEN

Once again Chala stood in the palace garden. This time he had no bishop to introduce him to a prince; but this time, he brought with him Bedane and Babilla Wami and the boys who had followed Bedane north to battle. There they all stood with him—all those who were still alive—Egersa, Ibbsa, Tula, Shiferaw, Mamo, Shasho. They wore new clothes, purchased with their army pay in the markets of Addis Ababa, and their clothes gleamed white. Each carried his spear and shield and waited patiently.

Five days from Teglat Meda, they had delivered their grain to Kanyazmach Didda at Warra Ilu, along with two stray cows they had discovered along the way. But the squad did not remain at Warra Ilu. They rode south, toward Addis Ababa. The second night out from Warra Ilu, Egersa examined Chala and pronounced him well. He snipped his patient's stitches and pulled them out. After Chala had bathed his face in the cold water of a mountain stream, all the boys stood around commenting on his appearance. They laughed and said that he looked like a fierce shifta. But Chala had not cared to banter. His mind was fixed on the whereabouts of Father Haile. There had been no word of the priest at Warra Ilu.

Chala turned away from the fire and stared into the dark of the night, and soon the conversations of his friends ended. They too were introspective, thinking of Dabale and Wondimu and Taffa, lost forever; and thinking too of what they had done in rage at Teglat Meda, for that was something unlike any of them had ever done before. Each thought of his own part in it. Not one of them wanted to talk about it, fearing where conversations might lead, and where accusations might lie. All they wanted to do now was to go home, or go to the west with Dejazmach Baltcha, or laze around Addis for a few days and eat at the Adarash and bathe at the hotwater springs. Each had a different idea, but the one thing that they all wanted to do was to meet the Emperor. They had learned that he was ahead of them now, riding south fast on his big gray horse, eager to reach his capital. So at daybreak they were all in the saddle again, and pounding once again toward Addis Ababa.

Now they stood waiting in the garden, and presently Prince Daniel came to the door of the palace and said, "Are you all here? Are you all ready?"

"All ready, Your Excellency," said Chala. He turned to survey his compatriots and received a shock. Bedane was not there. He was nowhere to be seen. Chala whirled around. "Prince Daniel, sir! Your Excellency! We are not ready. My brother, Bedane...."

"He is over there," boomed out Shiferaw. "Over by that wall. With a girl."

All of them looked toward the high stone wall at the far edge of the compound. Sure enough, there was Bedane. Even at that distance, he was unmistakable. He was standing with a girl who looked at him and touched his arm, and they were looking only at each other, and they were not aware of time.

"Tula!" said Chala, alarmed. "Tula, please, run over there and get him. We cannot have the Emperor wait. Please. Run!"

Tula took off at a lope that soon changed into a charge, and as he approached them Bedane and Helena looked up and saw him coming. Tula stopped in his tracks and called out, "Bedane, sir! The Emperor comes! Please come!"

Bedane and Helena looked at each other once again, and barely nodding to each other, both said, whispering, "Later." Then Helena watched Bedane as he ran lightly across the wide compound and took his place in front of the squad, next to Chala and Babilla Wami.

And out of the doorway strode Menelik, Menelik the Second, Emperor of All the Ethiopias, Guardian of the Faith, Elect of God, Conquering Lion of the Tribe of Judah, King of the Kings of Ethiopia, and each of the soldiers of Arusi dropped to one knee, and lowered his head, and dropped his spear and shield to the ground, and stayed like that.

All of them except Chala who, true to form, looked up and grinned at the Emperor. Menelik looked at him, shocked, and walked over to him quickly and said, "Chala, my boy! What has happened to you? What has happened to your face?" Then, at once he said, "Get up, lads, get up! Welcome to my palace. Who will tell me what happened to my friend Chala here?"

The warriors leapt to their feet. Shiferaw raised his voice. "He got that from an Azebo, Janhoi, but Chala got the son-of-a-bitch," he said, looking directly at the Emperor.

"Oh?" said Menelik, a twinkle in his eye. He looked at the squad members, who all seemed to be staring at the sky, or at the walls of the palace, or off into space somewhere. They were all petrified. When Shiferaw was talking, you never knew what would come out of him next. They were embarrassed beyond words.

"Yah," said Shiferaw. "Speared him right through the guts."

"And where did you find a doctor to sew you up so nicely," asked Menelik, looking intently at Chala and running his thumb along the scar cut.

"My friend, Your Majesty. My friend Egersa Regasa. He is the hakim of this squad. He is right here."

Menelik looked up, and Egersa bowed politely.

"Good work, hakim," said Menelik. "Nicely done. Now Chala, how did it happen that you were out spearing Azebos?"

Chala looked up at the Emperor, who looked as tall as a thundercloud, and just as powerful. "I was...." he said. "I was...."

"Your Majesty, if I may," said Bedane, and he bowed low.

Menelik breathed deep, and swelled himself up to his greatest height. He looked like a great lion. "You may," he said regally.

"Your Majesty, my name is Bedane Negassa, and I am Chala's brother. Sir, Your Majesty, sir..." Bedane's voice started at a whisper, but grew in strength as he went on. "Chala was guarding Bishop Haile Mikael of Ba'le on the journey south. They were attacked by a raiding party of Azebo, as you know. Chala did what he could, and got his man, but that is when he was injured, and that is when the Bishop was taken. By the time we arrived, it was too late to save the Bishop."

"Ah, yes. The Bishop," said Menelik. "Let me tell you about the Bishop. Do not worry about him. The Bishop, Father Haile, is well. Did you hear that, Chala? He is well. When I received your message, I was with Ras Mengesha. Ras Mengesha offered to get him back, and he did. He sent his special warriors of the desert. Until a day ago, Father Haile was at Ras Mengesha's palace in Makelle. The Russian doctors healed him."

"Thank God!" said Chala, and tears streamed down his face.

"He was ill-used by the Azebo," continued the Emperor. "If it were not for you boys, if you had not told Us, he would be dead by now, I believe."

Menelik paused. "We are grateful to have him back. Further, We are gratified that We have such soldiers as you in Our army." Menelik glared fiercely at the men. "To show Our appreciation for the deeds you have done, I have some things for you which you may enjoy." Menelik clapped his hands, and servants appeared carrying folded silk shirts of shimmering green and blue in their arms. They were the kind of shirts that were worn only by Imperial soldiers who had proven themselves most valiant in battle.

"Meto Aleka Babilla Wami," said Menelik. "Come forward."

Babilla did so, and dropping to his knees before the Emperor, he bowed low to the ground.

"Babilla," said Menelik, "as aleka, you did great service to Us. We do not forget. Take this green shirt, worn only by the greatest of our warriors. You have earned it."

Without rising or looking up, Babilla Wami reached out his hands and felt the soft touch of green silk as the shirt seemed to float into his hands. Then he remained kneeling.

"Hamsa Aleka Bedane Negassa," said the Emperor, "you have also earned your green shirt. We have heard of your exploits and your leadership, and we predict a fine future for you."

Bedane followed Babilla's example, and bowing, received his shirt.

"Chala," said the Emperor. "My good friend Chala. What would We have done without you? You always seemed to show up at the unlikeliest of times, for no good reason; yet every time you did, good things happened to Us." He paused. "Except for that bicycle business. Of course, perhaps that was good too. Perhaps it would be well for every emperor to get knocked on his.....ahem.....knocked to the ground by a kid on a bicycle at least once during his rule. Sometimes We become too haughty, and We lose sight of the ground."

Menelik ran his thumb over Chala's scar once again. "In the old days, there was a thing known as the King's Touch. It was said a king could heal a person just by touching him. I am too late to heal your wound, Chala, but perhaps, if you are also hurt inside, this touch might help."

Chala's heart was leaping inside him, and he knelt and said, "Whatever hurts I had, your words about Father Haile have already taken away, Your Majesty. I am content."

"Good," said Menelik. "Accept this green shirt from Me. The next time we meet, stay off the bicycle. Now, as for the rest of you...."

The squad knelt as one man.

"You have acted valiantly. All of you. I have had reports. Excellent in battle, and doubly excellent in friendship and loyalty." The Emperor's voice became low. "I know you have lost friends—good friends—boys you have known since you were shepherds together. I cannot bring them back. I can ask you to honor their memories and their deeds, and never let their memories die. And because of your excellent service, I give each of you the blue silk shirt given only to great warriors."

Prince Daniel ordered the shirts to be given to the kneeling figures. As the servants finished distributing the garments, Bedane called out, still with his head pressed against the earth, "Your Majesty! We are not the great men you think we are! We do not deserve this honor."

Then there was silence for a long time.

Finally, Menelik himself ended the silence. "Look at Me, Bedane Negassa," he ordered quietly. "Why do you say that?"

Bedane poured out to the Emperor all that had happened at Teglat Meda, and when he had finished, he added, "For this reason, we are not worthy. We acted like thieves, not soldiers. We acted like shiftas. We do not deserve Your thanks, or these presents."

Again there was silence for a long time. Then Menelik said, "This little town of Teglat Meda; how many people did you kill there?"

"None, Your Majesty."

"And how many maimed, injured?"

"None, sir. But we...."

"And their animals. How many cows did you take? How many horses and mules and donkeys? How many chickens and goats and sheep?"

"None, Your Majesty. But we burned their homes, and all the food we could not carry, we burned also. We left them to starve."

"The people of the town had set a trap for anyone who found their food, and your friend was killed by it?"

"Yes, Janhoi."

"You did not act with wisdom," said Menelik. "You acted from anger, and that is not good. But the people of Teglat Meda did not act with wisdom either. They acted from fear."

Menelik paused. There was no sound except for the birds that chirped in the bushes that surrounded the little garden. Then the Emperor sighed and said, "Boys, you are not guilty of this crime. You acted from anger because your friend had been killed. And you did not act like shiftas. You were ordered to find food for our army, which was starving. Now, the people of the town: neither are they guilty. They were just protecting their food. They were doing that because they are used to armies coming through and ripping their hard-earned produce and animals from them. This has gone on for hundreds, thousands of years. It must stop! When I became Emperor, I ordered that this be stopped. Then, because this time there were so many of us on the move, with so few provisions, I ordered that soldiers could take provisions once again. You are not guilty of this. Neither are the people of Teglat Meda. I am guilty of this. I alone, your Emperor. And I say to you, what you did, you did out of loyalty to me. I take this bad thing upon my own head. I take the death of your friend and the burning of the crops and the houses on my head. And I resolve to never again allow this to happen. I will build this country so that there is no hunger; so that armies will not rampage across the length and breadth of it. I swear to you that I will do this. Now that the famine is over and our greatest enemy is defeated, now is the time to do this. I will do this for you and for the people of Teglat Meda and for all the people of Ethiopia. I, Menelik of Ethiopia, swear this! Get up!"

The boys stood and looked at the Emperor, and Menelik said, "This audience is over, but remember this: you are my valiant soldiers, and you are guilty of no wrong. I forgive anything you have done by my orders. Another thing: do not be afraid that I will forget you. If at any time you wish anything from Me, appear at My palace and ask for Me, and I will grant your request."

The boys stood silently.

"That is all, my faithful soldiers," said Menelik, and he turned and began to walk toward the palace.

"Sir!" yelled Shiferaw. "Janhoi! I know what I want right now! Will you give it to me, Sir?"

Menelik turned. He looked at a sea of embarrassed faces, then saw the one who spoke. He raised his eyebrows, questioning.

"Sir, I wish You to give me a Singer!"

"A Singer?" Menelik smiled. "What on earth would you do with a Singer, warrior?"

"Sir. I have seen those new machines in the market here. There are none like that in Meraro, or Bekoji, or Assella. I would take that machine back to Bekoji, to the marketplace there, and I would rent it to one of the tailors who works there. Soon the Singer tailor would have more business than any other, because the Singer machine is swifter than any seamster in the marketplace. The more money the tailor made, the more he would pay me. Then I would come back here to Addis and buy many more Singer machines from the Americans, and rent them to seamsters in many towns, and I would become rich!"

Menelik walked quickly back to the boys. His arm was raised and his finger was pointing directly at Shiferaw. He kept jabbing the air with his finger. "See this!" he kept saying excitedly, until he stood directly in front of Shiferaw. "See this, boys! See this! This is exactly what I have wanted. Just what I have wanted! Before the war, I made a proclamation: 'Farmer, farm!

Trader, trade!' That is what I said. This is what My Empire needs. What is your name, son?"

"Shiferaw Gonfa, Your Majesty." For once, Shiferaw's voice was low.

"Shiferaw, my son," said Menelik, "you shall have your Singer. You shall do with it what you said, and yes, you will become rich. But you will also become the cause that brings good clothing to My people. This is what we must do. This is what we all must do. Then our empire will be strong."

Menelik paused and turned toward Prince Daniel. "You will see to this, my Prince?" he asked.

Prince Daniel bowed low.

With a flourish of his cloak, Menelik turned once again and walked quickly toward the palace. At the door, he turned and said, smiling broadly, "Fare thee well, my good and valiant warriors! Fare thee well. Now go on over to the Adarash and have a good meal. Eat until you drop onto the floor! Farewell!"

And with that, he was gone.

Bedane began to chuckle to himself.

"What are you laughing at?" asked Chala.

Bedane drew his brother aside and said, laughing, "Shiferaw can't add two and two, but he knows how to make money!"

In the garden, gabis and shirts were flying through the air as the boys ripped them off and tried on their new silk shirts. Their happy voices filled the air.

Mamo and Babilla Wami were not trying on their shirts. They stood and looked at the beautiful silk in their hands and Mamo looked at Babilla Wami and said, "This is a just and good man, and he has forgiven me."

Babilla Wami replied, "It is a good decision to fight for a man like that. Shall we go and look for Dejazmach Baltcha? I think he might welcome some men who wear shirts such as these."

Ibbsa and Tula, Egersa and Shasho and Shiferaw were walking up the hill toward the Adarash, and Ibbsa said to Tula, "So that is what an Emperor does. He takes the sins of the people on his own back."

"No," said Tula, "that is what a *great* emperor does."

"And he takes their joys, too," said Egersa.

"And their lives," said Shasho. Shiferaw said nothing to any of this. He did not understand talk of this kind. Shiferaw was not one for speculation.

The pilgrim was dressed in the rags of an itinerant monk, staff in one hand, begging bowl in the other. Head thrown back, eyes closed, he sang his prayers up to the monks of the Monastery of Debre Damo.

Far up the cliff, the monks heard him and peered over the edge. They observed him and examined him as he prayed. When they were satisfied that he was alone, that he posed no threat, they lowered the rope chair over the side.

The itinerant monk clambered into the braided chair and the monks on top pulled and tugged. Legs dangling down, the monk from the World pushed at the side of the cliff with his feet, and the basket swayed to and fro in the hot still air of the afternoon. Back and forth went the basket, and around in circles, but always upward.

A hundred feet above the plain, the monks swung the boom of the rope ladder inward, grabbed at the worldly monk as he came swinging through the air, and hauled him to safety on the top of the amba.

As soon as he was disentangled from the ropes, the monk, looking around, saw the ancient church of Debre Damo. Seeing it, with fierce eyes he fell to his knees and prostrated himself, saying into the dust, "My name is Haile Mikael Tesfaye, an unworthy and sinful and evil priest. I have come to repent and to confess and to seek absolution for my great sins." Then he was silent.

There was no movement around him. There was only the silence of the sky and the dry, skin-cracking wind. Then he heard a man kneel next to him. He felt the pressure of a hand on his shoulder. The hand tugged at him, bidding him rise.

He rose to a kneeling position. Before him knelt a kindly-faced monk who smiled and held out a water-filled gourd to him. Haile Mikael took the bowl from the monk. "God bless you," said Haile Mikael. He raised the bowl to his lips and drank. The water was cool, and tasted good to him. "I beg an acolyte's hut, or, if there are none, permission to build one," said Haile Mikael. "I can work. I can pay with my hands. I need absolution or I will die in sin."

The kind monk said, "Alas, Father Haile, there are no huts. They are all taken. But you can have a choice of one of three small caves. They are filthy, and musty, and you have to scramble along the cliff face to get to them, but they will keep you dry. Perhaps you will like one of them. Come, let me show you."

For two weeks Haile Mikael remained at Debre Damo, living in his cave, going out of it before dawn every day to join the early morning prayers, then to mass, then back to the cave for contemplation before the noontime prayers. No one bothered him, or talked to him. They left him alone in his grief. In the afternoons, he drew water from the well and pounded the millet seeds to make bread. He took his turn on the rope, hauling up pilgrims and priests, beggars and mendicants, and lowering them down again. Then mid-afternoon prayers, the silent evening meal, evening prayers, and back to the cave for a fitful sleep full of demons and dragons and stones pressing into his thin bones. Slowly the fears and horrors of his life receded. Quietly, one by one, they were replaced by a kind of comfort. When the comfort came, he hugged it about him like a warm blanket. If it came at night, he sighed with thanks and slept in peace for a few minutes. If it came during the day, he wrapped it around him like a cloak and went into the church and showed it to the Christos like it was a new garment, thanking God over and over for its being. Not once did he think about theological matters. Not once did he think about the nature of God. He didn't care if there were three persons in one God or if there were three natures in one Godhead. Let the monks and the priests in the worldly places care about that! He didn't care. He cared that he might be forgiven.

One night, in the opening of his west-facing cave, in the middle of the night when terror and comfort were wrestling for his soul and his breathing came in labored gasps, he wiped tears from his eyes and gazed into the black heavens just in time to see a star shoot through the sky in a blaze of fiery liquid light and glory. Then another and another. He found himself staring into the sky, waiting for the next star to dive and glide through the heavens.

He was rewarded. "Ah!" said a small voice in his mind. He felt the corners of his mouth lift. Over and over through the dark hours of night stars shot across the sky. One huge one was so big and bright that it seemed to throw off sparks, and Haile Mikael thought in wonderment that he could hear it hiss and crackle like a faraway campfire. This pleased him so much that he fell into a deep sleep of peace, and he slept through the time for morning prayers. He didn't even hear the great stone bell that called the rest of the monks to prayer.

Later in the morning, after he finally woke, after he had cleared his head and sorted out his mind, he contemplated the stars shooting through the last night's sky, and he took them as a sign. He felt stronger than he had felt since the day he had been flayed, and he knew that the strength he had came from within, and was from the Spirit. And from his past life, he knew that it was time for him to confess, that if he waited he would grow fearful, and that fear would overcome the purity of his desire for forgiveness.

He left his cave in the middle of the morning and asked the first monk he saw to intercede with the abbot for him, that the abbot might find him a confessor. Then he sat on a rock and waited, and fidgeted, and twitched about, looking toward the north and south and east, all over that part of the country, and if he thought of anything, it was of the white honey of Adigrat. On his way to Debre Damo, he had passed through Adigrat, and at the doorway of a merchant's compound, a servant had placed a piece of injera in his begging bowl, and over it the servant had poured the purest, sweetest, most delicious honey Haile Mikael had ever tasted in his life. Now that is what Haile Mikael thought of as he waited for word of his confessor, and his heart was glad, for he thought his nightmare would soon be over.

And the monk returned, and told him to be at the altar of the church at eight o'clock the next morning.

And so he was.

The light of the morning sun streamed into the nave of the church from the heights above. It was broken into irregular patterns by the carved wooden latticework in the high windows. The stillness of the morning was broken only by the calling of birds in the great old trees that grew outside the church. Haile Mikael knelt in the aisle before the altar, face pressed to the stone floor. He waited, content.

After time passed, he heard the light sounds of bare feet against the stone floor. Whoever it was came toward him and stopped barely two feet from his head. Haile Mikael could feel the warmth of his clothing. The smell of the priest's burlap robes hung in the still air.

"Forgive me, Father," said Haile Mikael, "for I have sinned."

"So have we all," said his confessor.

"I have sinned greatly," Haile Mikael blurted out.

"And who has not?" asked the voice.

"I have caused the deaths of thousands. I am unworthy to be called a priest of God, or even a simple man."

"The smallest action that we take sets in motion—what?" asked the voice. "Who knows who has caused the deaths of thousands?"

"I know," said Haile Mikael. "I have caused death. I have caused it to come to thousands who were not prepared to meet God. I caused them to die with anger and fear in their hearts."

Then there was silence.

After a long time, the voice said, "Your clothing is that of a mendicant monk. But you must be a most powerful man, to send so many souls to their deaths. How do you know you did this?"

"I was a proud man," said Haile Mikael. "Like Lucifer, I carried the sin of pride in my heart. It was I, Confessor, who rallied the troops of Menelik in the great battle and sent them racing wildly against the Ferengi. I it was, I alone, who drummed the drum and sang the canticle and started the troops along the way."

The Confessor said, "We have heard the story of the battle. We have heard that it was the great Bishop Haile Mikael Tesfaye who led the Imperial troops into battle on that day, not a simple country priest."

"I..." said Haile Mikael. "Aye. I am....God help me, if it would help the world I would be a simple country priest in my little church and sit and praise the Lord, but I am not. Am not. Am not." Haile Mikael's breath came in gasps.

The confessor monk looked down at him and smiled. "You know, Bishop, I wondered about you when you came. Somehow, I did not think of you as some simple country priest."

"God help me. That is what I wish I had always been; and what I wish to be," said Haile Mikael. "Instead, I am a monster."

"You know," said the confessor, "I think.....I think that if you had been born to be a simple country priest, your church would have been situated on a tongue of land heading east from the town of Adua, and that thousands of souls carrying bodies of different colors and minds of different backgrounds and temperaments would have converged someday on your church and thrashed it into dust. That," the voice ended, "is what *I* think. Get up."

Haile Mikael rose slowly to a kneeling position, and put his right hand up to his temple. He moaned lowly.

"Look at me," said his confessor.

Haile Mikael looked up. "I am honored," he said. His confessor was the Abbot himself.

"Why?" asked the Abbot.

"You are known throughout the Empire for your holiness and wisdom. You have taken a part of your life to be with me, a sinner."

"Did I have a choice?" asked the Abbot. "I chose a little country monastery. Now I have an army before me filled with wounds and slashes, with broken bodies and unmended souls, all inside the soul of one terrified man. What can I do? How am I different from you?"

"You did not go to seek glory!" said Haile Mikael. "You sought God. And I have brought you grief!"

"True. I did not seek glory," said the Abbot. "But neither have you brought me grief. You have brought not grief, but God here, because you sought Him here; because you sought Him here, He found you here. Thank you for bringing Him here."

"Because I, a sinner, seek forgiveness, God is present here? How is that?"

"Am I to explain the ways of God?" asked the monk, smiling. "What can I do for you?"

"Can I be absolved of so great a sin?"

"I am not the one to ask," said the Abbot. "Come, let us sit together. It is better than kneeling on icy granite."

The two men sat on the priests' bench at the side of the altar.

"Who can I ask?" said Haile Mikael.

"Who did you ask before?" replied the abbot.

"I asked Jesus," said Haile Mikael.

"And what did He say?" asked the abbot.

"He said I should follow the reed," said Haile Mikael.

The abbot looked at him quizzically.

"He did," said Haile Mikael defensively. "We were sitting in the desert, and I was asking Him what to do, and He pointed to a small reed blowing in the wind in the desert sand and He said to follow the reed. And then when I was captured by the Azebo, and they were lashing me to death, I called on Him and He came and said that I had not followed the reed. I had tried to follow the reed, but I did not know how. I must follow the reed, but I do not know where to find it. Holy Father, I must follow the reed. I know I have not done that. He said I had not done that. And when I did not do that, I committed these crimes and sins. I was not on His path. But I do not know where His path is, or leads."

"The last part is easy," said the abbot. "His path leads to Him. But the rest of it is difficult. What you have told me bears no relationship to what you have asked. You asked to be forgiven your sins; now you talk about sitting with Jesus out in the desert."

"I am not crazy," said Haile Mikael.

"I know that," said the abbot, "or at least I think I know that. A crazy person usually does not wish to be rid of his delusion, as you wish to be rid of your sins. Nor do I think you are possessed by evil. But still, most people I know do not claim to sit around in the desert talking with the Christ. About a reed. If you do that....."

"I have done that," said Haile Mikael. "It was glorious. But I must find that path back to Him."

The holy abbot thought about what had been said. "So," he said at length, "you wish to be absolved of your sins."

"Please, Father," said Haile Mikael. "Intercede with God for me, a frightened sinner!"

"Not now," said the abbot, and rose from the bench.

"What!" said Haile Mikael.

"Not now," said the abbot. "I must have time to think about this. You have given me a big problem. I want time to study it." He looked at the distraught face of Haile Mikael. "One day, Father," he said. "I want one day. Give me that day to think about what you have told me. I need that time so that I can do my best to help you. This is not an easy thing to deal with."

"But what if I die!" said Haile Mikael. "I will die a sinner. I will go to hell."

"You should be safe here, for a day at least. Go back to your cave. Spend the day and night in prayer and fasting. I will do the same, and think about how to help you. Tomorrow morning, at this same time, meet me here, and perhaps we will be able to do something good for you in His behalf."

The abbot padded out of the church without another word. Haile Mikael sat, stunned. He sat and drank the coolness and beauty of the day into his soul, but he was not satisfied. He tortured himself with his thoughts.

Finally, he too left the church, and made his way to his cave.

The next morning at eight o'clock he was back in the church, prostrate before the altar, his arms outstretched, his eyes closed. Once again there was the sound of naked feet crossing the stone floor.

"Peace be with you," said the Abbot.

"And also with you," whispered Haile Mikael.

"I have thought all night about your request," said the Abbot. "It is a difficult thing for me to do this. Here, take my hand."

The Abbot helped Haile Mikael rise from his kneeling position, and together they walked over to the priest's bench. They sat facing each other.

"It is easy for me to absolve you," said the Abbot, "and to intercede with the Lord for you. That is the easy part. That is simple." The Abbot stopped talking, and seemed to be thinking. Then he said, "The hard part, Father, is to know whether you will forgive yourself. Can you?"

Haile Mikael stared at the older man.

"It is the sin of Pride, you see, that you carry within you. You are right about that. You are a proud man. But mixed with that sinful pride is the pride of so many people who saw you as a wonderful man; a superior man; a delightful and loving and saintly man. All that pride is within you too, and who can say if that is good or evil? How will you look on that? Can you separate that pride from the sin of pride, and be happy in it? What can you do with that?"

Haile Mikael sat and looked at the Abbot, with no words; no answer.

The Abbot's voice took on a distant sound. He seemed to be speaking to himself. "You thought that what you did was right," he said. "Possibly it was. True, many died. But probably, they would have died that day anyway, regardless of what you did. Eventually, they all would have died anyway; in whatever state of grace or sin, who is to say? This is something only God can say. The Lord, Father, did not give over His power to you to decide who died or who lived; nor did He allow you to determine the fate of those souls. That is something that occurs between God and each soul directly. So, even though you may have changed the course of the battle, you did not change the destiny of each soul who died. Or who lived, for that matter. No, Father, that is between each soul and God Himself."

The Abbot rose and stood in front of Haile Mikael. "Do you see," he said, "that you did not decide who lived and died? Your actions may have dictated that Death would be present for some, but who knows what else happened that day? In such a grisly winnowing of life as Death conducted that day, what was your part? Who can say? Was your part greater than the Emperor's? Or the Italian general's? I would say not. So, to take on the burden of the death of thousands is truly the sin of Pride. It is good that you recognize it as such. You will have to rip it out of your soul with mighty force. And you will have to be sure that the good pride that people felt in you does not go with it. That is a mighty task."

"I...I do not know how..." said Haile Mikael

"It will come to you," said the Abbot. "But you will have to give yourself time. That will be your time of penance. It may be a long time, but it will come. Now, kneel."

Haile Mikael obeyed quickly, sliding from the bench to the floor. He lowered his head.

"Lord," intoned the Abbot, "I beg forgiveness for this man who kneels before you now, contrite in his heart for all his sins, past and to come. Forgive him, please, and give him the strength to go on and do good in this world, so that many more souls will know of You and come to You in glory. For this is a great soul you have wrought, and he hath much to do for You in this world. Keep him from temptation, and deliver him from evil."

The Abbot made the sign of the cross over Haile Mikael, blessing him. Haile Mikael sighed as if a mountain had slid off his back. His hands went to the floor as he supported himself.

"Now," said the Abbot, "now let us talk about what you will do." He touched Haile Mikael's shoulder. Haile Mikael took a deep breath and rose back up to a kneeling position.

"Could I stay here? Is this the path I may follow?" he asked. "To stay here and pray with you and the other priests and brothers?"

"No," said the Abbot. "This place is a place of peace. Here are found men of peace, men who have made peace with themselves. You are not at peace. First, above all, you must find the Peace of the Lord. Then, perhaps, you may come back to us. To talk and visit, at least. But you must go, and not return until you have found that Peace. You alone can find it, and you cannot find it in a place, but only within. You know as well as I do that this is what you must do. And then, you see, you must also find the reed. So you must go."

"The reed," said Haile Mikael. "Yes, I must find the reed." He smiled.

"You are a blessed and lucky man, Father," said the Abbot, "to have been given such a worthy task. God must love you very much."

"You have given me much peace already, holy Abbot, and Hope, also."

The Abbot bowed to him. "You have found what we could do for you," he said. "Now you must go to decide your mystery."

"May I have one last day, at least?"

"Certainly," said the Abbot.

The rest of the day was glorious. Haile Mikael felt that it glowed with a special light. The night, too, was brilliant with stars and clear air. After mass the next morning, he said his farewells to all the priests and monks, took his bundle of poor belongings, and climbed into the basket. The monks lowered him to the valley floor, and as he swayed down the side of the cliff he smiled at the world, and laughed to himself in joy.

His feet hit the floor of the world, and he twisted his body out of the basket and tugged at the rope for a signal. The monks raised the empty basket. Haile Mikael stood looking up at it as it grew smaller and smaller and then disappeared over the rim of the amba. Then he stood looking around. "Which way is the Way?" he asked himself. "Well," he thought, "I will let my feet answer that."

With an inexplicable feeling of happiness and joy, Haile Mikael began to walk.

The wide road down from Addis Ababa to Debre Zeit was alive as usual with thousands of people going to and fro, driving huge herds of cattle and sheep and goats to market; with camel caravans from the lowlands to the east heading to the capital; and more people simply visiting friends and family along the way. Within this stream of commerce and humanity rode a few cavalrymen from Arusi. Those returning did not include Babilla Wami or Mamo. They had remained in Addis Ababa, waiting for Dejazmach Baltcha to form his army for the west. Now the group was reduced to Bedane and Chala, and Shasho, Shiferaw, Tula, Ibbsa, and Egersa . All of them led ancient, rickety pack horses that looked as if they were making their last trip. The boys had found them in the market in Addis, and had a good time laughing about their condition and haggling over their worth with the drover who was charged with selling them. They did not pay much for them, and when they had them, they loaded them down with goods from the market to bring home with them. Shiferaw took his pack horse over to the American company office that sold Singers, loaded his sewing machine onto the back of his new old horse, and rejoined his friends at the start of the road to Debre Zeit. Laughing, they started off, admonishing each other to treat their pack horses well, since if any of them died on the way they would have to redistribute the loads and burden the other animals.

They took up three of the six eastbound tracks, riding side by side and laughing and talking about what they would do when they arrived home, and commenting on how beautiful the day was. Across the valley of the Awash River to the south, the sacred mountain of Zukquala hung over them, and Chala told them about the monks on the top of that mountain, and of the crazy old man he had met there. As he spoke, he fingered the scapular containing the scroll of the nine angels that still hung around his neck. Shiferaw trailed along behind, keeping his pack horse close to him, checking the ropes, watching the load, protecting his financial future.

At Akaki, there was a road that went straight to the south, down along the Rift Valley to its lakes. Here the boys halted, and Chala said his goodbyes to each, and promised to visit each of them when he got home. Then, the air sharp in his nostrils, he headed Eagle down that valley road and rode fast for Lake Zwai. Under the looming Zukquala he rode. He sent Eagle splashing across the wide Awash. Alongside the shore of Lake Zwai he went, and with every step that Eagle took, Chala's heart grew lighter.

That night, he stayed at the western station of the island ferry. He could hardly sleep at all. The next morning he was up early, and drank coffee with the guards, and paid them to take Eagle and the pack horse around to the east side of the lake, and promised them more money when he would arrive there. They were good men and true Lati, and he knew Eagle would be safe with them. Then he went to the ferry and climbed aboard, and the ferryman let him help oar the boat across to the island.

He climbed quickly up the slope to the town of Debre Sion, then took the trail toward the south between the golden grainfields and the stately ensete groves, and in little more than half an hour he stopped at the gate of a peaceful home surrounded by giant ensete plants.

The owner of the house sat on a stool in the dooryard. He was intent on cleaning a rifle that lay across his knees.

"Sir?" said Chala.

The man looked up. "Who are you?" he said.

Chala bowed low and said, "Grazmach Birru, my name is Chala Negassa, from the district of Meraro in Arusi Province. I have been here before. I bring you news of Bishop Haile Mikael."

"Oh!" exclaimed Birru, standing up. "Of course. Come in."

Chala opened the gate and entered the yard. Arriving before the Grazmach, he bowed again. Birru looked at him, puzzled.

"When were you here?" he asked. "I don't seem to recall."

"With Father Haile," said Chala. "I accompanied him north to the battle."

Birru looked at the young man as he stood before him. He saw what appeared to be a young noble who wore good clothes, who wore a camelshair cloak over those clothes, who wore at his waist a scimitar. Startled, he saw that the boy also wore the green silk shirt of a decorated warrior. And this boy wore on his face the scar of a heavy fight.

"I remember a shy young peasant boy by the name of Chala Negassa," said Birru, a smile slowly beginning to play across his face. "Strange that you should bear the same name as that one. But stranger things have happened. You come, obviously, from Addis. Come, sit down. Would you like some coffee?"

"Thank you," said Chala.

A servant was summoned, and brought cups of coffee out of the house, and an extra stool for Chala. He and the Grazmach sat sipping the coffee, and Chala told Birru the story of his adventures with the Bishop, and assured him that Haile Mikael was safe and that he would be returning south someday soon. "Doubtless he will visit you," he ended.

"Thank you for this news," said Birru, "but will you stay for dinner? There seem to be pieces of your story that still must be told. Like how you received that shirt, for example. I would like to hear that. And my family would like to hear that too, I will bet."

Hearing this invitation, Chala could not believe his good fortune. He saw his opportunity and spoke. "Sir," he said, "There is another matter I wish to speak to you about." He paused. "Just to you," he said.

"Speak," said Birru, intrigued.

Chala put down his coffee, took a deep breath, and stood. "Sir," he said, "I have come to you to ask for the hand of your daughter in marriage."

Birru blinked, and his face showed no sign or emotion. For a long time he sat, just looking at Chala. Then he said solemnly, "Chala Negassa, you seem to be a remarkable young man, but I must say that you really look very young to be talking of marriage. And my daughter has scarcely turned twelve, still too young to be given to anyone."

"It is true that I am young," said Chala. "When I came before, I was fourteen. Now I am fifteen, only a year from marriage age. I wanted to ask anyway. I have loved your daughter ever since I heard her play and sing in that house in the village. I wanted to be sure to ask early, for I felt that many would ask. Besides," he said, "Prince Daniel says it is common to arrange marriages early. He said I should ask."

"Who?" asked Birru, startled.

"Prince Daniel Gebre Medhin. And Princess Helena, too, said I should try. She said you should always try, that there was no harm at all in asking."

"I suppose the next name you mention will be that of Menelik himself," said Birru.

"A thousand pardons," said Chala, embarrassed. "I did not mean to mention names like that. I meant to wait until you asked about my family and friends. But I could not wait. I am sorry."

Grazmach Birru sat and looked wise, as he had learned to do when judging cases at the Tuesday court. 'Well,' he thought to himself, 'if all problems were as pleasant as this, it would be a happy world.' Then Birru said thoughtfully, "There are other people to consider."

Alarmed, Chala blurted out, "There are others who have asked before me?"

"No, no. Calm yourself," said Birru, "but we must know more about you. And by others, I meant my wife Aster, and my daughter Almaz herself. You really should speak with her about this too, don't you think? Or do you know something that I don't?"

Chala raised his eyes and looked at the face of the Grazmach. "Oh, no, sir. I have not said anything to your daughter. I would not. This is too important to me. I would never go behind your back."

But Birru was not looking at him. His eyes were fixed on something in the distance. "Behind my back?" he asked, grinning broadly. "You had better look behind your own back, and see who is coming up the lane."

As Chala whirled around, Birru laughed and clapped him on the shoulder. "She is pretty, isn't she?" he said. "You will stay for dinner with us? You never did answer that, you know."

And Almaz, her arms full of bundles from the market, walked into the yard and stood there, her eyes full of wonder and delight.

Bedane sat on the floor in the main room of his parents' tukul high in the hills outside of Meraro. His father sat across from him on a new carved stool, a gift that Bedane had brought from Addis. In the kitchen, Bedane's mother brewed special coffee as a celebration for the homecoming of her son; and outside, the wind whispered gently across the golden grasses that grew fast under a cloudless sky.

Tsehai brought the coffee on a tray, knelt, and served it to Negassa, Bedane, and herself. She continued to kneel, and sipped silently from her cup.

"Well," said Negassa, and cleared his throat. "Well," he repeated.

The three sat in silence for a long time. Then Negassa said, "So! How are you?"

"I am well," said Bedane quietly.

"The battle went well?"

"Very well, Father. We could have driven them into the sea if Atse Menelik had given us the word."

"And why did he not?" asked Negassa.

"We ran out of food and water. He chose to send us home instead. He said that we had done what we had set out to do, and no more was needed."

"We have heard that it was a great battle," said Negassa.

"We killed eleven thousand of them," said Bedane. "We lost seven thousand of our own."

"Aiyee!" said Tsehai quietly.

"And how did our boys do?" asked Negassa, his eyes gleaming with memories of battle.

"We broke their center, Father. We came down on them like lions and broke their center. And they were good troops in the center. We would have had our hands full if it had not been for Uncle Bedasa."

"Bedasa!" said Negassa. "How is he? Have you seen him?"

"He is in Addis," said Bedane. "Father, Bedasa has been made Turk Bashaw of the Empire!"

"What!" exploded Negassa. "My little brother Bedasa is made Turk Bashaw? The ruler of all riflemen? What have I missed? How did this happen?"

"He was taken from us, Father. He was made leader of a special section of troops. Machine-gunners. He trained them. They had their guns on royal mules, and they brought them right into the battle. They took the flank of the Bersaglieri and raked them. It was when the Italians turned to attack them that we came down on them."

"He is all right?"

"He is splendid," said Bedane. "He wears a green silk shirt." Bedane paused. "Just like this one," he said, reaching into his bag. He pulled out his shirt and spread it before his mother and father.

"Indet!" exclaimed Negassa. "How glorious is this! My son has gained an Imperial honor! How did this happen?"

"When Uncle Bedasa was taken from us, Babilla Wami became our aleka. I was chosen to be his hamsaleka."

" Tsehai, our son was highly regarded!" Negassa smiled, then laughed. "And how was life under the direction of the Wild Warrior?" he asked.

"He was a good leader, Father. He knows a lot. He has joined the army of Dejazmach Baltcha, and they are off to the west, to Kaffa again, to finish that fight. Mamo went with him."

"Hmmmm," said Negassa. "So the army life sat well with Mamo, did it? I can see that." He paused. "Tell me, how are the other boys you took with you? How did they fare?"

Bedane dropped his head. He spoke slowly. "Three are dead," he said. "Dabale died at the battle. Wondimu and Taffa died on the way home. Wondimu died in a battle with bandits south of Amba Alagie. Taffa died in an accident. It......it....." He fell silent.

"It is too bad," said Negassa quietly. "This kind of thing happens."

"So many out of so few!" exclaimed Tsehai. "Wey! Such a price to pay. So many young men!"

Negassa cleared his throat. "So," he said, "None died of disease?"

"You were right about that, Father," said Bedane, brightening. "You were right to tell me to bring Egersa. He was an excellent hakim. He knows all about the wild leaves and roots, and he is very good with stitches, too. Wait 'til you see Chala!" he laughed.

"Chala!" shouted Tsehai and Negassa both together. "You have seen Chala?" "Where did you see him?" "Where is he?" "He is well?" "How is he?"

Bedane grinned. "He found us as we were scouting on a hill above Makelle," he said. "Babilla Wami thought he was a ghost. It was the only time I have ever seen Babilla Wami frightened. But it was not a ghost. It was Chala. He stayed with us for a few days." He paused, and Negassa and Tsehai were silent, waiting. "The next time was after the battle, when we were trekking south, and the bandit Azebos attacked. They took Chala's bishop prisoner, and that is when Wondimu died in battle against them, and where Chala was wounded. He is all right, though," he added quickly. "Egersa patched him up. Then Chala—we thought he was raving—insisted that we take him to Sokota, where he knew of a talking wire....."

"A what?" said Negassa.

"A talking wire. It sends messages over great distances. A man called an 'operator' taps on a metal thing, and a message is sent. So Chala was raving and rambling on about saving the bishop, and he convinced Kanyazmach Didda to have us take him to Sokota, and Didda demoted Babilla Wami to be the head of our squad, and I became second to him, and Mamo went down to third, but it didn't make any difference. We were just all friends again, and it was but a short detour on the way home. Then, when we got to the talking wire station, Chala convinced the Imperial Guards there to send a message to Atse Menelik, and they did, and His Majesty instructed Ras Mengesha to get Bishop Haile Mikael, and Ras Mengesha sent Danakil warriors to get him, and they got him, and he is safe and recovering from his wounds at the palace in Makelle, and the Emperor told Dejazmach Baltcha to tell Chala to...to..."

Bedane paused. Tsehai and Negassa just looked at him for a long while. Then Negassa leaned over and felt Bedane's head with his hand. "I thought you might have a fever," he said. "You say Chala told these Imperial Guards to send a message to Atse Menelik? And they did?"

"Yes, Father."

"You are sure you were not hit on the head or something?"

"I am fine, Father."

"All right. So you are fine. You are not mad. So, what did the Emperor tell Baltcha to tell.....to tell.......Chala? Our Chala."

"Baltcha told Chala that he should not worry, that the bishop would be all right, and to meet Atse Menelik at the palace when we returned to Addis. And to bring us with him."

Negassa stared at his son. He spoke slowly. "Are you about to tell me that you met Atse Menelik himself?"

Bedane answered directly. "His Majesty gave me this shirt. Chala has one too. It seems Chala and Atse Menelik are great friends." Bedane shrugged his shoulders.

Negassa sat in silence, looking at his son.

"Bedane," said Tsehai, "where is Chala? Why is he not telling us this himself?"

Bedane looked at his mother. "Chala came home with us a part of the way," he said. "He left us at Akaki, and said he had friends to see on an island in Lake Zwai....."

"What!" yelled Negassa.

"The house of the demons!" shouted Tsehai. "You are crazy! How can you talk such things? Why are you doing this to us!"

Bedane felt like the entire Italian army was firing down on him from a great height, but he held his ground. "Chala says there are no demons there," he said. "He says the island in Lake Zwai is the home of ancient Amharas; that it is a sacred spot; that it is called Debre Sion."

Negassa and Tsehai looked at each other, speechless.

"I am not crazy, Mother," said Bedane. "I know it sounds crazy, but it is not. You can ask Egersa, or Shasho, or Tula, or any of the other boys who came home with me. It will be the same story. In the market in Bekoji, you can hear Shiferaw tell how the Emperor gave him a Singer machine to start him off as a trader. I am not crazy. But you will see for yourselves. Chala will be here within a few days. You may not recognize him. He wears fine clothes and a camelshair cloak, and he carries a Japanese scimitar. He looks like an Amhara prince. But under everything, it is Chala. Oh, and he has a scar, too, on his cheek, but you will see that it has healed nicely."

"You are sure of what you say?" asked Negassa, after a silence.

"I am, Father," said Bedane. "Ask any of the boys."

"All of this is difficult to take in," said Negassa. "It rolls across my mind like green clouds across an orange sky. But although your tales are strange, you seem to be....like....like yourself. You were always a level-headed boy. You seem the same."

"I am the same, Father. Here, Mother, look at this!" Bedane pulled a package from his bag. "I have brought this for you."

Tsehai took the package, which was wrapped in paper. It was pliant. She could squeeze the paper in her hand and listen to it crinkle. She unwrapped the gift. Soon, in folds of shimmering white, she held in her hands the most beautiful shamma she had ever seen. She folded the garment around her head and over her shoulders. The wide border was of red and gold thread. "Oh, Bedane," she said, "it is beautiful. So soft," she said, stroking it.

"This goes with it," said Bedane, handing her a small leather pouch. Tsehai opened the pouch and out fell a pair of golden earrings. "Oh," she said. "Oh!"

"And for you, Father," said Bedane. Out of the bag appeared a magnificent pistol. "It is called a Colt," said Bedane. "It is from America. I have a hundred rounds that go with it. See."

While Negassa cradled the revolver in his hands, Tsehai rose and left the room. Soon she returned, carrying what appeared to be a bundle of clothes in her arms. "See, Bedane," she said. "We have some news too. Here, meet your sister. Her name is Ahdu, and she is very new."

Bedane took the little baby from his mother. "Oh, she is beautiful, Mother," he said. He smiled. "Soon we will be a family again. Chala will be here, and you will have three children, strong and happy."

"And then *you* will marry," said Tsehai, "and you will have children, too. And thinking of that, there is a young girl over the next hill named Askale, who still waits for you, and who is now of marriageable age. She has blossomed like a flower in the last few months. She is a beauty."

"I am surprised she is not already married," said Bedane. "I thought she would have had many suitors."

"Oh, she has had many interested in her," said Tsehai, "but only one appealed to her, and he was away at war. But now he has returned. When will you see her?"

Bedane handed the baby back to his mother. "I don't know if I will see her," he said. "You see, Mother, I have met someone."

"Oh, dear," said Tsehai softly.

"You met someone?" said Negassa. "When did you have time to meet someone?"

"We met at Makelle," said Bedane. "First, at Makelle. She was with the army."

"A camp follower!" exclaimed Negassa.

"A princess!" said Bedane.

Negassa snorted. "They are all princesses until you get to know them!" he exclaimed, and he laughed.

"Negassa!" said Tsehai. "Negassa Merga! Is that what you think of *me?*"

"Oh, you know what I mean," growled Negassa. "You know. A young man. Falls in love. Runs after....." His words trailed off into a mumble. Tsehai's bright eyes were throwing daggers at him.

"A princess, Father," said Bedane quietly. "A real princess. Her name is Helena, and she wishes me to return to Addis. She wishes me to be her bodyguard."

"You saw her again in Addis?"

"Yes, sir. At the palace."

"And she wants you for her bodyguard?"

"Sir, she wants me for more than her bodyguard."

"And you know this because....."

"Sir, just, I know this."

"Oh, my," thought Tsehai. "If he is truthful, and if he hasn't gone crazy, this princess will use him, and make mincemeat out of him, and throw him away. And he will lose his chance with Askale. And then, ah! Who knows? His life will be a wreck. Unpredictable. Ah, what a mess."

These were Tsehai's thoughts, but to Bedane she said, "Son, I cannot understand all these things you have said to us. It is like....it is like you have come back from another world. But here is what we will do. We will have a little feast tonight, just the four of us. Ahdu and I will make the best food you have ever tasted. We will have a glorious dinner. And you can tell us your stories until you fall asleep. You will have the best sleep you have ever had. And tomorrow will be a beautiful day. Now, you and your father drink some tej and light a fire in the yard, and I will make dinner." And Tsehai, Ahdu at her breast, went into the kitchen.

Negassa said, "Come on, son. Let's have a glass of tej. Bring it outside. I will show you the cattle. They are fat! Three good years in a row. I still cannot believe the famine is over and the drought is gone. But things are good! Good! Come, we will build a fire in the yard."

That night, fires were lit in the yards of many homes in Meraro. They signaled the return of brave sons from battle. All through the night, they shone like the stars in the sky. And over the next few weeks, more and more fires were lit throughout the valleys and hills of Arusi, as the boys came home.

For the next fifteen years, during the reign of Menelik the Second, Conquering Lion of the Tribe of Judah, Elect of God, King of the Kings of Ethiopia, peace reigned throughout the Empire. The rains fell, the harvests were good, and the land prospered.

No one knew when the rumor began. No one could remember who brought the story, or when they had first heard the strange tale. It was spoken of in the court of the Emperor Himself. The courtiers whispered it—the princes, the princesses, the rases, the warriors, the diplomats—all of them knew of it. In the churches and monasteries it made itself known, and in the towns and countryside all over the Empire. In the years after the battle, while the power of Menelik waxed and the nation grew strong, the story came into being, seemingly out of the thin air.

So it was said—a new holy man had arisen, and he was unlike any other holy man the world had ever seen. He was a hermit, and he lived somewhere deep in the Danakil Desert. Companions he had none. He kept the silence of the desert as willingly, as faithfully, as the rocks and sands which surrounded him. Together he and the rocks and the sands raised their prayers day and night to God.

The story said that Mengesha Yohannes, the Ras of Tigre, knew where he was, and that always when the Ras went into the desert to visit his warrior friends he would inquire of them after the hermit. For the Danakil kept watch over the holy man, and no man dared to visit him, for they would have to walk beyond the dark, cold eyes of the desert warriors to arrive at the hidden hermitage. And no man dared the Danakil.

It was said that the holy man had strange powers; even that he could talk with the Christos Himself. It was said that in his past the holy man had been a powerful man of the Church—a bishop, in fact. It was said that he had been the first to march against the enemy at Adua, and had rallied the army to victory when it stood confused and shaken. It was said that he had forsaken a brilliant career at court for the strength and peace of the desert. All of this was said, and some contended that he was the reincarnation of Saint George; but others said no, that he was indeed Saint Michael himself come to earth. No one could understand how Saint Michael, a spirit, could take on a human form; but then, it would not have been the first time that a spirit had taken on a human form.

All of these theories were rumor and conjecture. But the truth remained. There was a holy man in the desert, one who could speak with God, and who interceded daily with the Lord on behalf of the whole of Ethiopia.

And the thin reed blew in the desert wind, and the desert did not comprehend it.

So it is said...

So it is written...

NOTES

ETHIOPIA IN 1895

ETHIOPIAN WORDS AND TERMS

These words are given in the order in which the reader encounters them in the book. There are many other words and expressions which are almost immediately defined in the text, usually within two or three lines, and so are not recorded here. The following, however, tend to appear unannounced and, especially in the beginning of the book, seemingly out of the blue.

Debtera – a Coptic priest who specializes in teaching.

Tukul – the traditional-style house of the Ethiopian highlands

Shemagale – an elder

Shifta – bandits

Teff – a small grain that thrives in the highlands. When ground, it provides the flour used to make injera

Injera – the unleavened bread of the highlands which forms the basis of every meal

Indet! –an Amharic expression of surprise

Menelik yimut! An oath – "May Menelik die if I am not telling the truth!"

Tej – honey mead

Tella – home-brewed beer

Berbere – a prime candidate for the title of 'hottest pepper on earth'

Ensete – the False Banana plant – the basic food source for the Gurage people

Ferengi – the word used to describe foreigners, especially Europeans

The Negarit – the war drums of the Ethiopian rases (dukes)

Meto Aleka – Oromo title – leader of a hundred

Hamsa Aleka – leader of fifty

Kanyazmach – in an Ethiopian military formation, leader of the right wing

Grazmach – leader of the left wing

Dejazmach – leader of the center, and superior of the Kanyazmach and Grazmach

Wareda governor – a district governor

Shum – a leader of a town or village; equivalent of a mayor

Shint – about what it sounds like. Urine.

Bashaw – leader of the riflemen of the Emperor

Ge-ez – the ancient language of the Amhara and Tigre peoples, pre-dating Tigrinya and Amharic. Orominya, the language of Chala and Bedane, is derived from an entirely different language system.

Shamma – a very delicate and beautiful shawl-like garment worn over the shoulders and head. It was made of the finest cotton, and it was exquisitely woven

Askari – African troops in the service of the Italian army

Negus – king

Negusi Negast – King of Kings, Emperor.

Janhoi, Atse – honorifics applied solely to the Emperor.

Ras - duke

NAMES

In Ethiopia, people are named in a manner similar to Norse naming. Thus, sons are given a first name and attach to that name the name of their fathers. Yohannes Yohannes is John, son of John, or John Johnson. Daniel Selassie is Daniel Trinity. Haile Selassie is The Power of the Trinity, etc. So in the family of Negassa Merga, his sons are named Bedane Negassa and Chala Negassa. Negassa's brother Bedasa, uncle of Chala and Bedane, is Bedasa Merga. Negassa's wife, Tsehai, does not take the name of her husband, but is known by her original name and her father's name: Tsehai Jara.

Pronunciation of Ethiopian words: Generally, each vowel is attached to a consonant, so that, for instance, Bedane is pronounced Be da ne, not Be dāne. Mikael is Mik ā el. Mekele is Me ke le. Tewodros is Te wo dros.

Names of major fictional characters in order of appearance:

Chala Negassa – younger son of Negassa Merga and Tsehai Jara

Debtera Markos – Chala's teacher.

Negassa Merga – father of Chala and Bedane

Tsehai Jara – mother of Chala and Bedane

Bedane Negassa – older son of Negassa Merga and Tsehai Jara

Bedasa Merga – uncle of Chala and Bedane; Meto Aleka of the Meraro cavalry

Tamrat Bekele – friend of Negassa

Emebet – wife of Tamrat

Babilla Wami – famed Oromo warrior, known as The Wild Warrior of Kofele, Aleka of the Meraro cavalry

Kanyazmach Didda Bokku – leader of the right wing of Ras Mikael's cavalry, superior officer to Bedasa Merga and Babilla Wami.
Haile Mikael Tesfaye – bishop of Ba'le Province

The young warriors who followed Bedane Negassa into battle: Mamo Galata, Wondimu Gemechu, Egersa Regasa, Tula Urga, Dabale Ariti, Shifaraw Merga, Shasho Megenasa, Taffa Bulcha, Ibbsa Biya

Additional characters:

Askale – young girl picked by Negassa and Tsehai as a marriage partner for Bedane
Bashaw Indelibu – almost mythical old warrior who aids the cavalry with a gift of cattle
Dejazmach Wube – leader of the center of the cavalry detachment under Ras Mikael
Grazmach Roba – leader of the left wing of the cavalry under the leadership of Ras Mikael
Father Bekele – a priest of the Lati on the island of Lake Zwai
Grazmach Birru Goshu, shum (similar to mayor) of the Lati of Lake Zwai
Weizero Aster – wife of Birru Goshu
Almaz – daughter of Birru and Aster
Paulus [Wild Paul] – deranged old monk of the abbey at the top of Mt. Zukquala
Leul-Ras [Prince] Daniel
Princess Helena
Princess Mentuab

Historical Ethiopian figures who appear in the novel:

Emperor Menelik II - reigned 1889-1911
Empress Taitu
Abuna Mattewos – the head of the Orthodox Coptic Church of Ethiopia
The Itchegie – the head of all the orders of monks in Ethiopia
Menelik's Rases – a Ras being the equivalent of a Duke: Ras Mengesha of Tigre, Ras Alula of Asmara, Ras Attakim of Begemder; Ras Makonnen of Harar; Ras Mikael of Wollo; Ras Gobena of Ba'le; Ras Tafari Makonnen (son of Ras Makonnen) of Harar
King Tekle Haimanot of Gojjam
Wagshum Guangul, hereditary King of Wag and Lasta
Dejazmach Baltcha - principal war general of the Ethiopian army. An Oromo, appointed by Menelik
Minister of the Pen (Secretary of State) Gebre-Selassie Wolde-Aragaye

Fitaurari Gebre Iyesus, commander of the Imperial Army
Fitaurari Damtew Ketema – former Ethiopian envoy to Russia
Balambaras Gebre-Medhin Wolde-Amanuel
Alawon – an Ethiopian spy in the Italian camp
Abba Nega [translation – Father Of The Dawn] – Ras Alula's horse, famous
    throughout Tigre and Eritrea

Historical Italian figures who appear in the novel:
General Oreste Baratieri – leader of the Italian forces
His generals and major officers:
    Generals Albertone, Arimondi, Dabormida, and Elleni
    Colonel Galliano
    Major Tomasi Toselli
    Captain Isthia
    Lieutenant Barrada

Almost all of these historical figures, on both sides, have speaking parts in this story. I have put these words in their mouths, relying on my knowledge of history in determining what they might have said under the circumstances in which they found themselves.

Except for Menelik's admonition to his subjects—"Traders, trade! Farmers, farm!"—and his proclamation of war, nothing of what they say here is in any way a quote. I tried my best to discern the characters' motivations by studying their notated historical actions. So much went wrong on the Italian side during the Battle of Adua, I felt that there must have must have been ulterior motives on the part of at least one, and possibly three, of the Italian generals. My interpretation reflects my own suspicions.

Some of the actions I describe during the historic battle may or may not have occurred. History is not clear on exactly what happened. There are many interpretations, some conflicting in major details. What is known with some certainty is that Albertone advanced to the wrong place, relying on an inaccurate map which most people agree was compiled by Baratieri.

Also known is that the column led by Dabormida inexplicably ended up in the Mariam Shavita Valley, where it had no reason in the world to be. It was cut to pieces there. Some say this column was overrun early in the battle; some say it put up a fight longest and was the last division of the Italian army to retreat from the field. I don't think anyone knows for sure today. More evidence on the course of the battle has recently come to light through scholarly research, but this is ongoing. I am not entering that fight. I have based the battle portion of the story on what I was able to find out from the available sources, and I then 'improved' on it, as Mark Twain was fond of saying.

What I do know is that Ethiopia is an extraordinary nation filled with natural beauty and wonderful people. I also know that this story, and my interpretation of history, may please some people and greatly displease others. A battle currently rages within and among the various cultures of the nation as to which way the future should turn. Fingers are pointed at current and historical actions of individuals, factions, and ethnic groups. I hope these differences can be resolved peacefully and amiably. The extraordinary people of this nation deserve the best outcome.

GEOGRAPHY

Major mountains and mountain ranges of Ethiopia:
Ras Dashan – highest peak in Ethiopia, located in the High Simien, 15,000'+
The High Simien – the major range of northern Ethiopia
Encuolo – high peak in Arusi, to 14,000'+
K'ech'a – high peak in Arusi, to 14,000' +
Galamont – range in Arusi Province
Chercher – range in Harar Province
Entoto – the peak upon which Addis Ababa is built
Amba Alagie – a rugged mesa which straddles the main north/south trade route
Magdala – an amba which was the stronghold of Emperor Theodore
Zukquala – an extinct volcano which is considered a sacred mountain; home of the monks
The Ba'le Highlands – to 14,000'+

Rivers: the Blue Nile, the Takkezze, the Mareb, the Awash, the Omo, the Wabi Shibelli

Provinces and principalities: Adal, Arusi, Begemder, Eritrea, Fatagar, Gemu-Gofa, Gojjam, Gondar, Hamazien, Harar, Illubabor, Kaffa, Last, Manz, Quara, Shoa, Sidamo, Tigre, Wag, Wellega, Wollo

Arusi Provincial towns: Assella [capital of Arusi], Bekoji, Dida, Gunguma, Lemu, Meraro, Moto, Sagure, Siltana

Major Ethiopian towns and cities:
Addis Ababa – New Flower, founded by Menelik II in 1889
Adua – city in Tigre, site of a major historical battle
Ankober – ancient capital of Manz and Shoa Provinces, before the rise of Addis Ababa

Asmara – capital of Eritrea
Axum [in Tigre] – original capital of Ethiopia, home of Makeda of Saba
Debre Berhan – market town on the Addis Ababa-Makele route
Dessie – capital of Wollo Province
Gondar – medieval capital of Ethiopia, known for its castles
Harar – walled city in eastern Ethiopia, close to Somalia and The Ha'ud
Jimma – capital of Kaffa
Lalibela
Makele – capital of Tigre Province

WRITINGS

The **Kebra Negast** – translation: The Glory of the Kings. This is the history of the kings of Ethiopia, as recorded in the official chronicles of the royal courts. It spans the years from the re-establishment of the Solomonic Dynasty in the 12th Century to the end of the reign of Haile Selassie in 1974, and also records such significant happenings as the reign of Ezana in c 350 AD +/-; the reign of Caleb c 550 AD+/-; the original story of the visit of Makeda, the Queen of Sheba and Axum, to Solomon of Jerusalem; the seduction of Sheba by Solomon; and the subsequent birth of Menelik I, first Emperor of Ethiopia.

The Fetha Negast – translation: The Law of the Kings. This is a record of the laws of the Ethiopian Empire.

References: an amazing number of books regarding Ethiopian history, geography, and culture have been written over the years. Now, those books have been supplemented by all kinds of media entries. The internet is filled with Ethiopian sites, and each site leads on to others. It is a fascinating study, if you wish to pursue it. I urge you to do so. Not enough is known about this beautiful mountain land of legend and mystery. Make the study of this wonder of East Africa your own and it will reward you with knowledge beyond your wildest expectations.

ACKNOWLEDGEMENTS

First, a writer can't write unless he/she has the absolute support of someone who loves him/her very much and is willing to put up with forty years of mutterings and listening to stories of places and people she has never been to and, until recently, has never met. In my case, this person is named Joan Bowker. I don't know how she has been able to stand it, but she has! Thank you, Joanie!

Second, if you don't have an editor/publisher who is willing to get down in the trenches and fight with you over commas and make you realize that the smallest things can expand a manuscript into greatness, you are just plain out of luck. And that applies to the big things, too, like telling you when you're wrong as wrong can be about anything, even things you just know you have exactly right. Boy, am I lucky to have Pat Goudey O'Brien of Tamarac Press on my side, and at my side, saying "I just took two weeks plucking all those extraneous commas out of your manuscript. Now leave them out!" Thank you, Pat!

Third, this manuscript has been vastly improved by the changes suggested by Negesse Gutema, who grew up in Bekoji, was in the second grade when I was teaching eighth grade in Bekoji School there, and who now lives in Essex Junction, Vermont, where he is an engineer working for a major global company. We reconnected a few years ago. I invited him to read the story, and subsequently we spent four or five months meeting every two weeks to talk about the accuracy of the account and educate each other about Ethiopian history in general. It was great, Negesse. Thank you!

I also wish to thank the members of the League of Vermont Writers. If any writer ever had a base of support better than the League—well, there is no support group better than the League, with its constant supply of new ideas, nationally known lecturers, and access to agents and attorneys well-versed in the field of intellectual property. Thank you, League members!

And I would like to add many, many thank yous to those who have read this book and made valuable suggestions: Richard Bowker of Boston; John Coyne of Peace Corps Worldwide; Ted and Marie Tedford; Debby Patterson; and Hank Lambert.

This book would never have been possible had I not met and known the good people of Bekoji, Ethiopia. I spent two years with them, and because of them, the riches and knowledge I have received in the many years since then are incalculable. I have dedicated this book to them. If you're going to have a home town, you would be lucky to have it named Bekoji, and have it sitting up there in the mountains at 9,000 feet altitude. It's a great town. Thank you, people of Bekoji!

About the Author

Born in 1940 in Brooklyn, New York, a baseball throw away from Ebbets Field, Dan Close grew up on the south shore of Long Island, where he enjoyed rambling about the bays and wetlands and fishing for snappers and flounder in Great South Bay.

He has lived and taught in a variety of places across the globe, including Long Island, Manhattan, the Bronx, St. Croix in the Virgin Islands, Shiprock in Navaholand, and at 9000' altitude in the little mountain town of Bekoji, fabled home of Ethiopia's Olympic-gold-medal-winning long-distance runners, long before it had attained that reputation.

He is the author of several books, including What the Abenaki Say About Dogs; A Year On The Bus; and Stories From The Arusi Hills, which was selected for the official 50th Anniversary Peace Corps Collection of the Library of Congress. His previous works have been favorably reviewed by writers as diverse as Jodi Picoult and Rusty DeWees.

He currently lives in Underhill, Vermont with his life partner of forty years, Joan Bowker.

When he isn't writing something, he can be found stacking wood, splitting kindling, breaking rocks, muttering about the state of his garden, painting the deck, listening to Joan playing her harp, shoveling snow, driving hither and yon, traveling, and wondering what's going to happen next. He is generally happy, and, at 72, he is not an old curmudgeon, even if the weather is somewhat unstable these days and gets to his joints occasionally.

www.ingramcontent.com/pod-product-compliance
Lightning Source LLC
Chambersburg PA
CBHW050612110726
47899CB00001B/83